Praise f

"Gedge excels at setting the scene and subtly evoking a sense of the period as she tells a timeless story of greed, love, and revenge."   —*Kirkus Reviews*

"Gedge makes the past so accessible. You can imagine walking between the pillars into a magnificent hall and watching it come alive with the smell of the fresh paint on the frescoes."   —*The Globe and Mail*

"Gedge vividly renders the exotic, sensuous world of ancient Memphis, the domestic rituals of bathing and dressing, the social ambience of superstition and spells."   —*Publishers Weekly*

"Gedge has such a terrific feel for ancient Egypt that the reader merrily suspends disbelief and hangs on for the ride."   —*Calgary Herald*

"Her richly colourful descriptions ... hit the reader with photographic clarity."   —*The Ottawa Sun*

"Gedge has brought Egypt alive, not just the dry and sandy Egypt we know from archaeology, but the day-to-day workings of what was one of the greatest and most beautiful kingdoms in the history of the world."   —*Quill & Quire*

PENGUIN CANADA

HOUSE OF ILLUSIONS

PAULINE GEDGE is the award-winning and bestselling author of eleven previous novels, eight of which are inspired by Egyptian history. Her first, *Child of the Morning*, won the Alberta Search-for-a-New Novelist Competition. In France, her second novel, *The Eagle and the Raven*, received the Jean Boujassy award from the Société des Gens des Lettres, and *The Twelfth Transforming*, the second of her Egyptian novels, won the Writers Guild of Alberta Best Novel of the Year Award. Her books have sold more than 250,000 copies in Canada alone; worldwide, they have sold more than six million copies and have been translated into eighteen languages. Pauline Gedge lives in Alberta.

ALSO BY PAULINE GEDGE

Child of the Morning

The Eagle and the Raven

Stargate

The Twelfth Transforming

Scroll of Saqqara

The Covenant

House of Dreams

The Hippopotamus Marsh:
Lords of the Two Lands, Volume One

The Oasis: Lords of the Two Lands, Volume Two

The Horus Road: Lords of the Two Lands, Volume Three

The Twice Born

HOUSE OF
ILLUSIONS

PAULINE
GEDGE

PENGUIN
CANADA

PENGUIN CANADA

Published by the Penguin Group

Penguin Group (Canada), 90 Eglinton Avenue East, Suite 700, Toronto, Ontario, Canada M4P 2Y3
(a division of Pearson Canada Inc.)

Penguin Group (USA) Inc., 375 Hudson Street, New York, New York 10014, U.S.A.
Penguin Books Ltd, 80 Strand, London WC2R 0RL, England
Penguin Ireland, 25 St Stephen's Green, Dublin 2, Ireland (a division of Penguin Books Ltd)
Penguin Group (Australia), 250 Camberwell Road, Camberwell, Victoria 3124, Australia
(a division of Pearson Australia Group Pty Ltd)
Penguin Books India Pvt Ltd, 11 Community Centre, Panchsheel Park, New Delhi – 110 017, India
Penguin Group (NZ), 67 Apollo Drive, Rosedale, North Shore 0632, Auckland, New Zealand
(a division of Pearson New Zealand Ltd)
Penguin Books (South Africa) (Pty) Ltd, 24 Sturdee Avenue, Rosebank, Johannesburg 2196,
South Africa

Penguin Books Ltd, Registered Offices: 80 Strand, London WC2R 0RL, England

First published in a Viking Canada paperback by Penguin Group (Canada),
a division of Pearson Canada Inc., 1996
Published in Penguin Canada paperback by Penguin Group (Canada),
a division of Pearson Canada Inc., 2002
Published in this edition, 2007

1 2 3 4 5 6 7 8 9 10 (OPM)

Copyright © Pauline Gedge, 1996

LIBRARY AND ARCHIVES CANADA CATALOGUING IN PUBLICATION

Gedge, Pauline, 1945–
House of illusions / Pauline Gedge.

Sequel to: House of dreams.
Originally publ.: Toronto : Viking, 1996.
ISBN 978-0-14-316743-3

I. Title.

PS8563.E33H69   2007   C813'.54   C2007-903367-9

ISBN-13: 978-0-14-316743-3
ISBN-10: 0-14-316743-X

Visit the Penguin Group (Canada) website at **www.penguin.ca**

Special and corporate bulk purchase rates available; please see
www.penguin.ca/corporatesales or call 1-800-810-3104, ext. 477 or 474

HOUSE OF
ILLUSIONS

Part One

KAMEN

I

IT WAS THE BEGINNING of the month of Thoth when I first saw her. I had been detailed by my commander, the General Paiis, to escort a Royal Herald south into Nubia on a routine assignment and we were on our way back when we put into the village of Aswat for the night. The river had not yet begun to rise. It was flowing slowly, and although we were making better time on our return than we had on the journey out, we had covered hundreds of miles and were very eager to reach the familiar comforts of the Delta.

Aswat is not a place I would choose to visit. It is little more than a huddle of small mud houses crouched between the desert and the Nile, although there is a rather fine temple to the local totem, Wepwawet, on its outskirts, and the river road wanders pleasingly through shady palms as it enters and then leaves the village. The Herald whom I was guarding had not planned to beach our craft there, indeed he seemed very reluctant to do so. But a frayed rigging rope on which we had been keeping an anxious eye finally parted and that same afternoon one of the crew sprained his shoulder, so with bad grace my superior ordered that the oars be shipped and a cooking fire built on the bank not far from Aswat's place of worship.

It was sunset. As I alighted I could see the temple's pylon through the trees and a glimpse of the canal up which visitors to the God might float. The water was red with the glow of Ra's setting. The air was warm and full of dust motes, and but for the rustle and twitter of nesting birds the silence was unbroken. Unless the peasants here had conceived a violent hatred for Pharaoh's messengers, I would have no work to do this night. But mindful of my duties I left the beach where some of the sailors were already gathering what wood they could find and the rest were wrestling with fresh rope for the rigging, and I checked the river road and the sparse trees for any danger to my Herald. Of course there was none. If there had been any possibility of real harm on this journey, my General would have assigned a seasoned soldier to guard the King's man.

I was sixteen years old, two years out of school and into my military training, and had seen no action at all apart from the rough and tumble of the training ground. I had wanted a posting to one of Pharaoh's eastern forts where the foreign tribes pressed against our borders with longing eyes fixed on the lush fecundity of the Delta. There I might have been called upon to unsheathe my sword, but I suspect that my father used his influence to keep me safely in the city of Pi-Ramses for I found myself a member of General Paiis's household guard, a position of monotonous ease. My military education continued, but most of my time was spent patrolling the General's walls or standing outside the doors of his house, watching a steady stream of women come and go, nobles and beautiful commoners, drunk and happily dishevelled or elegant and deceptively cool, for Paiis was handsome and popular and his bed was always full.

I say my father, and so I think of him, but I have always known that I was an adopted child. My real father was killed in one of Pharaoh's early wars and my mother died giving birth to me. My foster parents had no sons and were glad to take me in. My father is a merchant, very rich, and he wanted me to follow in his footsteps, but something in me yearned for the soldiering life. To please my father I went with him on one of his caravans to the country of the Sabaeans where he trades for rare medicinal herbs, but I was bored and increasingly embarrassed as he tried to interest me in the sights we passed and the subsequent negotiations with the tribesmen when we arrived. We exchanged heated words, and when we returned to Pi-Ramses, he gave in to my begging and enrolled me in the officers' school attached to the palace. So it was that I came to be walking towards the little temple of Wepwawet, God of War, on a still, warm evening in the month of Thoth, God of Wisdom, the village of Aswat behind me, the Nile rippling quietly on my right and the tiny barren fields of the peasants lying brown and furrowed on my left.

In truth I was curious to see inside the temple. The only link I had with my true parents was a small wooden statue of Wepwawet. It had stood on the table beside my bed for as long as I could remember. I had cuddled its smooth curves during the brief unhappinesses of childhood, paced furiously before it when my lamentably fiery temper was aroused, and fallen asleep night after night while watching the glow from my lamp illumine the God's long wolf nose and pointed ears. I never felt fear with him beside me. I grew up with the fanciful belief that my first mother had appointed him to guard me and no danger, human or demonic, could reach me as long as Wepwawet stood gazing with his steady eyes into the dim recesses of my room. The craftsmanship was simple but sensitive, the hand that had formed the spear and sword the statue carried, that had carefully carved the hieroglyphs for "Opener of the Ways" across the God's chest, had been devout as well as able, I felt sure. Who had made it? My adoptive mother did not know, and told me not to distress myself with fruitless fantasies. My father said that when I had been delivered to the house as a baby the statue had been wrapped together with me in the linen swathings. I doubted if either of my mysterious dead parents had actually put knife to wood themselves. High-ranking officers do not do the work of artisans and somehow I could not imagine a woman fashioning a God of War. Nor could I believe that the statue came from the poverty of Aswat. Montu was the Mightiest God of War, but Wepwawet was also venerated throughout Egypt, and in the end I had to sensibly presume that my dead father, a military man, had purchased the statue for his household shrine. Sometimes when I touched the God, I thought of those other hands, the hands that had made it, the hands of my father, the hands of my mother, and I imagined that I felt a flow of connectedness with them through the oiled patina of the wood. On this peaceful evening I had been given the unexpected opportunity to enter the house of the God and pray to him in his own domain. I skirted the end of the canal, walked across the tiny forecourt, and passed under the pylon.

The outer court was already full of evening shadows, its paving blocks dim beneath my feet, the unadorned pillars on either side shrouded in the coming darkness but for their crowns which still glowed in the last light of the sun. As I approached the double doors leading to the inner court, I stooped down, unlatched my sandals, removed them, and was raising a hand to pass through when a voice stopped me.

"The doors are locked."

Startled, I turned. A woman had emerged from the shelter of one of the pillars and was in the act of lowering a bucket onto its pediment. She tossed a rag after it, put a hand to the small of her back, stretched, then came towards me, her step brisk. "The officiating priest locks the doors to the inner court at sunset," she went on. "It's the custom here. Few villagers come to worship during the night. They work too hard during the day." She spoke off-handedly, as though she had made the same explanation many times and was only partially aware of me, yet I found myself looking at her carefully. Her accent held nothing of the harsh, slurred speech of Egypt's peasants. It was clipped, precise and well modulated. But her bare feet were rough and splayed, her hands coarse, the nails broken and grimed. She was dressed in the formless garb of the female fellahin, a thick shift falling to the knees and secured with a length of hemp, and hemp also held back her wiry black hair. Her deeply brown face was dominated by a pair of clear, intelligent eyes whose colour, I realized with a shock, was a translucent light blue. Meeting them, I was immediately tempted to drop my gaze and the urge annoyed me. I was a junior officer of the King's city. I did not give way before peasants.

"I see," I replied more abruptly than I had intended, switching my attention to the inoffensive temple doors with what I hoped was a casual authority. "Then find me a priest to unlock the doors. I am guarding a Royal Herald. We are passing through your village on our way home to the Delta and I wish to perform my devotions to my totem while I have the opportunity." She did not bow and back away as I had expected; indeed, she moved closer to me, and those peculiar eyes narrowed.

"Really?" she said sharply. "What is the Herald's name?"

"His name is May," I offered, and saw the sudden interest die from her face. "Will you fetch a priest?"

She scanned me, taking in the regulation-issue sandals in my hand, the leather belt from which hung my short sword, the linen helmet on my head and the armband denoting my rank that hugged my upper arm and of which I was so proud. I could have sworn that in that moment she had correctly assessed my position, my age and the limits of my power to command her. "I do not think so," she said smoothly. "He is enjoying his evening meal in his cell and I do not wish to disturb him. Have you brought a gift for Wepwawet?" I shook my head. "Then it would be better to come back at dawn, before you set sail, and say your prayers when the priest begins his duties." She turned as if to leave but swung back. "I am a servant to the servants of the God," she explained. "Therefore I cannot open the doors for you. But I can bring you refreshments, beer and cakes or perhaps a meal. It is also my duty to see to the needs of those who journey in the service of Pharaoh. Where are you moored?" I thanked her, told her where our craft rested, and then watched her pick up the bucket and walk away through the gloom. She carried herself as regally as my older sister who had been trained in correct deportment by our nurse, a woman lured into our employ from the harem of the King himself, and I was left staring after her straight spine with a vague feeling of inferiority. Annoyed, I put on my sandals and made my way back to the boat.

I found my Herald sitting on his camp stool moodily staring into the flames of the fire the sailors had kindled. They themselves squatted in the sand a little way off, talking quietly. Our craft was now a bulk of darkness against a fading sky, and the water rippling gently against its hull had lost all colour. He glanced up as I approached.

"I suppose there's no chance of a decent meal in this forsaken hole," he greeted me wearily. "I could send one of the sailors to the mayor and demand something but the prospect of being surrounded by gawking villagers is too much tonight. Our supplies are running low. We will have to make do with flatbread and dried figs." I crouched beside him and turned my face to the fire. He would eat and retire to sleep in the cabin of the boat, but I and the one soldier under me would rotate watches while he snored. I too was tired of indifferent food, hours spent in boredom and discomfort on the river, too many nights of broken sleep, but I was still young enough to be excited by my duties and proud of the responsibility that had me yawning and leaning on my spear in the small hours when nothing stirred but wind in the sparse trees along the Nile and overhead the constellations blazed.

"We will be home in a few days," I answered. "At least the journey has been uneventful. In the temple I met a woman who is bringing us beer and food."

"Oh," he responded. "What did she look like?" The question took me aback.

"She was as anonymous as any other peasant but she had unusual blue eyes. Why do you ask, Lord?" He gave a snort of annoyance.

"Every Royal Herald plying the river knows about her," he said. "The light-eyed crazy one. We try not to stop here, but if we must, we do our best to stay hidden. She works for the temple, but under the pretext of hospitality she pesters us to deliver a package to Pharaoh. I have met her before. Why do you think I was so anxious to bypass this mudhole?"

"A package?" I asked, intrigued. "What is in it?" He shrugged.

"She says that it is the story of her life, that once she knew the Great One, who exiled her here for some crime or other and if only he will read what she has written he will forgive her and lift the banishment. What she has written!" he finished scornfully. "I doubt if she can even scratch her name in the dirt! I should have warned you, Kamen, but it is a small damage done. She will annoy us briefly, but we will at least enjoy a meal."

"So no one has actually seen inside the package?" I pressed.

"Of course not. I told you, she is insane. No Herald would risk embarrassment by carrying out such a request. And put away any romantic notions you may have, young man. Peasants in stories told by nurses may end up in the presence of the Lord of All Life, but in reality they are dull, stupid animals fit for nothing but raising crops and tending the herds they resemble."

"She has an educated accent," I ventured, not sure why I was defending her, and he laughed.

"She has acquired it through years of annoying her betters who have been luckless enough to encounter her," he retorted. "Do not be kind to her or she will importune you all the more. The priests who employ her should control her behaviour. Soon no one at all will want to stop at Aswat, to trade or worship or hire workmen. She may be harmless but she is as irritating as a cloud of flies. Did she mention hot soup?"

Full dark had fallen by the time she came to us almost soundlessly, appearing out of the dense shadows and pacing into the flickering orange light of the fire like some barbaric priestess, her hair, now freed from the hemp, rioting about her head and waving on her breast. She had changed her shift, I noticed, but the one she now wore was no less crude than the garment in which she had been washing the temple floor, and she was still bare-footed. She bore a tray which she set ceremoniously before us on the collapsible table my Herald had called for earlier from the boat. Bowing to him, she then lifted the lid from a pot and proceeded to ladle a savory-smelling soup into two smaller bowls. Beside them were dishes of fresh barley bread and date cakes and, best of all, a flagon of beer. Her movements were graceful and delicate. She offered the soup first to the Herald and then to me with head bowed, both hands around each bowl, and as we began to spoon up the admittedly delicious broth, she poured the beer and unfolded two spotless linen squares which she placed carefully and unobtrusively on our naked knees. Stepping back, she stood with her arms at her sides as we demolished the food, coming forward only to refill our cups or remove the empty plates, and I wondered as I ate if perhaps she had been a servant in the home of some local dignitary, or if the Chief Priest of Wepwawet, a peasant himself but of necessity more highly educated than his neighbours, had taught her how to behave. At last the dishes were piled on the tray and covered with the now soiled linen and my Herald sighed and shifted on his stool.

"Thank you," he said gruffly and, I thought, grudgingly. At his words the woman smiled. Her mouth parted to reveal even white teeth that glinted briefly in the light of the fire and I realized suddenly that she was beautiful. The dimness hid her chafed hands, the fine lines around those strange eyes, the dull dryness of her wild hair, and I stared at her boldly for a moment. Her gaze rested on me, then returned to my Lord.

"We have met before, Royal Herald May," she said softly. "You and your entourage put in here last year when your skiff was holed. What news from the Delta?"

"No news," May replied stiffly. "I am returning to Pi-Ramses from the south. I have been away for several weeks." Her smile widened.

"And of course momentous events may have taken place in the north of which you are unaware," she chided him with mock solemnity. "Therefore you can give me no news. Or is it that you do not wish to encourage me in conversation? I have fed you, Royal Herald May. In return, could I not sit here in the sand and enjoy your company for a while?" She did not wait for permission. Sliding to the earth, she crossed her legs and settled her shift across her lap, and I was reminded of how the scribe in my father's household would sink to the floor and use just such gestures to place his palette on his knees in order to take the dictation.

"I have nothing to say to you, woman!" May snapped. "The food was very welcome and for that I have already thanked you. There is nothing happening in Pi-Ramses that could be of the slightest interest to someone such as yourself, I assure you."

"I have embarrassed him," she said, turning her face to me. "This mighty Herald. I embarrass them all, the important men who hurry up and down the river and curse when they are flung upon the barren shore at Aswat because they know that I will immediately seek them out. It does not seem to occur to them that I might embarrass myself in the process. But you, young officer with the handsome dark eyes, I have not had the pleasure of meeting you before. What is your name?"

"I am Kamen," I answered her, with a rush of unworthy fear that she was about to make her insane request to me. I cast a sidelong glance at my Herald.

"Kamen," she repeated. "Spirit of Men. Might I suppose that Men is your father's name?"

"You might," I said tersely. "And I might suppose that you are making fun of me. I too thank you for the food, but my duty is the care of this Herald and he is tired." I rose. "Be pleased to take your dishes and retire." At once she also scrambled to her feet, much to my relief, and picked up her tray, but I was not to be reprieved so easily.

"I have a favour to ask of you, officer Kamen," she said, "a package to be delivered to the King. I am poor and cannot afford to pay. Will you take it for me?" Oh gods, I thought in exasperation. I felt shame for her as I shook my head.

"I am sorry, Lady, but I do not have access to the palace," I replied and she sighed and turned away.

"I expected nothing more," she called back over her shoulder. "What has Egypt come to, when the powerful will not hearken to the pleas of the destitute? It is no use asking you, Herald May, for you have refused me before. Sleep well!" Her scornful laughter trailed after her and then there was silence.

"Witless creature!" my Lord said curtly. "Set your watch, Kamen." He strode off in the direction of the boat, and I signalled to my soldier and began to fling sand onto the fire. The food was souring in my belly.

I chose the second watch, gave my soldier the perimeters of his patrol, and retired with my blanket under the trees, but I could not sleep. The murmur of the sailors' voices slowly died away. No sound came from the village and only an occasional muted splash revealed the presence of the river as some nocturnal animal went about its quiet business. The sky above me, latticed by branches, pulsed with stars.

I should have been content. I was on my way home to my family and my betrothed, Takhuru. I had successfully completed my first military assignment. I was healthy and vigorous, rich and intelligent. Yet, as I lay there, a restless sadness began to steal over me. I turned over in the sand, closing my eyes, but the earth beneath me seemed harder than usual, grinding against my hip and shoulder. I heard my soldier pace close and then stroll away. I turned again, but it was no good. My mind stayed alert.

I got up, strapped on my sword, and stepped through the trees onto the river road. It was deserted, a ribbon of greyness running through a shrouding of palms and acacia. I hesitated but had no real desire to see the village, which would differ little from a thousand others fronting the Nile from the Delta to the Cataracts of the south. I turned right, feeling increasingly insubstantial as the dark outline of the temple appeared limned in moonlight and the palm fronds above me whispered their dry night song. The water in the canal was black and motionless. I stood on its paved edge for a moment, staring down at my own featureless pale reflection. I did not want to go back to the river. I swung left and walked beside the temple wall. All at once I was skirting a ramshackle hut that leaned against the rear of the temple and before me the desert opened out, rolling in moon-drenched waves to the horizon. A line of palms marking the edge of Aswat's fragile cultivated land meandered away on my left, such a weak bastion holding back the sand, and all of it dim yet stark in the all-pervading streams of moonlight.

I did not notice her at first, not until she emerged from the deep shadow of a dune and glided across the ground. Naked, arms raised, head thrown back, I took her to be one of the dead whose tombs are untended and who wander the night desiring revenge on the living. But she was dancing with such vitality that my thrill of terror vanished. Her straining, flexing body seemed the colour of the moon himself, blue-white, and the cloud of her hair was a patch of blackness moving with her. I knew I should retire, knew I was witnessing a very private ecstasy, but I was rooted to my place by the savage harmony of the scene. The immensity of the desert, the cold flooding of moonlight, the passionate homage or expiation or act of intense pleasure the woman was performing, held me spellbound.

I did not realize the dance was over until she suddenly stood still, raised both fists to the sky, and then seemed to go limp. I could see dejection in the slump of her shoulders as she walked towards me, bent down to retrieve a piece of clothing, and came on more quickly. All at once I knew I was about to be discovered. Hurriedly I swung away but my foot hitched against a loose stone and I stumbled, falling against the rough wall of the hut in whose shadow I had been hiding. I must have grunted with the instant pain in my elbow for she halted, wrapping herself in the linen she was carrying and calling out, "Pa-ari, is that you?" I was caught. Cursing under my breath, I stepped out under the moon to come face to face with the madwoman. In the un-light surrounding us her eyes were colourless, but her lines were unmistakeable. Sweat glimmered on her neck and trickled down her temple. Strands of wet hair stuck to her forehead. She was panting lightly, her chest rising and falling under the two hands clasping the cloak to her. I had not surprised her for long. Already her features were composed.

"So it is Kamen, junior officer," she said breathily. "Kamen the spy, neglecting his duties to guard the illustrious Royal Herald May who is doubtless snoring in blissful ignorance aboard his safe little boat. Have they begun to teach young recruits at the military academy in Pi-Ramses how to spy on innocent women, Kamen?"

"Certainly not!" I retorted, confused by what I had seen and angered by her tone. "And since when do decent Egyptian women dance naked under the moon unless they are …"

"Are what?" she countered. Her breathing was returning to normal. "Insane? Mad? Oh I know what they all think. But this," she waved at the hut, "is my home. This," she jerked her head, "is my desert. And that is my moon. I am not afraid of prying eyes. I harm no one."

"Is the moon your totem then?" I asked, already ashamed of my outburst, and she laughed grimly.

"No. The moon has been my undoing. I dance in defiance under Thoth's rays. Does that make me mad, young Kamen?"

"I do not know, Lady."

"You called me Lady once before this night. That was kind. I did have a title once. Do you believe me?" I looked full into her shadowed face.

"No."

She grinned and a brief glint of some internal fever in her eyes gave me a stab of superstitious fear, but then I felt her fingers, warm and commanding, on my arm. "You have grazed your elbow. Sit down. Wait here." I did as I was told, and she disappeared into the hut, returning almost immediately with a clay pot. Sinking beside me she prised off the lid, took my elbow, and gently smeared a salve on the small wound. "Honey and ground myrrh," she explained. "The wound should not infect, but if it does, soak it in the juice of willow leaves."

"How do you know of these things?"

"I was once a physician, a very long time ago," she answered simply. "I am forbidden to practise my craft any more. I steal the myrrh from the temple stores for my own use."

"Forbidden? Why?"

"Because I tried to poison the King."

Disappointed, I looked across at her. She was sitting with her knees hunched and her arms encircling them, her gaze on the desert. I did not want this strange, this eccentric creature to be insane. I wanted her to be in her right mind so that I might add another dimension, unpredictable and exciting yet legitimate, to my knowledge of life. Predict-ability had protected me through all my growing years. I had enjoyed the security of predictable meals, predictable schooling, predictable affection from my family, predictable feast days of the gods. My predictable betrothal to Takhuru, daughter of established wealth, was planned and expected. Even this assignment had brought no adventure, only predictable duties and discomforts. Nothing had prepared me for quixotic women who dance frenziedly under the moon in peasant villages, but insanity would render this new dimension illegitimate, an aberration of a sane society best ignored and then forgotten. "I do not believe you," I said. "I live in Pi-Ramses. My father knows many nobles. I have never heard of such a thing."

"Of course not. Very few knew of it at the time and besides, it was years ago. How old are you, Kamen?"

"Sixteen."

"Sixteen." She stirred and put out a hand. The gesture was irresolute and oddly pathetic. "It was sixteen years ago that I loved the King, and tried to kill him, and had a son. I was only seventeen myself. Somewhere in Egypt my son lies sleeping, knowing nothing of who he really is, from what seed he has sprung. Or perhaps he is dead. I try not to think about him too much. The pain is too great." She turned and smiled at me sweetly. "But why should you believe me, the crazy Aswat devil? Sometimes I have difficulty believing it all myself, particularly when I am swabbing the temple floor before Ra has shaken himself to rise.

Tell me about yourself, Kamen. Is your life pleasant? Have your dreams begun to come true? Whom do you serve in the city?"

I knew that I should return to the river. My soldier's watch would soon be over. He would be waiting for me to relieve him and besides, what if some emergency had arisen on the boat? Yet the woman held me. It was not her now obvious insanity. Sadly I had to agree with my Herald's assessment of that. Nor was it the contradictions she presented, though I found them intriguing. She was something new, something that troubled and yet soothed my ka. I began to tell her of my family, of our estate in Pi-Ramses, of my battles with my father who wanted me to become a merchant like himself, and of my eventual triumph and admittance to the military academy attached to the palace. "I intend to obtain a posting to the eastern border when I have been promoted to senior officer," I finished, "but until then I am under the command of the General Paiis who keeps me guarding …" I got no further. With an exclamation she grasped my shoulder.

"Paiis! Paiis? That worm of Apophis! That granary rat! I found him attractive once. That was before …" She was struggling for control. Deftly I removed her hand from my shoulder. It had gone cold. "Is he still handsome and charming? Do princesses still plot to share his bed?" She began to beat at the sand. "Where is your pity, Wepwawet? I have paid and paid for my deeds. I have fought to forget, to abandon hope, and now you send me this!" Clumsily she scrambled up and ran past me, and I had only just got to my feet when she returned clutching a box. Her whole body was shaking as she thrust it at me. Her eyes were fierce.

"Listen to me without prejudice please, please, Kamen! I beg you for the sake of my ka, take this box to the house of Paiis! But do not give it to Paiis himself. He would destroy it or worse. Place it into the hands of one of the King's men who surely must come and go under your eye. Ask that it be delivered to Ramses himself. Make up any story you like. Tell the truth if you like. But not to Paiis! Think what you wish of me, but if there is any doubt in your mind, any doubt at all, help me! It is a small thing to do, is it not? Pharaoh is besieged with petitions every day. Please!"

My hand went to my sword with the instinctive reaction of my training. But I had been taught how to hold off hostile men, not obstinate women with only the most slender control over their minds. My fingers alighted on the hilt and rested there. "I am not the one to ask," I objected, keeping my voice calm. "I cannot approach such people as freely as you might think, and if I make your request to one of my father's friends, he will want to assure himself of its validity before risking loss of face before the One. Why have you not taken your box to Aswat's mayor to be included in his correspondence to the governor of this nome, and through the governor to Pharaoh's Vizier? Why do you trouble the Heralds, none of whom will ever help you?"

"I am an outcast here," she said loudly. I could see that she was striving to appear reasonable, but her body was rigid and her voice was uneven. "I am a daughter of Aswat but to my neighbours I am a source of shame and they shun me. The mayor has refused me many times. The villagers make sure that my words are not heard by denying my story to those who might help me. They do not want the scab torn off the wound of their humiliation. So I remain the madwoman, an irritant they can explain honourably, instead of an exiled murderess trying to obtain pardon." She shrugged. "Even my brother, Pa-ari, though he loves me, will do nothing. His sense of justice would be outraged if the King at last bent a sympathetic ear to me. No one will risk his position, let alone his life, for me." Holding the box in both hands, she pressed it gently against my chest and looked full into my face. "Will you?"

I heartily wished myself a hundred miles away, for pity, the one emotion sure to drain all strength from a man, had woken in me. Perhaps if I took the box the madness of her obsession would decline. I had only the faintest idea of what it must be like for her to make her way month after month, year after year, to the riverbank to face the ridicule of the men she was forced to approach, their dismissals, the contempt or worse, the compassion, in their eyes. I hoped she could not read my own. If I took the box, she would be relieved of that burden. I could throw it overboard. No word would come to her from the palace, of course, but she would be comforted by the thought that the King had simply chosen to continue her banishment, and peace might come to her. Such a deceit was unworthy of an officer in the King's service, but were not my intentions kind? Guiltily I sighed and nodded, my hands, as I lifted them to receive the box, sliding over hers as she stepped away. "I will take it," I said, "but you must surely not expect any answer from the King." A great smile spread across her face and she leaned forward and kissed me on the cheek.

"Oh but I do," she whispered, her breath warm against my skin. "Ramses is an old man, and old men begin to spend much time reliving the passions of their youth. He will answer me. Thank you, Officer Kamen. May Wepwawet protect and guide you on my behalf." Drawing the cloak more tightly around her she walked away, disappearing into the shadow of the hut, and I tucked the damnable thing under my arm and began to run back towards the river. I felt like a traitor, but I was already furious at my lack of will. I should have turned her down. "Well it is your own fault for allowing the moon to bewitch you," I berated myself as I stumbled through the trees. "Now what are you going to do?" For I did not think I was callous enough to fling the box into the Nile. When I reached my sleeping place, I hid it under my blanket, then hurried to relieve my soldier and spent the hours until dawn miserably pacing out the bounds of my watch.

While the sailors were preparing a morning meal, I stood in the inner court of the temple listening to a bleary-eyed priest chant the early salutations to the god. I could not see the form of my totem through the half-open door of the sanctuary. His servant blocked my view. Inhaling the thin streams of newly lighted incense that twisted towards me on the morning air and performing my prostrations, I strove to concentrate on the prayers I had wanted to say, but my thoughts refused to clear and the words stumbled over my tongue. By the time the merciless light of Ra had slipped fully over the horizon, I had finished rebuking myself for my weakness in allowing a mere peasant woman to manipulate my will and had decided to give the box back to her. I was angry with myself, but even more angry with her for foisting the responsibility of dealing with the thing onto me. If I kept it, the hard decisions would be mine and I knew I was too honest to simply drop it overboard and let the Nile receive its weight. As I knelt and stood, knelt and murmured my petitions with an absent heart, I kept glancing about the court in the hope of seeing the woman, but she did not appear.

The priest concluded his worship and the sanctuary doors were closed. With a cursory smile in my direction he disappeared into one of the small rooms that fronted the court, his two young acolytes scurrying after him, and I was alone. The box sat on the paving beside me, mutely accusing, a demanding orphan. Snatching it up, I hurried through to the outer court, jammed my sandals back on my feet and ran across the forecourt and around to the tiny shack that clung to the temple's rear wall. As I opened my mouth to call, I realized that I did not even know the woman's name. Nevertheless I raised my voice in a greeting and waited, aware that the sailors would be completing their final check of the boat and my Herald would be anxious to cast off. "Oh damn her!" I muttered under my breath. "And damn me for being a soft fool." Calling again I pushed tentatively against the woven reed mat that passed for a door. It gave, and I was peering into the dimness of a small room whose floor was packed dirt and whose walls were bare. A thin mattress covered a low wooden cot that was surprisingly well constructed, the patina of its smooth legs and sturdy frame gleaming expensively in the relative poverty of its surroundings. The table beside it and the stool at its foot, though simple, were also obviously the work of a craftsman. A crude clay lamp lay on the floor. The hut was empty, and I could not wait. Briefly I considered placing the box on the cot and fleeing but discarded the idea, not without another curse, as unworthy of me. Letting the reed mat fall closed behind me, I swung back towards the river.

As I ran up the ramp and onto the deck of the craft, my kit and blanket under one arm and the offending box under the other, my Herald gave a loud guffaw.

"So she has finally found her fool!" he chortled. "Are you going to drop it overboard, young Kamen, or will your principles get the better of you? How did she persuade you to take it? With a quick roll on her doubtless flea-ridden mattress? You are carrying a load of trouble there, mark my words!" I did not reply. I did not even glance at him, and as he shouted the order to raise the ramp and cast off and the boat slid away from the bank into the glittering morning, I realized that I did not like him at all. My soldier had saved bread and beer for me. I sat in the shade of the prow and ate and drank with no appetite while Aswat and its sheltering vegetation slid away behind us and the desert swept around the few fields and isolated palms remaining. The next village was of course not far away, but as I brushed the breadcrumbs from my knees and drained the last of the beer, a weight of loneliness descended on me and I fervently wished this assignment to be over.

2

THE REMAINING EIGHT DAYS of our voyage passed without incident, and on the morning of the ninth day we entered the Delta where the Nile divided into three mighty tributaries. We took its north-eastern arm, the Waters of Ra, which later became the Waters of Avaris and ran through the centre of the greatest city on earth. It was a relief to me to leave the silent aridity of the south behind and breathe the air of the Delta, more humid, heavy with the scents of gardens, alive with the reassuring sounds of human activity. Though the river had not yet begun to rise, there was water everywhere in ponds and placid irrigation canals, dimpling cool between the closely gathered trees, sparkling half-glimpsed in the tall papyrus thickets whose delicate fronds waved to the touch of a gentle breeze. White cranes stalked arrogantly in the shallows. Small craft plied to and fro beneath the dart of piping birds and our helmsman's gaze never left the river as he carefully negotiated through them.

At the Waters of Avaris the view changed, for here we passed the temple of Bast, the cat goddess, and then the wretched shacks and hovels of the poor who crowded around the huge temple of Set and who filled the air between the temple and the rubble of an ancient town with a frenzy of dust, noise and filth, but soon the scene changed again and we had reached the vast canal that encircled Pi-Ramses, the city of the God. We took the right-hand arm, passing the seemingly endless panorama of warehouses, granaries, storehouses and workshops whose quays ran out into the water like greedy fingers to receive the goods that arrived from every corner of the civilized world and through whose gaping entrances the loaded workmen filed in a constant stream, bearing the wealth that was Egypt on their backs. Behind them I caught a glimpse of the sprawling faience factories. Their Overseer was the father of my betrothed, Takhuru, and I felt a surge of elation at the thought that I would see her again after so many weeks.

Beyond all this confusion was the peace and elegance of the estates of the minor nobles and officials, merchants and foreign traders. Here was my home. Here I would disembark for a few days of leisure before returning to my post on the estate of General Paiis and my labours in the officers' school while my Herald sailed on through the closely guarded narrows that led at last to the Lake of the Residence. There the water lapped against steps of the purest white marble. The craft drawn up to them were fashioned of the finest Lebanon cedar and ornamented in gold, and the polite silence of extreme wealth cast a dreaming hush over lush gardens and deeply shadowed orchards. Here lived the Viziers and High Priests, Hereditary Nobles and Overseers, my future father-in-law among them. Here also a mighty wall surrounded the palace and environs of Ramses the Third.

One could not enter the Lake of the Residence without a pass. My family had access to the private domain, of course, and I had a separate pass enabling me to enter the house of my General and the military school, but today, as the helmsman pulled on the tiller and our craft nosed towards my landing steps, I thought of nothing but a good massage, a flagon of decent wine to complement our cook's fine dishes and the clean touch of scented linens on my own bed. Impatiently I gathered up my belongings, released my soldier from his duty, took formal leave of the Herald May, and ran down the ramp, my feet touching the familiar coolness of our stone watersteps with delight. I barely heard the ramp being withdrawn and the captain's command as the boat went on its way. Crossing the paving, I walked through the high metal gates which stood open, called cheerily to the porter who dozed on his stool within the entranceway of his small lodge, and entered the garden.

There was no one about. The trees and shrubs lining the path stirred lazily in whatever small gusts of wind managed to dive over the high wall that enclosed our whole domain, and sunlight spattered through their branches onto the beds of blooms dotted here and there in the haphazard way my mother liked. Striding along, I soon came to the Amun shrine where the family regularly gathered to worship and I turned right, angling towards the house porch through more trees. Between their sturdy trunks I could glimpse the large fish pond away on my left where the garden pressed up against the rear wall of the estate. Its reed-choked verge and stone lip were deserted, the wide green lotus pads dotting its surface were motionless. There would be no flowers on them for several months yet, but dragonflies darted over them, gossamer wings trembling and glittering, and a frog leaped among them with a splash and a quick ripple.

I had almost drowned once in that pond. I was three years old, insatiably curious, never still. Briefly escaping from my nurse who, I admit, was sorely tried, I trotted to the water, my hands eager for fish, flowers and beetles, and tumbled head first through the reeds. I remembered the shock, then the delicious coolness, then the onset of panic as I tried to draw breath from the dark greenness all around me and found I could not. My older sister pulled me out and tossed me onto the lip where I vomited water and then screamed, more in rage than in terror, and the following day my father directed his Steward to find someone to teach me to swim. I smiled as I entered the gloom of the porch and veered right, into the reception area, that memory coming fresh and vivid for a moment. Pausing, I let out a great breath of satisfaction, feeling the discomforts and tensions of the past few weeks flow from me.

To my left the big room was open, broken by four pillars between whose bulk the sunlight streamed. Beyond them the garden continued with its well close by the inside wall separating the house from the servants' quarters. The fruit orchard was so dense that the main wall running around the whole of my home could not be seen. Far to my right a small door led out to the courtyard where the granaries stood, and across the expanse of white-tiled floor the opposite wall held three doors, all closed. I looked longingly at the one nearest the pillars, for behind it was the bath house, but I crossed in the direction of the third door, my sandals leaving little siftings of grit as I went. I had almost reached it when the middle door opened and my father's Steward came towards me.

"Kamen!" he exclaimed, smiling broadly. "I thought I heard someone come in. Welcome home!"

"Thank you, Pa-Bast," I replied. "The house is so quiet. Where is everyone?"

"Your mother and sisters are still in the Fayum. Had you forgotten? But your father is at work as usual. Do you return to the General at once or shall I have fresh linen placed on your couch?"

I had indeed forgotten that the females of the family had decamped to our little house on the borders of the Fayum lake to escape the worst heat of Shemu, and would not come back to Pi-Ramses until the end of next month, Paophi, when everyone hoped the river would be rising. I felt momentarily dislocated. "I have two days' leave," I answered him, shrugging off my sword belt and handing him my kit together with the sandals I had also slipped off. "Please do have my couch made up, and find Setau. Tell him everything in my kit is filthy, my sword needs cleaning, and the thong on my left sandal is coming unstitched. Have hot water taken to the bath house." He continued to stand there smiling, his eyes on the box under my arm, and all at once I became painfully aware of it weighing against my side. "Take this to my room," I said hurriedly. "I picked it up on my journey and have no idea what to do with it." He took it awkwardly, his other hand loaded with my belongings.

"It is heavy," he commented, "and what strange knots have been used to tie it closed!" I knew that the remark was not an inquisitive one. Pa-Bast was a good Steward and minded his own business. "A message has come from the Lady Takhuru," he went on in a different vein. "She asks you to visit her as soon as you have returned. Akhebset came here yesterday. He wants you to know that tonight the junior officers will be celebrating in the beer house of the Golden Scorpion on the Street of Basket Sellers and if you are home by then he begs that you join them."

I grinned ruefully at Pa-Bast. "A dilemma."

"Yes indeed. But you could pay your respects to the Lady Takhuru after the evening meal and go on to the Golden Scorpion later."

"I could. What is our cook offering tonight?"

"I do not know but I can ask."

I sighed. "Never mind. He could serve stewed mice on chopped grass and it would be more toothsome than a soldier's fare. Don't forget the hot water. At once." He nodded and turned away and I took the few steps to the third door and knocked sharply.

"Enter!" my father's voice commanded and I did so, closing the door behind me as he rose from behind his desk and came around it, arms outstretched. "Kamen! Welcome home! The southern sun has burned you to the colour of cinnamon, my son! How was your journey? Kaha, I think we have done enough for now, thank you." My father's scribe rose from his position on the floor, gave me a quick but very warm smile, and went out, his palette in one hand and his pen and scroll in the other. Indicating that I should take the chair facing the desk, my father regained his own and beamed across at me.

His office was dim and always pleasantly cool as the only light came from a row of small clerestory windows up near the ceiling. As a child I had often been allowed to sit under his desk with my toys while he conducted his business and

I had been fascinated by the squares of pure white light they cast on the opposite wall, light that gradually elongated as the morning progressed and slid down the jumbled shelves until those uniform but fluid shapes began to creep towards me across the floor. Sometimes Kaha would be sitting cross-legged in their path, his palette across his knees and his reed pen busy as my father dictated, and the light would slither up his back and seep into his tight black wig. Then I knew I was safe and could return to my wooden goose and the little cart with real wheels that turned and in which I loaded my collection of pretty stones, brightly painted clay scarabs and my great pride, a little horse with flared nostrils and wild eyes and a tail of real horsehair protruding from its rump. But if Kaha chose to take up his position slightly closer to my father's chair, then my toys would be forgotten and I would watch, tranced with something akin to fear, as the healthy bright squares slowly became distorted rectangles that oozed down the shelves and began to seek me out with blind purpose. They never quite reached me before my mother called me for the noon meal and, of course, I realized as I grew older that it would have been impossible for them to do so once the sun stood over the house. Later I spent my mornings at school, not under my father's desk, but even as a man full grown, sixteen years old and an officer of the King, I could not laugh at that childish fear.

Today it was an early afternoon light that diffused gently through the room, and I sat and regarded my father in its soft glow. His hands and face were heavily lined and toughened with years of travelling the caravan routes in blazing heat, but the runnels of his face had set in their own routes of humour and warmth and the blotching and coarseness of his hands only served to accentuate their strength. He was an honest man, bluff and straightforward, a masterful bargainer in the hard market-place of medicinal herbs and exotica but fair in his dealings and he had made a fortune doing what he loved. He spoke several languages including that of the Ha-nebu and the peculiar tongue of the Sabaeans and insisted that the men who led his caravans, though citizens of Egypt, shared a common nationality with those with whom he traded. Like the priests he belonged to no class and so was accepted into all circles of society, but he was in fact a minor noble, a distinction he did not particularly value, as, he said, he did not earn the title. Yet he was ambitious for me and proud of the convoluted negotiations that had netted the daughter of a great noble for my future wife. Now he sat back, running a beringed hand over his bald scalp to where the last of his grey hair clung in a semicircle between his large ears, and raised a pair of bushy eyebrows at me.

"Well?" he prompted. "What did you think of Nubia? Not too different from the trek into Sabaea we took together, is it? Sand and flies and plenty of heat. Did you get along well with your Royal Herald?" He laughed. "I see by your face you did not. And all for an officer's pay. At least the army is teaching you to keep your temper, Kamen, which is a good thing. One rude word to His Majesty's servant and you would be out on your ear." He sounded regretful and I grinned openly at him.

"I have no intention of being flung out of the army on my ear or my rump or even my nose," I said. "Nubia was boring, the Herald an irritable man, and the whole assignment without incident. But it was better than sitting on a donkey day after day nearly dying of thirst, wondering if the desert brigands were going to attack and steal all the goods we had bartered so hard for and knowing we had to do it all over again in a few months."

"If you get a posting to one of the border forts as you so foolishly desire, you will have your fill of heat and boredom," he retorted. "Who can I leave my business to when I die, Kamen? To Mutemheb? Trading is no occupation for a woman." I had endured this argument many times before. I knew there was no barb in his words, only love and disappointment.

"Dear Father," I said impatiently. "You can leave it to me and I will appoint good stewards ..." He waved me to silence.

"Trading is not an occupation that can be delegated to servants," he pronounced loftily. "There is too much room for dishonesty. One wakes up one morning to find nothing but destitution and one's servants in possession of the estate next door."

"That is ridiculous," I cut in. "How many caravans do you still lead in person? One in ten? Once every two years when you become restless? You trust your men as an officer must trust his soldiers ..."

"Now YOU are becoming pedantic," he smiled. "Forgive me, Kamen. You must be longing for a bath. How was the river on the way back? The sailors were surely praying for Isis to cry so that the rising current would be stronger than the prevailing north wind and would float you home. How much longer did it take to come than to go?"

"A few days," I shrugged. "But we did not make sufficient time to put in where we had intended to each evening. My Herald had planned to spend his nights enjoying the hospitality of mayors who set good tables but more often than not we ate bread and dates on the bank of the Nile. By the time we were forced to camp overnight in Aswat, he had become decidedly disagreeable. There was a woman at Aswat who brought us food …" My father's glance sharpened.

"A woman? What woman?"

"Just a peasant, Father, half-mad. I went into the temple of Wepwawet to pray and she was there, cleaning. I spoke to her because the doors to the inner court were locked and I wanted them opened. Why? Do you know of her?" His bristling eyebrows drew together and his eyes were suddenly clear and very sober.

"I have heard of her. She pesters the Heralds. Did she pester you, Kamen?" The subject should have been a joke, but his gaze remained steadily grave. Surely he is not so protective of me that my encounter at Aswat has upset him! I thought.

"Well not exactly pester," I replied, though of course that was just what she had done. "But she did make a nuisance of herself. She tries to thrust a box at everyone important who passes, something she wants given to the One. Apparently she had already tried to give it to May, my Herald, on a previous occasion, and he had refused, so she attempted to force it on me." The gaze that had defeated so many foreign hagglers with sacks of herbs at their feet continued to bore into me.

"You did not take it did you, Kamen? I know the painful and fleeting compassions of youth! You did not take it?"

I had opened my mouth to confess to him that I had indeed taken it, that she had pressed it to my chest under the moonlight, half-naked, her strange eyes burning in her shadowed face, that something more than a naïve compassion had moved me, but a peculiar thing happened. I had never lied to my father, not once. My tutors had drummed into me the serious nature of lying. The gods did not like deceit. Deceit was a refuge of weakness. A man of virtue told the truth and took the consequences. As a child I had told the lies of anger and panic—No, Father, I did not hit Tamit because she was teasing me—but I had usually retracted those lies when pressed and taken my punishment, and as I grew older there was no need for retractions. I loved and trusted the man who was regarding me so solemnly, yet as I sat there staring back at him, the conviction began to grow in me that I must lie to him. Not because I was ashamed of giving in to the madwoman's desperation, no. Not because my father might be annoyed or might laugh. Not even because he might demand to see the box, might open it, might … Might what? I did not know why the truth had to be hidden from him. I just knew in the depth of my ka that to admit that the box even now lay on my couch upstairs would be to end … end what? Damn it, end what?

"Of course I did not take it," I answered coolly. "I pitied her but did not wish to feed her madness. The situation was very embarrassing though." And I had better make up some story for Pa-Bast, I told myself suddenly, in case he mentions the box in casual conversation. Not likely but possible. Although my father's stance did not change, I sensed a loosening in him.

"Good!" he said briskly. "We must cherish the insane as favourites of the gods but we must definitely not encourage their insanity." He rose. "I managed to obtain antimony on the last trip," he went on, changing the subject completely, "and a large amount of sage herb from Keftiu. The Sabaeans sold my caravan Steward a small quantity of yellow powder they call ginger. I have no idea to what use it may be put. I am going to visit the Seer in person after the sleep. The antimony is for him and he will pay a good price for it, but I am hoping he takes this ginger as well." Coming around the desk, he slapped me heartily on the back. "You stink," he said amiably. "Take a bath, a mug of beer and a rest. If you have the energy, dictate a letter to your mother and sisters in the Fayum. Too bad you were unable to take the detour on the way home and visit them." I was dismissed. Standing and hugging him, feeling his strong arms through the thin linen of his shirt, I ruthlessly quelled the seed of shame inside me. I left the office feeling all at once very tired.

Crossing the reception hall, I went through the centre door and mounted the stairs beyond to where the sleeping quarters were. My room was to the right, with two large windows. Because the upper storey of the house was smaller than the lower, I could step out onto the roof of the lower storey if I wanted, walk to the parapet, and look down upon the granaries, the servants' courtyard, the formal entrance and beyond the main wall the craft-choked Waters of Avaris. To the left of the head of the stairs were my sisters' rooms which overlooked the north side of the garden and straight ahead were the double doors behind which my parents slept. My door swung wide to my touch and with thankfulness I went inside.

The box sat on the fresh linen of my couch, smugly dominating this, my sanctuary, and before I stripped the limp and dirty kilt from my waist so that I could go down to the bath house, I grasped it by a handful of those odd knots with which it was secured and flung it into one of my cedar chests, letting the lid fall with a thud. I still had no idea what to do with it. Even unseen it contaminated the air. "To Set with you," I said under my breath to the woman who had already caused me so much inconvenience, for Set was the red-haired god of chaos and dissention, the totem of the city of Pi-Ramses to be sure but doubtless with followers as far away as miserable Aswat. Oh forget about it, I told myself as I left my room, went back down the stairs, and turned abruptly right at their foot, entering the warm humidity of the bath house. You're home, Takhuru is waiting, you can get drunk with Akhebset, and in two days you will be back at your post with General Paiis. Deal with it later.

The hot water I had ordered was already steaming in two large urns and my servant Setau greeted me as I stepped up onto the bathing slab. While I scrubbed myself vigorously with natron and he deluged me with the scented water, he asked me about my journey and I answered him readily enough, watching the grubby film of my weeks away go sluicing through the drain in the sloping stone floor. When I was clean, I went outside and lay on the bench just within the thin shade of the house so that Setau could oil and massage me. The hottest hours of the day had begun. Beyond the shallow terrace the trees barely moved and the birds were silent. Even the continual low rumble of the city outside the wall was subdued. As my servant's capable hands kneaded the knots from my muscles, everything in me began to relax and I yawned. "Never mind my feet,

Setau," I said. "At least they are clean. When you have finished pounding me, bring beer to my room, and please have a message sent to Takhuru. Tell her I'll come to see her at sunset."

Back in my own quarters I lowered the reed mats covering my windows, drained the beer Setau had promptly brought, and fell onto my couch with a groan of pure satisfaction. The little statue of Wepwawet gazed at me serenely from his post on my bedside table, his elegant nose seeming to quest the air and his tall ears pricked to receive my words as I drowsily saluted him. "Your temple is small but pretty," I told him. "However, your devotees at Aswat are strange indeed, Wepwawet. I devoutly hope I do not have to encounter them again."

I slept deeply and dreamlessly, and woke to Setau's movements as he raised the mats and placed a tray at my feet. "I did not want to wake you, Kamen," he said as I stretched and sat up, "but Ra is sinking and the evening meal is already over. Your father has been to the Seer's house and returned. He instructed me to let you rest but doubtless the Lady Takhuru is even now pacing her garden in expectation of your presence and I did not think you would want to incur her displeasure." I smiled at him slowly and reached for the tray.

"That is all too easy to do," I replied. "Thanks, Setau. Find me a clean kilt will you, but don't bother to get out my best sandals. If you've mended the others, they will do. I want to walk to the Noble's house. I need the exercise." The tray was heavy with milk and beer, a small loaf of clove-scented barley bread, steaming lentil soup and a bed of dark lettuce on whose quivering crisp leaves sat a square of yellow goat cheese, a piece of grilled duck and a scattering of raw peas. "Oh gods," I breathed. "It's good to be home."

While I devoured the food with an alacrity which would have earned me a stern rebuke from my old nurse, Setau moved about the room, opening my chests. I saw him hesitate when his glance fell on the box and he lifted it enquiringly. "This will crush your starched linens," he said. "May I place it elsewhere?" He was too well trained to ask me what it contained and I resisted the urge to increase his curiosity by trying to explain it away.

"Put it on the bottom of the chest, then," I suggested carelessly. "It's not something I need to deal with immediately." He nodded and did so, then went on laying out my gold-bordered kilt and tasselled belt, my plain gold bracelet and the earring set with beads of jasper. When I was ready, he painted my eyes with black kohl and helped me to dress. I left him to tidy everything away and went briskly down the stairs. My father stood at the bottom, talking to Kaha, and as I came up to them he eyed me critically. "Very handsome," he commented cheerfully. "Off to dally with Takhuru are you? Well keep your hands off her, Kamen. Your marriage is still a year away." I did not rise to the familiar bait. Bidding them both a good night I crossed the reception hall and out into the orange flush of the setting sun, thinking as I did so that I must remember to talk to Pa-Bast about the box.

Turning left outside the main gate, I swung along the path that ran beside the water, inhaling the cooler evening air. The watersteps I passed were thronged with the inhabitants of neighbouring estates and their servants as they prepared to take to the river in search of a night of revelry, and many of them called greetings to me as I passed. Then for a while I walked with dense trees on my left until I came to the sentries guarding the Lake of the Residence. Here I was challenged, but the words were a formality. I knew these men well. They allowed me to pass and I moved on.

The Waters of Avaris spread out into the great Lake that lapped with a suitably dignified slow rhythm against the sanctified precincts of the Great God Ramses the Third himself, and the estates between me and the towering wall protecting him from the common gaze were also walled. The tops of lush trees leaned discreetly over these massive mud-brick constructions, dappling me in a gradually deepening shadow as I paced beneath them. Where they were broken by tall gates that let out onto marble watersteps and sleek craft whose brightly coloured flags trembled in the evening breeze, the soldiers clustered. I saluted them happily and they shouted back at me.

Along this hallowed edge of the Lake lived the men holding the health of Egypt in their hands. Their power infused the kingdom with wealth and vitality. Under their direction the balance of Ma'at, the delicate web that wove the laws of gods and men together under Pharaoh, was maintained. Here lived To, Vizier of both the South and the North, behind his gates of solid electrum. The High Priest of Amun, Usermaarenakht, with his illustrious family, had his titles incised into the stone of the pylon under which his guests had to pass and his guards were decked in gold-tooled leather. The mayor of the holy city of Thebes and Pharaoh's Chief Taxing Master, Amunmose, favoured a life-sized statue of the God Amun-Ra, once totem of Thebes alone but now the King of all the gods, standing with folded arms and gently smiling face on the paving between watersteps and gate. I did him homage as I stepped past his mighty knees. The home of Bakenkhons, Overseer of all Royal Cattle, was relatively modest. Here a party was about to embark, the women in filmy linen encrusted with jewels that flashed red in the dying light of the sun, the men wigged and ribboned, their oiled bodies gleaming. I waited respectfully while they were handed onto the cabined raft rocking at the foot of the watersteps. Bakenkhons himself answered my obeisance with a warm smile and the raft was poled away in a swirl of dark water. I went on.

The shadows were lengthening, stretching over me now and fingering the verges of the Lake, and as I came to the precinct of the great Seer, I paused. The wall enclosing his house and grounds was no different from the walls I had already passed. It was broken halfway along by a small and very simple gateless pylon so that passersby were able to glance into the garden itself. Within the left-hand base of the pylon an alcove sheltered a taciturn old man who had been the Seer's porter for as long as I could remember and who had never once returned my greeting as I came and went. My father, who regularly had business with the Seer, told me that the ancient one only addressed those who turned in under the pylon and then only to send to the house for permission for the visitor to proceed. Not that he could have prevented anyone from pushing through into the garden, I reflected. He was too frail. Yet the Seer employed no guards outside the wall. Inside the house there were soldiers, or so my father said, who did their work with quiet and unobtrusive efficiency, but standing there with one hand against the still-warm brick of the wall, my eyes on the distorted shadow that marked the entrance to the Seer's domain, I understood why no weapons were needed outside. The pylon was like a mouth perpetually open to swallow the unwary and I had seen people on the path describe an unconscious semicircle as they went by. Even in the harsh light of noon I myself had often veered closer to the watersteps. Now, as the pylon's long silhouette snaked across the path, I had to force myself to straighten and go on.

I had never been allowed to accompany my father in his dealings with Egypt's greatest oracle. "The man runs a perfectly respectable household," my father had told me rather testily some years ago when I had asked him why I could not go with him, "but he is fanatical regarding his privacy. I would be too if I suffered from his affliction."

"What affliction?" I had pressed. All Egypt knew that the Seer had some terrible physical ailment. In his rare public appearances he was swathed from hooded head to bandaged toes in white linen so that even his face was invisible. But I had hoped that given the frequency of my father's visits some more specific information might be forthcoming. "Is the Seer deformed?"

"I do not think so," my father had replied carefully. "His speech is more than sane. He walks on two legs and obviously has the use of both arms. His torso seems pleasingly slim for a man of middle age. Under his windings of course. I have not had the privilege of seeing him without them." I had been nine at the time this exchange took place, and with a young boy's natural curiosity I had waited my chance to squeeze Pa-Bast for more. But he had been even less co-operative than my father.

"Pa-Bast, you are a friend of Harshira, the great Seer's Steward," I had begun after pushing my way with my usual bluntness into his little office where he was bent over the scroll on his desk. "Does he talk much about his illustrious Master?" Pa-Bast had looked up and fixed me with his level gaze.

"It is not polite to intrude without knocking, Kamen," he had reproved me. "As you can see, I am busy." I apologized but stood my ground.

"My father has told me what he knows," I said, completely unabashed, "and his words have distressed me. I wish to include the Seer in my petitions to Amun and Wepwawet but I must be exact in my prayers. The gods do not like vagueness." Pa-Bast sat back on his chair and smiled thinly.

"Do they not, young master?" he said. "Nor do they look indulgently on the hypocrisy of young boys who wish to acquire salacious gossip. Harshira is indeed my friend. He does not talk about his Master's personal affairs and I do not talk about mine. I strongly suggest that you concentrate on the state of your own affairs, namely the sorry showing you are making in the study of military history, and leave the Seer's business to the Seer." His head had gone down again over his work and I had left him utterly unrepentant, my curiosity unslaked.

My marks in military history improved and I learned, more or less, to mind my own business, but in my idle moments I continued to ponder the power and mystery of the man to whom the gods revealed their secrets and who, it was said, could heal with a glance. Heal all but himself, that is. As I hurried past the dark maw of his pylon, I thought of him now wound in linen like a corpse, sitting motionless in the dimness of the silent house whose upper windows could sometimes be glimpsed beyond the dense life of his garden.

Once past his domain my mood lightened and before long I was turning in at Takhuru's gate. The guards waved me through and I strode the sandy path that snaked between thick shrubbery. A straight line would have brought me quickly to the house's imposing, pillared façade but Takhuru's father had laid out his estate to give an impression of more arouras than he really had. His walkways curved around stands of doum palms, ornamental pools and oddly shaped flower beds before leading to the broad paving of his courtyard, and the building itself could not be seen until one had turned the last bend. The affectation amused my father, who said that the estate reminded him of a mosaic designed by an overly enthusiastic faience worker intent on giving those who saw it a headache. He had not, of course, made the remark in public. I found the effect slightly suffocating.

If the grounds were crowded with foliage and various embellishments, the interior of the house seemed always empty, cool and spacious, its tiled floors and star-spangled ceilings breathing an old-fashioned peace and gentility. Furnishings were sparse, simple and costly, the servants well trained, efficient and as silent as the polite air through which they moved. One glided towards me as I walked into the hall. Good manners demanded that I pay my respects to Takhuru's parents before seeking her out, but the man informed me that they had gone to dine on the river with friends. The Lady Takhuru could be found on the roof. Thanking him I retraced my steps and took the outside stairs.

In spite of the fact that the sun had now set and the streamers of red light being dragged rapidly towards the west held little heat, my betrothed was sitting in deep shadow against the eastern wall of the windcatcher, half-buried in cushions. Though she was cross-legged, her spine did not touch the brick, her narrow shoulders did not slump, and the filmy folds of her yellow sheath decorously hid her knees. Beside her were her gold-thonged sandals, set neatly together. To her right, a tray held a silver flagon, two silver cups, two napkins and a dish of sweetmeats. Before her the sennet game waited, each playing piece on its appointed square. Hearing me come, she turned her head and smiled happily, but that rigid little back did not bend. Her mother, I reflected as I approached, would have approved. Taking her hand, I pressed my cheek against hers. She smelled of cinnamon, an expensive but pleasant addiction she had, and of lotus oil.

"I am sorry to be later than I intended," I said to forestall the expected complaint. "I arrived home dirty and very tired, and when I had bathed I slept longer than I should." She affected a pout, and releasing her fingers she waved me down opposite her, the sennet board between us. She was wearing the bracelet I had given her last year when we were officially pledged to one another, a thin circlet of electrum around whose rim tiny golden scarabs marched. It had cost me a month of labour amongst the cattle belonging to the High Priest of Set during my leisure hours, and it looked beautiful on her elegant wrist.

"Providing you dreamed about me, I don't mind," she replied. "I have missed you a lot, Kamen. All I do from dawn to dusk is think about you, especially when Mother and I are ordering linen and dishes for our home. Last week the wood carver called. He has finished the set of chairs we ordered and he wants to know how much gilding to use on the arms and whether the rests are to be decorated or left plain. I think plain, don't you?" She raised her black eyebrows and the flagon of wine at the same time, hesitating until I nodded. I watched her white teeth catch a portion of her lower lip as she poured, and her dusky eyes, heavily kohled, met mine. I took the cup and sipped. The wine was delicious, bringing a rush of saliva to my mouth. I swallowed appreciatively.

"Plain or fancy, I don't really care," I began, and then seeing her crestfallen expression, I realized my mistake. "I mean that I cannot afford much beyond simple gilding," I added hastily. "Not yet, not for some time. I have told you that my soldier's pay is not large and we must try to manage on it. The house itself is costing me a small fortune." The pout was back.

"Well if you would accept my father's offer and learn about faience, we could have everything we wanted now," she objected, not for the first time. I answered her more sharply than I had intended. The argument was not new but the feeling that swept over me was, a depression mingled with anger at her blithe selfishness. My mind flooded suddenly with a vision of the modest hut where the Aswat woman lived, with its clean poverty, of the woman herself, her rough feet and coarsened hands, and I gripped my cup tightly to prevent the anger spilling over.

"I have told you before, Takhuru, that I do not want to become an Overseer of the Faience Factories," I said. "Nor do I want to follow in my father's footsteps. I'm a soldier. One day I may be a general, but until then I am happy with my choice and you will just have to learn to accept it without complaint." The words had an admonitory sting to them which I regretted as I saw her flinch. The affected pout was replaced by a watchfulness. She paled and sat back. Her spine found the wall and she straightened unconsciously, laying her ringed and hennaed hands in her yellow lap and lifting her chin.

"I am not accustomed to poverty, Kamen," she said evenly. "Forgive me for my thoughtlessness. You know of course that my dowry will be ample enough to provide for everything we might need." Then she gave an artless and unselfconscious grimace that restored her to young girlhood, and my anger was gone. "I did not mean to sound arrogant," she went on apologetically. "It's just that I am afraid of being poor. I have never done without anything I wanted, much less needed."

"My dear, silly little sister," I chided. "We will not be poor. Poor is one table, one stool and one tallow lamp. Have I not promised to care for you? Now drink your wine and we will play sennet. You have not asked me how my assignment went." Obediently her nose disappeared into her cup. She licked her lips and wriggled forward.

"I will be cones. You can be spools," she ordered. "And I have not asked you about your journey south because I am not interested in anything that takes you away from me."

I sighed inwardly and we began to play, throwing the sticks with a clatter onto the still-warm roof on which we sat and talking intermittently of nothing in particular while the last of Ra's light was pulled from the treetops around us and the first stars appeared.

We had known each other for years, first as toddlers reeling about our respective gardens while our parents dined together and then as students in the temple school. She had soon returned home with a rudimentary education considered appropriate for young women who would be required to do no more than run a household for their husbands while I had continued to study and then entered the military school. We had seen less of each other then, meeting only when our families joined for parties or religious observances. My father had begun the negotiations that ended in our betrothal. Such a thing had seemed natural to me until Takhuru began to talk of houses and furniture, of utensils and dowry, and I realized that I would be eating, talking and bedding with this girl for the rest of my life.

I did not think that the reality of a marriage contract had been brought home to her yet in spite of her dreams. She was a spoilt only child, the late product of her parents who had lost a daughter many years ago. She was lovely in a delicate, fragile way and I supposed that I loved her. In any case, the die was cast and we were almost irrevocably tied to one another whether we liked it or not. Takhuru in her innocence liked it. I had liked it too in a purely unreflective way, until now. I found my eyes fixed on the fastidious way her fingers found and grasped a cone, the way she would occasionally smooth her sheath as though afraid that I might see further than her knees, the way she pursed her mouth and frowned before making a move. "Takhuru," I said, "do you ever dance?" She looked across at me, startled, her features dim in the twilight.

"Dance, Kamen? What do you mean? That is not my vocation."

"I do not mean in the temple," I replied. "I know you are not trained for that. I mean dance for yourself, in the garden perhaps or before your window, or even under the moon, just for joy or perhaps in rage." She stared at me blankly for a moment and then burst out laughing.

"Gods, Kamen, of course not! What a strange thought! Why would anyone indulge in such undisciplined behaviour? Look out. I am about to put you into the water. An unlucky omen for tomorrow!"

Why indeed?, I thought ruefully as she pushed my spool into the square denoting the dark waters of the Underworld and glanced up to laugh at me again. The move signalled an end to the game although I struggled for a propitious throw that would deliver me, and soon she swept the pieces into their box, closed the lid, and rose.

"Be careful tomorrow," she warned me half-seriously as she took my hand and we wandered towards the stairs. "The sennet is a magical game and you lost this evening. Will you come into the house now?" I bent and kissed her full on the lips, briefly tasting the cinnamon and the sweet, healthy tang of her, and she responded, but then she pulled away, always she pulled away, and I let her go.

"I can't," I said. "I must meet with Akhebset and find out what has been happening in the barracks while I have been away."

"You must indulge in a night of carousing you mean," she grumbled. "Well, send and tell me when we can go and look at the chairs. Good night, Kamen." Her attempts to control me, often unspoken, could be tiring. I bid her sleep well, watched that spear-straight back move from dimness into the sallow light of the lamps already lit within the house, and then turned to walk through the shadowed gardens. For some reason I felt not only tired but drained. I had done my duty by calling on her, placating her, apologizing for something I would not even have bothered to mention if she had been my sister or a friend, and I looked forward with far more eagerness to a night in the beer house with Akhebset and my other comrades. I would not have to explain myself to them, nor to the women who served beer and food or who inhabited the brothels where we sometimes met the dawn.

I had reached the river and here I paused, gazing down at the specks of starlight disfigured in the water's slow swell. What is the matter with you? I asked myself sternly. She is beautiful and chaste, her blood is pure, you have known her and been happy in her company for years. Why this sudden shrinking? A tremor of air stirred the leaves above me and for a moment a shaft of new moonlight lit the reeds at my feet. Quelling the spurt of panic it caused me, I turned and walked on.

3

I SPENT THE REMAINING one day of my leave nursing a sore head, dictating the most interesting letter I could conjure to my mother and sisters in the Fayum, and swimming in a vain attempt to rid my body of the admittedly enjoyable poisons I had fed it. I sent a message to Takhuru, arranging to meet her at the woodworker's home after my first watch for the General. I dined in the evening with my father and later made sure that Setau had cleaned and laid out my kit in preparation for the morning. I was due to relieve the officer on the General's door at dawn and I had intended to take to my couch early, but three hours after sunset I was still tossing restlessly under my sheet while the last dregs of oil in my lamp burned away and Wepwawet, although he stared straight out into the flickering shadows of my room, seemed to be eyeing me with speculation and a certain disapproval. At last I knew that until I had resolved the problem of the box I would get no sleep. Rising, I opened my chest, half-hoping that by some miracle the thing had vanished but no, it nestled comfortably under my folded kilts like some unwanted parasite. With a sinking heart I lifted it and placed it on my knees as I sat on the edge of my couch.

It would have been impossible to untie all the curious knots that held its lid tightly closed. If I had wanted to examine the contents, I would have had to take a knife and slice through the hemp, but, of course, I could not have brought myself to break into something that did not belong to me, was not intended for my eyes. Yet I longed to do so. Perhaps in her delusion the woman had filled the box with stones and feathers, twigs and handfuls of grain, imagining that she was enclosing the story of her life. Perhaps she could indeed write a few halting words and had scrawled the doubtless pitiful details of her life in the pathetic hope that the Lord of All Life might be impressed, or worse, had made up a story of plot and persecution out of her madness. Even so, I had not been given permission to open the box. What would happen to a luckless messenger who managed to have the box delivered to the palace and who saw Pharaoh open it only to find rubbish of one sort or another inside? Probably only ridicule, the sharp edge of the illustrious royal tongue, the titters of the surrounding courtiers. I could easily imagine myself standing before the Horus Throne, although the details of the audience chamber and the throne itself were, of course, vague in my mind as I had never seen either. I could see the divine fingers holding the jewelled knife, slicing through the knots, lifting the lid. I could hear the condescending laughter as the King extracted—what? A few stones? A grubby piece of stolen papyrus? I could also hear my career go sliding into oblivion and I groaned. My principles would not allow me to throw the box away or open it and I could not possibly give it to someone else to be made a fool of in front of the Good God. I considered asking my father for advice but discarded the idea. I knew him too well. He would tell me that the responsibility was mine not his, that I was no longer a child, that I should not have accepted the box in the first place. He already saw my judgement as faulty and believed that it was only a matter of time before I was forced to change my mind regarding my decision to become a soldier. This stupid act of mine would simply reinforce his opinion of me. I knew he loved me fiercely, but I wanted to make him proud of me also. I would not approach him with this matter.

That left only my General. I would take the box to him tomorrow, explain to him what had happened, suffer his annoyance or amusement. I remembered that the woman had implored me not to say anything about it to Paiis, but how sane was her request anyway? It was impossible that she should know anything about him but his name. The relief I felt at having made the decision was immediate and over-whelming. Laying the box on the floor, I climbed back under my sheets. Wepwawet seemed to watch my movements with a fatuous satisfaction. I was asleep within moments.

Setau woke me an hour before dawn and I rose, ate a light meal, and dressed myself in the uniform of my position as an officer in the house of the General. The spotless kilt, the oiled leather belt with its burden of dagger and sword, the white linen helmet, the plain armband denoting my status, gave me a feeling of belonging and I put them on with pride. Slipping on my sandals and tucking gauntlets into my belt, I picked up the box and left the house.

The garden was still hushed and dark but the moon had set, and in the east a thin ribbon of red divided the land from the sky. Nut was about to give birth to Ra in a gush of blood. I could have descended our watersteps and taken the skiff, but I was not in danger of being late this morning so I walked along the river path as one by one the birds began their first songs and a few sleepy servants appeared to sweep the steps and clean the river craft.

The General's estate was not far, indeed no destination was far in Pi-Ramses. His gates opened just beyond Takhuru's home. I glanced into her garden, for sometimes if she woke early she would take her fruit and bread onto the roof and wave at me as I passed, but there was only a servant shaking a hanging from which a cloud of dust spewed and hung glinting in the new light.

Once within the General's precincts I sought out the officer in charge, then received the report from the man I was replacing. Nothing untoward had happened while I had been gone. Stowing the box under a bush by the entrance, I took up my station in front of one of the pillars and settled contentedly to watch the lush garden fill with life and warmth. This week I guarded the General. Next week I would take up residence in the barracks for weapons drill. It was rumoured that my company might be going out onto the western desert for manoeuvres. By this evening the nagging problem of the box would be solved. I was a happy man.

My watch passed without incident. Two hours after dawn a litter arrived and carried away a pale and yawning woman who emerged tentatively from the house escorted by the General's Steward and an attentive maidservant who immediately unfolded a parasol and held it over her mistress's tousled head as she approached her conveyance, although the sun was far from its full force. The woman climbed onto the litter, giving me a glimpse of one taut calf, and the maid closed the curtains hurriedly, whether to shut

out the sun or the few eyes fixed on the scene I did not
know. Nor did I care. The litter was lifted, the maid walking
by her invisible mistress's side, and disappeared towards the
river.

A short time later the traffic into and out of the house
began in earnest; fellow Generals and lesser officers, Paiis's
household servants, an occasional boon-seeker, Heralds
and minor messengers, and I watched them all, challenging
the faces I did not recognize, greeting those I did, until it
was time for the noon meal. One of the men under me took
my place while I went to the kitchen behind the house for
my bread, cold duck and beer which I consumed sitting in
the shade in a secluded corner of the garden, then I
resumed my duties.

In the late afternoon I made my report to my replacement, retrieved the box, and entered the house, asking the
Steward if the General might see me on a personal matter.
I was in luck. The General was still in his office, though he
was due to leave for the palace soon. As a member of his
household staff I knew the layout of the premises intimately
and did not need an escort to arrive at the rather forbidding
double doors leading to his private domain. Knocking, I was
bidden tersely to enter and did so. The room was not
strange to me. Large and rather pleasant, it contained a
desk, two chairs, numerous chests bound in brass, an ornate
brazier and a shrine to Montu before whose likeness an
incense cup smoked. Because the few windows were cut
high in the wall, the light was always diffused, an advantage, I reflected, for a man who often began the work of the
day with burning eyes and a pounding head. Paiis was a
man of sensual appetites, less a field officer than a strategist

and military tactician, and I often wondered how he had managed to survive the years of rigorous physical training followed by an obligatory apprenticeship in the ranks of the army before being promoted. Not that he was soft. I knew that he spent a considerable amount of time swimming, wrestling, and drawing the bow, but I suspected that he did so in order to continue to pursue his real interests—vintage wine and the delights of sex—and his excesses in both were beginning to tell in spite of his discipline. Handsome and vain, he was nevertheless a good superior, impersonal in his commands and impartial in matters of judgement.

I approached him confidently, saluting as I came up to the desk, and stood to attention as best I could with the box under my arm. He smiled at me. I presumed that he was due to dine at the palace, for he was dressed sumptuously in red linen, his black, grey-flecked hair held back by a scarlet ribbon fringed with tiny golden arrows. Gold dust glittered in the oil on his broad chest and above his thickly kohled eyes and more gold gleamed around his wrists. He was as magnificently arrayed as a woman, yet the impression he gave was one of purely masculine power. I did not know if I liked him. One did not think of one's superiors in such terms. But I occasionally hoped that I saw my own future in his great wealth and position.

"Well, Kamen," he said warmly, indicating that I might stand easy. "I understand that you want to speak to me regarding something personal. I hope it is not a request for a different posting. I know I must lose you eventually but I shall be sorry to do so. You are a promising young officer and my household guard functions well under you."

"Thank you, General," I answered. "I am content to be

in your employ, although I do hope for a more active posting before I marry in a year's time. After that I daresay there will be less opportunities for soldiering away from Pi-Ramses." He looked amused.

"Your future wife will wish it so," he replied, "but marriage will only curtail your ambitions if you let it. Unfortu-nately for you there are few rough and dangerous posts to be filled these days, but I suppose you may continue to dream of sudden invasions." His face did not mirror the condescension of his words. He continued to smile at me kindly. "Now what is the trouble?"

I leaned forward and placed the box on the desk, inwardly bracing myself for my confession. "I have done a foolish thing, General," I began. "Have you heard of the madwoman at Aswat?"

"Aswat?" he frowned. "That mud puddle in the south? Wepwawet has a rather fine temple on its outskirts as I recall, but the village has nothing else to recommend it. Yes, I have heard of some woman who pesters those who are forced to dock there on the way to a more salubrious destination. What of her? And what is this?" He had pulled the box towards him, but then he paused, going very still as his gaze fell on the many convoluted knots holding it closed. "Where did you get this?" he demanded brusquely. His fingers, weighted with rings, began to move almost clumsily over the hemp, then he snatched his hand away and sat straight. His words were like an accusation and I was taken aback.

"Forgive me, General Paiis, if I have done something wrong," I said, "but I needed your advice. The woman gave it to me, or rather, I agreed to take it. You see, she importunes all travellers to deliver this box to Pharaoh. She tells a tale of attempted murder and exile and says that she wrote it all down. She's insane of course, no one listens to her, but I felt sorry for her and now I don't know what to do with whatever is in there." I pointed at the box. "It would have been dishonest to toss it into the Nile, and even more dishonest to cut the knots and examine the contents. I do not have the authority to approach Pharaoh even if I wanted to, and I do not want to!" Now a wintry smile twisted the General's lips. He seemed to be recovering from whatever had ailed him, but he still looked somehow diminished, and I noticed for the first time the tiny red tracks of weariness in his eyes.

"I am not surprised," he said wryly. "Only the mad would aid the mad in that way. But sometimes honesty and insanity have a great deal in common, have they not, my idealistic young soldier?" Once more his hand hovered over the box but then withdrew as though he were afraid it would contaminate him in some way. "What is this woman like?" he asked. "I have heard her spoken of among the Heralds but rarely and briefly, as a mild and usually humorous inconvenience, and I paid no attention. Describe her to me." Now it was my turn to frown.

"She is a peasant, and like most peasants she should be anonymous," I said slowly. "Her hair is black, her skin burned dark by the sun. But I remember her well. There was something different about her, something exotic. Her language and her accent were too refined for a mere villager and she had blue eyes."

When I finished speaking he stared at me for so long that at first I thought he had lost interest and ceased to listen, and then that he had been struck by some sort of fit.

An awkward silence fell. For a while I did not wish to appear rude so I continued to look into his face but the moment became embarrassing and I let my attention wander. It was then I realized that he had certainly heard me and was struggling to absorb the impact of my artless words, for he was gripping the edge of his desk with such ferocity that the skin around his rings was white. My heart began to pound.

"You know who she is!" I blurted, and at that he came to himself.

"For a moment I thought I did," he said quietly, "but of course I am mistaken. This is coincidence, nothing more. Leave the box with me. You were a sentimental idiot to accept it in the first place, Kamen, but no harm has been done. I acknowledge your misplaced sense of pity. You may go." His voice was strained, and as I watched he began to massage his temple as though his head had begun to ache.

"But General Paiis, Noble One, you will not throw it away?" I pressed. He did not look up.

"No," he said slowly. "Oh no. I will certainly not throw it away. But seeing you have chosen to foist the responsibility for it onto me, young man, you must leave all decisions regarding its disposal in my hands. Do you trust me?" Now he did lift his glance as he spoke the last words. His mouth had thinned and I swear that if I had been close enough to feel his breath it would have been cold. I nodded and came to attention once more.

"I am your obedient servant, General. I am grateful for your indulgence."

"You are dismissed."

I saluted, turned on my heel, and left his office, my mind

in a turmoil. Had I done the right thing after all? I had not thought of my action as divesting myself of a responsibility, and I did not believe that placing the box in the General's hands gave him the right to do with it as he wished.

I had bid my replacement on the door an absent good evening and was walking through the gate when it came to me that I did not in fact trust General Paiis in this matter. The woman had not trusted him either. She had warned me not to give the box to him and I had ignored the warning. He did know who she was. Not by reputation, not by gossip among the Heralds, but by actually standing face to face with her. I was increasingly positive of this. He had asked me to describe her and I had told him of someone familiar to him, someone, moreover, with the power to evoke a surprisingly intense response in him. He had recognized the knots first, and my words had confirmed that recognition. But what was between them? I wondered as I set off towards my home. What could possibly link a peasant and the rich and mighty Paiis? Whatever it was, the General was very troubled. Could at least some of the woman's story be true?

The whole encounter with my superior had left me filled with an uneasiness that had not abated by the time I reached my own watersteps. Sending Setau for beer, I sat in the garden by the pond, watching its surface gradually fade from blue to an opaque darkness and then become slashed with orange as Ra rolled towards the wide mouth of Nut. I was not sure what distressed me most, the possibility that the woman was not insane after all, the astonishing and oddly threatening suspicion that Paiis knew all about her or the fact that in relinquishing the box I had abandoned any opportunity to learn the truth. The adventure, as far as I was concerned, was over.

Ra sank below the horizon. The lamps in the house behind me were lit. What had been shade above me became shadow all around me. It was not until the aroma of frying fish brought me to my feet that I remembered the appointment I had made with Takhuru. She would be furious. For once I did not care.

IT WAS JUST AFTER my disturbing meeting with the General that the dreams began. At first I ignored them, thinking that they had to do with the tongue lashing I received from Takhuru when I visited her to apologize for forgetting our visit to the woodworker. I had lost my temper with her, grabbed her wrist and shouted, and she had responded by slapping my face, kicking me in the ankle, and stalking away. Once I would have run after her, but this time I too turned on my heel and left her ridiculously crowded garden. After all, I had tendered an apology for nothing more than a lapse of memory, but she had behaved as though I had neglected to appear at the signing of our marriage contract and had accused me of caring for no one but myself. Now it was her turn to grovel. Of course she did no such thing. Takhuru's blood was noble, her character proud and selfish.

A week went by. The month of Thoth merged into the month of Paophi, hot and endless. The river was close to its highest level for that year. A letter arrived from my mother stating that she was planning to remain on our estate in the Fayum for another month. I dictated a sequence of watches for my men at the General's house, then took my gear into the barracks and spent the week on the training ground sweating out my irritation with Takhuru. We did not go out onto the desert. I returned home having been grazed with a spear across my shoulder blade. The accidental wound was not serious and soon closed, but as it healed it itched and I could not reach it in order to scratch.

Akhebset and I got noisily drunk and woke one dawn in the bottom of someone's skiff with a whore between us. There was still no word from my betrothed and none from the General. I had imagined that he would let me know what he had done with the box, but I walked his halls and watched his door without seeing or hearing from him. I was in a peculiar state of mind, restless and agitated. My sleep became fitful, and then I started to dream.

I was lying on my back outside, staring up into a clear blue sky. The feeling was one of utter contentment and for a long time I remained motionless, full of a wholly satisfying and unreflective comfort. But presently I sensed movement and the sky was blocked out by a huge shape coming steadily closer. I was not afraid, merely diverted. As it came into focus I recognized it as a hand, the hennaed palm curled around the stem of a pink lotus bloom. Then it slipped out of focus again and I felt the flower tickle my nose. Vainly I tried to grasp it, flailing arms that were suddenly clumsy and unresponsive, and I woke with my arms above my head, the scab on my shoulder throbbing and my sheets wet with sweat. My room was dark, the house full of night silence. I sat up trembling, consumed by a terrible fear that was completely at variance with the pleasant details of the dream, and had to force myself to reach for the cup of water on the table beside my couch. My fingers were like sticks, barely obeying me. I drank and gradually became calm. Saying a prayer to Wepwawet, I settled to sleep, and the remainder of the night was uneventful.

It took me several hours the next morning to shake off the effects of the dream and by evening I had almost forgotten it, but that night it came again, identical in every way, and again I woke to darkness and fear. The third night it was repeated, and I began to sleep with fresh oil in my lamp so that I would see the friendly sanity of my own four walls when I opened my eyes with my heart skipping and my limbs weak.

On the seventh night the dream became more complex. There were rings on the orange-painted fingers and a whiff of perfume that mingled with the scent of the lotus as it brushed against my nose. The smell added a sense of desperation to the terror and I fought to make my fingers do my bidding, but try as I might I could not grab the petals. I woke gasping for breath, ran to my window, and tearing aside the rush matting covering it, I leaned out, sucking up the mild night air. Out there the moon was setting, tangled in black treetops. Directly below me the grain bins that huddled against the wall of the house cast fat shadows across the peaceful courtyard and then there was the surface of the Nile's tributary, moving silently as it flowed towards the Great Green. Going back into my room, I gathered up my pillow and sheets and stepped out the window onto the roof, but lying looking up at the stars was too much like the dream and I soon returned to my couch. This time I could not sleep again. Curled in on myself I waited out the dark hours until the grey light that preceded Ra's rising began to seep into my room.

Drowsiness came with it and I tumbled at last into a deep slumber. I was late taking my watch that morning.

I decided to try drinking myself into such a stupor each night that no dream could penetrate the fug of wine fumes in my head. Instead of water, the cup beside my couch held Best Wine of the Western River that I quaffed without appreciation, but all I accomplished was a sore throat and a pounding head to add to the effects of the dream. I thought perhaps exercise might render me so exhausted that though I dreamed I would not wake up or even remember what was in the vision but it did no good. My fellow guards commented on my haggard looks, and I began to wake and stumble through my days in a daze of tiredness. I knew I should mend the rift that had appeared between Takhuru and myself, knew I should take her a gift and tell her I loved her, but she remained silent and I could not summon the energy to take any initiative in her direction.

On the fourteenth night, halfway through the month of Paophi, there was another change. It was as though the dream was the work of a magic artist who first sketched a bare outline and then proceeded to add not only many grades of colour and subtleties of definition but odours and finally sounds, for on that night, as the lotus caressed my face and I made my vain attempts to capture it, a voice began to croon. "Little one, darling one," it half-sang, half-chanted. "Pretty, pretty little boy, sweetness of my heart," and in the dream I smiled. The voice was female, young and lilting, slightly husky. It did not belong to my mother or my sisters or Takhuru, yet it sent waves of shock through me. I knew it, knew it in the blind marrow of my bones, and I woke with sobs aching in my chest.

Throwing on a linen shift, I went unsteadily along the hallway and knocked on my father's bedroom door. After a moment a slit of light appeared under it. I waited. Finally he opened, his face puffy with sleep but his eyes as always clear and alert. "Gods, Kamen," he said. "You look terrible. Come in." He motioned me inside and followed me, closing the door. I sank into one of the comfortable chairs that flanked his window. He took the other, crossed his naked legs, and waited for me to speak. I forced myself to breathe deeply against the already easing constriction in my chest. Gradually my body became still. My father jerked his head at the half-empty cup of wine that stood on the small table between us. He had obviously been reading before he retired, for a scroll lay beside the goblet, but I shuddered and shook my head. "I should think not," he said drily. "You've drunk half my stock in the last couple of weeks. What's wrong? Is Takhuru being difficult?" I shifted in the chair.

"Tell me about my mother," I said. His eyebrows shot up, then he understood.

"Your mother is dead," he answered. "You know that, Kamen. She died giving birth to you."

"I know. But what was she like? I've seldom thought about her. When I was a child, I imagined her as rich, young, beautiful, always laughing—the fantasies one would expect. What is the truth, Father? Did you know her well?"

He looked at me for a long time, the remaining band of his grey hair sticking out in tufts, the rumpled linen of his short sleeping kilt lying bunched above the bony protrusions of his knees, the fold of his old stomach hanging over it, and I loved him so much at that moment. Then he reached for the cup himself and took a deliberate sip. His eyes over its rim did not leave my own.

"I did not know her at all," he replied. "The messenger who delivered you to this house simply told us that she had died in childbirth and your father was likewise dead, in the King's service."

"But surely the man did not just turn up out of nowhere and drop me into your arms! There must have been enquiries from you regarding the possibility of adopting an orphan, negotiations, an agreement! You must know something about my origins!" He glanced into his cup, sighed, set it back on the table, and folded his arms.

"Why are you asking me these things now, Kamen? You haven't cared much about them before."

Quickly, awkwardly, I told him about the dreams, and as I spoke they came back to me in all their strange mixture of pleasure and horror, so that by the time I had finished, the tightness in my chest was back and it was hard to draw breath. "I think I may be dreaming of myself as a baby," I finished thickly, "and the hand that descends is my mother's. But it is a hennaed hand, Father, covered in expensive rings. Was my mother a noblewoman? Or is the dream mixing fact and wishful fantasy?"

"You are an astute young man," my father said slowly. "I never met your real mother but I knew a little about her by reputation. She was indeed young and beautiful and very rich when she gave birth to you. She was not a noblewoman."

"What was she then? Was she from a merchant family like this one? Do I have grandparents, here in Pi-Ramses perhaps? Do I have other sisters or perhaps a brother? How could she be an officer's wife and be very rich?"

"No!" my father broke in emphatically. "Put that idea right out of your head, Kamen. You have no brothers or sisters, and as for grandparents, we were not told of any other family you might have."

"But rich. You said so yourself." The pain in my chest was growing so that I wanted to press my fist to it. "Was my father wealthy? What of his family? Surely the army archives will hold records of my father's lineage and service!" My father's lips tightened. Colour began to creep up his neck.

"No. I have checked the records myself. There is nothing. I have told you all I know, my son. I beg you, be content with that." He had called me "my son" deliberately but I could not let it go.

"Nothing in the records? Not even his name? What was his name?" And why had I never asked that question before, or any of the other questions crowding into my mind? Had I been tranced for sixteen years? My father leaned forward and placed a hand firmly on my thigh. His skin was very hot.

"Kamen," he said loudly, "understand and believe this. I know nothing about your natural father except that he was a military officer, even though I anticipated this conversation some years ago and did my best to discover who he was. I have just told you everything possible about your mother. I love you. Shesira, my wife, loves you. Mutemheb and Tamit, my daughters, your sisters, love you. You are handsome and healthy and lack for nothing. You are betrothed to noble blood. Be content. Please." He sat back and his hand went to his head, smoothing down the wiry grey disorder of his hair in a familiar gesture of what I knew to be discomfiture. "As for the dreams, they will pass. You are of an age that signals the beginnings of mature reflection and that is all. Now go back to bed. Wake Setau and take a massage to help you sleep." He rose and I stood with him. He embraced me, holding me tightly, kissed me on both cheeks, and led me to the door. "Light incense for Wepwawet," he told me as I slipped out. "He has always been your guide."

Yes he has, I thought as I made my way back to my own room. He is my link with my true past, and he is not only a God of War but also the Opener of the Ways. I wish that he would speak to me. Perhaps he is speaking to you, another part of my mind responded. Perhaps he has sent the dreams in order to impart some urgent knowledge.

But another, more sinister thought occurred to me and I paused, my hand on the latch of my door. My mother's spirit has come to me. It needs something. It has ceased to rest. It will torment me until I understand. Where is her tomb? My father's tomb? Gods, what is happening to me? I turned from my door, ran down the stairs, and roused my servant. Under his capable hands my body relaxed and the stabbing in my chest went away, but it took me a long time to fall asleep.

For the one glorious night following I rested completely. It was as though talking with my father had leached some of the dream's potency, and I woke refreshed and eager to begin my duties. The scab on my shoulder came loose, leaving no more than a thin red scar. I was invited by Akhebset's family to a boating party to celebrate the good height of the annual flood and I accepted happily. Outside in the garden, as I headed for the General's house, the gardeners were sorting the new seeds to be planted, and all Egypt seemed to be in festivity, matching my mood. But that night the dream returned like some recurring fever, and dawn found me on my knees before Wepwawet, incense cups in my hands and prayers of desperation on my lips. I muddled through my watch like a man drugged with poppy, then returned home, bathed, changed my linen, and set off to see Takhuru.

I was admitted to her entrance hall and left to wait for so long that I was about to leave, but in the end a servant bade me follow him to her private quarters. I was past feeling any annoyance at her for this petty revenge, and when I was announced and she rose from her cosmetic table, I put my arms around her and held her tightly. She resisted, her body stiffening, but then she melted against me and her hands crept up my naked back. She had been painting for the evening but her hair had not yet been braided. It foamed around her head and I pushed my face into it, smelling its cleanliness and the hint of cinnamon that always clung to her.

"I am so sorry, Takhuru," I said. "I have been stubborn and callous. Forgive me for shouting at you and ignoring you for so long." She pushed me away, waved her body servant out of the room, and turned back to me with a radiant smile.

"I too must apologize," she put in. "I expect you to be perfect, Kamen, for so you are in my dreams, and that is not fair. Did I hurt you much when I kicked you?" Her eyes danced. "I hope so!"

"I was lame for days!" I protested, imitating her familiar pout, and she laughed, taking my hand and leading me to a chair. Gathering up her voluminous shift, she perched beside me on a stool, twining her fingers around mine and laying them on my knee.

"I have missed you, but not much," she announced. "My friend Tjeti got betrothed and there was a big party with mountains of food and professional dancers and hordes of young men to keep me amused. I would have invited you but you were too mean."

"I'm sorry," I repeated. "Come with me to the boating party Akhebset's parents are giving. I do not want to go without you."

"Why not?" she retorted with a return to her usual asperity. "You might as well be betrothed to Akhebset, for you have more fun with him than with me." It was true, I thought guiltily, but then it struck me that perhaps that was my fault. Perhaps I took Takhuru far too much for granted, and did not think of ways to enjoy ourselves that would please both of us the way I did with Akhebset.

"Well would you come with me to the beer house and drink and gamble?" I teased her. She looked up at me solemnly.

"Yes I would if it meant that I could be having fun with you. But Mother would never allow it." I could see that she was serious, and the picture of dainty Takhuru, with her jewelled sandals and spotless linen, her aristocratic fastidiousness and her sensitive nose, sitting aghast amid the rough and tumble of the beer house and trying to enjoy herself for my sake, made me smile.

"One day I will take you," I promised. "But after we are married, so that your father cannot demand your dowry returned and the contract torn up!"

There was a moment of silence during which she scrutinized me carefully. Then she placed her other hand over mine, imprisoning my fingers. "Something is wrong, isn't it,

Kamen?" she said softly. "You look ill. No, not ill perhaps, but hounded. Do you want to tell me about it?" Her perceptiveness startled me, for she often seemed entirely self-involved. I did indeed want to tell her about it, but I had feared her inattention. Now I kissed her fingers impulsively.

"Thank you, Takhuru," I said. "Yes, please listen to me. I have already spoken of this to my father but he cannot help me." I proceeded to relate the dreams and then my somehow unsatisfactory conversation with my father. She hardly moved except to draw in a quick breath or nod or frown until I had finished. Then she scrambled to her feet, and going to her cosmetic table, she began to toy with the pots and jars there, her expression closed. I waited.

Presently she said, "I think you are right when you surmise that the hand belongs to your real mother. What of the messenger, Kamen, the man who took you to your father's house? He must have collected you from somewhere."

"Yes, of course. But my father told me that the messenger simply arrived with me, said that my mother had died in childbirth and my father in Pharaoh's wars, and handed me over." She turned to me, leaning against the table, and folded her arms. "With no warning? No scroll to be signed?"

"Nothing. My father had begun to enquire in the city about a child to adopt and then the messenger just appeared." Takhuru seemed about to speak, closed her mouth, then came to me and knelt by my chair.

"Forgive me, Kamen, but don't you think he might be lying to you? The peasants might take in orphaned children without caring about their lineage, but your father is wealthy and a minor noble and would not accept a son from just anywhere, a baby that might be diseased or carrying the seeds of a later deformity. I find it hard to believe that your parents decided to adopt a boy, began to ask among their friends, and then lo, you appear as if by magic."

I did not want to hear these things. Takhuru's words were giving form to the vague suspicions that had been haunting me. I remembered the touch of my father's hot palm against my skin. "Be content. Please," he had said, and something in me had flinched. But I loved him. I trusted him. He had always set great store by honesty, and growing up I had been punished more severely for lying than for any other childish infraction. He would not lie to me—would he?

"He would not lie to me," I repeated aloud. "What would be the point?"

"He would lie if there was something that must be hidden from you, something that might hurt you," Takhuru re-joined. "But what could it be, presuming that what I said earlier was true and he would not have accepted a child without first making sure that it was suitable for his family and his future lineage?"

"Future lineage." I bent to her, all at once chilled. "Takhuru, your father agreed to a betrothal with me in spite of the fact that your blood is fully noble and your lineage more pure than my father's, in spite of the fact that my true lineage, my blood roots, are entirely unknown. Perhaps they are not unknown. Perhaps your father and my father share some knowledge that must be kept from me." We stared at each other. Then I laughed. "This is ridiculous! We are building a pyramid of supposition out of a few grains of sand." She reached behind her, pulled forward a cushion, and sank back onto it, crossing her legs under the floating shift. Her back straightened and I smiled inwardly.

"Nevertheless I shall ask my father about it," she said firmly. "Don't worry, Kamen. I shall not be obvious. Perhaps I will suggest that I am worried that I might not be marrying a man worthy of my station after all and my children's blood might not run pure. I am an arrogant and snobbish girl, am I not? And I do not care that I am so. He will not think my question strange. If he will not answer, I shall search his office. He has many chests full of scrolls. They are mainly concerned with the running of the faience factories, accounts and workers and things like that. Very dry and boring. But I might find something about you. Our fathers signed the betrothal contract last year. Do you think it might say something?" I looked at her in genuine amazement.

"You have astonished me twice today!" I exclaimed. "I am betrothed to a devious little witch who wishes to frequent the beer houses!" She giggled and tossed her head, very pleased with herself. I slid off the chair, pulled her against me, and kissed her. This time there was no hesitation, no resistance. She kissed me back fervently.

"I have a suggestion for you," she said when we had extricated ourselves from one another, flushed and panting. "Take a gift and go and consult the Seer. He does not read for common folk but your father has dealings with him and he will doubtless See for you. Ask him about the dreams, about your birth. If anyone in Egypt can help you, he can. Now you had better go. We are entertaining one of the Royal Butlers tonight and I am not nearly ready." I made as if to kiss her again but she squirmed away and I did not persist. It came to me as I was crossing her hall, now redo-lent with the tantalizing aroma of good food and the murmur of servants' voices in the dining room beyond, that my betrothed was a girl with a hitherto unsuspected taste for intrigue.

4

HER SUGGESTION regarding the Seer had been a good one, and later that evening I dictated a request for an audience to Setau, who doubled as my scribe on the few occasions when I did not want Kaha, my father's scribe, to know my business. Asking him to deliver it personally in the morning, I went through the now dusky garden and out to where our boats rocked. Untying the skiff from its mooring pole, I picked up the oars and pulled myself into the current.

Night had merged water with bank and bank with the growth along the path so that I seemed to be rowing both on and through an ocean of warmly penetrable darkness that encapsulated me. I encountered no one else, heard nothing but the creak of the oars and my own rapid breath. The dreamlike state in which I drifted was infinitely preferable to the nightmares of unconsciousness, and it was a long time before I turned the skiff for home.

No word came from the Seer for several days during which I continued to work and the dream continued to haunt me. I did not hear from Takhuru either. But my mood had changed from agitation to one of patience and optimism. I no longer felt helpless. My prayers to my totem continued also, and briefly I considered addressing my dead mother directly when I woke sweating and gasping, but I was afraid to leap that particular gulf. It was said that the dead could do no real harm unless the living invited them by calling their name or speaking to them, and I did not know if the owner of that hand meant me good or ill.

On the fifth day a terse message came for me from the Seer. "To Kamen, Officer of the King," it read. "Present yourself at the door to my house one hour before sunset tomorrow." The note was not signed. The papyrus on which it had been written was plain but expertly prepared, the surface smooth to the touch, and the scribe's hand was exquisite.

I hid the scroll under the kilts in my chest and went through my jewels, wondering what an adequate gift for the Seeing might be. What did he receive from the princes and nobles for whom he gazed into the future? His chests must be full of expensive trinkets. I wanted to put something different into those hands that no one but his servants, Pharaoh and the High Priests of the temples had seen. Then my own hands touched an ebony box and I drew it out reverently, lifting the lid. Inside lay the dagger my father had given me when I entered the military school. The gift had been an expression of selfless love on his part considering he had not wanted me to go soldiering at all, and a lump came to my throat as I drew it out. It had no real function. It was a ceremonial piece, something for a collector, for he had purchased it from Libu tribesmen. The serrated edge of its blade curved wickedly away from a hilt of chased silver set with milky green moonstones. I valued it above everything else my father had given me, but I knew in my heart that nothing less would please the mysterious man who would tell me of my origins. Setting it before Wepwawet, I put my other jewellery away.

That night I did not dream, and I woke with a sense of anticipation. On my way to the General's house, as I crossed our still-gloomy entrance hall, my father's Overseer of Caravans bid me a terse good morning. He was squatting outside his employer's office, a black face atop a bundle of coarse brown linen, and his passage over the tiles had been marked by a narrow smattering of fine sand. I returned his greeting, hearing a murmur of voices beyond the closed door to the office, my father's and another, and surmised that either a caravan had just returned or was about to set out. I wondered if my father would be travelling with it, seeing that the rest of the family was still in the Fayum, and felt a sense of relief at the thought. I had become so preoccupied with the enigmas of my life that dealing with the people and events of the household had become a distraction.

So had my daily duties. I was bored with standing at the General's door for hours and I no longer found his visitors interesting. I preferred the night watches, for then I could patrol his halls in peace, but I had recently fulfilled my night assignment and had to take my turn in daylight. That day, as I shifted from one foot to the other and the sword at my waist felt heavier than ever before, I wondered if the dream would have invaded me if I had been able to sleep during the sunlit hours.

But the time passed and at last I was able to hurry through my garden in search of a bath and a small meal before setting out for the Seer's house. As I was running up the stairs, the door to my father's office opened and he called me.

"Kamen, wait a moment." I turned. He was looking up at me, clad only in a thigh-length kilt and sleeveless shirt, his big feet bare, his sparse hair awry. "I have a caravan going into Nubia," he said. "I think I'll go with it as far as Thebes. I want to pray in the Amun temple and I can stop at the Fayum and see your mother and sisters on the way back. I'll be gone for a couple of weeks, perhaps longer. Will you be all right?"

"Yes, of course," I assured him quickly. "You know I will. I have Setau, and I presume Pa-Bast will stay here. Why do you ask?" He blew out his cheeks.

"Because I've been worried about you, but I must say you're looking better. Are you still dreaming?" He asked the last question diffidently and I knew he did not want an affirmative answer. A flash of resentment went through me.

"No," I half-lied, for I had not dreamed the night before. He smiled in relief.

"Good! Work hard, exercise regularly, eat sparingly, and the night demons will fly away. I leave at dawn and will be back sometime next month. I'll probably bring the women with me."

"Fine. Then may the soles of your feet be firm, Father." He held up a hand in acknowledgement of the blessing and padded back into his office and I continued on to my own room. I wondered, as I summoned Setau and stripped for the bath house, why my father should want to go all the way to Thebes to pray, for several Amun shrines were scattered about Pi-Ramses, but I supposed that it gave him a good excuse to visit his merchant friends there and spend some time in the Fayum. It was also true that the shrines were small and very public, little more than stone niches containing the God's image and an altar for incense and offerings, and no priests attended them to hear petitions. One prayed surrounded by busy crowds and noise. By the time I was standing on the bathing slab and Setau was handing me fresh natron, I had forgotten my idle speculation. It was enough that I would have the house to myself for many days.

Scrubbed clean, oiled, perfumed and in my best white linen, I approached the Seer's pylon as the light was beginning to change, his scroll in my hand and the dagger under my arm. I did not want to stop here. I wanted to hurry on to somewhere safer, for I knew that soon the thin evening shadows would lengthen and by the time I left the Seer his garden would be drowned in darkness, but I forced myself to step between the square stone columns. As I did so a form uncurled from behind one of them and barred my way. An ancient face peered up at me from bowed shoulders, its eyes sharp and unfriendly. The voice, when it came was reedy but strong.

"Oh it's you," it said pettishly. "Kamen, Officer of the King. Give me that." A gnarled hand shot out and snatched the scroll. I watched bemused as the old man unrolled it and scanned it quickly. "I've seen you come and go," he went on, glancing up. "You work for Paiis and pay court to Nesiamun's haughty daughter. I knew you'd be stopping at the Master's gate sooner or later. Everyone wants to. Few get this far." He slammed the scroll against my chest. "Go forward." The words fell on my ears like a part of some formal ritual so that I found myself bowing to the waspish old man, but I was bending to emptiness. He had shuffled back to his lair.

The path ran only a short way before dividing. One fork plunged to the right and appeared to end a long way away at a high wall I could barely glimpse through the dense foliage crowding the strip of beaten earth. The same thick tangle of trees, smooth palm boles and spreading shrubs gathered beside the fork that ran straight ahead. It obviously led to the house and I took it, striding swiftly to give myself confidence. But before long I found myself crossing an open space in the centre of which was a fountain spewing water into a large basin. Stone seats flanked it, and at the other end the path divided again. I went left but had to retrace my steps for the way only led to a fishpond choked with lily and lotus pads. A large sycamore, its branches tortuously knotted, leaned over the water. Taking what I now presumed to be the central path, I walked between thorn hedges, passing a much larger pool on my right that was surely intended for swimming. A small hut stood at one end of it. Further on I skirted a shrine. Behind the offering table stood a startlingly lifelike statue of Thoth, God of Wisdom and Writing. His long ibis beak cast a curved shadow over the small altar and his round black eyes followed me as I did him a courtesy and moved on.

Suddenly the trees fell back and I was pushing through a gate set into the low wall of a paved courtyard. The house stood before me, its entrance pillars white but now tinged with pink, painted brightly with birds flying towards the roof and vines tendrilling upward. Gingerly I approached it. No one seemed to be about, and there was no sound but the slap of my sandals against the paving. Before the gaping entrance I paused, briefly overcome by the same shrinking I had felt as I stepped under the pylon, but even as I drew a

deep breath and pushed myself forward, a servant materialized from behind the nearest pillar, held up a hand, smiled,
and disappeared within. I waited, my back to the courtyard,
my eyes on the dimness where the servant had vanished.

Then the space was almost completely filled by the
largest man I had ever seen. He reminded me immediately
of the sacred Apis Bull, for his massive shoulders and the
thick neck holding up his wide head exuded an animal
power. His stomach cascaded over his calf-length kilt in an
exuberant display of excess. If I had clasped him around his
chest my fingertips could not have touched. Not that I
wanted to do such a disrespectful thing. Just the thought of
it gave me an inward shiver, for he could have broken my
arms without blinking. Yet he was not a young man. His
jowls were deeply grooved, his temples and full mouth
lined. I felt sure that the starched linen helmet he wore hid
a shaved skull, for there was no discernable hair on his
body. He inclined his head.

"Good evening, Officer Kamen," he rumbled. "I am
Harshira, the Master's Steward. You are expected. Follow
me." His black eyes, nested in folds of flesh, appraised me
coolly before he turned and glided away, his step almost
silent and his great body moving with surprising agility. I
did as I was told.

A huge room unfolded beyond the entrance, its gleaming tiled floor broken by several more white pillars. Cedar
chairs inlaid with gold and ivory stood about haphazardly,
together with low blue and green faience-topped tables. A
servant was moving to light the lamps that stood about on
tall pediments, and as he did so the scenes of feasting and
hunting on the walls leaped into life. I would have liked to

examine them, but Harshira was already passing through double doors on the other side of the hall into a much smaller antechamber and I hurried to keep up with him. Here I was confronted with a set of stairs on my left, running up into darkness. Straight ahead a passage led right through the house to a row of pillars and more garden beyond, now suffused with the red glow of Ra's setting. To my right, several closed doors were set into the wall. The Steward approached one of them and knocked. A voice answered.

"You may go in," Harshira said, opening the door and standing aside. I walked through and the door closed softly behind me.

The first thing that struck me was the odour, a blend of sweet herbs and spices. There was a faint whiff of cinnamon that brought Takhuru's face vividly to mind, myrrh and coriander, and other scents I could not identify, but the fragrance overriding them all was jasmine. The second impression I received was one of extreme orderliness. Shelves filled the room from floor to ceiling and the shelves were crowded with boxes but they were stacked neatly and each bore a papyrus label. To my right and almost hidden by the jutting shelves was a small door. Another door faced it on the opposite wall. Directly ahead of me was a window, but between it and where I was gathering myself for an obeisance a large desk sat. The scrolls on it were lined up with a military precision. A scribe's palette rested beside a plain but finely wrought alabaster lamp in which a new flame burned. Everything shone with cleanliness. I absorbed these details swiftly, my glance travelling the room with great rapidity, before I bowed to the man sitting behind the desk.

Or at least, I presumed it was a man. He was muffled entirely in white linen from the enveloping hood that covered his masked face to the wraps on his feet. The hands folded on the surface of the desk were encased in white gloves. Nowhere could I see any exposed skin, and as I fought to control my shock, I was devoutly glad. Whatever horror lay under all those swathings, I did not want to see it. Yet though I could see nothing of his face, the Seer's eyes were on me. He had not missed my quick scrutiny, for he chuckled—a dry, harsh sound.

"Does my humble workplace meet with your approval, Officer Kamen?" he asked mockingly. "With your expectations also? I doubt it. The young who consult me appear to be disappointed. They want dimness and mystery, flickering lamps and a haze of incense smoke, spells and whispers. I must confess that I take an altogether unworthy delight in their disappointment." I wanted to clear my throat but forbade the nervous impulse.

"I had no such expectations, Master," I replied, amazed at the steadiness of my own voice. "Your gift of Seeing allies you to the gods. What do the trappings matter?" He sat back, his spotless wrappings rustling gently.

"Well said, Officer Kamen," he said. "Bright and conscientious, my brother Paiis called you, and you are cautious and tactful also. Oh? You did not know that Paiis was my brother? But of course you didn't. You are an honest young man and a good officer, trained to ask no questions of your superiors and to kill without reflection. Can you kill without reflection, young Kamen? How old are you?" I felt his eyes. I knew his attention had not wavered from me for a moment and my scalp prickled. Once again I had to repress a strong urge, this time to put a hand to the back of my neck.

"I am sixteen," I answered. "I do not know if I can kill, for the necessity has not yet arisen. I do my best to be a good soldier." I did not like his patronizing tone and something in my voice or stance must have betrayed me. He folded his arms.

"All the same, there is a tiny seed of mutiny in you, waiting for the water of insult or injustice to sprout," he remarked. "I sense it. You are not the man you think you are, Kamen. Not at all. You interest me, standing there all earnestness and hidden affront. Light will penetrate the Underworld before you retreat an inch, though you give an impression of polite pliancy. Paiis said I would find you entertaining. What do you want of me?"

"How did the General know I was coming to consult you, Master?" I asked. There was a small movement under the mask. He was smiling.

"I told him, of course. He dines here often and we talk of many things. When there are no more engrossing subjects, we discuss our own lives. I thought he would like to be told that one of the officers of his guard was coming to see me." He stirred. "Would you like to see me, Kamen?" A pang of fear shot through me.

"You are playing with me," I said. "If you choose to reveal yourself, I would be honoured. If not, I am content." Now he laughed aloud, the sound choked off by his mask.

"You deserve to be a courtier," he declared. "And you are right. I am playing with you. I apologize. Now I repeat. What do you want of me? You may sit." One white-gloved hand indicated the chair in front of the desk. I bowed again and lowered myself into it, placing the ebony box on the desk. Now that the moment had come I was at a loss for the right words.

"I am an orphan," I began haltingly. "My parents adopted me when I was only a few months old ..." He set an elbow on the desk and held up his palm.

"Let us not waste time. Your father is Men. Like you, he is an honest man who has amassed a considerable fortune through his sense of adventure and an astute nose for business. He is my most reliable source for rare herbs and physics. Your mother is Shesira, a good Egyptian wife who requires nothing more than a peaceful household. You have an older sister, Mutemheb, and a younger, Tamit. There is nothing extraordinary about your family. Now why are you in distress?" The rules of polite conversation obviously meant nothing to this man. He was capable of piercing to the heart, combining his gift with a keen ability to observe. No doubt in the aristocratic social circles he frequented he could be as smooth as scraped papyrus while he coldly assessed those into whose eyes he looked, but here with his petitioners there was no pretence.

"Very well," I said. "I have been happy with my life, lacking for nothing, until a few weeks ago when I began to dream ..." Carefully I described my night visitor, the hennaed hand, the voice that came with it, and my growing belief that I was seeing and hearing my real mother. "I know nothing about her or about my real father," I finished. "My adoptive father knows nothing either ..." He pounced on my hesitation.

"You think that your father knows more than he is

telling," he stated flatly. "Had you questioned him about your origins before you began to dream?"

"No. It was the dream that prompted my questions." I found myself almost babbling then, pouring out the interview with my father, Takhuru's perceptive comments and her plan to find our betrothal contract, my own suspicions, and all the time he sat there unmoving, his exceptional concentration fixed on me like a beam of noon sunlight.

"Describe the rings on the hand. Describe the voice," he broke in. "Tell me about the lines of the palm if you can. I must have a clear vision of what you see if I am to help you." I did so and then fell silent.

He crossed his legs, placed his hands in his lap, and I could feel him withdraw into himself. I waited, my gaze wandering the room. Outside the sun had now set and the last of Ra's glow diffused through the window. To my right I could see, without actually turning my head, the small door beside the laden shelves. There was something odd about it, something disturbing, but before I could decide what it was, the Master stirred and sighed.

"So you do not want to see your future," he said. "You want to know who your mother was, and perhaps your father too. Where they came from. What they were like. You have set me a difficult task, Officer Kamen." I interpreted this as an indirect query regarding payment and I leaned forward, lifting the lid of the ebony box.

"I have brought you something very precious to me," I said, "but your gift is worth the sacrifice. My father purchased it in Libu." He did not even glance at it.

"Keep your trinket," he said, rising and coming around the desk, shrugging the white robes higher on his shoulders as he did so. "I do not ask for payment from you. You have already done me a great service though of course you are not aware of it." I rose also and backed away as he passed me. I did not want to be too close to him. "Follow me," he commanded and I did so, turning right along the passage that led out into the rear garden where only the tops of the trees were tinged with scarlet. Their trunks and the ground around them were drowned in shadow.

Just beyond the exit there was a small paved space in the centre of which stood a simple stone pedestal. On it was a vase, a large flagon and a stoppered pot. The Seer ap-proached the pedestal, and lifting the flagon he briskly poured water into the vase. "Stand here beside me but not too close," he ordered. "Do not move or speak except to answer any question I may put to you." I did as I was bid, inhaling a rush of jasmine as he took the pot and removed the stopper. The perfume in the office that overrode all the other odours must have been from his body. I watched him carefully tip a small quantity of oil on top of the water, wait a moment, presumably for the oil to settle, glance at the sky which was rapidly paling to the purest of blues, and then bend over the vase. His hood fell forward. His gloved hands grasped the sides of the pedestal. "Praise to Thoth," I heard him murmur. "The Vizier who gives judgement, who vanquishes crime, who recalls all that is forgotten. The remembrancer of time and eternity, whose words abide for ever. Now, Kamen. Slowly and with every detail. Your dreams from the beginning. Omit nothing. See them as you speak."

I began, feeling awkward and foolish, but those emotions soon fled and my voice grew stronger, blending with the warm evening breeze that caressed my face and stirred the Master's coverings and becoming disembodied so that the words seemed to flow not only from me but from the quiet trees and the stone beneath my feet. Soon there was nothing but my voice and the dream, and the dream and the voice became one so that I was no longer flesh but a vision in the mind of a young man standing in a night-hung garden, suspended between reality and illusion.

The Master raised a hand, shaking back the sleeve of his cloak so that for a brief moment I saw his wrist between cloak and glove, and the skin seemed ashen in the fading light. "It is enough," he said. "Be silent." I closed my mouth and the world assumed the sanity of its familiar forms around me.

I waited. I was used to standing still for long periods, and by the time the Seer lifted his head, passing his hands over the vase and closing his fingers in a ritualistic gesture of dismissal, the stars had begun to appear. He straightened and stared at me. "Truly Thoth is he who recalls all that is forgotten," he said huskily. He sounded very tired, and as he spoke he put out a hand, fumbling for the lip of the pedestal as though he needed its support. My heart leaped. His gift was true. He had Seen for me. He was about to tell me all I wanted to know. Now my knees felt suddenly weak and I realized that my back was aching. "Thoth, the exact plummet of the balance," he went on, and laughed. The sound was without humour, a bleak, unlovely bark. "My dear Officer Kamen, you are far more interesting than my brother could ever have imagined. I must rest. The Seeing always exhausts me. Come. We will talk by the fountain."

He turned away and stumbled, righting himself, then strode around the side of the house, tucking his hands into his sleeves and walking quickly, his head down. I followed once more, crossing the courtyard and going through the low gate until we made our way to the little clearing and the seats and the fountain, now spewing a silver stream into its dark bowl. The Master slumped onto one of the seats and I followed suit tensely, my hands locking between my knees. Watching him gradually recover was like seeing a dry, crumpled leaf dropped in water become supple again. I could wait no longer.

"What did you see?" I asked urgently. "Please, Master, do not torment me with riddles!" After a pause he nodded reluctantly.

"Before I tell you anything, answer me one question," he said. "Why did you decide to become a soldier? Life as your father's successor would have been easier and more reasonable."

The only light left in the garden now came hesitantly from the rising moon and from the sifting of stars. The being across from me had become increasingly insubstantial as the daylight vanished. He sat motionless as a corpse, indefinable as a ghost, nothing but darkness within the deep shelter of his hood. There was no face to speak to. I shrugged.

"I don't know. It was just a strong desire. I always thought it was because my true father was one of Pharaoh's officers." The hood moved from side to side.

"Not your father." The muffled voice was timbreless. "Your grandfather."

Heat flushed through me. Leaning forward I grasped the Seer's arm, struggling for breath. "You know who I am!" I shouted. "You know! Tell me what you saw!"

"Your grandfather was a foreigner, a Libu mercenary who took Egyptian citizenship at the conclusion of Pharaoh's early wars forty years ago," he said, making no move to shake himself free of my clutching fingers. "He was not an officer. His daughter, your true mother, was a commoner. She was a beautiful creature but ambitious. She rose to wealth and favour."

"You saw this in the oil? All this?" I was unconsciously jerking his arm, and now he pulled himself away from me. Coming to myself, I regained my seat. I was trembling.

"No," he replied shortly. "In the oil I saw your dream, but opened out like a scroll. You as a baby, lying in grass outside the place where you lived with your mother. She came to you, kneeling on the edge of the blanket on which she had placed you. She was smiling. In her hennaed hand was a lotus flower. Other lotus blooms were scattered about her. She tickled your nose with the petals and you laughed, trying to catch them. I recognized her face, the flawless oval of it, the bow of her soft mouth. I knew her once, a long time ago."

"Where? Here in Pi-Ramses? Where did we live? What of my father? What was her name? Is she indeed dead?"

He raised an arm and suddenly, terrifyingly, the hood fell back. His features were still completely hidden beneath the tight mask with its tiny slits for eyes and no opening at all for his mouth, but his hair fell in a thick shower to his shoulders and it was the purest white, so white that it seemed to generate a light of its own. Even in the dimness of the hour I could see that no colour polluted it at all. What about the rest of him? I wondered breathlessly. Is that his deformity? To have no colour at all in his skin? What of his blood? "She lived in a place of great comfort," he said hoarsely, "here in Pi-Ramses. I cannot tell you the name of your father, Kamen, but I can assure you that Takhuru need not concern herself regarding your lineage. It is a high one. Your mother is indeed dead. I am sorry."

"Then my father is a noble? Am I an illegitimate child?" It would explain much, I thought excitedly. If my real father was a noble, then, of course, my adoptive father would have no hesitation in taking me and Nesiamun no qualms about marrying me to his daughter. Perhaps my father actually knew the man whose seed had given me life. That would explain his reluctance to tell me anything.

"Your real father is indeed noble," the Seer confirmed, "and yes, you are a bastard. I attended your mother at your birth and she died a few days later." He ran a weary hand through that alien hair and stood. "I have told you enough. Now you must be content." I got up and went to him, barring his way, thrusting my face close to the thick mask.

"Her name, Master! I must know her name! I must find her tomb, make offerings, say the prayers so that she will stop invading my sleep!" He did not back away. Instead he stepped closer, and even in my near frenzy I could swear that I caught a glint of red in those eye slits.

"I cannot tell you her name," he said firmly. "It would do you no good. She is dead. And I promise you that now you know as much of the truth as you need, she will not enter your dreams again. Be content, Kamen. Go home." He began to walk away. I ran after him.

"Why can't you tell me her name?" I called furiously, desperately. "What difference will it make if she is dead?"

He stopped and half-turned, speaking over his shoulder so that the starlight fell on his silver head and half the sinister mask, leaving the rest in darkness.

"You are a brave and very stupid young man," he said contemptuously. "What difference? If I tell you her name your curiosity will be inflamed even further, and dead or not you will still feel impelled to explore her history, find her relatives, drive yourself insane trying to conjure her personality, wonder what traits in you are yours and which hers. Do you want to distress yourself further, Kamen? Disrupt your family? I do not think so."

"Yes I do!" I shouted. "I must know! If the gift I brought might oblige you to reveal everything you saw, then take it, take it, but please, Master, give me her name!" He put out a gloved hand, an imperious warning.

"No," he said firmly. "To know it would bring you nothing but grief. Trust me in this. Be grateful for the life she gave you and fulfill your own destiny. Do not ponder hers any more. This interview is at an end." Then he was gone, melting into the shadows, and I was left shaking with anger and frustration.

I do not now remember walking home. It did not occur to me to doubt the Seer's vision or his word. His reputation as a genuine oracle and prophet had been established long ago. But his arrogance inflamed me, his haughty words keeping time with the rhythm of my feet, until I came to myself, exhausted and despairing, outside the door to my quarters. I suppose I should have been overjoyed that he had recognized her, had known her, but of what use was such knowledge to me if he refused to share the most useful detail? What was I to do now?

Pushing into my room where Setau had left a lamp burning, I shut the door behind me and stood gazing at things that were no longer familiar. Everything had changed. Only hours ago that was my couch, that my table, that the chest whose lid was left partly open when I removed the dagger. Now they seemed to belong to someone else, to a Kamen who did not exist any more.

I began to pace, too overwrought to go to bed. I wanted to rush to my father's room, wake him, shout my news into his sleepy ears, but what if I saw the knowledge I had just acquired mirrored in his face? What if he knew about her already? I did not want to see a confirmation of his deceit. There would be time for an explanation from him later. Besides, he was going away in the morning and I wanted to hold tight to my high regard for him a little longer. It was very likely that he knew who my father was too. He was a noble, the Seer had said. Nesiamun would not be ashamed to have me for his daughter's husband.

Was the one who had given me life a friend of my adoptive father? I began to consider the men with whom he conducted business, those, like the Seer, who bought from him, those who invested in his caravans, those he welcomed into our home to dine. They all treated me with a more or less disinterested politeness. Was any one of them warmer in his conversation than the rest? Did any one of them take more trouble than the others to enquire into my doings? What about General Paiis? He was a notorious womanizer and had surely produced more than one bastard in the course of his second career. I rather fancied myself as his son. But he and my father did not move in the same circles, although my father had used his influence to procure my position in Paiis's household. Had he used more than just influence? Perhaps a small blackmail? At that thought I laughed aloud, pausing by my window and mentally shaking a finger at my own foolishness. Such conjecture would lead nowhere but into the wildest fantasy.

Then what of my mother? Should I return to the Seer and pester him until he told me everything he knew, for I had a strong feeling he was withholding much? But I did not think that the mighty man could be either bludgeoned or coerced into saying or doing anything more for me unless he himself chose to do so. I could tell Akhebset and my fellow officers at the military school the whole story and ask them to circulate in the city, alert for any clue that might lead me to her. Yes, I would do that, but Pi-Ramses was vast and such a method of detection had very little chance of success. I could do what Takhuru might even now be doing. I could search the scrolls in my father's office. After all, he would be away for several weeks. The thought of rifling the contents of his chests left an unpleasant taste in my mouth. Such underhandedness was abhorrent. I would speak to him first, and investigate his records only as a last resort.

At that I yawned, the fever giving way to a sudden fatigue. I did not yell for Setau to come and wash the kohl from my face. Stripping off my linen and my jewels, I tossed them all in a heap on the floor and swung onto my couch, drawing up the sheet. For a while the evening's events rolled through my mind—the massive bulk of the Steward Harshira and his black eyes, my first sight of the Seer behind his desk, his white-gloved hands folded on its surface, my shock when he pushed back his hood to reveal hair like solid moonlight, then one of the servants running after me as I was making my way back through the garden, my dagger in his hands—until it all dissolved into unconsciousness.

I did not dream. Something in me knew that I was now forever safe from that particular haunting and I slept deeply until the moment when I found myself wide awake and sitting up, my hands gripping the sheet. The lamp had gone out, leaving a stale aroma of spent oil in the air, and all I could see was the faint square of my window, but it did not matter. It was not fear that had jerked me back to consciousness, it was the sharpness of a revelation. I knew now what it was about the small door in the right-hand wall of the Seer's office that had disturbed me earlier. At the time I had been unable to explain the moment of dislocation, but as I sat there staring into nothing I could see it clearly, the neatly packed shelves, the plain cedar of the door, the hook on its edge aligning cleanly with the hook sunk into the wall, and the rope passing through both hooks to hold the door closed.

Rope. And knots. Many knots, complex and impossible to undo unless one knew how they were tied, knots that ensured the security of whatever lay beyond. Or within. Everyone used knots to fasten chests and boxes. I did so myself. Usually they were simple, tied quickly to keep lids tight against dust, sand and vermin. If added privacy was needed, one smothered the knots in wax and left the impression of one's ring pressed into it. But the knots holding that door in the Seer's office closed were so intricate and elaborate, an ordered tangle of convolutions, that it would take many minutes to pry them undone. Worse, one would never be able to retie them in the same pattern. They were unique. And I would have staked my life on a wager that the knots I had seen out of the corner of my eye were woven by the same person who formed them to hold closed the cedar box I had so resentfully carried from Aswat.

I was afraid to move. I sat frozen on my couch, terrified that with even the twitch of a finger the direction of my thoughts might be lost. The same knots. The same person. The same person? But it was not possible that the Seer had tied the ones I examined so carefully on the box the madwoman had pushed into my unwilling hands. She had told me that the box contained the story of her life. Then logically she herself had laid the contents inside, closed the lid, and tied the rope. There was not even a hint from her that the Seer had given the box to her already secured, or that she had found it, on the riverbank say, after nobles from Pi-Ramses had stopped at Aswat. She had not deviated from her insistence that inside the box was her story, a story of poison and exile for which she wished to be pardoned.

Then how was it that both she and the Master knew how to tie identical knots? There was only one explanation. The woman was sane after all. And at that thought I felt as though something that had been twisted inside me ever since I encountered her began to untie and loosen. She was sane. She was telling the truth, and a desperate, bitter truth it was. She had said that she was once a physician, but where? She had not told me that. But the Seer was also a physician. Could it be that once, a long time ago, she had been his colleague here in Pi-Ramses, had visited his house to conduct consultations, had watched him tie the clever knots binding shut the door I had seen in his office? If that was so, if it was so, it was possible that she too had known my mother. Somehow I must return to Aswat, talk to her, tell her my story even as I had listened to hers, and ask her about my mother. How I would find an excuse to leave the General for the time it would take to go there and return I did not know. But I vowed I would find a way, even if it meant resigning my post.

I was unable to sleep again. I sat on my couch, knees drawn up, my body composed but my mind a confusion of conjecture and speculation, until just before dawn I heard a flurry of activity in the courtyard below. Getting up, I went to the window, stepped through, and walked to the edge of the roof. Just beyond the grain-storage bins torches flared, and in their wavering light servants ran to and fro, loading the horses that stood by the gate while the dogs that accompanied the caravans to kill desert vermin and warn of danger loped about barking with excitement. I saw Kaha with his scribe's palette and a rather dishevelled Pa-Bast conferring over a pile of sacks, and then my father appeared, cloaked and booted, and I drew back. I did not want him to see me, bid me take care while he was away, give me his wide smile. There was something between us now, and until I had explored and understood it I could not freely meet his gaze.

The unruly cavalcade finally moved out, through the gate into the service court and then left through the servants' entrance, and the cacophony of thudding hoofs and babble died away, leaving churned earth over which Pa-Bast and Kaha picked their way, entering the house beneath me. The sky in the east was paling.

Setau came in, greeted me, laid the early meal on my table, and without a word began to sort through the jumble of linen and jewellery I had thrown on the floor the previous night. I forced myself to swallow the fresh, warm bread, the brown goat cheese and sweet, wrinkled apples, all the while wondering what I could say to my General today. I had to get to Aswat and back before my father returned from Thebes. He would be gone for three weeks at the most. Aswat was closer than Thebes and I surely needed no more than one day with the woman there, but I did not think that the General would release me at once, if he was willing to allow me leave at all. What could I do if he refused me out of hand? To disobey him would be seen as desertion and the penalty was, of course, death. What argument would compel him? I still had no clear idea of what I would say. I was determined, but I was also afraid.

However, I need not have worried, for I had been at my post outside the General's door for less than an hour when his Steward approached me. "Officer Kamen," he said, "you are summoned. The General is in his office." Surprised, I followed him into the house, continuing on when he vanished, until the familiar cedar door loomed ahead. I knocked and was bidden to enter.

Paiis was at his desk. A tray with the half-eaten remains of his first meal sat on the floor and he himself was only half-dressed. He had flung a short kilt around his waist and his feet were bare. The room smelled strongly of the lotus oil that gleamed slickly on his broad chest and had not yet been washed from his unkempt hair. He glanced at me from under swollen lids.

"Ah. Kamen," he said brusquely. "Revise your list of guard duties so that you can be replaced for a while. You are to meet with one of my mercenaries at my watersteps in four days' time and escort him to Aswat where he will arrest the madwoman. You will then be responsible for their safety and well-being until he delivers her to the prison here. Your juniors can see to the provisioning of whatever craft you choose from my boats, and make sure that you select something with a cabin that is walled not just curtained. You will not put in overnight at any village or moor close to any habitation, nor will you speak of this assignment to anyone. You will report to me personally as soon as you return. That is all."

I stared at him, shocked. His words were so completely unexpected that for a moment I could not collect my thoughts. Then I blurted, "But why, General?"

"Why?" His black eyebrows shot up. "Because you are ordered to do so."

"Yes," I floundered. "I am ordered, I will obey, but may I ask why she must be arrested?"

"Not really," he responded curtly. "If every serving soldier questioned his orders, Egypt would be in chaos in a week. Do you want to refuse me?" I knew that to do so would result in an unfavourable testimony to my senior officer at the military school and a check to my career and besides, it was as though fate had conspired to put me in the very place I desperately needed to be. Yet this made no sense at all. Why send a Delta soldier and an expensive mercenary all the way to Aswat when a message to the governor of the nome in which the woman lived would surely be sufficient? Were there no prisons closer to Aswat? And for Amun's sake, why arrest her at all? I was treading on perilous ground by not saluting and turning on my heel but I persisted.

"No, General," I said. "I am well aware that to refuse an assignment means a negative assessment to my immediate superior. But to send two men from Pi-Ramses on such a routine mission seems to me inefficient."

"Does it indeed, my insubordinate young officer?" he said, a quick, cold smile coming and going on his face. "Perhaps I should be pleased that you are so concerned to prevent the wasting of the country's time and resources. I like you, Kamen, but you are sometimes lacking in the proper attitude a soldier must adopt towards those who carry more responsibility than he. This is not a meeting to plan any strategy, nor is your opinion required. Do as you are told."

I should have left the matter there. After all, I was completely sane and the woman to be arrested was not, according to all convictions but my own. To press the General was an act of madness but I could not help myself. The whole matter grew more nonsensical the longer I considered it. "Your pardon, General Paiis," I pressed. "But I wish to make two observations."

"Then hurry up!" he snapped. "I have not even been bathed this morning." Then why the speed of this summons? I wondered but did not say so aloud. Instead I went on.

"Firstly, the woman at Aswat is harmless. She is a nuisance, nothing more. Has she committed some recent crime? Secondly, why send me?"

"That is not an observation, it is a question, you young idiot," he said wearily. "And in answer to it, an answer I am not really required to give as you know, it is customary to have the criminal to be arrested identified in person. You have not only seen but talked with her. Any other soldier I might choose to send might make a mistake."

"Then a member of her family could identify her. Or one of the villagers."

"Would you point a finger at a member of your family in such a situation?" he asked. "And as for the villagers, I want this done as quickly and quietly as possible. The villagers have suffered enough at her hands. So have the King's Heralds and anyone else of note who wishes to conduct their own business or the business of Egypt in peace, without the certain prospect of harassment at the hands of this importunate woman. Their complaints have at last been heard. She is to be incarcerated for a time. She will be treated kindly but firmly, and when she is released, she is to be warned that on pain of an even wider exile she is not to bother the travellers on the river any more."

"I see," I said, but I was wondering again why the local authorities at Aswat were not dealing with the complaints, and why a man as powerful and influential as Paiis was concerning himself with this mundane affair. Suddenly his words penetrated and my head jerked up. "An even wider exile, my General? So she was exiled to Aswat? That part of her story, at least, is true? Did you open the box, and did you find her words as she swore?"

He got up and came round the desk, bringing with him a gush of lotus perfume and a tang of male sweat. Folding his arms he leaned towards me. "I did not open the box," he said distinctly, as though speaking to a small child. "I disposed of it as you should have done. I threw it away. I used the word exile inadvisedly. She is a native of Aswat, and her own madness has exiled her there. That is all I meant. You are in danger of losing not only your commission in this house but also any credibility you have been building as a mature soldier with a fine future by what I can only describe as a youthful obsession with this woman's pathetic fate." He grasped my shoulders and his expression softened. "I will forget that you had the effrontery to question your orders in this matter if you agree to carry them out diligently and then put all thought of Aswat out of your mind. Agreed?" Now a genuinely warm smile lit his handsome features and I responded, stepping out of his grip and bowing.

"You are generous, my General," I said. "Do I know the mercenary you have selected for the task?"

"No. I have not yet chosen the man. But in four days I expect you to be ready to begin the journey. Now you are definitely dismissed."

I saluted and went to the door. As I turned to close it behind me he was still watching me, arms across his chest, but his expression was no longer benign. Those compelling black eyes had gone blank.

I finished my watch for the day, then spent the evening rearranging the rota for guard duty and giving my instructions for victualling the boat I had chosen. Paiis had several skiffs, rafts and other craft, but I wondered why he had not commanded me to take one from the army's small harbour adjoining the barracks on the Lake of the Residence. I also wondered why I was not to tie up overnight where I could be observed. The whole exercise smacked of something excessively clandestine and I did not like it. Why try to keep the straightforward arrest of one miserable peasant woman a secret? Particularly as she was to be interned for a short time and then released. Why not instruct the mayor of Aswat to place her under house arrest instead? The more I thought about it the more ridiculous the whole affair began to seem, and my delight at being actually thrust into her presence was gradually overshadowed by an uneasy puzzlement.

Paiis had not destroyed the box, of course. It was obvious to me that he had not only opened it but found something important inside, something vital enough to prompt her secret arrest solely on his own authority. That was also a presumption on my part, but not once had he intimated that his order to me came from someone else through him. As long as the woman remained a nuisance, pestering men who regarded her as insane and brushed her off, Paiis was able to ignore her. But I had changed all that. I had accepted the box. I had put it into his hands in spite of her warning, and precipitated his decision to act. If these things were so, then I was the cause of her imminent arrest. I would obey the General, of course. To refuse would be unthinkable. But I would do so cautiously. I began to wish that I had thrown my principles to the winds and cut away those convoluted knots and read the sheafs of papyrus I no longer doubted had been inside.

By the time I arrived home, full night had fallen. Although a lamp was burning in the entrance hall, the house had a neglected air and the silence that met me as I crossed the tiles was somehow hollow. I had not missed my sisters' light footsteps or the sound of my mother's voice as she saw to the daily ordering of our lives, but now I longed to hear her calling, "Kamen, is that you? You're late!" and to see Tamit come running, her kitten at her heels. I felt all at once lonely and rootless, wanting the security of family and the cosy predictability of my childhood.

Passing my father's office, I paused. He too was gone. There was no chance of encountering him if I pushed open the door, approached the boxes in which he kept his accounts, began to remove the scrolls … A soft footfall behind me brought me to myself. I swung round. It was Kaha, his scribe's palette under one arm, the leather pouch in which he kept his papyrus dangling from his wrist and a lamp in his hand. "Good evening, Kamen," he said smiling. "Is there something you require in the office?" I smiled back wryly.

"No thank you, Kaha," I replied. "I was just standing here thinking how empty the house feels with everyone away, and now I myself have to leave it. I am ordered to go south in four days' time."

"That is unfortunate. You have only just returned," he said politely. "Do not forget to send a letter to the Lady Takhuru, acquainting her with your enforced absence." His eyes were twinkling and I laughed.

"I am sometimes a forgetful lover," I agreed. "Remind me again. Sleep well, Kaha." He inclined his head and walked past me, disappearing into the office and closing the door behind him.

Summoning Setau I stripped, bathed and ate, telling him that he could visit his family in their Delta village if he wished while I was away, and when he had bid me a good night I poured a few grains of myrrh into the small incense cup I kept beside the statue of Wepwawet, lit the charcoal beneath, and prostrating myself I prayed fervently that this journey would result in an answer to the riddle of my birth and that the god would protect me in my search. When I had finished, I stood and regarded him. His long, aristocratic nose pointed past me, the tiny eyes were fixed on something I could not see, but I seemed to hear him murmur, "I am the Opener of the Way," and I was content.

I received no further instructions from the General and I served my remaining three days without incident. Kaha had told Pa-Bast I was leaving, and the Steward assured me that the household would be intact when I came back. The words were a formality. Pa-Bast had ruled the family as kindly and ruthlessly as he ruled the servants for as long as I could remember.

On the second day I went to see Takhuru. She pouted less at my news than I had supposed she might, and was warmer in her embrace than I had expected, probably because she was bubbling with excitement over what she called "our mystery." With Takhuru, bubbling meant being slightly flushed and moving with a little less formal precision than usual. I watched her, amused and, I must confess, mildly aroused, but I was not sorry to leave her. The responsibilities of my other world were beginning to weigh on my mind and I hoped that the mercenary would prove to be a more congenial travelling companion than the peevish Herald.

After my watch on the third evening I inspected every cubit of the boat I had selected, opened every sack of flour, picked through the baskets of fruit, and made sure that the jugs of beer were still sealed. Army regulations required such a scrutiny, though it was often unnecessary. As for weapons, I would be providing my own and so, I presumed, would the mercenary. We would be sailing with a cook as well as six rowers, all chosen by me, for the pull upriver would be hard. The flood was at its height and the current flowing strongly north towards the Delta. I had thought, before my first assignment south, that sitting on a boat for hours, watching Egypt glide by, would be delightful. So it was, for the first day. Then it had become boring, increasingly so with no congenial conversation to while away the time. Surely a mercenary, inhabiting the outer desert of Egyptian society, would prove cheerful and unpretentious.

I spent several hours in the beer house with Akhebset, wending my way home a little unsteadily under a full moon riding high in the placid sky, and expected to go straight to bed, but a yawning Setau rose from the mat beside my couch as I let myself into my room. "Here," he said, holding out a scroll. "This came for you some hours ago. I thought I should wait up for you in case it requires an immediate response." I took it and broke Takhuru's family seal, unrolling it carefully. "Dearest brother, come at once if you can," it read. "I have amazing news for you. I will be at home until sunset but then I must go to a feast at my uncle's estate." The characters were crudely drawn, the lines of glyphs uneven, and I realized that the words had not been dictated to a scribe but laboriously written by Takhuru herself. This concerned something she did not want her father to know about. It could only mean that she had carried out her promise and rifled his office. What had she found? "Amazing news" the scroll said. Amazing indeed if it had prompted her to struggle with a task she hated, namely putting pen to papyrus. Takhuru did not like to read, and wrote nothing at all in spite of the benefits of a better education than most girls received.

I let the scroll curl in on itself and stared unseeingly at my servant, standing patiently by the couch. My first instinct was to rush out of the house but I checked it. Even if I did so the night was half-spent. I did not relish the prospect of trying to wake her without rousing her household and besides, I was due to leave Pi-Ramses at dawn. Reluctantly discretion prevailed. Whatever she had discovered could wait until I returned. Had I not waited sixteen years already? Patience, my teacher used to say, is a virtue worthy of cultivation if one wishes to achieve an estimable maturity. At that moment I cared nothing for estimation or even maturity, but I did not want to begin my assignment in an exhausted condition or worse be caught by Nesiamun's Steward trying to scale his walls. I handed the scroll back to Setau.

"Burn this," I said, "and in the morning send to Takhuru. Tell her that I received it but too late to call on her regarding its contents. I will visit her the moment I return from the south. Thank you for waiting up for me." He nodded and took the papyrus.

"Very well, Kamen. I've set out your kit for tomorrow and I'll be leaving for my home in the afternoon, but I'll be back in about a week. I wish you success." He let himself out quietly, and when he had gone I fell into a beer-saturated slumber.

However, I was at the General's watersteps just before dawn, my mind determinedly clear of all but my duty. One by one my sailors arrived, greeted me amiably, and went about their business. The cook and his assistant were already on board. I stood at the foot of the ramp as my surroundings gradually took on life and colour and the birds in the bushes clustering to either side began to pipe drowsily.

At length, to my surprise, I saw the General himself come swinging down the path from the house and emerge under his pylon. Just behind him a slightly shorter figure strode. He was cloaked and hooded in folds of brown wool. I was briefly reminded of the Seer until the General halted and the man, with a short bow to Paiis, slipped in front of me to ascend the ramp and disappear into the cabin. His sinewy ankles were a darker brown than his garb and a thin silver chain was wound around one of them. His feet were bare. The hand that had appeared to push back his hood slightly as he stepped onto the ramp was also the rich brown, almost black, of skin that is perpetually exposed to the sun. I caught the flash of a silver thumb ring before the sleeve of the cloak hid the fingers once more. Somehow I doubted whether this passenger would be more friendly than my last commission and I turned dismally to my superior. "Good morning, General," I said as I saluted. For answer he handed me a scroll.

"The confirmation of your instructions, Officer Kamen," he told me. "In the unlikely event that you encounter some emergency it will enable you to appropriate whatever supplies or transportation you might need." Such authorization was customary and I nodded, tucking the scroll into my belt.

"I presume that the mercenary also has written instructions," I commented. "What division is he from?"

"No division at present," Paiis answered. "He has been seconded to me alone. He cannot read, therefore his instructions were verbal. Nevertheless you will obey him implicitly."

"But, my General," I protested hotly, "in any situation of impending danger requiring a decision it is surely my duty ..." He cut me off with a swift, almost savage gesture.

"Not this time, Kamen," he said deliberately. "This time you are an escort, not captain of guards. If all goes well, you will have no decisions to make. In the event that something does go wrong, you will obey him without question." Seeing my expression he clapped a commiserative hand on my shoulder. "This is no reflection on your competence," he tried to assure me. "In truth, it is in fact a confirmation of my faith in your ability. I look forward to your report when you return."

Something in his tone shivered through me and I glanced at him quickly. He was smiling with what I supposed was meant to be the fatherly concern of a superior for a promising junior, but behind it, behind the sallow skin and dark-circled eyes, the face that bore the marks of yet another night of dissipation, was a curious withdrawing. His eyes left mine, lowering and then sliding to where the sailors sat waiting, oars shipped, and the helmsman was sniffing the morning air from his perch on the prow, one arm slung over the high arch of the rudder. "You had better cast off," he finished abruptly. "It will be a long, hard pull to your destination with the flood at the full. May the soles of your feet be firm." His voice cracked and he coughed, then laughed shortly. I saluted once more but to his receding back, for his head had gone down and he had turned quickly on his heel and was walking away.

I also turned, and at my movement the helmsman straightened and the sailors bent, ready to pull in the ramp as I came on board. Still I hesitated. It was not too late to change my mind. A sudden griping in the belly, a swift attack of fever. I could send to one of my subordinates who would be only too glad to leave the tedium of guard duty on the General's door in exchange for two weeks on the river. But then what? An awkward apology to Paiis? A scroll handed to my training master—"Kamen cannot be trusted to carry out his duty without question and has therefore been dismissed from my employ. He should be demoted to the ranks until such time as ..." The sun was growing hot on my shoulders and I could feel a trickle of sweat break out on my scalp. I did not think that the strengthening warmth of the day was entirely responsible. With an inward wrench of surrender I ran up the ramp, waved to the servant to let go the mooring ropes, and shouted "Under way!" to the helmsman.

An awning had been attached to the rear of the shut-tered cabin and I settled under its shade while our craft swung away from the General's watersteps and the sailors prepared to negotiate the channel that would take us through the Waters of Avaris and from thence south on the flood-swollen Nile. On impulse I rapped on the wall of the cabin. "You might wish to come out and enjoy the river breezes," I called, but there was no reply. Well, I thought, signalling to the cook's assistant to bring me water, if you prefer to swelter in that dark place you're welcome. I turned my attention to the slowly unfolding panorama of the city and the cool liquid sliding down my throat.

5

AT ANY OTHER TIME of the year the journey to Aswat would have taken approximately eight days, but we were slowed by the height of the flood and by the restrictions General Paiis had set. The Delta, and the succession of heavily populated smaller cities soon gave way to towns and then long stretches of deserted fields drowned in placid water that mirrored an equally peaceful blue sky. Sometimes we were forced to tie up early because the further miles offered little privacy and I had been warned not to stop in sight of any village or farm. Sometimes the river growth was lush and dense, but the river flowed without providing us the shelter of a small bay. It was heavy work for the sailors, pulling against the strong north-flowing current, and our ponderous progress exaggerated my own increasing boredom and a growing uneasiness that I could not dispel.

The first three days set the pattern of our confinement. After putting in at some lonely spot just after nightfall the cook and his assistant would light the brazier and prepare a meal for everyone. I would eat with the others but the mercenary was served in the cabin. Afterwards I would leave the boat, and taking a little natron, I would wash myself in the river. By the time I returned, the brazier would have been extinguished and the litter of the meal cleared away. The sailors would gather under the prow to talk or gamble and I would pace the deck, my eyes on the dusky bank or the moon-soaked surface of the river, until I was ready to sleep. By then the sailors were already rolled in their blankets, dark humps together, and I too would lay out my pallet, place my dagger under the cushion I used for a pillow, and gaze at the stars until my eyelids grew heavy.

I knew that the mercenary came out during the dark hours. I heard him once. The door to the cabin creaked gently, and the soft thud of his naked feet came to my drowsy ears through the planking of the deck. I was instantly alert but took care not to move. Next there was a quiet splash, and then for a long time, nothing. I was just sinking into unconsciousness again when he climbed back onto the deck, and this time I opened my eyes. He was padding to the cabin, water pooling around him as he went, both hands wringing out his hair in a spatter of barely visible droplets. He coiled to open the door and for just a moment he seemed to resemble something inhuman, sleek and feral, before he slipped inside and the illusion was gone. I presumed that he too was washing away the sweat and grime of the day, but the thought did not make me feel any kinship with him.

He continued to remain hidden during the interminable hours of daylight while I sat or lay under the awning with nothing but a thin layer of wood between us, but I became more and more uncomfortably aware of his presence as we floated south. It was as though his aura, powerful and mysterious, soaked through the walls of the cabin and began to penetrate me, invading my mind, intensifying that vague anxiety with which I grappled until it was betrayed in a physical restlessness. Occasionally he cleared his throat or moved about, but even the sounds he made seemed secretive. I wanted to order the awning taken down and re-erected under the prow, but the rest of the men had taken that place for their own and besides, such an act would be admitting to myself that my apprehension was fast becoming a most unflattering fear. If he had come out once in sunlight, if he had rapped on the wall and spoken one word, I believed that the impression he had given would be gone, but he remained invisible as the days flowed on and only appeared, briefly and stealthily, to immerse himself in the Nile when the darkness could cloak him.

I began to sleep more lightly, waking sometimes even before that small creak betrayed him and watching tensely, through half-closed lids, as he crept naked to the side of the boat and lowered himself over with an ease that I unwillingly envied. I was well muscled and very fit, but he, at least twice my age as far as I could judge, moved with a control and a suppleness that spoke of years of physical discipline. Again I wondered where Paiis had found him and why he was being wasted on such a dull and routine assignment as the arrest of a peasant woman. I thought that he was probably a desert tribesman. For many hentis the Medjay, the desert police, had been recruited from among the people who wandered the sandy wastes with their flocks and herds, for even Egyptians could not endure the many months of hardship needed to patrol our arid western border with the Libu. But I did not think that this man had come from the ranks of the Medjay, or if he had, that he had been recruited for long. The wildness of the desert still clung to him.

For some time I turned all these things over in my mind, recalling the General's words to me when he gave me this commission and my own questions regarding it, and as I did so the conviction I had felt then, that something was wrong, became certainty. Paiis had not become a general because he was an expert at making love. He was a logical thinker, a sensible man. He knew, as well as I, a mere junior officer knew, that all that was necessary for the arrest and internment of this woman was a written order to the mayor of her village who was perfectly capable of having her escorted to the nearest town. Yet here I was, sleepless on my pallet in the middle of the night, with a complement of men and a stock of provisions, on our way to Aswat as though she were at the very least a criminal of some importance. And the man in the cabin. He was not the mayor of her village. He was not a Herald. He was not even a serving soldier in any division active at present in Egypt. What was he then? My thoughts skittered away from that question.

Nevertheless, on the seventh night out, when he had glided across the deck and over the side, I got up, and being careful to stay low and not show myself above the level of the railing, I slunk to the cabin. He had left the door open so I did not have to be concerned that it might squeak and give me away. Still almost on my hands and knees, I went in. The interior was almost completely dark and very stuffy, smelling acridly of his sweat. I dared to pause for a moment, although every nerve in me screamed to be quick, and gradually my eyes adjusted until I could make out the dented cushions on which I supposed he spent most of his time, and a bundle beside them. With a curious reluctance to touch it, I lifted the coarse folds of the cloak and shook them. Nothing fell out, but under the garment there lay a leather belt, thonged to hold two knives. One was short, little more than a blade for gutting a kill, but the other curved wickedly and was roughly notched at intervals towards its point so that as it was withdrawn it would rip and mangle a victim's flesh beyond repair.

This was not a soldier's weapon, I knew. A soldier had to be able to work fast, strike or slash, withdraw and strike again. This knife would require not only great strength to pull out of a wound but also time. Not much, certainly, but more than a soldier in the heat of a battle could afford. This was a dagger for one killer, and only one prey. Vaguely aware that my heart had begun to beat erratically I knelt and ran my hands under the cushions. Coiled beneath one of them I found a length of thin copper wire wound at either end around two small, grooved blocks of wood. A garotte. I replaced it with shaking fingers, made sure that the cloak covered the belt once more, and backed out of the cabin.

I had only just lain down again under the awning and pulled a blanket over my shoulders when I heard the faint whisper of the man's foot regaining the deck. Closing my eyes tightly, I willed myself to stop trembling. The door gave out its tiny sound, and from the far end of the craft one of the sailors sighed and began to snore. I did not dare to sit up for fear the man inside, inches from me, would realize that I was not asleep. Had I left everything as I had found it? What would happen if he suspected that I had gone through his belongings while he swam? Would he be able to smell my presence? For I knew now what he was. Not a soldier. Not even a mercenary. He was an assassin, and Paiis had hired him, not to arrest the woman, but to kill her.

Even then I tried not to believe it. Lying there rigid while the stars wheeled slowly overhead, desperate to get up, to swim, run, anything to release the mental fever that had seized me but afraid to so much as twitch a toe, I did my best to think of one reason after another why the situation was as it was. I was grossly mistaken about the man. He was a foreign mercenary who, of course, preferred to carry and use the weapons he had been trained to use in his own country. That was perfectly acceptable. Someone of great importance, a Prince perhaps, had been harassed by the woman and had demanded her imprisonment and Paiis, because of the high standing of the man complaining, had done everything he could to make absolutely sure that nothing would go wrong. A quick message to the mayor of her village would not do. But why the secrecy? Why was the man hiding himself? Why was I commanded to proceed with a minimum of exposure?

Try as I might, it was impossible to justify any of the weak arguments my thoughts, in a pathetic effort at self-defence, presented, and in the end I was left with the inescapable conclusion that the man I trusted and in whose hands my welfare, to a large extent, lay had lied to me. I was not bringing a loss of freedom to the woman at Aswat, I was bringing death, and I did not know what to do.

My first reaction, as I allowed the truth to come clear, was a cold and selfish anger towards the General. He had used me, not because I was a capable soldier but because I was young and inexperienced. A more seasoned officer would perhaps have smelled something bad at once and refused the assignment on some clever pretext, or puzzled over it without the insecurity that had assailed me, and been confident enough to take his concerns to someone higher than Paiis. Another General perhaps.

But, of course, there was another reason why Paiis had chosen me for his dupe. He had to make absolutely sure that the assassin's blade would slide into the right woman. If he killed someone else by mistake, there could be many unforeseen complications. He could have sent one of the many travellers who had been accosted over the years but none of them, I thought bitterly and with a sense of shame, would be naïve enough to accept the flimsy story of arrest, not sitting in a boat with an arresting officer who did not speak and did not allow his face to be seen. You fool, I told myself. You arrogant fool, imagining yourself superior in some way, deluding yourself that Paiis respected your abilities and singled you out for them. You are nothing but an anonymous tool.

The man inside the cabin sighed in his sleep, a long exhalation that ended in a rustle as he shifted his body on the cushions. I could try to kill him now, I thought stupidly. I could creep into the cabin and run my sword through him while he dreams. But am I really capable of killing a man on the battlefield, let alone in cold blood as he lies unconscious before me? I have been through the motions, that is all. Paiis knows that too. Naturally he does. And supposing I try such a thing, and succeed? And supposing I have built a house of smoke out of my own fears and phantoms and this man is innocent of all save eccentricity? I felt my bowels loosen at the terrible thought. I am a soldier under orders, I reminded myself. Those orders are to escort a mercenary to Aswat and assist him in his orders. I do not know what those orders are, apart from the falsehood the

General told me. A sane and obedient young officer would shut his mind to all speculation and simply do what he was told, leaving the rest to his betters. Am I obedient? Am I sane? If I am right in my horrible assumptions, will I stand by and let the man kill, without any trial, without any written execution directive? And oh gods, I must talk to her about my mother. I had thought there would be time on the journey back, but if I am right and she is to die and I am to let it happen because that is my duty, how am I to speak with her first?

I had never felt so alone in my life. What would Father do in this situation? I asked myself, and even as I asked it, the answer became clear. Father was a man who had built his life on risks. He was not afraid to throw everything he had into a new caravan, with no guarantee of further riches at the other end. He was also honest and moral in his dealings. "Kamen," he would say, "no matter what the cost you must not allow this thing. But you must make absolutely sure that your suspicions are confirmed before you disobey your superior and throw your career away."

Miserably I turned onto my side and rested my cheek against my palm. The voice had begun as my father's but ended as my own. I would have to confirm my suspicions beyond any doubt. I was not foolish enough to assume that I could walk into the cabin and ask the man what his intentions were, therefore I had to wait until his actions proved me right, and in doing so I was putting my own life in danger. For if he was an assassin, he would not allow me to come between himself and his pay. I meant nothing to him, and as nothing he would brush me aside. By my reckoning we were about three days out of Aswat. I had three days to decide what to do. I began to pray to Wepwawet, steadily and coherently, and I did not stop.

We tied up just out of sight of the village on a hot, breathless evening when the sun had sunk below the horizon but the last of his light still tinged the river pink. I vaguely remembered the bay in which we berthed, wider now because of the flood, the trees clustering along its pleasant curve half-drowned, and I knew that the river path bent sharply inland to pass behind the sheltering thicket. Anyone walking from Aswat to the next place would go by without knowing that the boat was there. I did not allow the cook to light the brazier and we fed on cold rations— smoked goose, bread and cheese—while the light continued to fade and the activity of the many birds around us died away until the only sound was the quiet gurgle of the water as it poured towards the Delta.

I had forced myself to eat without appetite and had just drained my beer when there came a sharp rapping on the wall of the cabin. With a sense of shock I realized that the sound had come from inside. I waited, suddenly dry-mouthed in spite of the beer, and then his voice came, muffled by the wood. "Officer Kamen," he said. "You can hear me?" I swallowed.

"Yes."

"Good. We are at Aswat." It was more of a statement than a question, but I answered.

"Yes."

"Good," he repeated. "You will wake me two hours before the dawn and you will lead me to this woman's dwelling. You know which it is." He spoke with a heavy, guttural accent. His Egyptian was clumsy, as though he did not use the language often or had not learned it correctly, but the coldness and sureness of the delivery left me in no doubt as to the clarity of his mind. Paiis must have told him everything I had myself confessed. Otherwise how would he know that I could lead him straight to the woman's home? I took a deep breath.

"It is not kind to rouse her from her sleep in order to arrest her," I said. "She will be frightened and confused. Why not do it tomorrow morning after she has had a chance to wash herself, and dress and eat? After all," I added daringly, "she is not being detained for any major crime. She may not be mad enough to be under the special protection of the gods but she is certainly not fully in control of her faculties. An arrest in the darkness would be cruel."

There was a moment of silence during which I imagined, chillingly and with certainty, that he was smiling. Then I heard him stir. "Her neighbours, her family, they are not to be disturbed," he said. "The General tells me this. If we go in the morning the village will be up. People will be about. They will see, and be distressed. Her family will be notified later." I exhaled loudly enough for him to hear.

"Very well," I agreed. "But we must be quiet with her, and gentle." I waited for a reply but there was none. My throat was now so parched from sheer nervousness that I could have drunk the whole beer barrel dry and I was about to signal to the cook to bring me more, but I changed my mind. My wits must not be clouded.

I needed one more piece of confirmation. As the darkness deepened and the chatter of the sailors gradually gave way to the subdued sounds of the night river, I lay stiffly, senses alert although my eyes were closed. Time passed but

I was not tempted to sleep. I was beginning to think, with enormous relief, that I had been completely mistaken, when I heard the familiar creak of the cabin door. Cautiously I opened my eyes. An oddly misshapen shadow was moving across the deck and it took me several seconds to realize that the man was not naked this time but shrouded in his voluminous cloak. He disappeared over the side. I sat up and crawled quickly to the railing. He was just entering the trees, and even as I watched he blended with their shadows and was gone.

I sat back on my heels and stared at the planking of the deck. I did not think that he had gone to kill, not without the final identification I was to provide. No. He was scouting, assessing the layout of the village, its tiny alleys and open squares, routes of escape if that became necessary, even perhaps a suitable burial place for her body, out on the desert. He would return in two or three hours and then sleep, waiting for my call.

I had gone back to my pallet and was composing myself for a long and anxious wait when a piece of knowledge struck me with the force of a khamsin wind and I cried out aloud, clapping my blanket to my mouth even as I did so. Once he had killed the woman, he would have to kill me too. I was to lead him to her. Unless he then sent me away on some pretext or other while he did what he was being paid to do, an unlikely happening, I would be a witness, able to hurry back to Pi-Ramses, to other authorities than Paiis, and spill the story of an arrest that was in reality an order to destroy. Would he calmly return to the boat and make up some story for my sailors? Tell them that she had fallen ill and could not be moved for some time but that I had been left to guard her? Or would he simply vanish into the desert after burying both of us, so that no one would ever know the truth? And what of Paiis? Was my death part of his original plan? Did he have a tale ready to tell my family when I did not come home? A lie was easy when there was no one to gainsay it. Oh, Kamen, I thought, you are indeed a gullible, innocent fool. You have put your head into the lion's mouth, but you can thank the gods that it has not yet closed its jaws.

My impulse was to jump up and rouse the sailors, blurt out my suspicions, command them to take us away from Aswat immediately, but a saner judgement prevailed. I had no proof at all. I would have to see this thing through, and seeing it through meant that by the time the sun rose either I would be branded an idiot in my own eyes forever or one of us would be dead. I cursed Paiis as I lay there, cursed myself, cursed the events that had led me to this moment, but my curses turned to prayer as I remembered my totem's temple so close by, and the prayers calmed me.

He came back just after the moon had passed its zenith, and this time he did not go straight into the cabin. When I saw him turn towards me, I closed my eyes and forced myself to relax, opening my lips slightly and breathing deeply as though in sleep. I felt him come to a halt. I could smell the wet mud on his feet as he stood there looking down on me, watching me, his very immobility a threat. The moment stretched, froze, stretched again, until I knew I must leap up screaming, but then I heard the squeak of the door and I was safe. Even if it had not been necessary for me to wait a decent interval while he himself drifted into sleep, I would not have been able to move. My knees shook and my fingers trembled. But after a while I managed to bring my body back under my control and without a sound I rose, working my way patiently across a deck still wet from his footsteps, and lowered myself over the side.

Beyond the trees was the path and I took it running, conscious that I did not have much time. It led me, as I had thought it would, to the edge of the modest little canal that connected the Nile with the paving before Wepwawet's temple where it veered, taking a route directly behind the building, past the woman's hut, and then back beside the river and on into the village itself. Panting I slewed with it, aware, even with the urgency of my mission, how good it felt to be on land, to be running unfettered, to be free under the dark lacery of palm fronds. I could keep going, I told myself. Just run on and on until Aswat is far behind me and I am safe and can make my way back to Pi-Ramses, but even as I was thinking these things I was slowing before the entrance to the ramshackle hut I remembered only too well.

For a few moments I paused, listening and catching my breath. The night was quiet, the vast landscape of the desert opening out to my right, its edge of small fields now only great pools of star-shot water sliding away before me. Everything was grey and still. The wall of the woman's house cast a black moon-shadow over my feet. I had half-expected to see her dancing on the dunes like a demented goddess but they lay empty. I could wait no longer. Grasping the tattered reed matting that served her for a door, I lifted it and slipped inside.

I knew where her cot was, and no more than four strides took me to it. Looking down I could make out the shape of her, one arm outflung towards me, her knees bent under the blanket, and as my eyes adjusted to the dimness, I could see her face also, half-hidden in a welter of disordered hair. Giving myself no more time to hesitate and so perhaps lose my nerve, I bent, clapped one hand over her mouth, took her shoulder with the other, and put my knee hard against her outer thigh. She jerked once, convulsively, and I knew she was instantly awake, but then she lay still. "Please don't be afraid," I half-whispered. "I mean you no harm, but it is very important that you don't cry out. May I take my hand away?" She nodded vigorously and I removed my fingers. At once her head came up and she shrugged me away from her shoulder.

"You can take your knee off me as well," she hissed. "It weighs like a boulder. Explain yourself quickly or I shall be forced to do you some damage." Swiftly and quite unself-consciously she sat up, swung her feet onto the dirt floor, and stood, taking the blanket with her and draping it around herself. Reaching to the table she snatched up the stub of a candle but I grabbed her wrist.

"No!" I whispered. "No light. Come outside so that we can talk freely. I don't want to be caught by surprise in here." I felt her hesitate and I waited, still holding her wrist. It was stiff with tension.

"I have nothing to steal," she said softly. "And if you had meant to rape me it would all be over by now. Who are you? What do you want?" Her tone was heavy with suspicion but the tautness had gone out of her so I let her go, moving to the door mat and lifting it. After a moment she gathered the blanket more tightly about her and followed, ducking past me and then pausing to inhale the night air.

Taking her elbow I guided her across the churned sand to the line of trees that began beside the temple and straggled between the desert and the path leading to the centre of the village, and I drew her into the tangled shadow where we could not be seen from any direction. Here we halted and immediately she turned to me and searched my face. "Yes," she breathed. "Yes. I thought I knew you and I was right. Wait a moment. More than two months ago, at the beginning of Thoth. In the temple, and then I caught you spying on me as I danced out there." She flicked a hand towards the rolling sand dunes. "You are the one who kindly took my box, the only one to take pity on me in many a long year. I am sorry, but I do not remember your name. Why are you here? Why the secrecy?" The smile blossomed on her face like the opening of an exotic lotus flower. "It has something to do with my box, doesn't it? I have hardly dared to hope that by some miracle you were an honest man and did not simply toss it overboard. You were able to bring it to the attention of Ramses, weren't you? Is he coming for me? Did he send you to me with a message?"

"No," I replied shortly. "You must listen to me, for there is not much time. I disregarded your warning and gave the box to General Paiis. I believed that you were indeed insane and I did not know what else to do, seeing that in all good conscience I could not throw it away. I am sorry!" The smile left her face to be replaced by a dawning incredulity. "I did what seemed to be the most honourable thing but I think I have only succeeded in putting you in terrible danger. I am here on the General's orders," I went on hurriedly. "and with me is a man I believe to be an assassin who has been sent to kill you. Just before dawn I am to lead him to your house. I had thought we were to arrest you for being a public nuisance, but whatever was contained in that box of yours has prompted an attempt on your life. I am convinced that you are to die."

She studied me carefully for a while. I stared back, but I could see no trace of fear in her face, only a thoughtful speculation. "So in the name of honour you handed over the responsibility you accepted quite freely to a man you had been asked specifically to avoid," she said at last. "That was a cowardly thing to do. But you are still a young man, therefore I forgive you for confusing honour with cowardice. I am not in the least surprised that Paiis has decided to get rid of me, seeing you were stupid enough to stir up all his old misgivings. And why, my fine young officer, are you disobeying your superior so flagrantly in bringing me this warning?" I was dumbfounded at her composure. "But perhaps you are not disobeying him at all," she went on drily. "Perhaps you have been sent to trap me, to frighten me into fleeing with your tale of an assassin, and thus I would violate the terms of my exile. Then he could quite legitimately have me arrested, thrown into prison, and forgotten."

Fingers steepled to chin she began to pace, the blanket dragging behind her, and I did not speak. She had been entirely correct in her calm assessment of the motive that had prompted me to take her box to Paiis. I was guilty of a wrong but I did not understand the larger situation, could not have understood what I was really doing when I placed the box on his desk. I was still out of my depth, so I watched her and kept silent. She sighed twice, shook her head, then laughed without humour. "No," she said. "He would not try to force me from Aswat. He knows that no matter what I will not go. For sixteen years I have kept the law. Paiis knows that mere tales will not cause me to jeopardize any chance I might have to regain the King's favour. In any case, if I was foolish enough to run I would have to be arrested with a legitimate warrant issued by the King's officers on the word of the mayor of Aswat. All that would be much too public for dear Paiis. He wants to bury the past. Literally. No." She stopped pacing and came up to me, looking directly into my face. "You choose to warn me first because you are indeed an honourable young man who must try to undo the harm he has done and secondly because you know that of course if I am to be murdered you must die too." She had grasped the whole situation with a speed and acumen that stunned me, and seeing my expression she laughed again. "I am not such a crazy woman after all, am I?" she chuckled. "How invincibly arrogant the young can be! So. I am to die just before dawn, when you have pointed the finger of doom at me?" She frowned. "He will not choose to make his move if we are together. That would decrease his odds of success. There would be more of a chance that something might go wrong. He will invite you to bring him to my threshold, then he will turn and kill you before entering and slaughtering me. That way he deals with one of us at a time and also it means that both our bodies are close by. Easier to drag off and bury." She fell to chewing her lip, then she held out a hand. "Well? Have you brought me a weapon?" I shook my head, bemused.

"I have only my own, my sword and dagger. I left the sword on the boat."

"Then give me the dagger. Otherwise how am I to defend myself? Do I throw my lamp at him?" I hesitated, looking into her sober face, and she exclaimed angrily, "You still have a doubt regarding his intention, don't you? You will not make a move until you are absolutely certain. But such scruples will get us both killed if your suspicions are correct. You must trust me. Listen. If you give me the dagger, I will swear by my totem Wepwawet to return it to you meekly and willingly if it becomes clear that the man on your boat is innocent of all save a desire to arrest me. Can you trust this oath?"

At her words my mind suddenly filled with a vision of the little wooden statue beside my couch at home, and I remembered all the prayers of desperation I had sent to the god over the last few terrible days. She was watching me anxiously, lips parted, fists clenched at her sides, and I smiled as a great cloud of uncertainty was lifted from my shoulders. It was as though the name of the god had at this moment become a password of mutual surety between us and for answer I unhooked the scabbard and handed her my weapon. She behaved as a soldier might, drawing out the blade and inspecting it carefully, testing its edge for sharpness before slipping it back into its sheath. "Thank you," she said simply. "Now what plan can we make? I think this. You will lead him here. I will shadow both of you. I can watch you on the path without detection. I think you will agree that he will attempt to kill you as soon as you have pointed out my house. As he prepares to knife you in the back I will cry out, and you will turn and kill him instead." I disagreed.

"It won't work," I said. "He needs me to identify you without any doubt. Supposing I point out your house and he kills me but you are not there? You might be sleeping at the home of a friend or relative. Then how will he find you? This is what he will think. In any case, if he knows his business, I will be dead before I can even turn around. This man can move in silence, and swiftly. And even if I am able to face him before his knife finds my back I do not know … I do not think … I have not yet drawn blood of any kind." Her hand was on my arm, warm and reassuring.

"I have killed," she said in a low voice, her grip tightening. "Twice I have killed. It is possible to murder and remain whole, but it is the remorse afterwards that can drive one to the brink of madness. Do not allow the prospect of shedding his blood to unman you. He is an animal, nothing more. He will certainly feel no such remorse after killing you." The hand was withdrawn and my skin felt cold where it had been. "If you are sure that he needs you to identify me with no room for error whatsoever, then he will be forced to face us in the same place at the same time," she went on briskly, "but that will not be his choice so beware! He will do his utmost to separate us at the last moment. It seems that we will have to improvise our defence after all, and pray that you are right in your assessment of his thoughts. I owe you a great deal for this," she finished, leaning towards me and kissing me gently on the cheek, "and I will do everything in my power to make certain that your bravery is not the last act of your life or mine. Keep your sword to hand, and pray!" She shrugged the blanket higher on her shoulders, glancing up at the sky, and as she did so an awareness of time passing rushed in on me.

"I must get back to the boat," I said urgently, for the moon had gone and the merest hint of dawn was in the air.

"Do not sleep again!" She nodded and I turned away from her, half-running back across the sand, but she called to me, "What is your name?"

"Kamen. I am Kamen," I answered without looking round, and I plunged into the shadow of the temple wall.

There was still no visible sign of sunrise as I waded to where the boat was tied, but its vanguard was all around me in the stirring of the breeze and a sense of invisible awakenings in the river growth. Quelling the need for haste that would have had me rushing on board, I stood knee deep in the water, my hands pressed to the side of the craft, and strained to hear anything unusual in the darkness, but all was quiet. Cautiously I grasped the deck rail and pulled myself up. The sailors still lay wrapped in their dreams, vague humps clustered under the prow, and the cabin sat like a squat sentinel, shuttered and silent. I crept to the awning, and lifting my blanket I carefully dried my legs. If the man noticed that they were wet and muddy, he might come to the correct conclusion. Then strapping on my sword, I went to the cabin door and rapped on it loudly. "Dawn approaches," I called. "It is time." There was no more than a hint of movement within before he emerged, cloaked and barefooted, bringing with him a miasma of stale hot air. He said nothing. He merely nodded and strode towards the side. "We must run out the ramp," I said. "We cannot expect the woman to climb to the deck." He paused.

"Not now," he replied curtly. "We will command the sailors later." With that he clambered over the side. I followed grimly. I had given him yet another chance to inadvertently prove himself innocent of my misgivings and a wave of despair swept over me as I left the shallows and padded after him through the sand. He was waiting. I came up to him and with a gesture he waved me past. "You lead me," he said.

Everything in me seemed to shrink and waver as I brushed by him and set off to cover the short, the very short distance to the woman's hut. I think until that moment the reality of it all, Paiis's treachery and my own imminent death, had been like a game in my mind, moves and motives of make-believe that I had played through as though when it was over I would wake the man and we would arrest the woman and sail happily back to the Delta.

But now as I trod the path through a darkness made thicker by the trembling fronds of palms and saw ahead the glint of water in the little canal leading to Wepwawet's temple, the full realization of my situation came to me. This was not some strange military exercise conjured by my training officer or a destructive spree devised by my fellow juniors. This was true, this was real, behind me padded a man who would end my life before Ra rose huge and shimmering over the trees on the other side of the river, and then it would all be over. I would never know what happens next. My spine prickled and a sweat of sheer panic sprang out on my body. He walked with such stealth that I was unable to hear his footfalls. I did not know how close he was to me, how much space there was between us. When he suddenly whispered, "Leave the path," I barely suppressed a shriek. I turned around.

"We must follow it because it passes her door," I whispered back. "It is not far."

We went on, and just as we veered with the path to skirt the temple wall, I fancied that I caught a glimpse of movement in the shrubs. Was she there? All at once the frantic beat of panic in my chest was gone, to be replaced by a numb fatalism. I had done all I could. The rest was up to the gods.

At her door I halted. Over the desert the night still hung, but as I glanced to the east I could see the faintest shredding of its cover. "She lives here," I said, not bothering to lower my voice. "It is wrong for two strangers to wake her so rudely. We can at least knock on the lintel." He ignored me, raising the reed covering and slipping inside. I did not follow. I knew she was not there.

When he emerged, he took my elbow. "The hut is empty," he hissed. "Where is she?" I pulled away from him and was about to reply when the bushes stirred and she stepped out. She was wearing the same coarse cloak in which she had hidden her nakedness when I had surprised her dancing under the moon two months ago. It was tied at the neck. One hand held its edge. The other was invisible but I knew that it gripped my dagger.

"An odd hour to be calling on me," she said warily, her eyes flicking from one to the other of us. "Who are you, and what do you want? If you are looking for a priest, he will arrive shortly to sing the morning prayers. Go back along the path and wait for him in the forecourt." She was completely calm, completely convincing.

I could sense that the man beside me was troubled. The moment before he replied was too long. I could almost read his thoughts. We were together, she and I, outside. What would he do? Would he say, "I am here to arrest you on a charge of public annoyance," and end the game my fevered mind had invented? For that second before he opened his mouth the three of us seemed suspended. Then I realized that I could see her more clearly, her face still indistinct and grey in the heatless light of early dawn. She was clutching the cloak too tightly.

"Is this the woman?" His voice was flat. I did not dare to look at him.

"It is."

"You are sure?" I gritted my teeth.

"Yes." He nodded then spoke directly to her.

"Woman of Aswat," he said, "I am here to arrest you on the minor charge of being a public nuisance. I am to take you north. Go into your house and gather up the things you might need." Shock coursed through me, and I could see that she too was dumbfounded. Her eyes widened.

"What? Arrest me? Is that all?" she almost shouted. "On what charge? Where is your warrant?"

"A warrant is not needed. You are to be held for a short time only." She glanced at me, at her door, then back to him.

"In that case I shall take nothing with me," she said deliberately. "The authorities can provide for me. I have had no warning! What will my family think if I simply disappear? Does the mayor of Aswat know about this?"

"They will be notified. Officer Kamen, go back to the boat and tell the sailors to run out the ramp and prepare to sail."

But of course. I swallowed. How clever, this farce, or how supremely irreproachable. I still did not know which, and we, she and I, would have to play it out to the end. I saluted, catching her eye as I turned to leave. Her face was expressionless.

Once out of sight I drew my sword and left the path, moving back into the undergrowth until I was concealed but could still see the way they would come. The light was stronger now. At any moment Ra would lift himself above the horizon and already the first drowsy pipings of the dawn chorus were beginning above my head. I was staking all my hope on the conclusion that he would bring her a little way along the path until he was sheltered on one side by the trees and on the other by the temple wall, and she would be ahead of him, walking unsuspecting with her back exposed. Would he try to tie her hands? If so he would find my dagger.

They came almost at once, she pacing ahead, he on her heels. She was looking at the ground. He was swiftly running his eye over his surroundings beside and behind, and even as I crouched, sword at the ready, he reached inside his cloak and drew out the garotte. His movements were fluid, easy, and his stride did not falter. Unwinding it he grasped the toggles, leaned forward, and in one graceful, brutal action brought it over and down against her throat.

Something, some kiss of air or tiny sound, must have warned her. Her hand came up, curling between the wire and her neck, and she half-fell, throwing him off balance. As I stood and leaped onto the path, I could see her other hand groping in the folds of her cloak. He was already recovering. Letting go the garotte, he hooked one arm under her chin, ignoring her flailing limbs, and the barbed knife appeared suddenly in his hand. She was trying to scream but could only make choking sounds.

Suddenly I was entirely calm. The sword steadied in my grip. Time slowed. I was closing, rushing towards them, but my mind registered a clot of mud on the swirling hem of the man's cloak, a perfectly round orange pebble on the path before my foot came down on it. He heard me come and his head half-turned but he did not waver. His elbow came back, ready to drive the knife into her side. It was then that I struck him, both hands on the hilt of my weapon, in the angle between neck and shoulder. He gave a grunt and fell on one knee, swaying. His knife clattered to the earth. I wrenched the sword free, blood following it in a welling tide, but even as he fell on all fours he was groping for his blade. I snatched it up, and with a shout I buried it in his back. He slumped into the dust, face down in the pool of dark red liquid spreading across the path. Briefly his fingers scrabbled among the small stones, then he groaned once and was still. I staggered to the wall, and leaning on my sword, I vomited until I was empty. When I could bring myself to turn I saw that the sun had risen. A gust of warm wind was stirring the stray hairs that had escaped from the man's glossy black braid and lifting the edge of his cloak in tiny billows.

She was sitting beside the body, cradling her hand from which a few drops of glittering blood were oozing. "Look," she said hoarsely, showing me the backs of her fingers. There were bruises already swelling on her throat. "The copper cut me to the bone. But he is dead. I examined him. There is no pulse." She glanced at me sympathetically. "You did well," she went on. "I was afraid that you might have believed his story and gone back to the boat. I can hardly speak, Kamen. We must bury him before any traffic begins on the path. Go into my house and bring my blanket and broom. Hurry." I was already recovering, but my legs were weak and I retraced my steps unsteadily to her door. It seemed that I had stood there with them both a thousand hentis ago, and left another Kamen still hovering in that darkness before dawn, full of fear and uncertainty.

Something in me had changed. I felt it as surely as I knew that the sun had risen. I had crossed the gulf between boyhood and manhood in one bound, and it had not happened because I had raised my sword and slashed a man to death. I had found myself compelled to face a challenge unknown to my young fellow officers and I had not refused to see it through. By the time I had returned to her with the blanket and her twig broom, the nausea had completely gone.

We rolled the body in the blanket, leaving the knife in the flesh so that no more tell-tale blood would spill onto the path, and used the broom to sweep into the bushes all trace of the murder. Then, working in a near panic of haste, we half-dragged, half-carried the corpse inside her hut. "It is no use trying to bury him out on the desert," she said. "The jackals would just dig him up and besides, how long would it take to make a hole deep enough? We would be out there all morning, and I am due to sweep the temple at once. If I do not go, someone will come looking for me." As she spoke, or rather croaked, for her throat was visibly wounded, she was busy attending to her hand, washing it and applying a salve. She held it up and winced. "I cannot help you," she added. "But you will find a spade against the outside wall. Put him under my floor. I have no intention of inhabiting this place again anyway. When I return, we can decide what to do." I had not considered the future. All my thoughts had been bent on saving her and myself. I could not afford to consider it now, either. The morning had begun. The sailors would be breaking their fast and would soon be wondering what had become of me. I fetched the spade and began to dig.

Her floor was of beaten earth, clean but hard. However, when I had broken through the first few inches, I found sand and the work went more quickly. Now and then someone would pass her door and I would pause and stand pant-ing, but no one rapped on her lintel. In the end her one room was a nightmare landscape of piled sand and I knew I could not continue without shovelling some of it outside, so I laid the body in the pit I had made and began the equally backbreaking task of covering it. It was then that she came back and we finished together, she awkwardly with a clay scoop, and we stamped down the earth and piled what little remained under her couch.

For a while we sat half-dazed side by side on the edge of the disordered bed, gazing at the churned floor, then I came to myself. "I must go," I said. "When I stand before my General, I will have to say that we tied up at Aswat and the man walked down the ramp and disappeared. I attempted to make the arrest myself but found that you had disap-peared also." I was suddenly conscious of an intense thirst. "It is over," I went on, rising stiffly. "Have you relatives who will give you a bed and help you to build another hut? What excuse will you use for abandoning this one?" She stared at me as though I had lost my wits and I felt her strong fingers bite into my forearm.

"It is not over," she said urgently. "Do you think that Paiis will trust your word? He will have instructed the assas-sin to return to him with some evidence that his assignment was fulfilled, and when you arrive with your guileless story he will know that something has gone wrong. If you lie convincingly, you yourself will be in no danger, but you can be sure that he will send another spy or assassin after me. No, Kamen. I cannot stay here and live in constant fear that next time there will be no reprieve. I am coming with you."

I recoiled. She was right, of course, but the prospect of being responsible for her indefinitely appalled me. I had believed that I could now question her about my mother and then happily set sail for the north and home, putting all this insanity behind me.

"But what of the terms of your exile?" I said hurriedly. "If you leave Aswat the local authorities will search for you, and then they will be forced to report to this nome's governor that you have run away. Besides, I can take you north as my prisoner but what will you do once we reach the Delta?"

"I have no choice!" she almost shouted at me. "Can't you see that? I am trapped here, a defenceless target. The villagers are ashamed of me and would not help me. My family would try to shelter me but eventually Paiis would accomplish his end. He will not let go, not now."

"But why?" I said. "Why does he want you dead?"

"Because I know too much," she replied grimly. "He did not take my persistence, my determination not to remain dumb and quiet, into account. He underestimated me. I will give you my manuscript to read on the way north, and then you will understand it all."

"But I thought ..."

"I made a copy." She slid off the couch and stood looking down on her hands, turning them over and over, the calloused palms, the rough skin of her knuckles, the thin red slash where the garotte had bitten into her flesh. "I have been nearly seventeen years in this place. Seventeen years! Every morning I woke vowing never to rest until I was released from this bondage. Every day in humility and shame I have cleaned the temple, cared for the priests who are also my hostile neighbours performing their three-month duty in the holy precinct, planted, tended and harvested my own food, and kept my sanity by stealing sheets of papyrus and writing down my story in whatever few dead hours I had to myself. I am not stupid, Kamen," she said, and to my astonishment I saw tears in her eyes. "I knew that even if I was able to persuade some kind-hearted traveller to take my box, there was no guarantee that the King would ever see it, so I copied each page as I completed it. For some time after I came here, I sent petitions to him through our mayor but they went unanswered. They probably went unread. But surely he has forgiven me after all this time! Forgiven and also forgotten. They say he is ill. I must see him before he dies."

"But once he dies, the new Hawk-in-the-Nest will review all judgements," I protested. "If what you say is true, would it not be better to approach his successor?" She laughed shortly.

"I knew the Prince also, when he was young and handsome and hid a cold ambition beneath an aloof but beneficent mask. He will not wish to be reminded that a peasant girl once bargained with him for a queen's crown. No, Kamen. My only chance lies with Ramses the elder and you must help me reach him. Wait here a little longer." A blinding shaft of sunlight fell across the floor as she lifted the reed curtain and went out.

This was my chance to run. I could be back aboard the boat within a very few minutes with the ramp hauled in and the sailors pushing us away from the shore. I had done what the gods required of me. Surely nothing more could be demanded. I had saved her life. What she did now was none of my business. I had my own affairs to settle. Indeed she had no right to further endanger my career by foisting herself upon me as though she were a beggar importuning me as I walked down the street. I did not want to know her story. I wanted to retreat to the Delta and the sane ordering of my days. She was like a disease I had contracted on my first trip south and could not purge away.

Yet I knew I would not run. Not because I was too weak of character to deny her but because her words were true and I did not relish having her die after all the trouble I had gone to in order to preserve her life. I still had choices, though she had none. I would read her manuscript. If I was unconvinced by her story, I would turn her over to the proper authorities in Pi-Ramses where she would be charged with violating her exile. I would not give her to Paiis, however, and he would not dare to admit that he had already given a command for her secret arrest on his own recognisance. I thought of the body beneath my feet and surrendered to the inevitable.

She was gone for a long time and I was ready to abandon her after all when she appeared, silhouetted against the hot sky, and beckoned me outside. Thankfully I left that dim, airless room and stepped, blinking, into the glare of mid-morning. She had washed and tied back her hair. Over one arm she carried a hooded cloak and in the other hand a leather bag which she thrust at me. "It was at my brother's house for safe keeping," she explained. "He has agreed to put about the rumour that I am ill and living with him and his family until I can resume my duties. My parents will be concerned and my mother will want to treat me, although she has retired as the village physician and midwife, but my brother will dissuade her somehow. I have seen little of her over the years. She has always disapproved of me. But my father will have to be told the truth eventually." She shrugged but her voice was thick. "I love my brother dearly. He has cheered and supported me through every foolish adventure and if harm comes to him as a result of this I will have one more burden of guilt to carry, but I can think of nothing else to do." She swung the cloak around her shoulders and pulled up the hood. "Let us go."

"Is there nothing you want to take with you?" I asked, indicating her hut, and for answer she made a gesture, part violent repudiation and part regret, before turning away.

"I have lived two lives already," she said bitterly. "I left Aswat all those years ago with nothing and I was sent back with nothing. I begin again from this arid womb and once more take nothing." To that there was no answer.

Together we made our way under the shadow of the temple wall and followed the path as it ran between the trees and the river. The fields were empty, and the path, much to my relief, also deserted, though I could faintly hear the chanting of the priests as we passed the temple's small canal and veered left. The ship could not be seen but I took her elbow, and pushing through the undergrowth, we came to the bay. I was all at once conscious of my filthy appearance. I was streaked with sand and soil that had stuck to my sweat, and I stank. While she waited just out of sight of the sailors whose desultory conversation drifted clearly on the limpid air, I submerged myself in the blessed coolness of the river and rubbed myself clean as best I could. Then we approached the craft. I called for the ramp to be run out and ushered her onto the deck.

A brief silence fell before I nodded to the waiting helmsman to mount to the helm, and the sailors busied themselves drawing in the ramp and preparing to push off. The boat quivered beneath me as it strained to free itself from the sand, and then we were swinging out into the north-flowing current and the lateen sails bellied with the breeze. We were free. We were going home, and elated and exhausted I lowered myself under the awning and the woman sank beside me. My captain approached, a question in his eyes, and I forestalled him.

"The mercenary had further business to attend to on behalf of General Paiis," I said. "He will be returning to Pi-Ramses on his own. Tell the cook to bring food and beer for the prisoner and myself and have the cabin aired and cleaned for this woman." He bowed and pattered away across the deck and I leaned back, closing my eyes. "I will eat and drink and then I must sleep," I sighed. "When the cabin is ready you may occupy it."

"Thank you," she said tartly. "I did not expect to spend the next ten days or so sprawling here in the sight of your crew." I smiled inwardly.

"You would if I ordered you to," I responded, still with my eyes shut. "I am the master aboard this vessel and you are my prisoner." She did not reply. I felt a tray being set by my thigh and caught a whiff of the beer that waited, dark and quenching, but for some time I did not move. Neither did she. When I finally opened my eyes and sat forward, I found her watching me, those clear blue eyes narrowed, her full mouth curved. "It is good," she said.

As the miles lengthened between us and Aswat, I began to relax. No soldiers appeared on the bank, shouting and waving for us to stop, as I had vaguely feared. No vessel pursued us. With a northerly current and a following wind we sailed steadily on, putting in at sunset each evening for fire and food. We no longer went warily. There was no need. While the sailors built a cooking fire, the woman would dive from the deck and swim vigorously up and down, her black hair trailing, her arms appearing and disappearing like brown fish. She did so with a purpose that reminded me of the exercises my training officer prescribed for improving the drawing power of the muscles that bent my bow.

I had begun to read her story and was immediately ensnared by it. The flowing hieratic script in which she wrote was confident and beautiful, her power of self-expression compelling. These were not the painful scratchings of a village woman but the assured phrasings of a well-educated scribe.

I read of how she had been born in Aswat of a father who had been a Libu mercenary for Pharaoh in his early wars and had been rewarded with the usual three arouras of arable land. Her mother served the village as midwife. She told of her early years, of her longing to learn to read and her father's refusal to allow her to enter the temple school, of how her brother had taught her secretly. She did not want to follow in her mother's footsteps, as was the custom. Restless and dissatisfied, she longed for more, and that longing was assuaged when a great Seer came to Aswat to consult with the priests of Wepwawet. The girl had fled to the Seer's barge in the middle of the night to beg him to tell her what the future held for her, and instead he had offered to take her away from Aswat. Here I had laid the manuscript aside in wonderment and hope, for the Seer's name was Hui.

I approached her one early evening when the sun had just begun to tinge the sky with the orange of its setting and the water foaming by beneath our hull had already become opaque. She was leaning on the rail with her arms folded and her face raised to the light breeze. Egypt was sliding by in a peaceful panorama of palm-lined fields behind which the bare dun hills sprawled, and white herons stood and stared at us amid a scattering of stiff rushes. She smiled at me as I came up, the coppery light blushing her skin, and held back her hair against the fingers of the evening air. "I still cannot believe that I am not at home on my cot in Aswat, dreaming of this freedom," she said. "It is a fragile thing, I know, and it may not last, but for these precious days I am spellbound with delight." I looked into her face with a shiver of anticipation.

"In all this time I have not asked you your name," I said levelly. "But I have begun to read the account of your life and I find that it is Thu." She laughed.

"Oh, Kamen, please forgive me for my rudeness!" she exclaimed. "Yes, my name is Thu, short, common, and entirely Egyptian, although my father is a Libu. I should have offered it before."

"You say in your manuscript," I went on carefully, "that the great Seer Hui took you away from Aswat. You told me when we first met that you were a physician once. Did the Seer train you?" Her smile faded to be replaced by a peculiar expression, of sadness perhaps.

"Yes," she replied simply. "He was, he probably still is, the most cunning and able physician in Egypt. He taught me well." I swallowed, eager and yet terrified to ask the question burning on my tongue. Do not form the words, some cautious self warned. Leave all as it is. Keep your fantasies. I ignored it.

"A short while ago I consulted him regarding a disturbing dream I could not shed," I said. "I am an adopted child. This dream had to do with my mother, my real mother. I had believed that she died giving birth to me. That is what I had always been told. In the course of his reading the Seer told me that my mother was a commoner and that my grandfather was a Libu mercenary. He also said that she was dead, but that he had known her slightly. According to him, she was beautiful and rich." I hesitated. My chest felt tight and I drew a deep breath. "I was pleased to accept this assignment from my General because it meant that I could come to Aswat and ask you if you could recall ever meeting a woman like that. Perhaps even treating her. But it may be that I am looking at her now. Are you my mother, Thu? It is not so unlikely, is it? Your father is Libu. Your son would be as old as I am now, wouldn't he?" Her expression became one of earnest sympathy and she laid a hand against my cheek.

"Oh poor Kamen," she exclaimed. "I am so sorry. It is true that there are certain coincidences that appear to join my early circumstances with your own but they are nothing more than that. Coincidences. Pharaoh employed thousands of foreign mercenaries in his early wars and gave them Egyptian citizenship afterwards. They dispersed throughout Egypt, settling on the arouras that were their reward for service and marrying village girls. I was beautiful once and rich, but all I had belonged to Hui or was a gift from the King, and as for nobility, I was granted a title and lost it. I was born a peasant. Dreams of a rich and beautiful mother must be a common longing among those such as yourself, orphans without a history. I am truly sorry that I cannot help you, Kamen," she went on gently. "The matter of your original parentage troubles you a great deal, I can see. I wish with all my heart that I had been able to bring you peace, but nothing links us save a few coincidences. Unfortunately there is no tangible evidence joining your blood to mine. I wish there were. I would be proud to call you my son."

"But it is not impossible, is it?" I persisted. "Many coincidences may weigh against a lack of evidence. Supposing it is true? Supposing that you are indeed my mother and for reasons of their own the gods caused us to meet in the manner we did, to right some great wrong perhaps ..." She looked at me quizzically and my voice trailed away.

"That is a leap we may not take, dear Kamen," she said softly. "If you are right, then the gods will unveil the truth to us in their own good time. Until then I think that for the sake of your sanity you must presume that your mother is dead." The Seer's words to me had been almost identical, and I felt immediately the same flash of rebellion.

"No, I cannot," I said emphatically. "She is already alive and breathing in my dreams and my imagination. I would like to question Hui further." She did not reply.

After a moment she turned back to her contemplation of the evening and I joined the captain who was ready to put in for the night. As I walked across the deck, I remembered, as though it had happened in another life, the message Takhuru had sent to me just before I left the city. She had discovered something important among her father's scrolls and so, I told myself resolutely, I may go on hoping, at least for a little while.

By the time we reached the mouth of the Fayum, I had finished reading the manuscript. Intriguing and horrifying, it nevertheless had the ring of truth about it and I put it back in the leather bag knowing that I would not give the woman over to the authorities. Young and innocent in spite of her ambition, used by unscrupulous men to advance a plot against the King, deserted by them when she failed, she was more sinned against than sinning, and her betrayal by the Seer, someone she both loved and trusted, had been a final and most bitter blow. For several hours I sat under the awning and pondered a tale of lust, treason and murder before turning my thoughts to the problem of what to do with her. I wished with all my heart that I might simply take her home and present her to the household as my mother, but she had spoken the truth when she said that nothing linked us but a series of vague coincidences and my own great need.

I knocked on the cabin wall and presently she appeared, tousled and sleepy, just as the canal leading to the wide Lake of the Fayum drifted past. She stood wrapped in a blanket, watching it, before lowering herself beside me. "Ramses gave me an estate on that Lake," she said. "I was a good concubine. He was pleased with me. After I tried to kill him, he took it all away from me. My land, my title, my child." She spoke without emotion. "I deserved death for trying to murder him but he relented and gave me exile instead. Those who used me in the attempt to rid themselves of a Pharaoh they despised went free. Paiis, Hui, Hunro, Banemus, Paibekamun."

"I know," I said. "I have read it all."

"And do you believe my words?" It was the question she asked the most, her tone always urgent, and in that question she betrayed her own defencelessness. I clasped my hands around my knees and looked up to where the white triangles of the sails billowed and flapped against the blue of the sky.

"If General Paiis had not hired the assassin, I would doubt you," I said. "Your story is compelling, but without the corroboration of an attempted murder I would not have believed." Now I looked at her. "As it is, I must ask you how you intend to bring the plotters to justice after all this time. Do you have any friends in Pi-Ramses?"

"Friends?" she repeated. "No. There is Great Royal Wife Ast-Amasereth, if she still lives and still controls the King through her web of spies and her political acumen. She was no friend to me, but her interest lay in keeping Ramses secure on his throne, so perhaps she may listen to me." She sighed. "But it was all too long ago. She may have died, or lost her authority. A royal court is an intricate game of move and countermove where everyone schemes openly or in secret to influence and thus share the power emanating from the Horus Throne. The dancers come and go, sway forward and swirl back. Old faces vanish. New ones take their place." She pressed one finger to her temple and leaned against it in a gesture of both thought and defeat. "Pharaoh's present malady is nothing more sinister than old age and he has suffered no accident or serious illness in years, therefore I presume that the plotters have relinquished their plan to destroy him. They still live and prosper. The only evidence against them was my word, is still my word, and I think that no one now will remember me. I want them to pay for what they have done to me, but I don't know how to accomplish that end. All I can do is somehow bring myself to the feet of Ramses and beg to have my exile rescinded. Any revenge I take on Hui I must contrive myself." She shot me a keen glance. "You wonder what to do with me when we reach the city," she said. "But look at me, Kamen. I no longer resemble the pampered Lady I once was. I can sit in the market-place and hire myself out as a servant while I ponder what to do. I owe you my life. I do not intend to embarrass or endanger yours any further."

Her words were generous, but to toss her into the maelstrom of the city without so much as a pair of sandals for her feet was unthinkable. I could not hide her in my house as one of our servants. Pa-Bast's sharp eye would spot her eventually. Perhaps Takhuru would shelter her. Nesiamun's estate was vast, much larger than ours, and employed many more people both inside and out.

But could I hide her at all? What of my captain, the sailors, the cook and his assistant? Would they at some time, in some beer house, innocently let slip the knowledge that I had told them the mercenary had stayed on in Aswat with further business on the General's orders? Such gossip would come to Paiis's ears eventually. All I could do was pray that it came to him after the woman had found her way into the palace.

She was sitting with her head now resting on the knuckles that were digging into her temple. She seemed calm enough, and I supposed that nearly seventeen years in Aswat must have taught her the kind of patient fatalism I had yet to learn. If she was aware of my scrutiny, she gave no sign. I studied the pleasant curve of her jaw, the uncompromising slope of her small nose, the tiny lines that radiated from the corners of her eyes. She had pushed her unruly hair behind one ear, revealing a slender neck burned almost black by the sun, and all at once I could see her as she must have been with kohl encircling those exotic blue eyes, with red henna on her mouth and her hair soft and gleaming, surmounted by a circlet of jewels. As though she had read my thoughts, she repeated suddenly without turning round, "I was beautiful once."

"You still are," I replied, a lump in my throat. "You still are."

6

IT WAS MIDDAY when I tied the woman's hands behind her and led her down the ramp and onto the busy quay of Pi-Ramses' warehouse district. We had made good time. The return journey had taken eight days, and I congratulated my sailors and gave them three days' leave. I had let it be known that I was to be met in the city's central district by an escort from the prison. There were always soldiers at the quays, waiting to conduct precious cargo to the temples or the palace. Some of them could be presumed to be waiting for me. Dismissing my men and telling them to return the boat to the military pier for inspection before I had it returned to the General, I led the woman into the shadow of one of the warehouses, slipped the rope from her wrists, and together we merged with the crowds. She had raised the hood on her cloak, and attracted no attention.

The day was pleasantly warm. The month of Athyr was about to give way to Khoiak and the worst of the summer heat was over. It would be a long, dusty walk to Takhuru's gate, but try as I might, I had not been able to think of any other way to reach it without suspicion. I pushed through the usual noisy city chaos of braying donkeys, creaking carts and shrieking stallkeepers with the woman behind me, my mind on the problems ahead. Would Takhuru be at home?

How could I take the woman past Nesiamun's gateguard? How much time did I have before Paiis received word that my sailors had returned and I still lived?

The throngs became less dense as we moved away from the warehouses and into the district of the markets. People clustered about the goods on display, and we were able to walk more quickly. Trees began to appear, under whose grassless shade the old men crouched in their dirty loincloths, gesticulating and croaking to one another as the city foamed around them. Occasionally I glanced back but she was always just behind me, her bare feet covered now in white dust, her cloak brushing her ankles. We wove our way through a group of worshippers clustered about a small Hathor shrine, and a whiff of incense smoke stung my nostrils briefly before we were past it. The Feast of Hathor on the first day of Khoiak was fast approaching and all Egypt would be celebrating the Goddess of Love and Beauty.

I thought of my women as I strode along. Takhuru, lovely and wilful, with her fit, pampered young body. My mother, Shesira, always exquisitely dressed, always wearing some expensive necklet or bracelets or rings my father had lavished on her. My sisters, Mutemheb and Tamit, with their pale skin untainted by too much exposure to the sun, their delicate linens and fragrant hair oils and pots of precious perfumes. Behind me trudged a pair of coarse, splayed feet, a body kept wiry not by the indulgence of exercise but the necessity of hard work, a face touched all too often by the withering fingers of Ra. Yet I had not lied when I told her that she was still beautiful. Her glittering blue eyes held a wealth of knowledge and experience completely foreign to the women of my social acquaintance. Hers was an attraction without artifice. Arrayed in all the splendid accoutre-ments of the royal harem, she must have been an irresistible prize indeed.

I left her sitting under a tree with her feet in the water just out of sight of the guards at the entrance to the Lake of the Residence, and meeting their challenge I passed the familiar row of imposing gates and marble watersteps. The Seer's pylon cast no shadow in the mid-afternoon light but as I walked by I caught a glimpse of movement just beyond it and called a greeting to the old gateward. He did not respond. Smiling to myself in spite of the anxiety that filled me, I went on.

Nesiamun's porter welcomed me effusively and assured me that Takhuru was at home. I threaded my way through the abundance of garden statuary and entered the house, sending a passing servant to tell her that I was in the entrance hall.

I had resigned myself to a long wait. I was used to waiting for Takhuru. She was almost always late and never offered an excuse for her tardiness in the lofty and unreflec-tive presumption, I thought, that she was the centre of the world. But I had paced the hall and was about to seat myself in one of the fragile cedar chairs scattered about when she came running from the rear of the house. When she saw me she halted. I stared at her in amazement, for she had flung a loose tunic over limbs that gleamed with oil. Her face was unpainted and her hair had been piled haphazardly on top of her head. I had never before been allowed to see her in such disarray. "Kamen!" she blurted. "Did I keep you waiting? I'm sorry. I've been taking a massage. Forgive my appearance. I did not expect you so soon ..." Her voice trailed away. Her glance did not hold the mild disapproval I usually saw if I dared to present myself to her in less than spotless condition. My kilt was stained and wrinkled and the dust of the city clung to my legs and had sifted into my hair, but she seemed not to notice. She continued to stand there, one bare foot over the other, chewing her lip. After a puzzled moment I went to her, took her hot hand, and kissed her gently on the cheek.

"I have missed you, Takhuru," I said dutifully. "Are you quite well? You seem flustered."

"Well?" she repeated. "Oh yes, Kamen, thank you, I am very well. But I must talk to you at once. I have something very important to show you. It has been hard, waiting nearly three weeks for you to return. Come up to my room." I felt a rush of indulgent affection for her. She was looking up at me with flushed face and bright, expectant eyes, yet the tension in her fingers and her awkward stance betrayed an anxious desire of some sort.

"I will," I said. "But first I must talk to you. Something has happened, Takhuru, something rather terrible. Can I trust you?" She withdrew her hand.

"Of course."

"This is not some frivolous secret you can gossip about with your friends," I warned her. "You must swear to keep it to yourself. Hathor's feast day is coming. Swear by Hathor!" She took one step away. "I so swear," she faltered. "Kamen, you are frightening me."

"I'm sorry. Come into the garden where we will not be overheard."

She followed me into the glare of the afternoon without argument, and her silence, more than anything else, convinced me that something had deeply disturbed her, for otherwise she would not risk leaving the house undressed and unpainted for fear she might be seen. I led her into the privacy of the shrubbery, and pulling her down onto the grass I told her everything. I knew that I was taking an enormous chance, but if I could not trust Takhuru as my betrothed, what reason would I have to trust her as my wife? Paiis was a frequent visitor to her house. He and her father were old acquaintances. And Paiis was the Seer's brother.

As I spoke, relating the woman's story and then the dreadful events of the past weeks, it came to me like the unfolding of a piece of embroidered linen that the Seer must have known what Paiis had planned. Perhaps the instigation of Thu's destruction had even come from him. I had read the manuscript. Hui was a cold, ruthless man who had used a young girl and then abandoned her to the blind finality of a royal judgement. Would killing her now mean anything more to him than brushing away a bothersome fly? Particularly if the machinations of his past, so long forgotten, were in danger of at last being revealed? I had read and believed the story, damning and utterly convincing as it was. If it had fallen into the King's hands, might his reaction not have been the same? Supposing Paiis had opened the box, read it, and recognizing its power to persuade had passed it to the Seer, and together they had decided first that Thu must die and second that I must die also just in case I too had found it credible?

Takhuru watched me intently. She did not interrupt. Her eyes moved from mine to my mouth and back again and she sat completely still. At last I fell silent, and after a while, during which she was obviously deep in thought, she touched my knee. "You believe all this, Kamen?" It was the woman's oft-repeated question. I nodded.

"Yes, I do. I have now staked my career and perhaps my very life on its veracity."

"Then I believe it too. And she is outside, by the river? This peasant woman? What do you want me to do with her?" I did not miss the note of mild disdain as well as apprehension in her voice. I could not blame her for either.

"There are many servants in your employ, Takhuru. Tell your Steward that she followed you in the market-place, begging for a position, and you could not refuse her plight. Put her in the servants' quarters but be sure that any work you give her keeps her well out of sight. Perhaps she could tend the gardens." Takhuru wrinkled her nose.

"Why can't you take her to your house, Kamen, and let her tend your garden?"

"Because," I pointed out gently, "we have far fewer servants than Nesiamun, and Pa-Bast would simply turn her out or pass her on to another household. Please do this for me, Takhuru." My begging did not sweeten her. Instead she spoke sharply.

"For you, Kamen, or for her? Or for both? Is she beautiful? After all, you were on the river with her for days and days." I sighed inwardly. Oh women!

"My dearest Takhuru," I said. "You have heard me well. I know you have. She was beautiful once, the beloved of the King, but that was seventeen years ago. Now she is nothing more than a woman desperate for our help. She needs us. And will you try to think of some way she can slip into the palace?" At that Takhuru brightened.

"If she was once a concubine, she must know the palace well," she said. "I will ponder this problem with her. Actually, Kamen, I have never seen a concubine and I am most interested." She leaned forward earnestly. "I do understand the gravity, and the strangeness, of it all," she insisted. "I will treat none of it lightly. But, Kamen, my news for you is even more momentous. Will you hear it now?" I got up.

"No," I said brusquely. "Not now. Get me a servant's armband for her, Takhuru, so that she can pass the guards. She has been waiting for a long time and must be hungry and thirsty. I will go and fetch her." Takhuru made as if to speak again. Her mouth opened, then closed in a firm line and she scrambled up and walked away. Before long she was back with a thin copper bracelet dangling from her fingers.

"I told the Steward that I had hired a new servant," she said, handing me the band. "Bring her to my room, Kamen, and then I simply must talk to you." That expression of eagerness coupled with hesitancy flitted across her face again before she turned towards the house. I made my way quickly through the garden and out the gate.

The woman was asleep under her cloak in the shade of one of the sycamores, both hands pillowing her brown cheek, her hair spread over the grass. I watched her briefly, noting the way her long black lashes fluttered as she dreamed, then I squatted and touched her shoulder. She came awake at once, eyes opening to fix me with their straight blue stare. I gave her the armband. "I have spoken with Takhuru," I said. "I told her everything. She has agreed to take you into her employ and keep your secrets."

"You trust her." It was a statement, not a question, and I nodded.

"I don't know what tasks you will be set," I offered, with a vague and irrational feeling that I should apologize to her for suggesting that she work at all, and once again she seemed to divine my thoughts. She smiled, pushing the armband over her knuckles and shaking it onto her wrist.

"I am used to hard labour," she said matter-of-factly. "I do not care what kind of work I am ordered to do. All I ask is that your betrothed allow me time to swim every day and if possible keep me away from all guests and visitors."

"Good. Then we will go."

We passed the guards, and as we did so she held up her wrist without slowing or looking at them. They hardly bothered to acknowledge either of us, and soon we were hurrying across the small shadow the Seer's pylon was beginning to cast. Thu turned her face away, and I was painfully reminded of her story, of how many times she had come and gone from these watersteps, resplendently garbed in all the finery the harem and an adoring King could provide. She made no comment and I remained quiet.

It was the hour of the afternoon sleep, and the garden was deserted. We slipped quickly into the house, across the empty entrance hall and up the stairs. Takhuru was waiting for us and answered immediately to my knock. I was amused to see, as we entered her room, that she had managed to be washed and painted while I was gone. The folds of her gossamer-thin white linen sheath were held to her tiny waist by a belt of interweaving gold ankhs. More ankhs studded with moonstones encircled her long neck and hung from her earlobes. Her cosmetician had sprinkled her face and shoulders with gold dust. The contrast between such rich elegance and the stained and tattered garb of my companion was startling, yet it was the peasant who dominated the space in which we all stood. She put out her arms and gave Takhuru a deep obeisance. Takhuru inclined her head, and the two women surveyed one another in silence. Then Takhuru said, "What is your name?"

"My name is Thu," the woman replied equably.

"I am the Lady Takhuru. Kamen has told me all about you. I am sorry for your plight, and I have promised him that I will do all I can to help you. My Steward believes that you importuned me in the market-place and out of pity I hired you. I expect that such an excuse for your presence here might offend you seeing that once you had your own servants," she went on hurriedly, the haughty Takhuru giving way to an anxious kind-heartedness I loved but seldom saw, "but it was all I could think of. You will have to do what he tells you until Kamen and I can decide how to extricate you from this nightmare." With the slight emphasis she put on some of her words I suddenly understood that my betrothed had put on her finery out of a feeling of insecurity not arrogance, and was making clear her prior claim on me. I was flattered and amused.

"I am very grateful to you, Lady Takhuru," the woman replied smoothly. "I assure you that I am not in the least offended in having to serve when once I was served. I will do my best not to endanger either of you. After all, Kamen saved my life." Takhuru smiled.

"He did, didn't he? It hasn't really sunk in yet, any of it. I shall summon you soon to talk to me and explain everything better. Now if you go down to the rear of the garden you will find the servants' quarters. My Steward should be there. Tell him to give you food and beer and a place to sleep and something to wear."

"Thank you." The woman bowed and let herself out with an unobtrusive grace. When she had gone, Takhuru turned to me.

"She is not at all the way I imagined," she said frankly. "I thought she would be, well, sturdy and solid, but if you disregard the evidences of poverty and neglect you can see someone quite fine underneath. Her speech and manners owe nothing to village life."

"I love you, Takhuru," I said. "Not only are you generous and beautiful but I keep finding pieces of you I never knew were there." She smiled and blushed.

"That is an appalling admission seeing that we have known each other since we were children," she retorted. "I, on the other hand, know perfectly well that under your boring and distressingly responsible exterior lies a man who would throw everything proper away with a snap of his fingers if it became necessary. And you have done just that. I love you also. I am intrigued with this adventure. Do you think that one day we may find ourselves in the presence of the One because of it?"

"No," I said shortly, suddenly afraid that she did not after all understand the gravity of the situation we were in. "If we are lucky I will be left alive and your family will remain in ignorance of the whole matter. This is not a game."

"I know that," she whispered, and all at once the Takhuru who had greeted me so oddly was back. She was searching my face carefully. "Kamen," she said slowly, "the message I sent you, the one you had to ignore because you were going south. I have something to show you. Something about your father." I was immediately alarmed.

"What is it? Has there been an accident? Is he injured? Dead?"

"No, not Men," she said. She took a deep breath, blew it out, and went to her tiring chest. Kneeling, she lifted the lid, rummaged about among her clothes, and withdrew a scroll. Getting up, she approached me with a strange caution, holding it close to her body.

"I found this when I was investigating my father's office," she said, her voice thready. "It was in a box of old lists of employees and faience production for previous years. If it is genuine, you may indeed one day stand before the One. You have a right to do so. You are his son." She held out the scroll with both hands, as though she was bestowing a precious gift or an offering to a god, and I took it in a cloud of sudden confusion.

The papyrus was stiff, as though it had not been unrolled for some time. It had once been sealed but half the seal had broken away. I noticed almost dispassionately that my fingers were shaking. Something in me had heard and understood her, and was tremulous with shock although my conscious mind still slumbered. "What are you saying? What are you saying?" I stammered like an idiot. Numbly I felt for a chair and sat down heavily. The black, formal hieroglyphs danced before my eyes. She came and put a firm hand on my shoulder.

"Read it," she said.

The letters had ceased to gyrate, but I had to grip the scroll tightly to keep it steady enough to obey her. "To the Noble Nesiamun, Overseer of the Faience Factories of

Pi-Ramses, greetings," it said. "In the matter regarding the lineage of one Kamen, now residing in the home of Men the merchant, you may rest assured that the aforesaid Men is a man of integrity and has not tried to link an adopted son of base and uncertain parentage to your daughter who is of pure and ancient stock. The Lord of the Two Lands, the Great God Ramses, has seen fit, for divine reasons of his own which may not be questioned, to place his son, the aforementioned Kamen, into the care of the merchant Men to be raised by him as his own. Although the said Kamen is the son of a Royal Concubine, he is nevertheless blessed with the blood of the divinity, therefore do not hesitate to allow a marriage contract between your house and the house of Men. You are commanded, however, to obey the injunction of utter secrecy imposed upon the merchant Men when first he received the child Kamen into his care. Dictated to the Royal Scribe of the Harem Mutmose, this fourth day of the month Pakhons, in the twenty-eighth year of the King." It was signed, "Amunnakht, Chief Keeper of the Door."

For a long time I felt nothing. My head, my heart, my limbs were frozen. I stared into the room unseeing. This is what it is like to be dead, be dead, be dead, I thought over and over again. But gradually I became aware of a hand on my shoulder, a woman's hand, Takhuru's hand, I was in Takhuru's quarters on a warm afternoon, no, not me, a King's son was here, a King's son, I, Kamen, was indeed dead, and then a dizziness washed through me and I doubled over.

With my eyes screwed shut I pressed my forehead against my knees until it receded. Takhuru's hand was removed. When I was able to straighten slowly, I saw her sitting on the floor in front of me, calmly waiting. "It was a terrible shock for me," she said. "It must be doubly so for you. It was your mother who came to you in your dreams, Kamen, and your will was bent on finding her. Who would have thought that a question you had not yet asked would be answered first?" I licked my lips and tried to swallow. I felt light and empty, like a winnowed husk.

"I suppose the scroll is genuine?" I managed.

"Of course it is. Amunnakht is indeed the Keeper of the harem door. His word is law within its precincts. Besides, who would be mad enough to forge such a scroll? Not only use the Keeper's name but also express the will of Pharaoh without his knowledge or permission? His sons may not marry without that permission. It means that when the matter of our betrothal was mooted, your father told my father it was all right to join us because your lineage was in fact higher than mine. My father did not believe him. He applied to the Keeper for confirmation. The Keeper went to Pharaoh for permission both to reassure my father and to obtain the Great One's permission for you to marry. You are a royal son, Kamen."

"My father knew," I said, anger beginning to flood my emptiness with a frightening speed. "He knew all of it. He must know which concubine bore me. And yet he denied everything, he lied to me in my distress! Why?" Takhuru shrugged.

"The scroll makes it clear that your father was bound to secrecy. He could not tell you the truth." But I was not ready to forgive him. That blind, strong anger pulsed hotly through me so that I wanted to take my father by the throat and pound and pound him. My fists curled, and then I realized that it was my real father I wanted to smash into the dust. The Great God himself. I was a royal son.

"Why did Ramses give me away so quietly?" I said vehemently. "There are dozens of royal bastards in the harem, as young officers in the army, in positions in the administration. Everyone knows who they are. They may not be accorded the worship due to legitimized princes but their parentage is not hidden. Why was mine?" She leaned forward and grasped my wrists.

"I do not know, but we can find out," she said. "Give yourself time to become used to the idea, Kamen. Do nothing foolish. Perhaps you were born under excessively unlucky omens. Perhaps your mother was so beloved of Pharaoh that he could not bear to keep anything that reminded him of her. That peasant woman Thu. She was a concubine at about the same time you were born. I will ask her what she remembers of those days. And what I say is true. You are royal. You can request permission to come into your father's presence and will not be refused." She gave my arms a little shake. "You know that I loved you before I discovered you were of royal blood, don't you?" she said solemnly. I tried to smile but my mouth felt heavy.

"You are an outrageous snob, Takhuru," I half-whispered. "Now what do I do? How must I view myself? What am I? Are my thoughts and habits, my likes and dislikes, rooted in the royal seed? Must I remake myself? Try to know myself anew? Who am I?" She pulled me down beside her and strained to embrace as much of me as she could.

"You are my Kamen, brave and honourable," she murmured. "We will do one thing at a time. First you will go home and have Setau bathe you. Tomorrow you will break into your father's office and confirm this scroll by the undoubted existence of the other."

"Tomorrow I must stand before the General and lie," I answered, and she laughed.

"You can stand before him and secretly know that your blood is the purest in the kingdom," she said. "He will not dare to raise a hand against a King's son!"

But I was not so sure. For a long time Takhuru and I sprawled on her floor, alternately kissing and drowsing in the sleepy afternoon. Her room was security, normality, a last affirmation of the man I used to be. Not until I felt sane enough to pass through my own door did I leave her.

I remember vividly the short walk home. It was as though my old eyes had been replaced by new ones, and I saw the sparkle of bright light on the water, the outline of the trees against the sky, the dark yellow patches of sand beside the path, with remarkable clarity. The soles of my feet were sensitive to every surface beneath them, my ears responded to the myriad sounds of life, insect, bird and human, on the Lake. I was reborn, and yet I was the same. No longer did I inhabit the world on sufferance, feeling that I was filling a place that was not mine.

Once within my own domain I washed, changed my linen, and set out again, this time for Paiis's estate. I would have liked to wait until the next day to give him my report but I knew I must speak to him before he heard from elsewhere that I had returned. He would be expecting the assassin to be admitted to his office. Instead, it was I who shouldered past his Steward and saluted.

He did not rise from behind his desk in shock, but I saw his body tense with the urge to do so. He controlled it immediately and his eyes, by the time they met mine, were empty of any panic. I admired his self-possession, keeping my own expression carefully solemn. "Kamen," he said unnecessarily. "You have returned. Make your report." His voice did not waver, but it was uncharacteristically shrill.

"My General," I began, "I am sorry to have to tell you that I have failed to carry out your orders. I assure you that it was not from any lack of effort. I know my duty." He made an impatient gesture. He was now not only fully in command of himself but alert with suspicion, and everything in me rose to meet that challenge.

"Don't babble," he cut in testily. "What went wrong with so simple an assignment?" I was tempted to laugh, but I recognized the desire as an invitation to a mildly reckless hysteria.

"I escorted the mercenary safely to Aswat as you required," I said calmly. "Our nightly berths were in quiet places where we could not be seen, also as you required. Once we had arrived a little way out of the village, I accompanied the mercenary to the home of the woman three hours before dawn but she was not there. The mercenary was angry. After asking me where she might be, he told me to wait outside her door. I did so. He did not return, and neither did she."

"What do you mean, he did not return?" Paiis snapped. "How long did you wait? Did you search for him?"

"Of course." I allowed myself a fleeting expression of wounded pride. "But I was mindful of your admonition regarding secrecy. It made any thorough search difficult. I could have spent days questioning all the villagers and ransacking their houses, but as it was, I walked the alleys and the fields until the morning was far advanced. I waited a further day, hidden on board the boat, but the mercenary did not come. That evening I went again to the woman's house but with no success. She also had not come back. I had to make a choice between making myself and my crew increasingly visible to curious peasants or leaving for the Delta. I chose to set sail. The responsibility is mine. I hope I have acted as a good officer should. I would like to suggest that you send a message to Aswat, commanding a local authority to make the arrest. Someone who knows the woman's movements and habits." Had I gone too far? His dark eyes regarded me thoughtfully, coolly, but I had no difficulty in holding his gaze. I hoped there was enough apology in mine.

As I looked at him, it was brought home to me that the assassin was only a tool. Paiis himself was the impulse that moved the tool, his the original force that set the instrument in motion. I did not think that he hated the woman, or me either for that matter. His motive was not tangled with emotion; in fact, I believe that he liked me a great deal. His was a decision of self-preservation. He had seen a potential danger. He had carefully calculated the need for and degree of involvement. And then he had acted. All talents necessary in a senior military commander. Thu had said that he would try again. Looking into those eyes that gave nothing away, I knew that she was right.

He grimaced and leaned back, and the moment of appraisal had passed. "I am sure that you acquitted yourself as well as could be expected," he said crisply. "I may say that I am puzzled by the behaviour of the mercenary and I will of course investigate his odd disappearance. Do you think he met with some misadventure?" I did my best to look taken aback. I was, I reflected, becoming a very good actor.

"Misadventure?" I repeated. "Oh I do not think so, General. What misadventure could have befallen him on such a mundane assignment? I must say that I neither liked nor trusted him. He kept himself secluded in the cabin and would speak to no one for days. I suspect that he simply felt the call of the desert once we had left the more populated areas and answered it without the sense of duty that would keep a more civilized man from abandoning his task. He is a desert dweller, is he not?" Paiis glanced at me sharply.

"I suppose that is obvious," he said, "and I daresay we will not see him again. Tell me, Kamen, that box you brought to me. Did you open it?"

"No, my General. It would have been dishonourable to do so. Besides, since the woman is adjudged insane, I did not think there would be anything interesting inside it. Those knots were remarkably intricate. I could not have retied them." Now he smiled.

"How comforting is a sense of honour," he murmured. "A man with such an apprehension of what is right need make no difficult decisions. Ma'at has made them for him. You are dismissed, Kamen, but before you go, I should warn you that your time of service in my house is coming to an end. You have guarded me well but we both need a change. You will return to officers' school for further training and reassignment."

A dozen thoughts sped through my mind. He has just now decided this. He has not believed a word I told him and will no longer feel safe with me pacing his halls at night. He will not take the chance that I did not read the manuscript and he wants me back in the barracks so that he can kill me at his leisure. A training-ground accident perhaps. He is going to use his influence to have me posted to Nubia or one of the eastern forts. With great effort I let none of these conjectures show on my face. I saluted. "I am content in your service, General," I said, "and I hope I have not displeased you in some way or my care of your household has been less than acceptable."

"I have no complaints, Kamen," he assured me, rising. "But you are a young man. You need to move on to something more challenging, something that will further develop your abilities. I will keep you under my eye, of course. I have a proprietary interest in you." Now he grinned openly, with an impudent, boyish confidence, and I wanted to smash the smile from his face.

"Thank you, General," I said. "You compliment me. I shall be sorry to leave your employ." With that I turned smartly on my heel and left his office, my gut churning with both relief and rage.

As I strode along the path beside the water, I imagined myself in the presence of Pharaoh, my father. He had explained the reasons why he had thrown me away. He had not begged my forgiveness, for surely those reasons had been divinely correct, but he was looking down on me with loving indulgence as I knelt before him. "Is there anything I can do for you, Kamen?" he asked me kindly. "Some favour I may bestow?" "Yes," I answer humbly but firmly. "You may deliver the General Paiis into my hands. He has done me a great wrong." At that point I came to myself. A boatman passing on the Lake recognized me and called a cheerful greeting. I raised an arm in response then burst out laughing at the silly fantasy, at myself for my presumption, at Paiis for his arrogance. The outburst was a cleansing one and I answered our gate warden's small bow and turned towards the entrance hall in a better frame of mind.

There were messages waiting for me from my family. My father had arrived safely in the Fayum having despatched the caravan and caught a boat north. He would spend a week seeing to the affairs of the estate with his Overseer, judging the state of the soil as the flood receded and deciding what crops should be planted, before escorting the women home. My mother and sisters had dictated long, gossipy letters so full of the flavour of their language that I could almost hear their voices as I read. I loved them all very much, but there were now too many secrets between my father and myself, and perhaps my mother also, and until they were removed, I would be on one side and my family on the other.

I sent Setau with word to Pa-Bast that I would be out for the evening meal. I had not seen Akhebset for some time and besides, I had a need to lose myself in the rough and tumble of the beer house. All of it, Paiis and the woman and my lineage and my fears, could wait until the morning to enfold me again. I would get drunk with my friend and forget it completely. Laying aside my weapons and uniform, I wrapped a short kilt about my waist, slipped a pair of old sandals on my feet, and catching up a cloak I left the house.

I drank a great deal of beer, but try as I might I could not wholly obliterate the memory of the last week. Its events and emotions, its tension and shocks, remained in my consciousness and throbbed faintly beneath the singing and raucous laughter. I told Akhebset that I was soon to leave the General's house. I wanted to tell him more, to pour it all into his ear. We had known each other since the days of our initiation into the army, but I did not want to risk losing his friendship or put him in danger, however remote that possibility. So we quarrelled and diced and sang, but I walked home sober as the moon set, and I fell into an unsatisfied slumber.

I woke late feeling jaded and I lay on my couch for some time, watching Setau raise the window hangings and straighten up my room while the meal he had brought sent its tempting aroma into the air. I was in no hurry to rise. Having completed a long assignment, I was due the obligatory two days to myself, so I lay on my back in a shaft of strong sunlight, not hungry, until Setau said, "Are you ill this morning, Kamen? Or just being lazy?" At that I sat up and swung my feet onto the floor.

"Neither," I replied. "Thank you, Setau, but I don't want any food, just the water. I think I will swim, and then I want to see Kaha if he is not busy. Don't bother to lay out anything for me. I can dress myself when I get back." He nodded and took the laden tray away, and when he had gone I drained the jug of water he had left, slipped sandals on my feet, and made my way to the Lake.

The morning was clear and sparkling, pleasantly warm without a draining heat, and I slid beneath the surface of the gently lapping water with a sigh. For a while I simply hung suspended in the coolness, content to see the distorted blur of my limbs, pale in the limpid depths, and feel the sun on my head, then I began to swim. There was sanity in the rhythmic action, in the flow of liquid against my lips and the sound of my measured breaths. When I began to tire, I pulled myself onto the bank, and by the time I had walked through the garden I was dry again. In my room I wrapped a clean kilt about my waist, combed my hair, and went down into the hall, sending a passing servant for Kaha. I was entirely calm. I knew what I must do.

He came at once, his palette tucked under his arm, a smile on his lively face. "Good morning, Kamen," he greeted me cheerfully. "Do you want to dictate a letter?"

"No," I said. "I want you to help me search the scrolls in my father's office. You know them all, Kaha. I could go through them myself but there are many years of records in there and it would take too long."

"Your father always asks that the office remain closed while he is away," Kaha responded thoughtfully. "I only deal with the correspondence that cannot wait until he returns. Is it an urgent matter?"

"Yes it is. And I assure you that I have no intention of disturbing his business affairs."

"May I ask what you are looking for?" I regarded him reflectively for a moment, then decided that I might as well answer him honestly. He was my father's loyal servant, and whether he agreed to assist me or not, he would feel bound to tell my father that I had delved into his accounts.

"I want to find a letter from the palace," I said. "I know that Father has occasionally supplied the Overseer of the Royal Household with rare goods. I am not talking about such requests. This scroll will date from the year of my birth." His gaze sharpened.

"I entered your father's service three years after that," he said. "Your father's affairs were in order and I did not need to examine any earlier records. But of course there are boxes from those years." He hesitated. "Kamen, I risk your father's displeasure if I open his room for you," he reminded me. "Yet I will do so if you can assure me that this matter is indeed of the gravest importance and does not concern something he has forbidden you to explore."

In this case the literal truth is closer to a lie, I thought to myself swiftly, but if I tell Kaha the spirit of the injunction concerning the secrecy and not just the bare words of command, he will refuse to let me through that door. After all, Father did not forbid me to investigate my roots. He simply advised me to leave it all alone.

"It is indeed very important," I told him. "I know my father's order about the office, but it is vital that I find the scroll. I have not been forbidden to explore this matter, indeed I have been pursuing it diligently and have reached the point where I need to examine certain information Father has. It is unfortunate that he is not here to consult and I am in a hurry." Kaha frowned, obviously indecisive. His long fingers rapped absently on the wood of his palette.

"Can you not tell me more?" he asked finally. "I want to help you, Kamen, but your father's long-standing order is quite explicit."

"You have free access to the office," I argued. "You come and go. Could I not slip in with you while you are attending to the daily business and talk to you while you work?" He was weakening. I could see it in his eyes. Then he capitulated.

"I suppose so," he said doubtfully. "You are indeed the drip of water that wears away the rock! But you will stand before your father when he returns and tell him of this matter?"

"He does not have to know," I said as he turned away, cracking the dried wax that had been plastered across the sliding bolt of the office door. He slid back the bolt and walked in and I followed, closing the door behind me.

"Yes he does," he retorted with his back to me. "If a man cannot trust his scribe, who can he trust?" He began to break the seal on several scrolls already lined up neatly on the desk's surface and I went at once to the shelves.

Each box contained the records of the year whose number was painted in black ink on its end, facing me. Kaha was obsessively neat. "Year thirty-one of the King," I read. That was last year. The shelf above it contained the boxes from the previous ten years beginning with "Year twenty of the King." In that year I was six. My heartbeat sped up as I ran my fingers along the boxes on the next shelf up, the one that began with "Year ten of the King." The dating on the first seven boxes was in a different hand from Kaha's. I lifted down the one designated "Year fourteen of the King," glancing at the scribe as I did so. His head was down over the scroll in his hands. Placing the box on the floor, I raised the lid.

"Make sure that you keep the scrolls in order," Kaha said suddenly. He was still not looking at me. I did not reply. Quickly I scrutinized them, expecting at any moment to see the remains of the tell-tale royal seal, but it was not there. I went through them again. Nothing. I replaced that box and took the ones from the years before and after year fourteen, going through them with increasing agitation, but again there was nothing. Sliding them back on the shelf, I approached Kaha.

"It's not there," I said, aware that my voice sounded choked. "Not in the business records. Where are Father's private papers kept?" Kaha pushed himself away from the desk.

"Enough!" he said crisply. "You know better than to even ask me that, Kamen. You will have to wait until he comes home."

"But I can't wait, Kaha," I said. "I'm sorry, but I can't."

I walked around the desk, stood behind the scribe, and hooking my arm under his chin I grasped my wrist, imprisoning him. His head was forced back against my chest. "With one sharp twist I can break your neck," I said. "You can tell my father how I threatened you and laid hands on you and forced you to give me what I want. Now where is his private box?" Kaha sat perfectly still in my grip. The hands in his lap were relaxed.

"Kill me if you like," he said thickly, and I felt the movement of his throat against my forearm. "But I don't think you will. You know what the consequences would be. This will do you no good, Kamen. It might be better to explain to me why you are so desperate." With an exclamation I let him go and flung round the desk. Sinking onto the stool in front of it, I passed a hand over my face.

"I am trying to find out who my parents were," I said. "I have good reason to believe that although my father denies it, he knows, and the scroll I seek will tell me all."

"I see." His stare was level and composed. I had not frightened him at all, indeed, I now felt foolish under the careful regard of those dark eyes. "Then surely, Kamen, if your father declines to give you the knowledge you seek, it is not my place to allow you to disobey him."

"Kaha," I said heavily, "I am no longer the child who used to play under this desk with his toys while you sat cross-legged beside it and took my father's dictation. If you do not bring out the box I need, I will tear the office apart until I find it. I no longer care what my father might say. I am not afraid of him. And you have no authority over me."

"Kamen I am very fond of you," he said, "but let me remind you that you have no authority over me either. I am answerable directly to your father and no one else. My position in this house depends on it."

I stood up. Coldly I went to one of the chests under the shelves, and kicking apart the wax seal on the string wound about the two knobs holding it closed, I opened it and began to toss its contents onto the floor. He watched me silently. The chest contained more scrolls but also small boxes and things wrapped in linen. Roughly I opened and unwrapped. There were gold trinkets, bars of silver, an uncut piece of lapis lazuli that must have been worth our whole house, loose gems, Sabaean coins, but not the thing I sought. Kicking through the debris, I approached a second chest. The lid crashed against the wall. I bent.

"All right, all right!" Kaha shouted. "Gods, Kamen, are you insane? I will give you what you want. Call Pa-Bast as a witness that I do so only under powerful duress." But there was no need to summon the Steward. He loomed in the doorway, staring aghast at the chaos I had made. I gave him no chance to speak.

"You see all this?" I said shakily. "I did it. Kaha tried to stop me. He will now give me what I seek because if he does not I will wreck this room. I mean it, Pa-Bast." I saw his glance quickly assess my state, Kaha's anger, the extent of the damage I had already done.

"Are you drunk, Kamen?" he enquired. I shook my head. "Then you had better give him whatever it is that has prompted this display," he said to Kaha. "If that does not calm you," he went on, turning to me, "I will have you confined to your room until your father returns from the Fayum."

"No you won't," I replied. "I am in my right mind. Everything will be fine. Kaha?" He nodded coolly, and going to another chest, he opened it and withdrew yet another box. This one was of ebony chased in gold. Lifting the lid, he held it out to me.

"I will hold it while you examine the contents," he said. "Do not disturb anything other than the thing you want."

I saw it at once. It resembled the scroll Takhuru had shown me. The papyrus was of excellent quality, tightly made and then expertly polished. This seal had come away intact on one side of the sheaf rather than breaking in two and the imprint on it was identical. I unrolled it slowly, the two men, the mess on the floor, the other contents of the box Kaha was still holding out, receding into nothingness. A mantle of composure seemed to suddenly envelop me and I read the hieroglyphs without a tremor.

"To the Noble Men, greetings. Having become acquainted with your desire to adopt a son, and having investigated your suitability both as a minor noble of Egypt and a man of good repute, it is our pleasure to place in your care this child, conceived of our holy seed and born to the Royal Concubine Thu. You will nurture and educate him as your own. In return we deed to you one of our estates in the Fayum, the legal survey of which we enclose a copy. We adjure you never to reveal the lineage of this child, on pain of our strongest displeasure. We wish you joy of him. Dictated to the Keeper of the Door, Amunnakht, this sixth day of the month of Mesore, in the fourteenth year of our reign." It was signed in a different hand, hurried and so heavy that it had scored the papyrus. The King's titles took up four lines.

So it was true. I was a king's son. This scroll confirmed it. And the concubine's name, my mother's name, was Thu. Could it be true after all, a miracle sent by the gods, that Thu of Aswat is also my Thu? Not so fast, I tried to tell myself soberly. Thu is a very common name. Thousands of women in Egypt answer to it. Yet I felt almost incoherent with excitement. I let the papyrus roll up. Kaha gestured with the box but I shook my head. "I will keep it for a while," I said. "Get a servant in here to put everything away." His eyes and Pa-Bast's were on the scroll in my hand and I searched Pa-Bast's face for any sign of recognition or remembrance but there was none. Without another word I pushed past him and strode across the hall towards the stairs.

I had almost reached my room when something happened to my thoughts. It was as though a waiting hand had descended, and with a few deft movements rearranged them into a new and startling pattern. The shock was almost physical, so that I stumbled and cried out, then I broke into a run.

Once across my own threshold I flung the scroll onto my couch and falling to my knees I wrenched open my chest and withdrew the pouch containing the copy of the manuscript the Aswat woman had entrusted to me. Sitting on the floor, I shook it out and began to feverishly riffle through the sheets of papyrus. It was somewhere towards the end of her account. I found it and read rapidly. "Every afternoon when the heat started to abate, I took him onto the grass of the courtyard and laid him on a sheet, watching him kick and flail his sturdy limbs under the shade of my canopy and crow at the flowers I picked to dangle before his eyes and place in his fist." She was speaking of her son, the son she and Pharaoh had had together, the son who had been taken away from her when she was exiled to Aswat in disgrace. Not enough, not quite enough, I thought incoherently. My dream, yes, the words bring it back to me with horrible clarity, but can it be more than coincidence? But it fitted the pattern that had formed inside me and was now throbbing insistently.

Something else fitted too. I had been too burdened and anxious on the journey back to Pi-Ramses from Aswat to do more than feel the horror and pity of her story without any reflection, but now I found another passage that I had skimmed too quickly. "Many coats of oil had been added to give the wood the soft patina I saw and felt. Wepwawet's ears were pricked up, his beautiful long nose quested, but his eyes gazed into mine with calm omnipotence. He wore a short kilt, its pleats faultlessly represented. In one fist he clutched a spear, and in the other a sword. Across his chest, the hieroglyphs for 'Opener of the Ways' had been delicately chiselled and I knew that Father must have taken the time to learn from Pa-ari how to carve the words."

I turned and regarded the peaceful, intelligent face of the god who had stood beside me for as long as I could remember, and Wepwawet gazed back at me smugly. "Opener of the Ways," I whispered. "Can it be? Is it possible?" I crammed the squares of papyrus back into the bag, got up, and lifting the little statue I pushed it in also. Then I ran back down the stairs and out into the garden. She had given the totem her father had carved to Amunnakht, the Keeper of the Door, and begged him to see that it went with her son wherever he might go. Had he gone to the home of Men the merchant? I was about to find out.

I ran the short distance to Takhuru's house, the satchel bumping against my hip, my sandals sending up small spurts of sand. The sun was standing almost overhead now. The path was busy and I wove in and out of the groups of purposeful servants, brisk soldiers and loitering residents of the estates I passed. Many greeted me but I did not pause.

Panting, I veered in at Nesiamun's gate, managed a breathless word flung over my shoulder to the startled warden, and just had time to slip behind a spreading shrub as Nesiamun himself came towards me, deep in conversation with two other men. Behind them an empty litter was being carried, its tassels swinging scarlet and its gold-shot curtains glinting in the noon light. "We are delayed by a shortage of powdered quartz," Nesiamun was saying, "but that problem should be solved tomorrow unless of course the quarry men decide to strike. There are altogether too many incompetent overseers who have bought their positions without knowing the first thing about the manufacture of faience. I have great difficulty in firing them. Their relatives are influential and some are my friends. Still, the important thing is production …" His voice faded as he and his companions rounded a bend.

It was not difficult, in Nesiamun's garden, to remain out of sight. I stayed away from the winding path, thinking as I went how my last few visits to my betrothed had been conducted like the furtive forays of a secret lover. I felt all at once disgusted with the way my life had become one clandestine event after another, as though I had been acquiring a new layer of inner grime with each occurrence. I wanted to walk clean and free.

Approaching the house, I heard Takhuru's mother, Adjetau, laughing and the accompanying murmur of female voices above a clink of dishes. She was entertaining her friends in the entrance hall and I could not go in that way unless I wanted to be invited to sit and be offered wine and honey cakes under the inquisitive eyes of the nobles' wives. Nor was I dressed for polite concourse. I plunged deeper into the shrubbery, wondering what to do.

As I neared the pool towards the rear of the estate, I caught a glimpse of billowing white linen through the tracery of leaves. I crept closer. Takhuru herself had just left the water and was wrapping a voluminous sheet about her naked body. She stood straight, arms outstretched, hands grasping the corners of the sheet, and for a moment I saw her small breasts lifted in the action, her long black hair tendrilling against her elbows, the glistening water trickling over her belly to be channelled in the grooves to either side of her pubis and run down her inner thighs. She was a glorious sight and for a moment I forget all else. Then the sheet enveloped her and she lowered herself onto the mat by the verge of the pool and reached for a comb. I stepped warily out of the shadows. "Kamen!" she exclaimed. "What are you doing here?" I went to her quickly and squatted, glancing about for a sign of her body servant. "She has gone to fetch my sunshade," she explained, seeing my movement. "I decided to stay outside for a while to avoid mother's little group of gossipers. Are you bringing me another mystery?" I nodded.

"Perhaps." Taking the statue of Wepwawet out of the bag, I put it in her damp hand. "I want you to toss this among your cushions and jars," I said, indicating the jumble beside her. "Then I want you to send for the Aswat woman. When she comes, dismiss your body servant. It doesn't matter what you ask the woman to do. She can comb your hair or oil your limbs. It is important that she eventually notice my totem. I will be hidden and watching."

"Why?"

"I will tell you later, but now I want you to see her reaction to it without knowing why."

"Oh very well." she wrinkled up her nose. "Isis is coming with the sunshade. Can you give me no clue, Kamen?" For answer I kissed her and rose, and I had just regained the shelter of the shrubbery when her servant appeared and began to unfold the dome of white linen over her. Takhuru felt about in her belongings and produced a piece of cinnamon which she put in her mouth and began to suck. "Isis, go and bring the new servant to me, the one with the blue eyes," I heard her order. "I think she is working in the kitchens today. I want her here at once. You can go back to the house." Isis bowed and went away.

Takhuru settled back on one elbow. I saw her lips open to briefly reveal the piece of dark cinnamon caught between her teeth. She gazed levelly at the bright scene before her, then she raised herself and adjusted the thin gold anklet above her foot, pulling the sheet up around her thighs as she did so. She leaned back again. Her movements were slow and lazy, fraught with a sensuous purpose, and I realized suddenly that she was taunting me in a way that owed nothing to her youth and inexperience.

"You are like the Goddess Hathor herself today," I called to her quietly. She smiled.

"I know," she said serenely.

We waited. The time seemed long, but at last the woman came striding into the open area around the pool. She was wearing the dress of the house, a calf-length sheath bordered in yellow and pulled in at the waist by a yellow belt. Yellow sandals were on her feet. Her hair was pinned on top of her head and tied with a yellow ribbon. Approaching Takhuru she bowed gracefully and then stood still. "You sent for me, Lady Takhuru," she said. Takhuru sat up.

"You massaged me with such skill yesterday," she announced, "and I am stiff with swimming today. Please do it again. You will find the scented oil there." She pointed.

The woman bowed again and went to where the pot of oil rested. Wepwawet lay beside it, half-buried under a cushion. I saw the woman's brown hand reach out, then pause. My breath hitched in my throat. Her hovering fingers began to shake, then with a strangely animal grunt she grabbed the statue with both hands and turned towards Takhuru. I could see her face plainly. Her eyes were wide, the blue of them rimmed entirely in white. She had gone very pale. Lifting my totem, she pressed him clumsily to her forehead and stood there swaying as though she was drunk. Her throat worked. Takhuru was watching her as keenly as I. When she did manage to speak, her voice was ragged.

"Lady Takhuru, Lady Takhuru," she said. "Where did you get this?" She was now running uncertain hands over it as I had often done, feeling the smooth, gleaming lines of the god's kilted body.

"A friend gave it to me," Takhuru answered off-handedly. "It is well made, is it not? Wepwawet is the totem of your village, isn't he? Why Thu, what is the matter?"

"I know this statue," Thu said huskily. "My father carved it for me as a gift for my Naming Day long ago when I was still an apprentice in the house of the Seer."

"Are you sure it is the same one?" Takhuru asked. "There are hundreds of likenesses of the god. He is after all the Opener of the Ways." She touched Thu's arm. "You may sit, Thu, before you collapse." The woman sank onto the grass.

"I would know it blindfolded," she said more calmly though her voice still trembled. "One touch would tell me that it is my father's handiwork. Did I not see it beside my couch every day? Did I not pray before it? My Lady, I beg you to tell me which friend gave it to you." She was leaning towards Takhuru, her face strained, her whole body tense. "The last time I saw it was when I passed it into the keeping of Amunnakht, ruler of the King's harem, on the day I left Pi-Ramses to begin my exile. I beseeched him to see that whatever fate befell my little son, Wepwawet should go with him." I saw the bewilderment on Takhuru's face begin to give way to a dawning understanding. The woman pounded the earth with a clenched fist. "Do you see?" she cried out. "If I can talk to your friend, I might be able to find my son! Perhaps he still lives!" Takhuru stared at her, then her gaze swivelled to where I knelt. "Gods," she whispered. "Oh gods. Kamen, it's you."

With great difficulty, as though weak from some long illness, I came to my feet and walked unsteadily out into the clearing. I was able to come right up to the woman before my legs gave way again and I sank before her. I looked full into her face. "That statue is mine," I said, hearing my words coming from far, far away. "It was wrapped in the linen with me when I was delivered to the house of Men. I know that Pharaoh is my father. And you ... You are indeed my mother."

Part Two

KAHA

7

I WAS STILL A YOUNG MAN when I first came to this house and Kamen was but three years old, a solemn, intelligent child with even features and a desire to understand everything that was going on around him reflected in his straight gaze. I would have made a good teacher, for I always responded to such latent potential with an anxiety that it might not be allowed to develop, but in Kamen's case I need not have worried. His father took great care over his schooling, and nurtured and disciplined him as lovingly as one could wish.

There was something about the boy that drew me. He was like a face one glimpses briefly, forgets, and then begins to see everywhere, not connected to memory or event. Sometimes his father would allow him into the office while he dictated his letters. Kamen would sit under the desk with his toys, playing quietly, occasionally glancing out at me as I wrote, for we were on the same level, and I often wanted to touch him—reaching not for his soft baby skin but the thing inside, unconnected to anything I knew, yet familiar, that tugged at my consciousness.

Men's home was a happy and congenial place and Men himself a good master. I was an excellent scribe. I had been trained, in both literacy and disillusionment, in the great temple of Amun at Karnak, where I saw the worship of the god reduced to complex but hollow rituals conducted by priests who believed more in filling their coffers and demonstrating their self-importance than in the power of the deity or the needs of his petitioners. Nevertheless, the education I received was excellent, and when it was completed, I had my pick of noble households in which to ply my trade.

I also had a passion for the history of my country and chose to enter the employ of a man with similar interests. He was of the opinion, which I shared, that Ma'at was perverted in Egypt, that the past glory of our country, when the Gods who sat upon the Horus Throne maintained the necessary harmony between temple and government, had become tarnished. Our present Pharaoh lived under the thumb of priests who had forgotten that Egypt did not exist to fill their coffers and advance the aspirations of their sons. The delicate balance of Ma'at, the cosmic music that wove secular and sacred power to produce the sublime song that was Egypt's great strength, had become weighted with corruption and greed, and Egypt now sang weakly and discordantly.

Pharaoh, in his younger days, had led the army in a series of mighty battles against the encroaching eastern tribes who wished to appropriate the lush grazing fields of the Delta, but his genius did not extend to the battles begging to be fought within his own borders. His father had struck a bargain with the priests in the days when the foreign usurper polluted the Horus Throne, and the priests had agreed to help Setnakht regain the throne in exchange for certain privileges. Our present Pharaoh has honoured that bargain down all the long years of his rule and the priests have grown fat and bloated while the army stagnates and the administration has fallen into the hands of those of foreign blood whose loyalty extends only as far as the gold that they are paid.

My first employer greatly desired to see Ma'at healed and restored. He hired only those people who shared his love for Egypt's past and I, with my regard for history, was happy there. Besides, in my younger days I had a horror of routine and repetition and the thought of spending my days writing predictable letters for wealthy but unimaginative nobles was distasteful. I began my career as an Under Scribe to Ani, Chief Scribe of that odd household. I was then nineteen years old. For four years I lived in virtual seclusion in the home of that very strange, very private man, and I was content. He recognized and encouraged my ability to absorb, and regurgitate at will, any fact or figure, any historical event. Of course a good scribe must be able to remember his master's words during dictation or discussion and give them back to him when asked, but my facility in these things was greater than most, and my employer saw this.

He gave me a task I loved and for which I was eminently well suited, the education of a virtually unlettered young girl he had chosen to perform a service for Egypt and Ma'at. I knew of that service. I approved of it. And an affection for the girl grew in me as we studied together. She was beautiful and full of a raw, quick intelligence. She learned rapidly and like me she had a love and a reverence for the sacred language given to us by Thoth, the God of all wisdom and writing, in the days of Egypt's birth. I was sorry to see her leave the household and I missed her.

I myself left my employer when I began to fear that he and all those of his acquaintance were under the scrutiny of the palace. After all, the service the girl had been trained to perform was the murder of Pharaoh that would, we all hoped, result in the restoration of Ma'at. But Pharaoh had not died and the girl had been arrested and sentenced to death. That sentence, however, had been commuted to exile for no reason we could ascertain, and that worried me. My employer presumed that it was because Pharaoh had been so enamoured of the girl that no matter what her culpability he could not bear to snuff out her life, but I was not so sure. For all his faults, Ramses the Third was not a man to be swayed by emotion alone. It was more likely that the girl had imparted to the king some piece of information insufficient to bring us all to justice but enough to arouse the kind of suspicion that would result in a royal watchfulness. My employer did not agree. Nevertheless he understood my reason for going and gave me a superb reference. He also understood that although I was no longer under his admittedly comfortable roof, I had no intention of betraying him or the other confederates.

That was seventeen years ago. I had applied at the house of Men after having spent two unsatisfactory years on various other estates and seeing the restlessness within myself dwindle as I matured. I had kept faith with my first employer and worked honestly for the others. I had almost married the daughter of one of my employer's Stewards. And I had almost managed to forget my part in the plot to assassinate the King.

Men's house became my home. His servants were my friends, his family like my own. I watched Kamen grow into a steady, capable young man with an inner stubbornness that sometimes set him against the will of his father. When

he chose to enter the army, there were harsh words, but
Kamen prevailed. I never quite lost that feeling of having
known him before and it made him easy to love. When he
became betrothed, I knew it was only a matter of time
before he built a household of his own and I thought that
perhaps I would request a place with him as his scribe. In
the meantime my loyalty went to his father.

So I did not harbour my anger at him for long. He had
laid violent hands on me, but I had known he would not
hurt me. He himself was frustrated and angry. For some
time he had been preoccupied, absent in thought. He had
taken to drinking excessively, roaming the house at night,
and crying out in his sleep. I had heard him from my room
at the other end of the passage. I wondered if he was in
trouble, but it was not my place to ask him. His act in the
office seemed to me merely the culmination of weeks of
distress, and when he told me about the scroll he sought, I
began to understand. We all knew that he was an adopted
child, and like him we had not questioned his roots. Why
should we? Why should he? He was adored by his mother
and sisters, loved by his father, and respected by us servants
who had seen him grow. His life had been rich, charmed,
but now everything had changed.

After he had stormed out of the office, Pa-Bast had
summoned one of the house servants, and under my direction she set the office to rights. As I was telling her what
went where I was thinking deeply. Kamen had said that he
would confess all to his father when he returned. For myself
I had no fear of Men. He was a just man. But it was obvious
to me that Kamen did not really want his father to know
what he had done, otherwise he would not have waited until

Men was away to get into the boxes of scrolls. I fully appreciated the young man's growing need to at least find out from whence he had sprung. I suppose that a good son would have obeyed his father's injunction to leave the matter alone, but my sympathies were with Kamen. Surely Men was being unreasonable. Was there harm in Kamen's desire?

When the office was tidy once more and the door closed and bolted, I went in search of Pa-Bast. I found him in the kitchens behind the house, in conversation with the cook who had little to do while the family was away. When he had finished with the man, I drew him outside. "I have been thinking about the uproar earlier," I said. "It was really no more than a puff of desert wind, soon dissipated. Kamen is troubled. I don't want to increase his anxiety by adding his father's displeasure to his own private worries. Let us keep what happened to ourselves, Pa-Bast. The office is clean. If I approach Kamen for the scroll he took, and replace it tomorrow, can we agree to forget the whole matter?" Pa-Bast smiled.

"Why not?" he replied. "It is the first time Kamen has caused such a stir, and as you say, no permanent harm has been done. I do not relish yet another tempest when Men returns and learns that his son had a fit of madness and tried to wreck his office. Whatever is gnawing at Kamen is not something frivolous. We both know him well."

"It has something to do with his origins," I said. "Men is being foolish in trying to keep the information from him. Once satisfied, Kamen would be at peace and the whole thing would recede into his past, become no more than a symptom of his growing. Do you know who his birthing parents were, Pa-Bast?" The Steward shook his head.

"No, and I do not remember the scroll Kamen snatched from the chest. He came with that statue of Wepwawet entwined in the linen that wound him. The scroll must have passed from messenger to Men without my knowledge. And you are right. Men is behaving stupidly in letting a dune become a mountain."

"Then we are agreed?"

"Yes."

I did not feel disloyal towards my employer; indeed, I did not want to see a rift grow between father and son. Though they loved and respected one another, they were not much alike. I would speak to Kamen when he returned, replace the scroll, and that would be the end of it.

But Kamen did not return that day. I swam, ate a light meal, and wrote a letter to the papyrus makers requesting more sheets and a quantity of ink to be delivered. Evening faded into night, and still he did not come home. The next morning I rose and went at once to his room but Setau met me in the passage and told me that Kamen was not there. He had not slept in the house. I thought little of it. Kamen's vices were the relatively harmless indulgences of youth and I presumed that he had spent the night carousing with his friends and was sleeping off the beer at someone else's home. He still had a day to himself after fulfilling his latest military assignment and I did not concern myself overmuch with his absence.

Scrolls for my attention were delivered mid-morning and for some hours I was busy in the office, then I ate with Pa-Bast, napped for an hour, and took my regular afternoon swim in the Lake. Kamen had still not appeared by sunset, and that night his couch remained empty.

Two hours after sunrise I was crossing the entrance hall when a soldier came towards me. I halted while he came up and saluted. "The General Paiis has sent me to enquire into the whereabouts of the captain of his household guard," he said without preamble. "Officer Kamen did not return to duty this morning. If he is ill, the General should have been notified."

I thought quickly. The man's words released a flood of anxiety in me and my first impulse was to protect Kamen. He was far from irresponsible. No matter what wildness might entice him he would not simply neglect to show himself to take his watch at the appointed time, much less leave the soldiers under his command to fend for themselves. Could I concoct a plausible lie? Say that there was sickness in the Fayum and his father had sent for him urgently? But what if Kamen was even now walking through the General's gate, having overslept somewhere? No. His gear was still laid out on his couch where Setau had placed it. Then where was he? With Takhuru? For two nights? Nesiamun would never allow it. Had he fallen drunk into the river and been drowned? A possibility. Been set upon in the city and robbed and beaten? Another possibility but remote. I began to be afraid. Somehow I knew that he had not overslept, that he would not come home, that something terrible was happening and that I must lie for him.

"Tell the General that his father sent for him from the Fayum late last night," I said. "It was a family matter of the greatest need and he set out at once. Did the General not receive his message?"

"No. When will he return?"

"I don't know. But as soon as I have news I will pass it on to the General." The man swung on his heel and padded away and I turned to find Pa-Bast standing behind me.

"This has become a serious matter," he said to me in a low voice. "I wonder what we should do. I will send Setau to Akhebset's house to make enquiries there, and also to Nesiamun's Steward to ask if Kamen has been with the Lady Takhuru, but if we cannot run him to ground, then Men will have to be notified. I pray that Kamen is safe. I am reluctant to alert the city police and so make his disappearance public." I nodded. It has something to do with that scroll, I thought to myself, but I did not say so aloud.

"Send Setau out," I said. "There is nothing else we can do at the moment. If he comes back without news, we will talk again."

I had little to do that morning. I took a few scrolls to read into the garden and settled myself within view of the entrance, and when I saw Setau leave, I went back into the house. Kamen's door was open. The passage behind me was empty. Quickly I stepped to his chest, and opening it I saw the scroll lying on a pile of fresh linen, where Setau had undoubtedly put it when he tidied the room. Taking it, I closed the lid of the chest and made my way back outside.

Of course I had intended to tell Kamen what Pa-Bast and I had decided, and ask for the scroll to be returned, but Kamen was the gods knew where, and Men and the women would be coming home soon. If I had been a scribe who always observed the letter of the law, I would have taken the thing to the office and restored it to Men's private box, and indeed my conscience smote me once, but very mildly, as I unrolled it. I was worried about Kamen. I wanted to help him if I could, and the contents of the scroll might point me towards some useful direction.

At first the words that I read made no impact on me, or rather, the impact was so violent that I was stunned into a mental insensibility. Then I let the scroll roll up and placed it carefully with the others beside my knee. Clasping my hands together in my lap, I gazed into the brightness of the garden from the shade of the tree under which I sat. For a while I thought nothing, was not able to think, but gradually my mind began to recover from the blow it had sustained.

Now I understood why the child who had sat under his father's desk had evoked such a mysterious affection in me, his glance, his gestures, even his laugh, stirring a memory I had not recognized as such. Yet now it was all clear, pitilessly so, and I marvelled at the slow but inexorable weaving of the divine fingers that decreed a reckoning for every deed. Or so it seemed to me in that moment of revelation. For Kamen's mother was none other than the girl I had tutored in the house of Hui my master, the girl on whose fresh, unblemished mind I had inscribed the formula for Pharaoh's downfall according to the instructions of the Seer. I had grown to love her with the proprietary affection of a brother, and when she left to become a royal concubine, I had missed her. Then the plot had failed and she had been exiled, and I had torn myself from the womb of that household in answer to an imperative for self-preservation. That sense of danger was back, a throb of fear, because I knew without a doubt where Kamen had gone. I would have done the same. He had gone south to find his mother, and she would tell him everything, and we were threatened again, all of us, Hui, Paiis, Banemus, Hunro, Paibekamun, even Disenk who had been Thu's body servant, grooming her for the eyes of the King.

I was only a scribe. I had not instigated the plot but neither had I reported it to the authorities, and I had obeyed Hui's command to instil in the young and impressionable Thu a sense of the past glories of Egypt and a sorrow and indignation at the depths to which our country had fallen under Ramses the Third's inept rule. We had succeeded well. The peasant girl entrusted to our care, innocent, raw and full of dreams, went to Pharaoh's bed like a scorpion, beautiful, unpredictable and deadly. Like a scorpion she had stung him but he had recovered. And Thu? She had vanished into the south and Hui had thought her sting had been drawn. But he was wrong. The child she had borne had not concerned the Seer at all, yet he could prove to be the undoing of us, even after so many years, unless we moved quickly to prevent it.

Shaking off an almost insupportable sense of fatalism, I took up my palette, and laying it across my knees I wrote to Hui. There was no point in waiting to hear what Setau might say. I already knew that Kamen was nowhere to be found in Pi-Ramses. "Most Eminent and Noble Seer Hui, greetings from your erstwhile Under Scribe Kaha," I penned. "I am most honoured to be included in your invitation to dine tomorrow evening with your brother the General Paiis, the Royal Butler Paibekamun, the Lady Hunro, and such of your servants as were in your employ seventeen years ago, to celebrate the anniversary of your gift of Seeing. I wish you long life and prosperity." I signed it knowing that it was weak, but I could not think of anything else. I hoped that Hui would be able to grasp my meaning. I had given him short notice, but if he did understand me, he would command the others to cancel any other plans they might have.

Walking to the servants' quarters, I gave the papyrus to one of the men and ordered him to deliver it at once, then I made my way back to the noon silence of the house and replaced Pharaoh's scroll in Men's box. It was my duty to warn them all. I would do so tomorrow, and they would decide what, if anything, to do. Nothing more would be required of me, or so I hoped. Yet I was filled with dread and could not eat the meal that was set before me.

As I had predicted, Setau returned with no news of Kamen. His friends had not seen him. Nesiamun's Steward, questioned privately, had not seen him either. "We will give him one more day before telling the city police," Pa-Bast said. "After all, we are not his jailors. He may have gone hunting on the spur of the moment and neglected to tell us." But his voice lacked conviction and I did not reply. He was hunting sure enough, and if he found his prey, the lives of everyone in both Hui's and Men's households could be changed forever.

Hui did not acknowledge my message. Nevertheless on the following evening I told Pa-Bast that I was going to visit friends and I walked to the Seer's house through the red drenching of a perfect sunset. It was the third day of the month of Khoiak. The annual Feast of Hathor was over. Soon the river would begin to shrink and the fellahin would tread the fertile mud its flood left behind to spread the seed of their crops. Here the Lake would remain much the same. The orchards would drop their carpet of flower petals and sprout fruit, but the life of the city would go on, largely divorced from the burst of activity in the countryside.

Born and raised in Pi-Ramses I cared little for the eternal changelessness of the rest of Egypt, a very different sameness from the constant excitement of such a huge concentration of people. Whether I chose to take part in it or not, I needed to know that it was there and I was in the heart of it. My years at the temple school in Karnak at Thebes had been spent in dedicated study. I had had no time or inclination to explore a town that had once been the centre of Egypt's power but now existed only for the worship of Amun and for the funerals that took place regularly on the west bank, the city of the dead. But my thoughts turned to the south as I neared Hui's pylon and my heart quickened with memories. Was Kamen on the river, floating towards the arid hostility of the desert and the village of Aswat?

The old porter came hobbling out of his lair and graced me with a dark look. "Kaha," he said sourly, "I haven't seen you in a long time. You are expected."

"Thank you!" I retorted as I strode past him. "And a cheerful greeting to you too, Minmose. Have you ever lived up to your name?" He chuckled throatily as he shuffled back into his lodge, for his name meant Son of Min, and Min was a type of Amun, when once a year the god became the lettuce-eater of Thebes and reigned over all excesses of the flesh.

In spite of the seriousness of my visit I must confess that my step became lighter as I paced the Seer's elegant garden. I had been happy here. Much of my youth lay in the pink droplets of water splashing from the fountain and spoke to me from the early shadows under the trees. There I had sat with the young Thu's eyes on me in fierce concentration as I recited a list of the battles of the Osiris Pharaoh Thothmes the Third and expected her to give it back to me from memory. She had pouted because I would not let her drink the beer at hand until she got it right. And there I had paused on my way to the market to watch her go through her morning paces with Nebnefer, the Master's physical trainer, her supple body sheened in sweat as she worked under Nebnefer's shouted goads. Naïve and eager she had been in those days. When she left my care to begin her instruction under the Master himself, I had sorely missed our lessons together, and though we saw each other daily, it was not the same.

I wondered what had happened to the small store of clay scarabs she had been accumulating. I had given her one for every discipline she mastered and she had been dispropor-tionately pleased each time I placed one on her tiny palm. Little Libu Princess I had called her, teasing her for her haughtiness, and she had grinned at me, eyes alight. For years I had not thought of her, but now, as I came to the expanse of courtyard and began to cross it, the images of her took form and colour. She had been left-handed, a child of Set, with the peasant's superstitious shame at such a brand until I explained to her that Set had not always been a god of malevolence and that the city of Pi-Ramses itself was dedicated to him. "Take heart, Thu," I had said to her in response to the expression of uncharacteristic hesitation on her face. "If Set loves you, you will be invincible."

But she had not been invincible. She had soared to the sun like mighty Horus himself and then fallen back to earth in pain and disgrace. I sighed as I passed between the painted pillars fronting the entrance to the house and greeted the servant hovering within. "You may proceed into the dining hall," he told me, and I crossed the huge tiled expanse, the slap of my sandals echoing against the walls, and went through the familiar double doors on the right.

Lamplight met me, blending with the fading last rays of the sun that were falling briefly from the clerestory windows high above. A gush of scented air blew into my face from the flowers scattered over the small tables set before cushions and from the oil in the lamps. It held the faintest undercurrent of jasmine, the perfume the Master preferred, and such a chaos of memories struck me that I paused on the threshold, overwhelmed. Then Harshira the Steward came gliding towards me like a laden barge under full sail, his kohl-rimmed eyes beaming, and clasped my hands in his own vast fists. "Kaha," he rumbled, "I am more than pleased to see you. How have you been faring in the house of Men? I see Pa-Bast from time to time and we exchange our news, but it is good to greet you face to face." I met the warmth of his words with equal enthusiasm, for I had always liked and respected him, but my attention was fixed on the others.

They were all there. Paiis was wearing a short scarlet gold-bordered kilt that showed off the turn of his handsome legs, his chest covered in gold chains and a droplet of gold hanging from one ear. His black hair had been oiled back and he had hennaed his mouth. The Royal Butler Paibekamun had aged somewhat in the years since I had seen him. He was stooped and the skin of his cheeks had drawn ever tighter but his expression was as closed and disdainful as ever. I did not like him, and I remembered that Thu had not liked him either. He was a cold man, full of calculation. Paiis was lounging back on one elbow, wine cup in hand, but Paibekamun sat cross-legged and as straight as the curve of his old spine would allow. He did not smile at me.

Hunro did. Kohled, hennaed, glittering with jewels, her braided hair threaded with silver and the folds of her long sheath heavy with beads of carnelian, she would have been a fantasy of beauty if it had not been for the tracks of discontent etched from her nose to the corners of her mouth, which gave her a slightly sullen look, even as her lips rose. I remembered her as quick and lithe, trained as a dancer, possessed of a restless body and an agile, masculine turn of mind, but she seemed to have thickened in some indefinable way. She and Thu had shared a cell in the harem. Of an ancient family, with a brother, Banemus, who was also a General, she had chosen to enter the harem rather than marry the man of her father's choice. She had spent her life there, and looking at her discontented face now, I wondered whether she regretted her choice.

Then there was Hui, and at the sight of him everything in me loosened. He rose and stood looking at me, a column of whiteness broken only by the silver border of his kilt and the silver clasping his upper arm. He still wore the wide silver snake that had always twined about his finger. He had not changed much. I supposed that he must be close to his fifti-eth year, but his inability to tolerate much sunlight had preserved his features well. No colour had ever tinged that pale skin or crept through the long, luxuriant hair that now lay loose about his naked shoulders, but it did not matter, for all his life lay in the glittering red eyes that always seemed to catch whatever light was in the room. Because of his peculiar malady he went about swathed like a corpse. Only in the presence of his friends and trusted servants would he unveil himself, and yet he was possessed of an exotic and compelling beauty whose power I had forgotten until this moment. I walked forward and bowed to him. "Kaha," he said. "It has been a long time. Why must it take a common threat to bring old friends together again? Come. Sit. You are no longer my pert young Under Scribe, are you?" He snapped his fingers. Harshira immediately went out to supervise the presenting of the food and a servant approached me with a flagon of wine and a cup, which I took and held while he filled it, but first I made my obeisance to the illustrious company. Then I sank onto the cushions the Master had indicated. He regained his seat. "Well," he went on. "We will not discuss the business at hand until we have eaten and shared other more innocuous news. We are called here together on short notice but that does not mean our conversation must be brusque. Drink your wine, Kaha!"

His harper in the corner of the room now filling with warm shadows outside the flickering circles of the lamplight began to play, and a general exchange began. Talk ebbed and flowed. Servants laden with steaming trays moved unobtrusively to and fro and the wine in our cups was replenished several times, yet beneath the laughter and chatter ran an undercurrent of anxiety. I ignored it, filled as I was with a gladness to be there. My mouth remembered the skill of Hui's cook. My veins ran hot with Hui's wine. All around me his house whispered to me of my past, and surely if I moved my hand just so, closed my eyes just then, let my thoughts drift aimlessly for one moment, I would come to myself knowing that Men's house was but a dream of the future and above me, in her elegant room, a young girl knelt before her window, waiting eagerly to see the guests leave.

But gradually the night deepened, appetites were assuaged, and the servants placed a newly opened jug of wine at Hui's knee and departed. The harper picked up his instrument, bowed at our smattering of applause, and the door closed quietly behind him. Harshira took up his post, arms folded, before it. "Now," Hui said, "you summoned us with an unholy speed, Kaha. What is the reason?" I glanced at him, aware of all their eyes suddenly upon me, but in his red gaze I saw that he at least did not need his own question answered.

"I think that you, Master, and the General, know already why we are here," I said. "Seventeen years ago we spent many evenings like this. Although I was not an insti-gator of the hope that brought us together, I was a willing participant in its execution, and when it failed I knew myself to be more vulnerable to exposure and punishment than the rest of you. I am not a noble. I have no influence in high places, save through your good graces. Discovery would have meant death to me but not necessarily to you. I took the greater risk, and so I left this house and distanced myself from all that had happened. Yet I have kept faith with you. I still do. I am here because a new threat has arisen. None of you cared to wonder what befell Thu's son by Pharaoh when she was exiled. Perhaps you believed that to enquire into his fate would have invoked suspicion. Perhaps you simply did not care."

"I certainly did not care," Hunro broke in. "Why should I? Why should any of us? She was a grubby little peasant from nowhere without a scrap of gratitude or humility in her and the muddy blood in her bastard's veins surely negated any influence Pharaoh's seed might have."

"All the same, she was extraordinarily beautiful," Paiis murmured. "I would have given a great deal to plant my seed in her, and I warrant I could have given her more pleasure than that lumpish man. She still haunts me like a half-remembered dream."

"You speak harshly of one who was your friend," Hui broke in mildly, his eyes on Hunro, and she sneered.

"That upstart? I too was young and full of optimism. I did my best to befriend her at your request, Hui, but it was hard. Her arrogance knew no bounds, and in the end she bungled everything and got precisely what she deserved."

"If she had got what she deserved and what we hoped for her finally, she would not still be alive to trouble us now," Paibekamun's reedy voice came from the shadows. "I understand your panic, my Lady. After all, you knew what was in the oil Thu gave to poor little Hentmira to anoint Pharaoh with. You were there when Thu handed it to the unsuspecting girl. Who knows what voices in the harem could be awakened to speak against you?"

"And what of yourself, Butler?" Hunro shot back. "You retrieved the empty pot with its traces of arsenic mingled with the oil. You gave it to the Prince as Hui ordered you to do, when Thu believed you would destroy it. No suspicion fell on you because we all lied to implicate her and her alone!"

"Peace!" Hui said. "All of us lied. Any one of us could damn the others if he so chose. Thu was sacrificed to keep us free. She was a loss to me, although you, Hunro, may not think so. I picked her up out of the Aswat dung. I trained her, disciplined her, saw to every detail of her education. I made her. She was mine. Such an undertaking leaves its scars. I did not throw her to the jackals lightly."

"No indeed, my brother," Paiis said softly. "And you missed her with more than your heart, didn't you?" Hui ignored the remark.

"Let Kaha continue," he commanded. I nodded and put down my cup.

"Thu apparently wrote an account of her dealings with us," I said, "and as you all must know, she has spent years trying to persuade those unfortunate enough to put into Aswat to take her story to Pharaoh. Foolishly of course, because all she accomplished was a reputation for insanity. But now our safety is challenged from another direction. Her son has discovered his true parentage. He has spent the last sixteen years as the adopted son of my present Master, the merchant Men. Three days ago he managed to read the scroll denoting Pharaoh as his father and Thu of Aswat as his mother, and now he has disappeared. I believe he is on his way to Aswat to meet her. Who knows what plan of retribution they may concoct together? He will persuade her to leave her exile and try to confront Pharaoh."

"And so?" Paiis drawled. "What of it? They have no more evidence of any plot together than Thu had alone. After you read the contents of her ridiculous box, Hui, you burned it all. It is still her word against ours."

"Perhaps," Hui returned thoughtfully. "But you sent the young man south with an assassin on nothing but the merest chance that he was aware of the contents of the box. You did not want to take any chance, however remote, that he could do us some damage. I do not think he opened the box. Those knots were either undisturbed or had been retied by someone who had learned them from me. No. I believe that Thu did not trust to one copy of her justification alone. There is another."

"Which Kamen has probably read," Paiis cut in. "He lied to me four days ago when he told me that both the assassin and the woman had vanished. I did not commit myself to doubt until I had questioned his crew. I discovered from them that Thu was brought on board by Kamen and delivered by him to the prisons here in Pi-Ramses. Therefore he must have deduced the identity of the man travelling with him and disposed of him in some way. An enterprising young officer." He turned his lazy gaze on me. "So you are mistaken, Kaha. Kamen is not running off to Aswat. He is in hiding somewhere in the city and so is Thu. If he had taken up his post at my door, I would have had him arrested at once, but he was too clever for me. Temporarily, anyway."

"So you knew who he was!" I exclaimed. "How did you know?"

"I told him," Hui said quietly. "Kamen came to me some time ago for advice. He was being plagued by a dream he could neither interpret nor drive away. I agreed to look into the oil for him because Men and I do business together occasionally. Kamen suspected that the dream had to do with the woman who gave him life and I thought so also.

When I commanded a vision, it was Thu's face I saw. Thu."
He paused, swirling the wine around in his cup before
taking a deep draught. His red eyes met mine and he smiled
wryly. "The shock was immediate, but my gift does not lie.
The sober young officer with the square shoulders was none
other than the child Ramses threw away. Of course once I
knew, I could see both of them in him. He has the shape
and colour of Pharaoh's eyes and his build closely resembles
that of Ramses when he too was a young and vigorous king
bent on war. But the sensuous mouth is Thu's, and the
uncompromising nose, and the set of the jaw. I taunted
him. That was my mistake."

"But why didn't you tell me?" I asked sharply. "You knew
I was under his father's roof!"

"How would that have helped?" Paiis said. "You left my
brother's house out of your own fear. It was kinder not to
implicate you further." I did not like his tone.

"I left because I did not, and do not, believe that Ramses
commuted Thu's sentence out of sentiment," I responded
hotly. "He knows something about us, has always known it,
though the knowing has not been enough to haul us before
the courts. I had no desire to become the target of a secret
palace investigation."

"You must forgive us then," Paiis said without a trace of
apology. "But I still do not believe any such thing. We have
walked free for nearly seventeen years. Hui still treats the
royal family. I am still a General. Hunro still comes and goes
from the harem, and Paibekamun still waits on his Majesty
every day. You were a victim of your own fantasies, Kaha."

"Paiis proposed the elimination of both Thu and
Kamen," Hui said. "It was only a matter of time before

Kamen found her and as you say, Kaha, as a team they could be dangerous. But Kamen managed to foil the attempt on their lives and so now we must decide yet again what to do."

There was a hint of pride in his voice, almost as though he was recounting the exploits of a son, and I looked at him curiously. The warmth of the night and the wine he had drunk had produced a thin slick of sweat on his body. He lay back on his cushions, a wilting garland of flowers across his thighs, his heavy-lidded eyes half-closed, and it came to me forcibly that he was in love with his victim, that at some moment in the past his mystery, his aloofness, had succumbed to the lure of both her beauty and his complete domination of her. It had not made him weak. I did not know if it had even wounded him when he had engineered her disgrace. But it was there nonetheless.

The General also knew. He was watching his brother levelly, a half-smile on his lips. "We have two options," he said. "We can try again to murder both Thu and her son. They will not be difficult to find. Or we can finally make an end of Pharaoh, although to do so now at the end of his life seems foolish. He has already designated the Prince Ramses as his official heir, and Ramses is far more aware of the needs of his army than his father ever was."

"I say kill them all," Hunro broke in with a drunken vehemence. "Ramses because it is past time for a new administration and Thu and her spawn because I need not remind you that the Prince was charged with the investigation into our last attempt on his father's life and he is an honest man. It will matter little whether Thu and Kamen whisper into the ears of the dying Horus or the fledgling in the nest." Paibekamun leaned forward into the lamplight.

His shaven skull gleamed and the shadows of his long, knotted fingers moved like twisted spiders as he spoke.

"This is insane," he said. "There is not a shred of new evidence against us. What if Thu and her son do succeed in winning their way into the presence of the One? She has no new words to say and nothing to show. Ramses is infirm and often ill. He may pardon her, but if he does, it will be because of past passion and not as an expression of her innocence." I was surprised to hear the Butler's words, for both he and Hunro had shared an arrogant dislike for Thu out of a sense of their own superiority. Hunro's noble blood was enough to explain her disdain, but Paibekamun's ancestry was muddy, and like all ambitious upstarts he betrayed his insecurity by denigrating those he regarded as inferior. "Besides," he went on, "Banemus has a right to be consulted before any move is made."

"My brother has softened over the years as you, Paiis, must know," Hunro said scornfully. "He has spent his whole life as Pharaoh's General in Nubia and it no longer irks him to expend his military talents so far from the centre of power. With our failure so long ago he lost interest in the cause. I see him seldom. He would share your counsel, Paibekamun, to leave all as it is."

"And you, Kaha," Hui said, lifting his cup to me in a half-mocking, half-respectful salute. "You could have kept your news to yourself but you called us all together. What is your opinion? Shall we kill them all?"

You are a terrible man, I thought, looking into the face that was always as white as salt. Your mouth seldom speaks the message that your eyes convey. You know already how I feel, what words will come from my lips, and you have already judged me. "I agree with Paibekamun," I said. "Such slaughter is needless. Ramses is dying. Whatever comes of Kamen's discovery it cannot touch us, although it will doubtless wreak havoc within Men's family. Thu has suffered enough at our hands. Let her seek her pardon in peace. As for Kamen, he is innocent of all save the misfortune of having been born of Ramses' blood. Leave him alone!" One of Hui's pale eyebrows rose.

"A dispassionate and impartial summing up," he said sarcastically. "We have two extremes here, my unscrupulous friends. Clemency or doom? Such an intoxicating choice, is it not? Do you relish the taste of such power? Are you willing, any of you, to take the gamble that no one at court will listen or care what Thu screams from the palace roof? For scream she will. I know her better than any of you. Given her chance she will curse and rant and shake her fists until someone pays attention. For whether we like it or not she is one of us, stubborn, wily, deceitful and unscrupulous. Those dubious attributes can be used in the cause of right as well as wrong and Thu, my very dear partners in regicide, will pursue the righting of her particular wrong remorselessly. If we do not eliminate her she will find a way to mow us all down."

There was a deep silence. Each of us sat or lay immobile, staring at the floor, but I was aware of the growing tension. Hunro's chin was in her painted palm, her eyes glazed. Paiis was entirely prone. He lay on his back with his eyes closed, his wine cup balanced on his chest, its stem resting between two of his beringed fingers. Paibekamun had retired into the shadows.

Hui also was still, sitting with one knee raised and both hands folded on it, but when I glanced up, he was watching me steadily. You have already decided, I thought. You are going to sacrifice both of them on the altar of your safety. You love her and yet you will see her die. Such an inner control is almost inhuman. Are you human, Great Seer? What fills your mind when you enter the nothing world between sleep and waking? Are you vulnerable then, or does your will reach even into those mysterious realms? You will see her die.

He inclined his head once, his gaze still on me. "Yes," he whispered. "Yes, Kaha. I gambled once. I am too old to allow the dice to fall where they may a second time." He straightened and clapped his hands. All but Paiis started and stirred. "She dies," he said loudly. "I regret the necessity, but there is no other way. Are we agreed?"

"Why are you asking for our assent, Master?" I put in. "You and the General have already decided her fate."

"And Kamen's too," Hunro added. "Like a good son he will burn to right a wrong done to his mother whether she is alive or dead. He must go."

"I still think it is entirely unnecessary," said Paibekamun, "and we run the risk of dredging up old memories at court if we fail."

"If I fail again, you mean." Paiis sat up and smoothed back his hair. "Old memories will certainly be dredged up at court if we do nothing, Paibekamun, therefore the matter is settled. I will undertake to find the two of them through my soldiers and you, Hui, can make discreet enquiries of your noble patients." He nodded to me. "If Kamen should be stupid enough to return to his home, you will let me know at once. In spite of your affection for him, Kaha, you must see how dangerous it would be to allow sentiment to stand in our way. And we had better move fast." He stood. "If Thu is here in Pi-Ramses, she has broken her exile and the local authorities in Aswat will send to the governor of the Aswat nome for instructions. We will not be the only ones hunting her. Harshira, fetch my litter."

At that the rest of the gathering prepared to leave. Harshira went to order the litters and servants reappeared with cloaks. We all passed through the now dim hall and out onto the pillared entrance. I glanced up at the night sky, breathing deeply of the clean air. The moon had waned to a thin grey sliver and nothing but starlight illumined the wide courtyard which faded quickly into the tumbled darkness of the trees beyond the small gate.

Paiis was the first to leave, bidding us all a good night before stepping into his conveyance and giving a sharp order to his bearers. Paibekamun followed. Hunro took Hui's upper arms and kissed him on the mouth. "You are our Master," she whispered. "We honour you." Harshira had to help her onto her litter, but soon she too was swallowed up and the crunch of her bearers' feet died away. Hui passed the back of his hand across his lips.

"She is poison, that one," he said. "Seventeen years ago she was all movement and energy, dancing through the harem, charming Pharaoh at his feasts with her enthusiasm and vibrancy. Befriending Thu was a game to her and she played it well, concealing her disdain, but when Thu failed to destroy Ramses, it was no longer necessary for Hunro to pretend. Her vitality has soured to spasmodic flickers. The optimism of her youth gave way to resentment. I wish she were the target and not Thu." He gave me a weary smile, his face only half-visible in the uncertain light. "You and I knew Thu far better than the rest of them," he said. "To them she is little more than a threat to be eliminated, but to us she is a memory of simpler days when we still had hopes." The usual cynicism was absent from his voice. He sounded tired and sad.

"Then leave all as it is," I said impulsively. "There was never a great advantage to you in getting rid of Pharaoh, Hui. Whoever sits on the Horus Throne, you are still the Seer, the healer. Your brother stood to reap the greatest benefits on behalf of the army and his own career. As for Ma'at, did the gods not speak when Thu failed? Kamen is a very estimable young man. He deserves to live!"

"Oh does he now?" The jaded tone had returned. It was tinged with humour. "And who sits frowning over the balance and tries to weigh the worth of one royal bastard against the unique value of a gifted Seer, not to mention a mighty General? You have not lost your idealism, Kaha. It used to be directed at the reprehensible state of Egypt. Now it has shrunk to a concern over the fate of one woman and her child. It is not a matter of Ma'at any more. Only survival, yours included." I bowed.

"Then good night, Master," I said. "And to you also, Harshira," for the Steward still stood silently behind Hui. I walked away, suddenly so fatigued that the distance from the house through the shrouded garden to the Lake path seemed impossible to cover. I did not want to go. Part of me longed passionately to run back to Hui and beg to be returned to his employ but I recognized the urge for what it was—a desire for the womb in which I had been happy. That Kaha was gone, dissolved in the acid of the increasing self-knowledge that comes with maturity and brings with it a corresponding disillusionment. Hui's entrance pylon towered over me as I passed under it, its size exaggerated in the thick darkness. A faint glow of starlight was reflected off the surface of the water beyond it. I turned right and followed the deserted ribbon of path towards Men's house.

8

I MET NO ONE as I made my way to my room. Removing my linen, I lay down, but though I was very tired, I could not rest. The evening was played over and over in my head, the words with their weight of emotional inflections, the glances, my own tumultuous feelings. The overwhelming sense of the encounter was one of resignation. All these years the story of our plot had been left without a strong conclusion. Now it was time to pick up the pen and write a swift and definite ending, tidy away the threads left hanging. But the threads were two people and the final hieroglyphs would be written in blood. Well, what did you expect when you sent that message to Hui? I asked myself as I stared up into the dimness of the ceiling. Did you think that he would ignore everything? You were not very surprised to learn that they were already moving, that Paiis had already tried to kill Thu and Kamen or that Hui knew who Kamen was. And you were correct in hoping that nothing will be required of you. Only a small act of betrayal. Only a few quick characters scrawled on papyrus if Kamen comes home. Betrayal? The word echoed in my mind. Who are you, Kaha? What do you owe, and to whom?

I turned on my side and closed my eyes against a wave of sickness I knew did not come from the rich food I had eaten or the quantity of wine I had drunk. All those years ago I had tried to sever myself from what I had done, but the cutting had been performed with a dirty knife and my ka had become infected. I did not know what to do.

Kamen still had not returned by the time I took my first meal out into the sparkling morning. I was not surprised. I ate and drank disinterestedly and was just draining the last of the goat's milk from my cup when I saw Pa-Bast coming towards me over the grass. He had an unsealed scroll in his hand and his expression was grave. "Good morning, Kaha," he said. "This is a message from the Fayum. The family is setting out to come home today. They will arrive tomorrow night unless they choose to put in at On, which I doubt." He squatted beside me, tapping the scroll against his thigh. "I have sent no answer. None is needed. The servants are turning out the bedrooms. But there is the matter of Kamen." His eyes met mine, veiled and troubled. "I have sent for the Commander of the city police and there will be a thorough search. Have we done all we could?"

The thought that flashed across my mind was that a search by the police would serve Paiis very well, provided he found and disposed of Thu and her son quickly. He would make sure that the police found the bodies floating in the Lake or knifed in an alley, and everyone would presume that they had been murdered by thieves. Men would want to know how Thu came to be in the city and in Kamen's company. So would Thu's family at Aswat.

Like the prick of a fishbone in my throat I remembered her father's gift to her on her first Naming Day in Hui's house. He had sent her a statue of Wepwawet he himself had carved, a thing of simple beauty, a modest demonstra-

tion of his love for her, and of course, of course! I took a
deep breath. It stood now on the table beside Kamen's
couch. What a fool you are, Kaha, I berated myself. How is
it that you did not recognize it for the portent it was? He
loved her. Her brother, Pa-ari, loved her and wrote to her
often. And you, cowardly scribe, what of the affection you
felt for her? Lip service and nothing more, for you stood
aside while she was arrested and sentenced to death, and
you would have let her die with no more than a twinge of
self-righteous regret. "Yes we have," I answered Pa-Bast at
last. "When Men returns I will tell him about the scroll. We
cannot keep that a secret, Pa-Bast. I believe that its
contents prompted Kamen's flight. Call me when the
Commander arrives." He pulled himself to his feet and
went away, but for a while I remained with my back against
a tree, my hands pressed into the cool grass.

The empty dishes beside me had begun to attract flies.
They circled hungrily then settled on the rim of the cup,
their black bodies gleaming in the sun. Others alighted on
the crumbs and fruit rind, scuttling greedily to feed, and
watching them I knew what I must do. We had all fed off
her. I had used her to fuel the pride I took in my knowledge
of history and my ability to teach. Paiis had regarded her as
sexual prey, enhancing his lust. To Hunro she had been a
creature to despise, and in the hating Hunro had reassured
herself of her own superiority. And Hui? Hui ate her up.
Hui took everything from her. Hui moulded her, dominated
her, made her an extension of himself. He chewed up her
ka and spat it out re-formed. In so doing he had fallen in
love, not with Thu the woman but with Thu the other Hui,
Thu his twin.

More flies had come, lured by the debris. Crawling over each other they sucked up the flavours under their feet. With a sudden revulsion I picked up my napkin and began to swipe at them and they rose with an angry buzz but did not go away. I covered the dishes with the linen. Where would Kamen go? Where would he take his mother? He was a sociable young man with many acquaintances but none with whom he would trust such a momentous secret. Akhebset was his friend, but I did not think that Kamen would ask Akhebset to assume so great a responsibility. He could put her in the servants' quarters at the military barracks, but that would be like pushing her head into Paiis's rapacious mouth. He could have sent her to the Fayum and perhaps would have done so if the rest of his family had not been in residence there. That left Takhuru, his betrothed. His friend since childhood. Yes. He would take a chance with Takhuru. It would be not only the logical place for Thu, close to Kamen's home, but also a test of Takhuru's loyalty, although if Kamen had any doubts about that he surely would not trust Thu to Takhuru's care.

I left the plates for a servant to clear away and re-entered the house. In the office there was a little business to attend to, and I had just finished with it when I heard voices in the entrance hall. I went out to find the Commander of the city police and Pa-Bast coming towards him over the freshly washed floor. I stood silent while the Steward explained why the police had been called. "This is not a matter for public examination," Pa-Bast warned him. "The noble Men would not wish his son's disappearance gossiped about in every beer house in Pi-Ramses."

"Certainly not," the man agreed. "I am most distressed at your news, Pa-Bast, and of course we will do everything we can to find Kamen. It must be some consolation to you that the young man is a soldier and well able to take care of himself. Let us hope that he has simply been drinking and fighting. I presume that he took none of his clothes or belongings with him?" Pa-Bast answered the man's few but pertinent questions while I waited, and when he had gone the Steward sighed.

"None of this feels right somehow," he said. "We are in the midst of a mystery, Kaha. Well, the life of this household must go on and if I am not to earn a reprimand from the Lady Shesira I had better get to the market and stock the kitchen before she arrives."

"I want to talk to Takhuru this afternoon," I told him. "I would be grateful if you would hire a scribe at the market to keep the tally of the goods. It will be an inconvenience for you, Pa-Bast, but this is important." He shot me a keen glance.

"You know more about Kamen's fate than you are disclosing, don't you Kaha?" he said. "You have the welfare of this family at heart?" It was a question, not a statement. I nodded. "Then go," he went on. "But Setau has already been to Nesiamun. Kamen is not there."

"Perhaps not. Thank you, Pa-Bast." He grunted and turned on his heel and I went to my room for my best sandals and a clean kilt. I was afraid, for the moment I crossed Nesiamun's threshold I would be setting myself irrevocably against the man I still regarded as my true Master, but it was time to heal that inner infection. Slipping on the sandals and setting the wide golden armband of my status around my wrist, I left the house.

I was blind to the beauty of the day as I walked, weaving

my way absently through the intermittent groups of people passing to and fro and talking lightly. Some greeted me, their voices jerking me briefly out of myself, and I replied as best I could, but I did not stop for fear that my feet, once halted, would turn me about and return me to my room. But at length they did slow, and Nesiamun's porter came out to take my name and my business.

I waited. Presently a servant appeared to tell me that the Master of the house could not be disturbed. He was closeted with the General Paiis. But if I wanted, I could take some refreshment with the Master's Steward. His scribe, of course, was in attendance on him and could not talk with me. As soon as the Master was free, he would receive me. I considered quickly. This was an unforeseen calamity. I could only hope that Paiis believed I was there on the conspirators' behalf. "Actually I have been instructed by my Lord's Steward to question the Lady Takhuru once more on the matter of Kamen's disappearance, if she is willing," I explained. "My Lord returns from the Fayum tomorrow and we are in great distress." The man clucked his tongue sympathetically.

"I will enquire if she will see you," he said, and went away. Again I waited, looking about at the colourful profusion of statuary dotting Nesiamun's vast gardens, and as my eyes travelled the sun drenched arouras, I caught a glimpse of soldiers moving far towards the rear wall where the servants' quarters sprawled. So Paiis was chatting with his friend while his guard searched the estate. Such effrontery took my breath away. I glanced in the porter's direction but he had gone back into his lodge. Despair mingled with relief as I strained to catch another sight of the armed men.

What would the servants tell the Steward about this intrusion? What had the officer in charge said? That they were searching for a criminal? Paiis would not care what was or was not said. His confidence knew no check. I turned as a shadow fell across me. "The Lady Takhuru will see you," the servant said. "Follow me."

He led me through the ground floor of the house to a small room at the rear whose wide window gave out onto the garden. "The scribe Kaha," he said, and bowing he left, closing the door behind him.

She was sitting in an ebony chair facing the window, both beringed hands grasping the armrests, her gold-shod feet placed decorously side by side on a low footstool. A plain white sheath of what was clearly the finest grade of linen fell from her narrow shoulders and frothed about her calves. A gold band encircled her forehead, holding a tightly woven net of gold thread which imprisoned her luxuriant hair. She was fresh and lovely, yet as I performed my deep obeisance, my own arms outstretched, I saw how pale she was under the expertly applied kohl and the orange henna on her mouth. There was tension in those long, soft fingers as they grasped the lions' heads on which they lay, and she swallowed before she spoke. "Chief Scribe Kaha," she said huskily, "I gather that you are here to ask me yet more questions regarding the fate of my betrothed. I have already told his body servant, Setau, all I know. I am sorry." I straightened and looked her over carefully. She was clenching her jaw. The muscles along it were flexing, and her attention was not on me. It was on the garden. I was right, I thought in a wave of exultation. She knows.

"Thank you for seeing me, my Lady," I said. "I am aware that the General Paiis is with your father, and soldiers are searching your estate. Is Kamen safe?" Her gaze shot to me.

"What do you mean?" Those elegant fingers were inside the golden lions' mouths now, running back and forth over the sharp carved teeth. "How would I know whether Kamen is safe or not? I pray for him night and morning. Worry is robbing me of sleep."

"I worry also," I said, "but my concern is that he should not be found by the men out there. I think you share my fear." Still she would not give in, though I could see that she was close to panic. Beads of sweat sprang out along her upper lip and a vein in her tall neck began to pulse.

"I do not wish to speak with you further, Kaha," she said with as much haughtiness as she could muster. "Please go."

"My Lady," I pressed. "I did not come here today with the General. I do not desire Kamen's death, nor his mother's, but Paiis does. I am here to warn them. You do know where they are, don't you?" She slumped, very slightly, leaning back in the chair.

"I have no idea what you are talking about," she said stiffly, "but if you think Kamen is in danger and wish to continue, I will listen." My heart went out to her, but I repressed the smile that came to my lips. She was still as flighty as a cornered gazelle. I had already come too far to back away now.

With a last flutter of apprehension I began my story. If I had not read her aright I was putting my head into Paiis's noose, but I was a scribe, trained to interpret more than just the words spoken around me, and I had not been wrong about Takhuru. At my first words her eyes went wide and then did not leave my face.

It took a long time. I spoke of life in Hui's house, of Thu as a young girl hungry for knowledge, greedy for recognition, desperate to transcend her peasant roots. I spoke of her training as a physician and of the darker education that ran like a subterranean river through all our dealings with her. I told of her introduction to Pharaoh and her removal to the harem, a living instrument of destruction wielded by Hui's hand. Calmly I described how Thu had borne a son and fallen out of favour, and how she had come to Hui in despair and Hui had given her arsenic which she mixed with massage oil and gave to Ramses' current favourite, Hentmira, and how Hentmira had died but Pharaoh had recovered to sentence Thu to death after his son had investigated the crime. The sentence was commuted to exile.

Takhuru listened without interruption until that point. Then she raised a hand. "Let me understand this, Kaha," she said in a low voice. "You say you lived in the Seer's house and taught Thu. Moreover you were yourself privy to the plot against Ramses. When Thu was arrested, you could have given evidence that would have saved her and you did not. Why have you come to me now?" I admired her self-possession. She was determined to give nothing away. Yet though her hands were now folded in her lap, one foot was creeping to cover the other, a betrayal of her consternation.

I knew her suspicion, knew her resolve to keep Kamen safe at any cost, but time was passing and I could do nothing without her co-operation. I came close to her and touched her shoulder. "I have paid lip service to love," I said. "Love is a word I threw about when I was younger. Love for Egypt, love of Ma'at, love for the sacred hiero-glyphs given to us by Thoth, love for Thu's intelligence and perception. But Lady Takhuru, when those loves were put to the test, I ran away. Love for myself superseded everything else. I did not know until last night that I have been carrying shame with me."

"What happened last night?"

"I went to the Seer's house and met with him and the General and the Lady Hunro. There it was decided to kill Thu and Kamen before they could plead Thu's case to Pharaoh. Nothing has changed for them. They are as rapacious and callous as ever. But I have grown to love Kamen since I entered the service of his father, and Thu was like a sister to me. I cannot let them die. I must redeem my former cowardice."

"The General has moved swiftly," she commented, and the wariness had gone out of her voice.

"Yes. And he is not a stupid man. He has deduced that the only place Thu and Kamen can be is right here. If he does not find them openly today, he will send assassins in the night to slip onto your estate and search in secret. You cannot hide them for much longer."

"He has tried before. In Aswat."

"Yes. He will not give up."

She stared at me speculatively for a while, biting her lip, then she slid off the chair. "I have read Thu's account of her life," she said at last. "You corroborate what I already know. Come with me."

She led me back along the passage, across the entrance hall, and up the stairs at the rear. There was another passage, and then she was pushing open large double doors. At her brusque word I closed them behind me and found myself in her private quarters. Her body servant bowed and Takhuru gave her leave to go. Once more the doors opened and closed.

Walking to the far wall, Takhuru pulled open another door. Beyond was a small room containing chests and shelves on which were piled various wigs, scrolls, jewellery and folded linens. At the back I saw narrow stairs leading up into darkness. "Like everyone else, I sleep on the roof in the summer," Takhuru said. "Thu has been staying in the servants' quarters. It was fortunate that she was here with me this morning when Paiis arrived. Father summoned me to answer some of his questions. He wanted to know if any new servants had been hired within the last few days. I am afraid that although I told him no, the Steward has said yes out of innocence. Kamen was also here. He has been going about the city during the day and creeping past the porter at night." She laughed suddenly, and colour bloomed on her face. "To tell you the truth, Kaha, I have never before had so much fun. They are both quite safe here you know. My quarters are forbidden to all unless I give them leave to enter."

"I do not think so," I replied. "Any good assassin could scale the wall, come down those stairs, and slay with ease." The smile left her mouth. Leaning into the little room she called, "Please come out, Kamen."

There was the sound of scrambling footsteps and then Kamen appeared, stepping out of the dimness into the full light flooding from Takhuru's window. When he saw me, he came to an abrupt halt. His body tensed for action. His gaze swivelled to the double doors. But I hardly noticed him. A woman had emerged from behind him, dressed in the yellow sheath of the servants of the house. For a moment I did not recognize her. My memory of another Thu, the perfect oval of her smooth, painted face lifted to mine, fought with the reality of this darkly tanned body with its coarse, untended hands and corded feet, its finely lined face and wiry hair. But the glittering blue eyes were the same, clear and compelling, and the bare mouth was still softly sensuous. My throat went dry. "Thu," I whispered.

She strode to me and slapped my face with all the force she could muster. "Kaha," she ground out. "I would have known you anywhere, you and the others. Your faces have haunted my nights and bedevilled my days for the last seventeen years. I trusted you! You were my beloved teacher, my friend! But you lied and deserted me and I hate you, and I want to see you dead!" The pent-up passion of those lost years came pouring out in a deluge of fierce recrimination. Her eyes burned. Her body shook. Kamen put an arm around her but she shrugged him off. "I will see you suffer," she cried. "I want you to know what it is like to find yourself friendless, condemned, robbed of everything!" My own eyes were watering from the force of the blow and my cheek was stinging.

"I am sorry, Thu," I said. "Truly, deeply sorry."

"Sorry?" she flashed back. "Sorry? Will sorry give me back the years? Will sorry show me how my son grew? Damn you, little scribe. Damn all of you!" She started to weep, and her tears were more shocking than her rage. Then she came to me and laid her head against my chest. My arms went round her. "I loved you, Kaha," she sobbed. "I believed everything you told me. You were my brother in that sober household and I trusted you."

There was nothing I could say. The others stood frozen while she struggled to regain control of herself, her tears warm on my skin, and before long the storm was over. Moving out of my embrace, she wiped her face on a corner of her sheath and gave me a level glance from beneath swollen lids. She took Kamen's hand. "Well," she said. "I presume that you have come here with Paiis to take me away. You can try, but I will fight you. I have nothing to lose any more."

Kamen was watching me very carefully and I noticed that he was wearing a leather belt from which hung a short military sword. His other hand rested on its hilt. "No, Kamen," I said. "I have not come to help Paiis arrest you. He would not need me for that. I am here to warn you that, as you have probably suspected, you are both marked for death. You cannot stay here. The General has already eliminated every other possible hiding place and he is left with the logical choice. He may not find you today, but sooner or later he will send men here to search for you secretly. The Lady Takhuru is now also in danger. She knows too much."

"I had not thought of that," Kamen frowned. "How foolish of me. Then it does not matter where my mother and I go. But surely if Paiis does not find us here he will not suspect Takhuru?"

"Yes he will," the girl put in. "He must conclude that you have at least opened your heart to me about everything and he will want to make sure I am not left to talk to anyone else." She did not seem in the least perturbed, and I could not decide whether her composure came from a blithe reck-lessness or a lack of appreciation for her true position. I presumed the latter. Takhuru had suffered no hurt or check in her whole pampered life, and I did not think she could even begin to imagine any real threat.

"The city police are hunting you also," I told them. "Pa-Bast called them in this morning, Kamen. He is frantic over your disappearance, particularly as your family is due home from the Fayum tomorrow night." I could see the swift conjectures flitting through his mind.

"It might be a good idea to let them find us," he said slowly. "If we fell into the hands of the police, we would at least be safe from the General."

"Not necessarily," Thu broke in. Her voice was now steady. The glance she gave me was cool. "The city prisons are very public and the police have always been closely allied to the army. It would be child's play for Paiis to arrange an accident for us there. I suppose that by now it has been discovered that I have left Aswat and am therefore liable for prosecution. I wonder if Ramses will be notified?"

"I doubt it," I said. "Unless there is new evidence that would compel the reopening of your case, you would simply be rearrested, probably whipped, and returned to Aswat without Pharaoh ever knowing." Thu let go of Kamen's hand.

"You could have my case reopened, Kaha," she said. "You could provide the evidence you should have given on my behalf. I gave the King all your names and he said that he would remember them even though the only evidence at the time was my word." She grimaced. "The word of an attempted murderess. If you truly want to help me, take me into the presence of Pharaoh and speak for me!"

I had always believed that something similar had happened. That was why I had left Hui, and I had been right to do so, even though we had all peacefully prospered in the intervening years.

Takhuru had turned to her table. Now she poured wine and offered it to each of us, then she sat on the edge of the couch. Kamen joined her. But Thu continued to stand facing me, her wine untasted in her hand, her whole stance a challenge. I could have drained the cup in one gulp. I was thirsty with tension. "It would not be enough," I said. "It would be the word of a scribe against the reputations of three of the most powerful men in Egypt and a noble lady of ancient and honourable lineage. There is no evidence that may be held in the hand, Thu."

"Paibekamun had it," she said bitterly. "He was supposed to throw it away but he kept it and handed it over to the Prince. Still, that pot was evidence against, not for me. The gods know I was guilty, but guilty of a lesser crime. The corruption of a young girl was surely the greater evil." She shrugged. "But it does no good to brood. You are right, Kaha. Perhaps I can mete out my own justice. Kill them all myself, one by one." Then she laughed, and the Thu I had known was back. "Will you at least try to put my manuscript into Pharaoh's hands?"

"There is no time for that!" Kamen said impatiently. "We must find another hiding place and do it immediately. And you, Takhuru. What are we going to do with you? If the daughter of such an illustrious house goes missing, Egypt will echo from one end to the other with the furore!"

"That might not be so bad," the girl mused. "The greater the uproar the more difficult it will be for the General to quietly dispose of us. Already the situation is getting out of hand. First he plans the nice neat assassination of two anonymous people far from the seat of power. But that fails. The two victims are now right in the middle of a city teeming with life night and day. And to make matters worse, he must add a third, the daughter of a very prominent family who will not disappear without a palace investigation. Perhaps he will throw up his hands and relinquish the whole scheme."

"If Hui knew, he would forbid the murder of Takhuru," Thu said. "I know him better than any of you save Kaha. He is cold and manipulative but he is not wantonly cruel."

There was a thoughtful silence in which I became aware of the not unpleasant heat of full noon invading the room and the intermittent sounds of the routine of the house going on below us. Thu's mild taunt to me rankled, and as I sipped my wine I considered what I should do. I had not looked past my duty to salve my conscience by warning her and Kamen of their danger, but it was not going to be enough. I must purge away my old self completely, repudiate Hui and everything he had meant to me. The conviction that such a thing had to be done brought a pang of homesickness to me, but I reminded myself that Hui worked by deliberately cultivating just such a dependency. The wine filling my mouth tasted like old blood and I swallowed it with an effort and put down my cup.

"I see it thus," I said. "Lady Takhuru, it is necessary for you to collect your things and move to Kamen's house for a while. I was going to suggest that you hide on Men's estate in the Fayum but I do not think that Kamen would allow you out of his sight and his protection." Kamen, eyebrows raised at my words, nodded briefly.

"Go on, Kaha," he prompted.

"You and I, Kamen, will tell your father everything, and ask him to beg an audience of the Prince. It is no use trying to see Pharaoh. He is ill and the affairs of government are now mostly in the hands of his Heir. If Men accepts our story, we will tell Nesiamun where his daughter is and why she is with Kamen. The Prince may refuse audience to Men but he would see one of his most influential nobles without demur."

"What reason will you offer for disturbing the Prince?" Thu asked sharply and I smiled.

"The kidnapping of the daughter of the Overseer of the Faience Factories," I replied. "Takhuru is right. Such an act would impel the involvement of the palace soldiery." I turned to Thu. "Nowhere is safe for you," I told her. "The only place you can hide is deep within the bowels of the city. Kamen, do you trust Akhebset?"

"Yes, but I do not like the direction you are heading, Kaha," he said. "I will not abandon my mother to the vagaries of life on the streets of Pi-Ramses." Thu put a hand to his cheek and patted him gently.

"This is no time for sentiment," she chided him. "Do not make the mistake of building fond fantasies around me, Kamen. After all, I survived the hazardous maze of the harem. The alleys of Pi-Ramses pose no great threat to me." She met my eyes, and in that moment the relationship that had bound us years ago was reborn, an affection and mutual respect older than any other in this room. We had our own history. "You intend to set me loose in the city and use Kamen's friend as a go-between," she stated. "Good, Kaha. Very good. I never did have a chance to investigate the brothels and beer houses of Pi-Ramses." She put up a hand to forestall Kamen's angry protest. "It will be easier for me to evade the General's hunters," she said emphatically. "Do not waste your concern on me. Concentrate on your betrothed." Takhuru slid from the couch and approached Thu, her eyes sparkling.

"I want to go with you, Thu," she said. "I too have never had the opportunity to explore the city." At that Kamen exploded.

"Absolutely not!" he shouted. "I have told you before, Takhuru, this is not some game of invented adventure. Now do as I say! Pack up the things you will need and we will leave." Takhuru flushed. Her chin rose and she met his angry gaze, but hers was the first to drop.

"I do not know how to pack," she objected sulkily, and Thu moved forward.

"I do, my Lady," she said kindly, but there was a quiver of mirth in her voice. The two women disappeared into the other room, and Kamen and I looked at each other.

"It might work, Kaha," Kamen said in a half-murmur. "And if it does not, we will have to deal with Paiis and Hui by ourselves." There was a hard glint in his eyes that came from Thu herself.

"We must hurry," I said aloud. "We must leave this house while everyone is enjoying the noon sleep." There was nothing more to add and we waited resignedly for the women to emerge.

Thu had divested herself of everything that could betray her as a member of Nesiamun's staff. Gone were the sandals, the yellow sheath and ribbon, the copper armband. She was barefoot and clad in coarse, calf-length linen. It was Takhuru who now wore the livery of her father's household. Behind her she dragged a large and bulky leather bag. Kamen picked it up and swung it onto his shoulder. "We will go down and leave by the servants' entrance," he said. "Mother, there is a beer house on the Street of Basket Sellers called the Golden Scorpion. Akhebset and I drink there often. Meet him there every third night for word from me."

We stood ready to go, but all at once we were reluctant to move. Thu had folded her arms and was staring out the window. Takhuru was pulling at her unfamiliar sheath and Kamen, with pursed lips, gazed at the floor. I did not want to leave the quiet security of the room either, but each of us knew that its safety was spurious and its walls no protection against nightfall. At last Kamen looked up and was about to speak when a knock sounded on the door. "What is it?" Takhuru asked sharply.

"Your pardon, my Lady," came the muffled reply. "Your father's visitor has gone and your mother wishes you to know that the noon meal is prepared."

"Tell her that I ate late this morning and I will see her after the sleep," Takhuru called, and we heard footsteps receding along the passage. The girl smiled wanly. "I do not like the thought of worrying my mother," she said. Kamen reached out and smoothed her hair.

"It will only be for one night," he said with a trace of purely masculine impatience. "Would you rather stay here and risk being murdered in your bed?" Her eyes flared.

"I am not a fool to wish to spare my loved ones grief," she snapped, and went to the door. Kamen murmured an apology and we followed her.

We left the house cautiously but without incident. Nesiamun and his wife were eating in the dining hall. As we crept down the stairs, we could hear their voices and the deferential answers of the servants who waited on them. The rest of the house seemed empty. The members of the household who were not needed had retired to their quarters to rest. The garden also was temporarily deserted, the gardeners' tools lying beside the winding path. Takhuru led us to the enclosing wall of the estate, far to the rear, and crossing just out of sight of the servants' domain, we came by a circuitous route to the servants' entrance far beyond the main gates. It was guarded but the lone soldier on duty waved us through sleepily without more than a cursory bow.

We found ourselves on the path beside the water. At once we set off, walking in silence through the drowsy hour when occupations were laid aside, until we came to Men's gate. Here, in the shade of his wall, we halted. Thu embraced Kamen, holding him tightly. "The guards on the Lake do not seem to care who leaves the precincts, only who comes in," she commented as she let him go. "I will be able to go out without trouble. In three nights I will be at the Golden Scorpion. May Wepwawet open a way for us out of this predicament." She did not linger. Turning on her heel she strode briskly away and Kamen sighed.

"That is how I first saw her," he said. "Clad in rough linen with her feet bare. I pray I do not have to remember her that way. Well, let us go in."

As at Nesiamun's house we were careful not to be seen. It was vital that no servant spy us, at least until Men had returned, for although I knew all Men's staff and they were loyal servants, a chance word to a questing ear could destroy us. Luckily no one had decided to work through the daily lull. Kamen escorted Takhuru through the somnolent house to his mother's rooms and I went straight to Pa-Bast.

He was lying on his couch naked. He had unrolled the reed mat on his window so that the hectic brightness of the early afternoon could not disturb him and he was snoring gently as I moved through the dimness and shook him carefully. He came awake at once, struggling to a sitting position and running a hand over his cheek where the pillow had dented it. "Kaha," he said thickly. "Is there a problem in the house?"

"No," I answered. "But Kamen is here with Takhuru. He has put her in Shesira's quarters. It will be impossible to keep this secret, so you must go down to the servants' cells and impress on them the necessity for keeping their mouths shut. Lives depend on it, Pa-Bast." He was wide awake now, and he fixed me with the penetrating stare that all Stewards seemed able to develop in their dealings with inferiors. But I was not an inferior. My place in the household was equal to his.

"Thank all the gods Kamen is safe," he said. "You had better tell me everything. I suspected you knew more than you were prepared to disclose, but now I must ask you to confide in me if I am not to send to Nesiamun at once. I presume he does not know where Takhuru is."

"No. I do not think he has discovered her disappearance yet but he will in a matter of hours. It is a long story, Pa-Bast. Will you swear to hear it to the end without anger?" He nodded.

"You have always had my respect, Kaha," he said. "I will listen."

So I told him everything, and by the time I had finished the hour of rest was over. He interrupted me with a few pointed questions but otherwise listened attentively, his face betraying nothing, hiding his reactions as a good Steward should. I fell silent. Presently he left the couch and began to gather up his clothes, the long, loose Stewards' robe, the bracelet of his office, the red ribbon of Men's house that went around his shaved skull. He dressed with an automatic precision. I could tell that his thoughts were far away. Then he said, "I know Harshira, the Seer's Steward, very well. I know the General's Steward also. Not the slightest whisper of any of this has come to me through them."

"Of course not," I retorted. "They are loyal servants of their masters. They do not gossip. Neither do you, Pa-Bast. But I tell you that I know Harshira better than you. I lived in his company for years. He lied for Hui and so did I. I beg you to give me the benefit of your doubts and reserve your judgement until the Master comes home tomorrow." He finished tying on his sandals and stood for a moment looking at his small shrine to the Apis Bull, his totem. "I will swear by Thoth, the god who guides my life, that what I have told you is true. Speak to Kamen if you wish."

"I shall," he said heavily. "And I will do as you ask but only until the Master makes a judgement. Of course the Lady Takhuru must be chaperoned while she is here. Unfortunately the women's body servants went to the Fayum with them. I shall summon one of the house servants to see to her needs." He looked at me, frowning. "It is a terrible story, Kaha," he commented. "Full of evil if it is true." I breathed an inward sigh of relief. I had him.

"Thank you, Pa-Bast," I said.

We parted, he to talk to Kamen and to warn the servants even now rising from their pallets and I to go to my room.

I had little to do until the regular dispatches arrived in the morning when I would make sure that all correspondence was up to date in preparation for Men's return, and I was profoundly glad. Shedding my clothes, I lay on my couch exhausted. I thought of Thu, surely mingling now with the crowds in the markets of the city. She would go unnoticed for some time. I would like to have known whether an official search for her was underway. If it was, then other soldiers besides those of Paiis's would be hunting her. Where would she sleep? What would she eat? And what if all this was in vain? What if the gods had not relented towards her, if her years spent in expiation were not enough? It was said that if the gods cared nothing for you, they allowed you to live without consequences. Then surely they must care for Thu, who had suffered the consequence of her crime many times over. Did they care so much that they would allow her to die, struck down by an anonymous hand in some dark alley? Kaha you are imagining rubbish, I told myself sternly, and whispering a quick prayer to Thoth on behalf of all of us, I fell asleep.

I spent the long, anxious hours of the evening in Kamen's room with Takhuru. Pa-Bast had assigned a shy house servant to wait on her. The girl was in awe of her illustrious charge, clumsy and apologetic, but to Takhuru's credit she endured the fumbles with good humour. The Steward had given orders that Nesiamun's daughter was to be accompanied at all times, so the three of us had no opportunity to talk about our private affairs.

A late meal was served in Kamen's quarters. I was invited to join the two of them. The girl served her new mistress and having done so, mindful of the Steward's admonition, she retired to a corner where she sat watching us, her eyes wide. Our conversation was fitful and innocuous. Depression gripped all of us and the room was often full of a gloomy silence in which Kamen and I stared into our wine cups and Takhuru fingered the playing pieces of the board game Pa-Bast had provided to amuse her. Kamen looked very tired. His eyes were shadowed and the skin around his mouth seemed pale. I had no doubt that his thoughts were on his mother as darkness fell.

I was descending the shadowy stairs on my way to my room when I saw Pa-Bast talking to a man in Nesiamun's livery who was standing just inside the entrance. My heart stopped. Crossing the floor, I came up to them. A servant stood with them holding a lamp. They turned to me. "The Noble Nesiamun has sent to enquire into the whereabouts of his daughter," Pa-Bast explained swiftly. His face was a mask of polite concern. "She has been missing since mid-afternoon. Seeing that the son of this house is also missing, the Noble Nesiamun asks first if we have any news of either of them and second that our Master see him as soon as possible after his return." The servant's hand trembled and the lamp's flame flickered wildly. I shot him a warning glance.

"We are all in acute distress over Kamen's disappearance," I replied. "This news is horrifying. Has Nesiamun acquainted the city authorities?"

"He did so at once," the man said. "He has also sent a message to his friend the General Paiis, who has promised to mobilize all his soldiers in the search for the Lady Takhuru." I fought against the urge to meet Pa-Bast's eye.

"Then there is nothing more to be done," Pa-Bast said. "Tell your Master that the noble Men will send to him as soon as he returns." The man bowed and walked out into the darkness. Pa-Bast turned to me.

"Pray that Men comes home early," he said grimly. "Otherwise there will be a disaster."

I managed very little sleep that night, only drifting into an uneasy doze as the sun lipped the horizon, and I went about my business in the morning with an aching head and a sense of doom. Upstairs the house was very quiet. Either Kamen and Takhuru were still in bed or they had decided to be as invisible as possible. The hour of the noon meal came and went. I picked uninterestedly at a few figs and some goat cheese but drank a cup of wine, hoping that it would cure the hammer thudding in my brain. I went out into the garden and talked with the head gardener who was polite but did not really want to be interrupted. I stood on the slab in the bath house and doused myself repeatedly with cold water, but nothing dispelled the sickness in my head or the cringing of my ka.

In the late afternoon four of Paiis's soldiers appeared. I heard them arguing with Pa-Bast as, draped in linen and still dripping with water, I was about to make my way across the hall to the stairs. I paused in the concealment of the doorway and listened. "You will have to come back tomorrow when the Master is here," Pa-Bast was saying firmly. "I have no authority to allow such a thing."

"We take our orders from the General and he from the Prince," the officer in charge retorted. "Those orders are to search all the houses between the palace and the neck of the Lake. If you do not obey, you will be subject to discipline from His Highness. You must step aside, Steward." Pa-Bast drew himself up.

"If your orders originate in the palace, then show me the scroll with the Prince's seal," Pa-Bast insisted. "The General surely gave you written orders signed by His Highness. No noble living in this district is going to let you ransack his estate on your word alone." The man's face darkened.

"Perhaps you do not understand," he said. "These people are clever and dangerous criminals. They could be hiding anywhere in these precincts without your knowledge."

"No, they could not," Pa-Bast disagreed. "This is a modest household with few servants. I am the Steward. I inspect the servants' quarters every day. No stranger hides here." I closed my eyes. Oh do not allow yourself to be trapped by the detour of argument, I prayed silently to my friend. Stand on the first matter of the scroll of authority.

"We must make sure," the officer pressed. "We have been to three of the noble Men's neighbours. No one else has refused us, indeed they have been eager to do their duty."

"My Master is not at home." Pa-Bast's voice had risen. "Therefore the decision to let you in is not mine to make without written orders from the palace. Show them to me and you may enter. Otherwise go away." He turned on his heel and began to cross the hall, moving with the upright carriage and slow grace of his authority. His face was flushed with annoyance but his uncertainty was betrayed in the way his bottom lip was trapped between his tongue and his lower teeth. He knew, and so did I, that if the soldiers forced their way in there would be nothing we could do to stop them. Men did not employ guards. But the bluff worked. After a moment's hesitation the officer barked a short command to his underlings and they left. Light once

more flowed unimpeded across the floor. I let out a quaver-
ing breath and continued on my way.

An hour or so later another soldier darkened the door,
this time one of Nesiamun's retainers come to enquire once
more for any new information we might have on Takhuru's
whereabouts. Again Pa-Bast was forced to lie. He was
angry, not with the poor man who was obviously as
distressed as Nesiamun must be, but with the circumstances
that had driven him into a predicament that was untenable
for any good Steward. It was only a matter of time before
the city was scoured by the regular police for the woman of
Aswat who had broken the terms of her exile, and I could
only hope that they made their way to this door after Men
was back in residence. What if our master decided to stay
on in the Fayum to link up with his caravan on its return
journey? I shuddered at the thought.

But I need not have worried. An hour after sunset a roar
broke the peaceful tenor of the house and the hall exploded
in a flurry of noisy activity. "Pa-Bast! Kaha! Kamen where
are you? Come out! We are home!" As I made for the stairs,
passing Kamen's door as it began to open, I heard Shesira's
placatory tones.

"Don't shout at them, Men. They will know we're here.
Tamit, take the cat to the kitchen at once and then come
back and wash before we eat. Mutemheb, have the servants
take the clothes and cosmetic boxes upstairs. They can
leave the rest down here until they've gone to their quarters and eaten something. Kamen! My darling! Gods, have
you always been so tall?"

I knew that Men would go straight to the office to be
brought up to date on his business affairs before he relaxed

enough to eat, but in the moment before he called me to the office door, as I reached the bottom step and looked out on the cheerful chaos of their arrival, Kamen pushed past me and took his elder sister by the arm. He whispered something in her ear, warning her, I suppose, that his mother's room had been occupied. I hoped that he had had the presence of mind to hustle Takhuru into his room for now. She nodded, smiled at him, kissed him, and turned to the servants struggling with a mountain of chests and boxes.

Shesira waited with arms spread wide. "My beautiful son!" she sang. "Come and embrace me! Paiis is working you too hard. Either that or you are spending too many of your nights in the beer house. You look haggard. How is Takhuru?" I saw Kamen hesitate and I knew immediately what was passing through his mind. A comparison, unbidden but intense, between this soft and lovely woman brimming with the confidence of her station, and the stranger with the murky but exotic past who had consumed his emotions and capsized all the verities of his life. He moved towards her, suffered her eager grasp, then extricated himself in order to kiss her painted temple where the greying hair waved back.

"I look tired, Mother, that is all," he said. "Tell me, have you had a good rest? How are things in the Fayum? What will Father plant there this year?"

"I have no idea," she replied. "He and the Overseer tramped about and frowned and consulted. I want him to enlarge the house down there. It's so small you know, far too small for family gatherings when you and Takhuru produce grandchildren for me. The fountain in the garden is in a state of disrepair too, but your father keeps putting off the simple task of hiring a stonemason. Still," and here she favoured him with another wide smile that showed her even teeth, "it is a blessed place and I like to go there. Mutemheb has begun to fret at the days of idleness and it is always a struggle to persuade Tamit to continue with her lessons while we are away."

"Tamit will make a gentle wife and little more," Kamen remarked to her. "She is a good child, content and unambitious. Do not nag her too much, Mother." Her kohled eyes roved over his face.

"You are troubled, Kamen," she said in a low voice. "I can tell that all is not well with you. I am tired, hungry and in need of a bath, but come to me later this evening. Kaha! There you are! Tomorrow I want to take a complete inventory of all our household effects with you and Pa-Bast. Tybi is almost upon us and we always have the annual task completed by the Feast of the Coronation of Horus." She gave a sigh of happiness. "I do love coming home!" I bowed to her, and at that moment Men summoned me sharply over the heads of the servants still bringing in a stream of belongings. I had grabbed up my palette before coming downstairs. Clutching it tightly, I threaded my way through the commotion, and we entered the relative serenity of the office. Kamen followed me.

Men cast the customary critical eye over his holiest of holiest. His eyes crinkled as he bade us sit, Kamen on the chair and I in my correct place cross-legged on the floor beside him. "Well?" he said, lowering himself behind the desk with obvious satisfaction. "Is there anything important to go over before we eat, Kaha? Has word come back from the caravan yet? Kamen, are you in better humour than when I left?" Kamen gestured to me. Quickly I made my report. Men listened carefully, grunting occasionally, sometimes waving a hand dismissively to indicate that I might move on to something else.

"I have brought back the reports of my Overseer in the Fayum with regard to the crops I wish to sow and the projected yields based on the height of this year's flood," he said. "You can transcribe them into permanent record tomorrow. Shesira has been plaguing me about that fountain. Find a reputable stonemason, will you, Kaha, and send him south to fix it. Though I would rather tear it out and have a fishpond dug. The flies are bad in the Fayum. You can also write to the Seer and tell him that the herbs he has requested should arrive with the caravan. He will have to be patient. Anything else?" I looked up at Kamen. His arms were folded and he was swallowing as though he had a bone stuck in his throat.

"Yes there is, Father," he said, "but I think you should at least bathe and eat before you hear it."

"Serious is it?" Men's bushy eyebrows rose. "I would rather hear it now and then enjoy my food. Has Paiis dismissed you?"

"No." Kamen hesitated. Then he unlocked his arms and rose. Going to a shelf, he lifted down the small ornate chest in which Men kept his private documents. He placed it on the desk and leaned over it. "It is about the scroll in here," he said, "but I do not know where to begin. Takhuru is here, Father."

"What, here? In this house? Why didn't you bring her to greet us, Kamen? Will she stay and eat this evening?"

"No, she spent the night in mother's quarters. Her life is threatened. So is mine. Paiis is hunting us. We ..." Men held up a warning hand.

"Sit down," he ordered. "Kaha, go and bring Takhuru downstairs and then find Pa-Bast and tell him not to serve the meal until I say so. But he can bring a jug of wine in here immediately."

"Kaha must be present," Kamen said. "He is a part of it all." Men stared at him.

"My scribe? My servant? Has this house gone mad while I've been away? Kaha, do as you are told." I came to my feet, bowed, and left the room.

Takhuru was waiting quietly by Kamen's couch and together we went down. Fortunately we met no one. I could hear the voices of the women and the splash of water come echoing from the bath house. Knocking on the office door and opening it for the girl, I went in search of Pa-bast, and I returned to the office bringing the wine myself.

Kamen was speaking steadily, telling the story I knew so well. He had given the chair to Takhuru who sat rigidly, her face pale. Before I folded onto the floor in my usual place, I poured the wine. Men drank it at once and held out his cup to be refilled. His eyes did not leave Kamen as the young man paced. By the time Kamen fell silent and came to a halt before his father, the jug was empty.

For a long time Men said nothing. His hands were clasped on the desk, his face vacant, but I knew he was thinking quickly and deeply. Then he passed a palm over his bald pate in one slow, familiar gesture and sighed. "If it were not for the fact that I know your true parentage well, I would say that this story is the most ridiculous I have ever heard," he said heavily. "The General is an able and well-respected man without a slur to his name. Moreover, he is your father's good friend, Takhuru. The Seer treats the illnesses of the royal family, apart from being Egypt's greatest visionary. You are talking about two of the country's most influential men. What proof do you have that the Aswat woman has not fabricated the whole matter out of her madness?" Kamen pointed to me.

"Kaha spent several years in the Seer's employ. He was a part of the plot to use my mother against Pharaoh. Tell him, Kaha." At my employer's nod I did so as succinctly as I could.

"I have kept the knowledge to myself for a long time," I said finally. "I have not betrayed my former Master until now." It was a lame attempt to remind Men that as a scribe I could be trusted, but I do not think he heard my last words. He was frowning, his fingernails rattling against his cup.

"It is still not enough to take to the Prince," he said. "That is what you want me to do, isn't it? Go to the palace? But even if Ramses would consent to grant me a private audience, I could do nothing more than fill his ears with an unsubstantiated tale." Kamen leaned over the desk and I glimpsed Takhuru's agitated face framed briefly in the curve between his body and his arms.

"There is evidence," he said emphatically. "Under the floor of my mother's hut in Aswat. The body of the assassin I killed."

Men sat back. His mouth had thinned to a grim line. "You all realize that if there is some other more plausible explanation put forward, we will be in serious trouble," he said. "My Lady Takhuru. Have you anything to add?" The girl stirred.

"No," she whispered. "But I trust Kamen and I have spent some time listening to his mother. Also Paiis and his soldiers came to my house today. The General sent more soldiers here this afternoon. I beg you to help us, Noble Men." He glanced at her and then suddenly his face creased in a smile. He prodded me with his foot.

"Go and fetch Pa-Bast," he ordered. "Have you been recording this conversation on your papyrus, Kaha?" I rose and placed my palette on the desk.

"No," I said.

"Good. Be quick."

Pa-Bast was in the dining room talking with the cluster of servants. He came at my bidding, an enquiry in his eyes, but there was no time to tell him what had passed. Men got up from behind the desk as we entered. "It is obvious that you also have been seduced by this fantastic story, Pa-Bast," he said. "It seems that the world I knew has changed while I have been away. Go at once to the house of Nesiamun and ask him to come here. Do not send someone else. Go yourself. Tell him that I have returned and I need to see him urgently on the matter of his daughter's disappearance. Meanwhile we will eat." He clapped his hands. The Steward bowed himself out, and by the time we left the office he had gone.

It was customary for the senior staff, Pa-Bast, Setau, the other body servants, and myself, to eat with the family. The meal should have been a joyous occasion, but though Takhuru did her best to talk to Mutemheb and feign an interest in Tamit's artless chatter, her glance kept straying to the doorway and she ate nothing. Shesira watched her, and Men, though he fed with gusto, watched Kamen. The atmosphere of strain spread until even Tamit fell silent, and in the end the soft footfalls of the servants and the polite clink of the dishes on the trays they bore could be clearly heard.

The sound of voices and brisk steps in the entrance hall came as a relief. At once Takhuru pushed away her table and fled. With an exclamation Shesira made as if to follow her but Men stayed her with a sharp gesture. "Later," he said. "Kamen, Kaha, come with me." We went out. Nesiamun stood just within the entrance, his arms around his daughter, and when he saw Kamen his eyes widened.

"What is this, Men?" he said. For answer Men bowed and held open the office door.

"We can talk in here," he offered. "Pa-Bast, go and eat now."

Telling my part of the story to Nesiamun was far more daunting than recounting it to my employer. The Overseer of the Faience Factories was no kindly merchant. Of a high lineage and cold intelligence he stopped me frequently to ask a blunt question or challenge me with a contradiction. He could not weaken my account, of course, for I was laying the truth before him, but he gave me no quarter. When he turned at last to Kamen, his attitude was little different, but Kamen was free to answer him as his equal.

To and fro they went until at last Nesiamun said, "Paiis and I have been friends for years. I know him very well but I am under no illusions about him. He's a military genius, or would be if there were any wars to fight, but he is also a greedy and devious man. Is he treasonous and murderous also? You tell me that he is. I've known you as honest, Kamen, so I must conclude that you are either completely correct or utterly deluded by the concubine who bore you. Will you swear by your totem that you killed and buried an assassin at Aswat in order to save your own life and that of Thu?"

"Yes, I will," Kamen answered promptly. "And will you request an audience with the Prince? You are an important man, Nesiamun. He will not make you wait. The longer we hesitate, the more likely it is that the General will find my mother. If you make your submission on the grounds of your daughter's possible kidnapping, the Prince will see you at once. The city police are still searching for her, are they not?" Nesiamun nodded. "Then word of her disappearance has surely already reached the Prince's ears."

"You have thought of everything, haven't you?" Nesiamun retorted. "Did you bring her here to force my hand?"

"No, Father," Takhuru broke in. "Kamen would not do that. If you will not help, I will go to Ramses myself. He is the only one with the authority to protect us." Nesiamun turned and glared at her in surprise.

"You may not speak to me in that fashion," he rebuked her. "You are not married yet." He swung back to Men. "Surely we should approach Paiis and his brother and give them a chance to defend themselves before placing them under the eye of the palace," he said, but Takhuru grabbed his arm.

"No!" she blurted. "Father, I am afraid. You have not had time to ponder it all or you would understand. Am I not a sensible girl? Is Kamen not a truthful and upright man? You cannot believe that we would be gullible enough to be deceived by a fanciful story. Besides, there is Kaha. No one will hire a scribe with the reputation of a liar. Send to Ramses now, within the hour! Please!" For answer he rose.

"I want you to come home with me, Takhuru," he said. "I will deliberate, and give my response in the morning. Our guards can certainly protect you, if such protection is necessary." Quickly and smoothly Kamen interposed himself between them.

"Either Takhuru stays here," he said evenly, "or I will indeed kidnap her. She is right. You don't understand how vulnerable we all are. My mother is out there somewhere, sleeping in an alley or in the bottom of a boat or huddled in a doorway with the beggars. Do you think she broke her exile for no reason at all after nearly seventeen years? Will you help us or not?" Their gaze met and locked. Nesiamun did not give way, but his body loosened.

"Your sheer determination is a powerful persuasion," he said resignedly. "Very well. I will send a request for audience at once with the excuse you suggested. If you are lying or mislead, I will not be responsible for the consequences. Think of your mother tonight, Takhuru, and the pain you are putting her through, for I suppose I can tell her nothing of this conversation yet. Good night, Men." He did not wait to acknowledge Men's bow but left the room abruptly. We looked at each other.

"Do not worry," Takhuru said. Her voice was shaking. "He is angry and puzzled but if he did not believe us, he would have refused us outright and dragged me home by force. He will keep his word."

I doubt if any of us slept much that night. Kamen lay on a mattress in the passage outside Shesira's room. Shesira had asked no questions when her husband had told her that Takhuru would be sharing her quarters. Mutemheb had raised her eyebrows and cast her brother an amused look before wandering off to her own domain and Tamit, tired and fretful after a long day on the river, had gone to bed without protest. Men commanded Pa-Bast to send two of the gardeners to the main entrance of the estate with orders to turn away all callers but a messenger from Nesiamun, and he himself settled down beside the entrance to the house. He did not say so, but I could see that he was regretting the fact that he kept no soldiers in his employ. I retired to my own room where I tossed restlessly, my thoughts revolving once more around Thu.

There was no word from Nesiamun in the morning. With the return of the family the house shook off its somnolence. Men was in his office shortly after dawn, and I was with him in my usual place at his feet beside the desk. Even with the door closed and my master's strong voice dictating, I could hear the wonderfully reassuring sounds of everyday life. Tamit's high childish treble echoed down the stairs as she poured out a torrent of unintelligible protest that gradually faded under her mother's calming tones. A little later Mutemheb's musical cadences interwove with a flurry of chatter and the shushing of sandalled feet in the hall and I presumed that she had lost no time in inviting her friends to catch up on their news. Pa-Bast rebuked a servant. Someone far away in the depths of the house dropped something with a muffled crash and a curse. Life coursed through the rooms once more, a river of sanity and normality, but I knew that its cheerful flow was superficial. Beneath it was blind uncertainty.

It was hard to concentrate on my Master's words and difficult for him to keep his mind on his business. Once he stopped dictating in the middle of a sentence and looked down on me. "He kept calling that woman his mother," he said. "Did you notice? No matter how this tragedy is played out, nothing will be the same again. I must tell Shesira something soon. Kamen and Takhuru are upstairs, closeted together like two cornered animals. Why has Nesiamun sent no message?" I laid my pen on the palette.

"She is his mother, Master," I replied. "You should have told him his lineage before he found it out for himself. He is full of a protective anger on her behalf and a different kind of anger at you for lying to him. But one day he will rediscover his love for Shesira. She is in his memories, not Thu." He ran a bemused hand up the back of his neck and absently drew his fingers through the tufts of sparse grey hair.

"I suppose you are right," he agreed. "I wanted to keep him from growing up full of arrogant fantasies, but it seems I was wrong. I cannot abide this waiting! Where was I?" We continued with the dictation but he had lost the thread of his instruction and finally he dismissed me and vanished into the bowels of the house.

I did not attend the noon meal, nor did I go to my couch for the afternoon rest. I went out into the garden and lay on my back, watching birds dart by overhead against the limitless blue of the sky. I could not abide the waiting either. I wanted to rush to the palace, elbow my way past guards and courtiers, and babble out my story at the Prince's feet and so make a swift end. I was destroying my career as a scribe more surely than Kamen had risked his military future in taking the chances he did at Aswat. If he was vindicated, he would be in high favour with his half-brother, the Prince, but a scribe's career was built on trust and I had betrayed my previous Master. My motives would not matter to a future employer. Would Men continue to use me? And if not, would Kamen take me into his new household as I had secretly hoped? Such thoughts, unworthy though they might be, seemed to be reflected in the world around me so that the grass beneath me began to prick my skin and the flutter of leaves hurt my eyes. I had no family into whose bosom I might retreat, no wife in whom to confide. I was entirely dependent upon this family's good graces and therefore ultimately alone.

But towards evening a message did come from Nesiamun. The Prince had consented to see him regarding his daughter's disappearance, and he was expected to present himself at the palace the following morning. I waylaid the messenger as he was leaving. "Does anyone else know of this summons?" I asked him. He looked puzzled.

"Only my Lord's scribe and the Assistant Overseer of the Faience Factories," he told me. "They were present when the Herald arrived from the palace. Oh and, of course, the General Paiis was there also. He has been spending much time with my Master. He is very concerned with the family's troubles."

"Did he have anything to say regarding the message from the Prince?"

"Only that he was pleased my Master had wasted no time in approaching the court. He is a good friend to my Master. He has put many of his soldiers abroad to aid in the search for the Lady Takhuru." I thanked him and allowed him to go. There was no point in fretting about such a piece of bad luck. I could only pray that upon reflection Nesiamun had not taken our story more lightly than he should and had not allowed Paiis's smooth tongue to seduce him into an indiscreet word. Nesiamun was a forthright man, impatient with subterfuge, and Paiis was observant. It was possible that even if Nesiamun kept his counsel, the General might have sensed a hesitation, a discomfort, in his old friend. If so, what would Paiis do? Would he deduce the truth?

The answer came with brutal speed. The family was just finishing the evening meal when there was a commotion in the entrance hall. We rushed out to find the room full of soldiers and one of the gardeners Men had set at the front gate holding his hand to a bleeding temple. Men took one look and turned to the girls. "Tamit, Mutemheb, go upstairs," he ordered. "At once!" I caught a glimpse of their frightened faces as they did as they were told.

"I am sorry, Master," the gardener gasped. "I tried to keep them out." Blood was coursing down his cheek and soaking into the neck of his tunic.

"You did well," Men said evenly. "I thank you. Shesira, take him away and tend his wound." His wife stepped forward in protest.

"But Men ..." she began. He cut her short.

"Now please, Shesira," he said, still in that steady, quiet tone that the members of his household recognized as a symptom of extreme anger. Shesira closed her mouth. Putting her arm about the gardener, she led him away. Pa-Bast and I drew together. "State your business," Men demanded. The officer came forward, holding out a scroll. Men nodded coldly to me and I took it.

"I am here to arrest your son, Kamen, on a charge of kidnapping," the man said uncomfortably. "And before you ask, my authority comes from Prince Ramses himself."

"Impossible!" Men shouted, but I was unrolling the scroll and reading it quickly. It was sealed with the royal imprint.

"He is correct, Master," I said, passing him the offending papyrus. He skimmed it. His hands shook.

"Who has brought this charge?" Men demanded. "It is completely ridiculous! What is Nesiamun thinking of?"

"It was not the Noble Nesiamun who pressed the complaint," the officer said. "The General Paiis had words with His Highness after visiting the house of Nesiamun. The General has the strong suspicion that the Lady Takhuru is being held here."

"Where is your evidence?" Men cut in. "You cannot arrest on suspicion alone!"

"We do not need evidence in order to search your house," the man said obstinately. "If you do not turn your son over to us we will seek him here ourselves."

"No, you certainly will not," Men snapped. "Are you aware that Nesiamun has already been granted an audience with the Prince regarding this matter and is to appear before His Highness tomorrow? He does not suspect his own future son-in-law. Besides, Kamen himself is missing. I arrived home to find him gone and my staff in a desperate quandary. Did not Paiis himself send here because Kamen did not appear to take his watch, Pa-Bast?" Grim-lipped the Steward nodded. "You see? I do not know what arguments the General used to persuade the Prince to commit this outrage and I do not care. Kamen is not here. Get out of my house."

For answer the officer gestured to his men and they began to spread out. One put his hand on the office door. Two strode towards the stairs. With a cry Men sprang at them and Pa-Bast moved to bar their way. The officer drew his sword.

At that moment Kamen's voice rang out. He was standing at the top of the stairs. "No, Father, no! You cannot fight them! This is madness!" He ran down and came to a halt before the officer. "You know me, Amunmose," he said. "It is I, Kamen, your fellow. Can you really believe that I would kidnap the woman I love?" The man flushed.

"I am sorry, Kamen," he muttered. "I am simply carrying out my orders. I could make some excuse to the General, but this is a palace matter. I dare not disobey. Where have you been anyway? Where is Takhuru?"

"I am here." She came stepping regally down the stairs, every inch the affronted noblewoman. "What is this talk of kidnapping? I am staying here as an invited guest. My father knows this. Has he been notified of your intent to drag Kamen from his own home? I suggest that you return to the General and explain his mistake and I hope he receives a severe censure from the Prince." It was a brave effort and for a second I believed it might work. Amunmose hesitated, clearly nonplussed. Then his shoulders straightened.

"I do not know what is going on here," he said, "but I will leave it to the palace to sort out. You must come with me, Kamen, at least until this obvious error has been revealed. My orders are quite clear."

"No!" Takhuru shouted. "If you take him away he will be killed! He will never reach the palace! Where are you going with him?" The officer regarded her with a glint of amusement.

"Really, my Lady," he expostulated. "He is being taken into custody, not to the executioner. The General has the Prince's permission to put a few questions to him. As for you," he concluded pointedly, "if you are a guest here, then why is the city being combed for you as we speak? Go home to your father." He issued a brisk command and Kamen was flanked by an armed escort. At another command he was ushered to the entrance.

"Father, go to Nesiamun immediately and make for the palace," Kamen called. "Do not wait for the morning. Kaha, the manuscript!" Then he was gone. We stood immobile with shock. Takhuru began to cry.

"Gods, what a fool I am," Men ground out. "Pa-Bast, I am putting Takhuru directly into your care. No one must take her from you, not even her father's retainers. Kaha, get your cloak. We will take the skiff to Nesiamun's house."

I ran upstairs, but before going to my own room for my cloak, I entered Kamen's quarters. Setau was there. "I need the leather bag Kamen brought back from Aswat," I said to him hurriedly. "Get it for me, Setau. It is all right. He asked me to deliver it to the Prince and I intend to do so tonight instead of tomorrow. I will be responsible for it."

"Kamen has said nothing of its disposal to me, Kaha," he said, but he turned reluctantly to one of Kamen's chests and drew out the satchel.

"He would have taken it with him tomorrow if he had not been arrested," I told Setau, taking the bag from him. "Please trust me. And help Pa-Bast to keep an eye on Takhuru."

Swiftly I made my way to my own room, and snatching up a cloak, I wrapped it around Thu's manuscript. Then I went downstairs.

9

MEN WAS ALREADY WAITING outside, muffled in his cloak. "I have spoken to Shesira," he said as he started down the path. "If anyone comes to take Takhuru away, she is to be hidden inside the granary and the soldiers must be allowed to search without hindrance. What a damnable business this is!" I caught up with him and grasped his arm.

"Master, I do not think we should take the skiff," I said. "Paiis will have rightly presumed what our next move will be. His men will be watching your gate and Nesiamun's also, and he may even have soldiers lingering about the palace entrances. We should slip out through the rear wall and proceed behind the estates. Put a couple of well-swaddled servants in the skiff and tell them to row to Nesiamun's watersteps, but slowly. Of course, they should not speak."

"Good. Wait here," he breathed, and was gone. Before long he returned with Setau and a house servant, both wearing full-length cloaks. "Keep your faces in shadow until you are well away from the watersteps," he told them. "When you reach Nesiamun's steps, tie up but stay in the boat for a while and pretend to debate your next action. Kaha and I need time. We do not know for sure, but we believe that General Paiis's men are watching both establishments." He clapped them warmly on the shoulder and turned away and I followed him into the darkness.

Once at the rear of the gardens we used the lip of the well that was set hard against the perimeter wall to hoist ourselves up and over into the littered alley behind. It ran in a rough curve, in one direction back towards the narrow bottleneck of the Lake's entrance and in the other to the huge compound where the army lived and drilled. Many noble estates backed onto it to left and right but it was not used for traffic. It was choked with the offal and rubbish tossed over the walls by lazy kitchen servants, and inhabited by feral cats. We turned left, for Nesiamun lived close to the neck of the Lake and not far from the factories in his charge.

We met no one. Slinking along in the shadow of the succeeding estate walls, stumbling over unnameable refuse, our progress was slow. We perceived it to be less rapid than it really was, for each wall seemed to stretch away blackly forever, elongated in the tepid moonlight, and the pocked ground beneath our sandals was vague. But at last Men came to a halt, his hand on the mud brick. "I think this is it," he whispered. "I lost count somewhere. Surely that is the branch of the big acacia tree Nesiamun will not let his gardener fell. Kaha, climb on my shoulders. You will have to find Nesiamun. I am too old to go scrambling over walls."

I placed my precious bundle at the foot of the wall and removed my sandals. Men bent over, and balancing myself with one hand on the bricks, I hoisted myself up. I could just reach the branch that overhung the top of the wall. Heaving on it, I peered gingerly down into the garden. There was no movement as far as I could see. The tightly winding paths showed as dull grey ribbons weaving indistinctly through the motionless tangled shadows of shrubs and trees. I would have to be quick. Fighting the protest of muscles long unused, I managed to ease my knee onto the lip of the wall. My chin grazed the rough brickwork. With a kick I rolled and fell tumbling into the sparse grass on the other side.

I wanted to lie for a moment and catch my breath but I did not dare. Getting to my feet, I crouched and ran to the nearest cover, then I began to creep towards the house. It was not long before I saw the first soldier. He was stationed beside the path, leaning against a tree and looking towards the dark bulk of buildings. It was not difficult to work my way around behind him, but I was in terror lest I stumble on another one. I stayed away from the entrance. I was certain that several men would be sitting under the pillars and more would be dispersed between the water and Nesiamun's gate. No one would be able to leave unobserved by the main way.

At last I was touching the wall of the house itself, on the opposite side to the entrance. How was I to get in? A trained man could get onto the roof and perhaps wriggle through a windcatcher but the limit of my exercise had been a vigorous swim once a day and I was not equal to such a task. There were stairs from the roof into Takhuru's quarters, I remembered, but to use them I had to get to them. Closing my eyes, I succumbed to a momentary fit of despair. If I paced the house walls and found no way in, I would return to my Master, acknowledge defeat, and we would attempt to be admitted to the palace without Nesiamun's authority.

But as I slid around the corner, a pattern of weak light met me. It was coming from a waist-high window. Its reed mat had been lowered and the light seeped sullenly between the slats. I waited, eyes straining into the darkness beyond the reach of that light, but I could discern no human shape. Taking a chance, I crawled to the edge of the window and set my eye to one of the slits. I was looking into Nesiamun's office, a large room the limits of which were lost in gloom. Facing me and close enough to reach in and touch was his desk.

Nesiamun himself sat behind it. A scroll was open before him and his hands rested on its edges but he was not reading. He was gazing straight ahead. Carefully I scanned what I could of his surroundings. He appeared to be alone. I heard the distant murmur of voices from far beyond the invisible inner door. I tapped on the edge of the window. "My Lord," I called softly. He stirred. I pushed the mat aside. "My Lord it is I, Kaha. Can you hear me?" To his credit he did not start. Quickly he left his chair and came around the desk.

"Kaha?" he said. "What are you doing skulking in the garden? Go around to the entrance."

"I cannot," I explained quickly. "Your house is being watched by the General's men so that no one may leave. Kamen has been arrested for kidnapping your daughter. The General persuaded Prince Ramses to issue the order. We must go at once to the palace, for Paiis will murder Kamen and then seek his mother at his leisure if the Prince does not stop it. We cannot wait until the morning." He grasped the situation at once. His gaze sharpened.

"Where is Men?"

"He is waiting for us beyond your wall. His house is also under observation. He begs you to come now." For answer he bent down. I saw that he was tying on his sandals, and in another moment he had stepped out his window and was standing beside me.

Without speaking again, I led him back the way I had come, motioning him into silence as we circumvented the soldier by the path. We reached the big acacia without incident, but here he looked up at the looming height of his wall. "I cannot climb that," he said brusquely. "Wait." The shadows swallowed him and I squatted uneasily, suddenly desperate to be away from this place, but soon he returned, dragging a ladder. I rushed to help him set it in place and held it while he climbed, then I followed him, hauling the ladder up and letting it down on the other side so we could descend. Men rose from the pool of darkness where he had been sitting and the two men greeted each other soberly. I picked up my cloak and the bag.

"We had better hurry," Men said. "Sooner or later they will discover that we have slipped their net." The words sent an ominous shiver down my spine. We turned and began to retrace our steps.

Like wraiths we slipped past Men's estate and went on. Occasionally the strains of music drifted to us over the walls we walked beside. Sometimes we were assailed by the laughter and din of a feast that soon faded to be replaced by the rustle of overhanging branches and the furtive scratching of the cats that lived in that forgotten strip of the city. But at last we had passed the final estate before the huge royal and military compound began and we turned in towards the centre of the city.

By unspoken consent we took a circuitous route that led us beside the temple of Ra and into the anonymity of the night crowds. Lamplight flared out at us as we moved past the open doors of beer houses or flickered from the stalls of merchants eager to attract those citizens who loitered happily, enjoying the balmy night. But at the road that ran right, to the temple of Ptah, Nesiamun stopped.

"This is no good," he said. "We cannot hope to enter the palace complex by any back way. Every entrance, small and large, is heavily guarded and even if we could by some miracle bypass the royal mercenaries, we would be challenged again and again before we reached the Prince. Nor do we know where exactly he is. The palace is too much of a maze to go wandering about in without direction, and time is fleeing by. I think we should attempt the main entrance and I will bully the guards into taking us straight to where we want to go. If Paiis's soldiers are also hanging about there, they will have to explain to Pharaoh's men just why I should not be given admittance. I brought this." He extracted a scroll from the loose folds of his tunic. "It is the Prince's agreement to my request for an audience. It will secure us a successful hearing at the gates at any rate."

"Very well," Men agreed. "I am frightened for my son, Nesiamun. Every moment that passes is a moment in which I see his death. If Paiis triumphs, I will never forgive myself for dismissing Kamen's distress in so cowardly a way."

Nesiamun smiled coldly. "And Takhuru will never forgive me," he added. "Come then. We must head for the water."

It took us another hour to thread our way through the confusion of city streets and alleys until we found ourselves suddenly on a great green lawn dotted with palms. At its edge the Lake of the Residence lay, rippling darkly. To our left reared the mighty wall that completely surrounded the whole palace complex, but it was broken some way ahead by the tree-lined canal upon which the royal barges were tethered and up which the diplomatic commerce of the world flowed towards our God. The canal ended in a flight of broad, three-sided watersteps of marble that led up onto a wide paved court and beyond that the vast pylon that signalled the entrance to the holy domain itself.

In a tense silence we walked towards the court. A gorgeously arrayed litter, glittering in the light of the torches held by slaves, sat on the paving. It was empty, its silk curtains looped back, and its bearers stood in a knot, talking desultorily. They barely glanced at us as we approached and then passed them. Several barges were being tethered at the watersteps. Ramps clattered against the stone and across them flowed a crowd of laughing people. They dispersed around us, enveloping me briefly in a cloud of perfume and a dazzle of jewels, before trickling in under the pylon. Many of them called to Nesiamun, asking him why he was not dressed for the feast and where his wife was. The phalanx of guards protecting the entrance glanced over them keenly and then drew back.

Men grasped my arm and moved closer to Nesiamun who had fallen into step with one of the revellers and was engaging him in earnest conversation. The loud company hemmed us in. Then the shadow of the pylon passed over us and we were within the palace grounds. "If there is feasting tonight, the Prince will not be in his quarters," Men said hurriedly. "Nor will he like being disturbed."

"It is still early," Nesiamun replied. "Too early for him to go to the banqueting hall. We will try to see him before he leaves his rooms."

We had come to a place where the paved way split into three, each path running through trees and bordered by grass. Ahead, at the end of the central way, a row of columns reared, like four vast tongues of red flame in the light of the torches clustered at their bases. "The public reception hall," Nesiamun said tersely. We approached them, still a part of the cheerful throng, but we did not sweep under them. Nesiamun led us left in front of them, across the springing turf, but did not join with the left-hand path. "That leads to the harem," he said. "We must go between the harem and palace walls." He had brought us to a small gate beside the pillars where two guards in the blue and white imperial livery stood and warily watched us approach. One held out a leather-clad arm and we halted.

"If you are for the feast, you have come the wrong way," he said. "Go back to the main entrance." Nesiamun peremptorily held out his scroll.

"I am the Overseer of the Faience Factories," he replied. "I have been granted an audience with Prince Ramses." The man unrolled the scroll and read it quickly.

"Your audience is for tomorrow morning," he announced firmly. "The Prince entertains tonight. Come back at the appointed time." Nesiamun took back the scroll.

"The matter to be discussed with the Prince is very urgent," he pressed. "It has become more so since His Highness agreed to see me. It will not wait."

"Everyone wants the Prince's immediate attention," the soldier snapped. "If you were a minister or a general I would let you through, but what important business can the Overseer of the Faience Factories have at this time of day? I am sorry." Nesiamun stepped close to him.

"You do your job well," he said forcefully, "and for that the Prince should be grateful. But if you refuse us entry you will be even more sorry. At least send for a Herald. If you do not I will summon one myself." The man did not back away, but after a moment he spoke to his fellow.

"You may leave your post," he said. "Go and find a Herald." With a creak of leather and a clack of brass studding the soldier vanished into the night beyond the gate. None of us moved, but I could feel my master's tense impatience. He was breathing heavily, his thumbs hooked into his belt, and every so often he glanced over his shoulder to where more shimmering, torch-lit celebrants paraded towards the public entrance in a burst of happy noise. Nesiamun seemed calm but only, I think, in order to impress the officer barring our way. I knew that at the first sign of hesitancy we would be dismissed.

But we did not have long to wait. The guard resumed his place before the gate and the Herald saluted. "It is the Noble Nesiamun, is it not?" he said pleasantly. "I understand that you wish to have a message conveyed to His Highness. You are on the list of audiences for tomorrow you know."

"I know, but this will not wait," Nesiamun replied. "Go to the Prince and tell him that I am no longer concerned solely with the fate of my daughter. The life of a royal son is also at stake. My companion, Men the merchant, and his scribe, Kaha, will bear witness to the second matter. We beg for a few words with him at once." The Herald had been well trained. His expression did not change to either curiosity or doubt. He bowed again.

"I will speak to His Highness," he said. "He is still in his quarters but is about to leave for the feast." He strode away and the three of us drew back a little from the gate. Presently the two guards struck up a conversation with each other and ignored us. The path behind was quiet at last. Only single lights moved along it as an occasional servant hurried on his errands. I felt a wave of fatigue and my master's face in the dimness looked haggard. Was Kamen still alive? In the wash of my sudden exhaustion I did not believe so, and saw all this effort as futile.

The Herald did not come back for some time but when he did he nodded to the soldiers who stood aside from the gate. "I will take you to the Prince," he said, "but I have been commanded to caution you. If you are misrepresenting a case, you will be in peril of His Highness's extreme displeasure." His words should have warned me, but I was so relieved to be walking through the gate on his heels that I paid them no heed.

It was a short distance to the stairs that hugged the outside wall of the Throne Room and ran up to the Prince's spacious apartments. We were led across the grass, followed the palace wall, and turned around a corner. Another two soldiers stood by the bottom step but the Herald did not pause, and we followed him up the stairs. At the top was a landing and a tall double door on which the Herald knocked. It was opened and a dull light seeped out. We went through, and I found myself at one end of a dark passage that ran away to my left. Directly in front of me were more closed doors. The Herald knocked again and a sharp, authoritative voice bade him enter. The light that poured out this time was steady and strong and the three of us moved, blinking, into its radiance. "The Noble Nesiamun," the Herald announced and left us, closing the doors behind him.

In the moment before I bent, with the others, into an obeisance, I scanned the room. It was large and elegant. The walls glowed deep blue and a delicate beige, the colours of Egypt's desert so finely depicted here, and I remembered that the Prince had always loved the simplicity of our horizons and often went out alone into the sand to think or meditate or hunt. This predilection had set him apart from both his sociable brothers and those at court who had tried to plumb his mind to determine which political party he favoured in the days when his father had not declared an Heir and the ministers and powermongers scrambled to make themselves agreeable to all the royal sons.

This Ramses had wisely and modestly kept his counsel, expressing only his love for his father and his country while his brothers actively played for the throne. Hui had told me years ago that the Prince's seeming self-effacement and kindness hid an ambition as fiery as his brothers', but he was more clever and patient in his manipulations to gain his goal, winning men and women to his personality. If that was so, he had finally succeeded, for he was now Pharaoh's Heir and right hand, ruling Egypt for a father whose health was failing and who would soon leave Egypt to sail in the Heavenly Barque. Whatever dreams for Egypt's future he had he still kept to himself, but it was said that he was showing a cautious interest in the hitherto neglected army that would flower when his father died.

His furniture was also simple and expensively elegant, the chairs of gold-chased cedar, the brazier in the corner polished bronze, the triple shrine containing the images of Amun, Mut and Khonsu of gold inlaid with faience, carnelian and lapis lazuli. Lamps were everywhere, on the cluttered desk, the few small tables, standing in the corners. A scribe sat cross-legged by the desk, his palette across his knees, watching us impassively as we straightened from our reverence.

But I had no eyes for him or indeed for the Prince, for there was another man in the room, sprawled indolently on one of the dainty chairs. He came to his feet slowly with a familiar grace that sent shock bolting through me. I heard Men give a strangled grunt. My heart began to pound as I waited for the Prince to speak and release us from our desperate silence.

Paiis looked us over with a half-smile on his painted lips. "I greet you, Nesiamun," the Prince said mildly. "I was to have the pleasure of a meeting with you tomorrow but the Herald garbled some nonsense about a royal son in danger and you hanging on my gate. On General Paiis's recommendation I have already issued a warrant for the arrest of your son, Men, on a charge of kidnapping your daughter, Nesiamun, and it is only a matter of time before Paiis's men wring from him the location of the girl, so I cannot imagine why you are here together but state your business quickly. I am hungry."

"On the matter of the kidnapping, Highness," Nesiamun began, "the General acted precipitously. My daughter has been a guest in the house of Men without my permission and I beg you to rescind the warrant at once. The whole thing was a misunderstanding."

"Is that so?" the Prince broke in. "Then why is the whole force of the Pi-Ramses police combing the city for her?"

"I requested their assistance when Takhuru went missing from her home," Nesiamun replied evenly. "I did not know she was with her betrothed. She had left without a word. I am angry with her."

"No doubt." The finely feathered royal eyebrows rose. "So your son, Men, is to be blamed for nothing more than an excess of love?" He turned to Paiis who was standing with braceletted arms folded. "The young man was also temporarily missing, was he not? He did not appear to take his watch on your estate?"

"That is correct, Highness," Paiis said smoothly. "He has proved himself to be completely untrustworthy. In the end I traced him back to his father's house, where he was holding the Lady Takhuru. Men did not know that she was there."

"You bastard!" Men shouted. "It is all a lie! All of it! Where is my son? Is he still alive?"

"Why in the name of all the gods would he not be alive?" the Prince asked irritatedly. "And you." He pointed at me. "I do not know you. What are you doing here?" There was a sudden hush. Paiis was openly smiling at us but his eyes were on me and they were cold.

My moment had come. Taking a deep breath, I severed myself finally and utterly from my past.

"I beseech your indulgence, Highness," I said. "I am Kaha, scribe to my Master, Men. I think that it is my place to begin what will be a long story, but before I do, I ask you if you have ever heard these names repeated all together. The Seer Hui, the Generals Paiis and Banemus, the Royal

Butler Paibekamun, the Lady Hunro." His brows drawn in puzzlement he began to shake his head, then he paused and his expression changed. His face became immobile but his kohled eyes grew alert.

"Yes," he barked. "Continue."

So I did. With Thu's manuscript in my hands I told it all. As I spoke servants entered and left, moving quietly to trim the lamps and lay wine and honey cakes before us. No one ate. Ramses listened intently, betraying nothing of his thoughts as my voice filled the room. Nesiamun and Men stood with lowered heads, wrapped in their own emotions. Paiis watched, eyes narrowed, mouth thin, and I knew that if we did not succeed in convincing the Prince of the truth the General would exact an immediate and ruthless revenge. I was afraid but I struggled on.

Someone came to the door, was admitted, and began to speak, but the Prince raised a jewel-encrusted hand. "Later," he said, and his attention returned to me. The door closed softly. By the time I had finished my part of the tale, the Royal Scribe was surreptitiously flexing his cramped fingers and the lamps had all been replenished with oil.

Ramses considered me carefully. He pursed his hennaed lips. Then he turned deliberately to the General. "A very interesting story," he said casually. "Longer and more involved than the tales my nurse used to tell me but absorbing just the same. Paiis, what do you think of it?" Paiis's broad shoulders lifted in a disdainful shrug.

"It is a marvel of inventiveness woven with a few threads of truth to give it a poisonous sting, Highness," he replied. "I knew this man when he was in my brother's employ. Even then he was flighty and garrulous. You are, of course, aware that the woman who tried to murder the One years ago has defied her exile and is free somewhere in the city. It is my belief that she has formed an association with Kaha in order to discredit those who once showed her kindness and by lying, win a pardon. They brewed this fantasy together."

"And why would he do such a thing?" Ramses folded his arms. He was no longer looking at Paiis. His gaze was on a far corner of the bright room.

"Because he has been in love with her for years," Paiis answered promptly. "She had a facility for capturing men's baser emotions and evidently she has not lost it." A peculiar expression flitted across the Prince's face, almost a twist of pain.

"I remember her well," he said, and cleared his throat. "My father's concubine, to his undoing. I was placed in charge of the investigation into her culpability. No evidence was found to link anyone other than her with the crime." His eyes left the ceiling and swivelled to fix themselves on me. "Now why was that, if your story is true?" It seemed to me to be a naïve question, but I knew that this Prince was far from stupid. He wanted something put into words.

"Because instead of throwing the pot of poisoned massage oil away, the Butler Paibekamun kept it and gave it to you, Highness, so as to cast the blame on Thu."

"Thu," he repeated. "Yes. Gods, she was beautiful! And what was your lie, Scribe Kaha?" I dared to glance at the General. He was standing with his hands behind his back and his legs stiffly apart as though he were on the parade ground disciplining his troops.

"Go on, Kaha," he said. "Perjure yourself for the sake of a love long since swallowed by the past. Lie for this Aswat peasant." Anger gripped me for a moment, eclipsing my fear of him.

"I lied once in the past out of loyalty to you and to the Seer," I retorted hotly. "Out of loyalty, General! But I am a scribe, and still have a reverence for the truth. Do you think it is easy to stand here knowing that I am but a small minnow trying to swim in a river choked with sharks? That I can be eaten while the powerful continue to enjoy the freedom of the water? You will be granted more clemency than I, no matter how heinous your crime!"

"Peace, Kaha," the Prince put in mildly. "Egyptian justice extends without partiality over both noble and commoner. You have no more to fear from the judges than Paiis." I went down on one knee.

"Then prove it, Highness!" I cried. "My lie was this. My Master Hui told your investigators that Thu had asked for the arsenic to cure worms in the bowels and he did not suspect that she intended to use it against your father. Yet he told me, with great satisfaction, that he knew how it was to be really used, and he rejoiced that Egypt would be rid of the royal parasite." I faltered. "Forgive me, Highness, but those were his words. I am trained to remembered accurately such things. When I was asked what I knew of the matter, I repeated the lie of my Master. I also lied in the matter of the whereabouts of my Master on the night your father nearly died. Hui told us all in his household to explain that he had gone to Abydos to consult with the priests of Osiris for a week and had not returned until two days after the murderous attempt. It was not true. He was in his house all the time, and he gave Thu the arsenic with which to poison the Great God during the time he was purported to be away." I rose.

"It is certain that your word alone will not be sufficient," Ramses said. "Yet I am not prepared to dismiss this affair out of hand." He bent and whispered to his scribe. The man rose, bowed, and went out. The Prince turned to Men. "And you," he said. "What do you have to do with all this?" Men straightened.

"It is quite simple, Highness," he said. "My son, Kamen, is an adopted child. His real mother is this same Thu and his father is your father. He is your half-brother. Fate brought them together at Aswat. She told him her story, and since then the General has been trying to kill both of them for fear their testimony should carry a combined weight of honesty." Paiis burst out laughing, yet the sound had no ring of humour and the Prince silenced him with a savage and imperious gesture.

"So that is what happened to Thu's child," he said. "I have sometimes wondered but my father has kept his counsel. I repeat my earlier question now to you. What evidence is there for such a foul accusation?"

"If Kamen were here, as he should have been had the General not arrested him," Men answered, "he would be able to tell you better than I. The General sent your brother south to Aswat as escort for the very man commanded to assassinate him. Kamen began to suspect the man's true purpose, but he could not be sure until the moment when he attacked Thu. Then Kamen killed him. His body is buried under the floor of Thu's hut in Aswat. If your Highness will send men there, they will find it as I have said."

"Paiis," Ramses said. "Do you have any objection if I do as the merchant has requested?"

"Do not contribute to their fantasy, Highness," Paiis replied, and for the first time I saw the mask of his self-confidence slip. A sweat had broken out along his upper lip and he was glancing nervously towards the door. "It is all a total fabrication."

"That is not an answer." The Prince pointed at the bag now slung over my shoulder. "What have you brought, Kaha?" I did not want to part with it yet, not until I knew whether or not Paiis would triumph, but now I had no choice. Reluctantly I set it on the floor and opened it.

"Thu has spent the last seventeen years writing an account of her downfall from the time the Seer took her away from Aswat," I told him. "She gave it to Kamen and begged him to bring it to the attention of Pharaoh as she had begged so many travellers before. She did not know she was speaking to her son. Kamen took it, and like a good officer he went with it to his superior, namely the General. It disappeared. But Thu was clever. She had made a copy." I lifted it and held it out to him. "Guard it well, Highness. It is a compelling document." Ramses took it and smiled. The sight sent a chill through me, for all his divine power, all the acuteness of his perception, was gathered in the slow parting of those painted lips.

"You may sit, all of you," he said. "Take some refreshment while we wait. It seems as though I will not be feasting tonight." He snapped his fingers and a servant came forward. I did not want to sit. I was too tense. But obediently I folded onto a chair and my two companions did likewise. No one dared to ask what we were waiting for.

"You also, Paiis," the Prince said curtly. "Over there." He indicated a chair by his desk, and I noticed with a surge of hope that it was the one farthest away from the door. Paiis knew it too. He hesitated briefly, then lowered himself and crossed his legs.

The Prince seemed quite at ease in the silence that followed. He seated himself behind his desk, proceeded to unroll one of the numerous scrolls, and began to read while we watched him anxiously. The servant poured wine for us into silver goblets and passed the honey cakes. We drank a little. Suddenly Ramses said without looking up, "Is my brother still alive, Paiis?"

"But of course, Highness," Paiis responded with a mild indignation that deceived no one.

"Good," was the grunted response. The room sank into silence once more.

About an hour passed before the door opened and the scribe came hurrying forward. He was clutching a scroll. Bowing, he approached the desk. The Prince did not stir. "Your pardon, Highness," the man said, "but the archives were deserted and I had to go in search of the archivist. He was at the feast and was difficult to find in the crowd. Then it took him some time to discover the scroll you requested. But here it is." Ramses nodded.

"Read it to us," he said. The scribe unrolled it.

"To the Lord of All Life, the Divine Ramses, greetings," he intoned. "My dearest Master. Five men, including your illustrious son the Prince Ramses, are even now sitting in judgement upon me for a terrible crime. According to law I may not defend myself in their presence but I may petition you, the upholder of Ma'at and supreme arbiter of justice in

Egypt, to hear in person the words I wish to speak with regard to the charge against me. Therefore, I beg you, for the love you once bore me, to remember all that we shared and grant me the privilege of one last opportunity to stand in your presence. There are circumstances in this matter that I wish to divulge to you alone. Criminals may make this claim in an effort to avert their fate. But I assure you, my King, that I am more used than guilty. In your great discernment I ask you to ponder these names."

The scribe paused. As he did so the realization of what I was hearing suddenly broke over me and my breath caught. I had been right in my vague but persistent suspicion that Pharaoh knew who the plotters were, had known all these years, because Thu had told him. In the final extremity of her terror she had whispered the names to a scribe who had dutifully carried them to the King. That was why her life had been spared. Evidence had been lacking, but Ramses, being a merciful God, had given Thu the benefit of his doubt. She had worded her desperate last plea with grace and I had a momentary flush of pride. I had taught her well. I must have made a sound, for the Prince's head turned towards me.

Out of the corner of my eye I could see Paiis. He was no longer lounging back in his chair. He was sitting upright, hands gripping his knees, and he looked pale. The scribe went on reading, listing the names of those who had fired my youthful zeal and imagination and perverted the eager girl from Aswat. Hui the Seer. Paibekamun the High Steward. Mersura the Chancellor. Panauk, Royal Scribe of the Harem. Pentu, Scribe of the Double House of Life. General Banemus and his sister the Lady Hunro. General Paiis. Thu had not placed me or her body servant, Disenk, among the guilty, although she must have deduced at the time the part we both had played in her manipulation. Perhaps she had felt a fleeting sympathy for us as people like herself, commoners without the avenues of potential escape open to those of nobler birth. "I implore Your Majesty to believe that these nobles, among the most powerful in Egypt, do not love you and through me have tried to destroy you. They will try again." The Prince waved the man to silence.

"Enough," he said. Rising, he came around the desk and perched on its edge. "That scroll was dictated by Thu of Aswat almost seventeen years ago, three days before she was sentenced to death," he went on conversationally. "My father read it, and because of it, sent her into exile instead of to the Underworld, a fate better, I think, than she deserved. He is a just King, and would not allow execution as long as there was any doubt as to the guiltiness of the criminal. Later he showed me this scroll. We watched and waited but no further attempts were made on his august life and he began to wonder if she had lied and he should have let her die."

The royal calf began to swing to and fro, the seeds of jasper and green turquoise sprinkled over his sandals catching the light and glinting at the movement. He spread his hands, hennaed palms up. He might have been expounding on a point of government or a hunting technique, this handsome man with his dark eyes and perfectly fashioned body, but none of us were fooled. He was the Hawk in the Nest, the very understatement of his posture and casual tones only serving to emphasize his invincibility. He was the arbiter of our fate and we all knew it.

"Now this," Ramses went on. "If I were faced with a lesser crime committed so long ago I should perhaps dismiss the matter, reasoning that time and a slow maturing might render any punishment nonsensical. But treason and attempted regicide cannot be so easily ignored."

"Highness, there is no proof of either on the part of anyone named in that scroll!" Paiis broke in. "Nothing but words of envy and bitterness!" Ramses swung to him.

"Envy and bitterness?" he repeated. "It may be. But will a human being under the crushing weight of certain death spew forth lies? I do not think so, for he, or she, knows that the Judgement Hall is only a few heartbeats away." Now he slid from the desk, and leaning against it, folded his arms. "What if Thu told the truth?" he mused. "And Kaha here? What if there are plotters, and these plotters, having failed in their aim, bide their time until a new Pharaoh comes to the throne? And what if they decide that the new Incarnation of the God is not to their liking either, General Paiis? What if they make regicide a habit? No. I cannot ignore this." He came to his full height and his shoulders went back. He jerked an imperious finger at one of the patient servants. "Bring me one of my Commanders," he ordered. "And you," he pointed at another one, "go to the banqueting hall and tell my wife that I will not be eating publicly tonight. Then go to my father, and if he is not sleeping, tell him that I wish to consult him later." The two men hurried out. Paiis slid to the edge of his chair.

"Your Highness, I am the most senior of your generals here in Pi-Ramses," he said. "You do not need to send for a Commander. Command me." The Prince smiled and lifted his wine cup.

"Oh I do not think so, General Paiis," he said gently. "Not this time." He drank meditatively, savouring the bouquet, then licked his lips. "Forgive me if my trust in you should temporarily waver."

"I stand rebuked."

"Pray fervently that a rebuke is all you will receive!" the Prince shouted. Paiis did not seem perturbed. One of his eyebrows twitched. He patted his thighs twice and regained his seat. I unwillingly admired his self-control.

The Commander appeared shortly. He strode to the Prince and made his obeisance, then stood imperturbably to receive his orders. I saw his glance flick briefly in the direction of the General before returning to Ramses' face. "You are to take twenty men of my own division of Horus," Ramses told him deliberately. "Escort General Paiis to his estate. He is under house arrest." The man's expression did not change, but I saw his blunt fingers curl suddenly against the hilt of his sword. "If more men are necessary to keep him there, then detail them. The General is not to leave his arouras on pain of extreme discipline. You personally are not to leave his side until a search of his holdings is made and the merchant's son, Kamen, is found there. Kamen is to be treated with respect and brought here, to me, at once. I want a similar detachment to surround the home of the Seer. He also is under house arrest. Send to the harem guards and the Keeper of the Door and tell them that the Lady Hunro is under no circumstances to leave the precinct. The same injunction applies to Chancellor Mersura and the Scribe Panauk. Pentu the Scribe who plies his trade in the Double House of Life must be taken to the prisons of the city for interrogation."

In singling out Pentu for direct incarceration, Ramses had placed his finger unerringly on a weak link in the chain of conspiracy and he knew it. Pentu, like me, had no recourse to the higher echelons of power and would break under pressure. He had been little more than a messenger for Hui and the others, rarely entering their houses, receiving second hand from the Stewards the words he was to carry. I had seen him no more than twice during my time with Hui, and I did not think that Thu had seen him at all. He was guilty only of keeping his counsel, but he knew more than was safe. The Prince had proved himself capable of a subtle perception, and we had won the first round, Kamen, Thu and I. We had won!

"Send a captain you can trust south into Nubia," Ramses was continuing crisply. "He is to tell the General Banemus that he too is under arrest and is not to leave his post until a replacement can be found. Then he is to be brought back under guard to Pi-Ramses. I want the members of my division to join the city police in searching for a woman, Thu of Aswat. The police doubtless have a description of her. Or have you got her also, Paiis?" He did not even bother to look at the General.

"No," was all Paiis said.

"She is to be taken into the harem and guarded carefully. Are your orders clear? Repeat them. And one other thing. Send an officer and men to Aswat. They are to disinter and bring to Pi-Ramses a body that they will probably find under the hut of this same Thu. I will dictate a scroll of authority to be taken south to Nubia and one for the officer who will be in charge of Hui's house arrest." The Commander repeated the words, and at the Prince's dismissal, saluted and left. But he soon returned, and the room filled with soldiers. Paiis did not wait to be handled. He rose.

"You are making a grave mistake, Highness," he said coolly, and his eyes, as he looked at his superior, were like black glass. Ramses at last faced him directly.

"It may be so," he said, "and if it is so then you will be exonerated and restored to your position of authority and my trust. If your conscience is clear, you may rest in the knowledge that Ma'at will vindicate you. But I do not think so, my General," he finished in a whisper. "No, I do not." For a second I saw the hardness of Paiis's eyes light with a flash of clean hatred that revealed to me in all its nakedness the envy, ambition and petty arrogance that had consumed him all his life and had brought him to this end. It had not been enough for him that he belonged to one of the oldest and most revered families in Egypt. Paiis wanted to rule. Paiis wanted the throne with the army behind him.

The Prince and his General stared at each other, then Ramses' shoulders slumped. "Take him to his house," he said. We watched as the soldiers surrounded Paiis and marched him to the door. I had expected a parting glance or a word of acrimony from him but there was nothing, and in a moment the room seemed empty. The Prince turned to us. "As for you Nesiamun, Men, Kaha, go home," he said. He looked suddenly very weary. "I will take Thu's manuscript to my father, and we will read it together. When I have spoken with my brother, I will send him back to his betrothed. Go now."

"Thank you, Highness," Men said. "Thank you from the bottom of my heart." We scrambled up immediately, made our reverences, and walked out into the night. Nesiamun drew in deep breaths of the fragrant air.

"It is good," he sighed. "But I feel I have aged ten years in these few hours. You were not arrested for your part in it all, Kaha. Perhaps you will be pardoned."

"Perhaps," I answered, and followed my Master into the dimness.

Part Three

THU

10

THE AFTERNOON was still hot but not unpleasantly so when I left Nesiamun's house and walked quickly along the Lake path, feeling dangerously exposed in that elegant, quiet district. I had told Kamen that I did not fear the city, but my words had been a lie to reassure him. I knew little of Pi-Ramses. When I lived with Hui, my days were strictly regulated and my movement constrained to the house and gardens. All else was closed to me. I used to curl up against my window at night, after Disenk had smothered the lamp and gone to her mat outside my door, and gaze out into the darkness through the tangle of tree branches, wondering what lay beyond.

I had sailed through the city of course on my way from Aswat, but I had been excited and afraid and the scenes I had floated past remained jumbled together in my memory, a chaos of colour, shape and noise unconnected to that which had come before or to what followed. Sometimes the sounds of laughter and loud talk drifted to my ears from the unseen Lake. Sometimes torchlight reached me, flickering spasmodically from an illuminated barge that passed Hui's pylon all too quickly, so that in the end the bounds of my reality were Hui's walls and the city seemed a mirage to me, existing and yet ephemeral.

Later I had gone to the palace to treat Pharaoh's symptoms. Hui and I had ridden in a litter. I had begged him to
leave the curtains raised as we went and he had done so, but
there was still only the Lake path with its thin traffic and
the sun on the water and more estates, more watersteps.
When I was admitted to the harem, the route Disenk and I
took was the same. I came to know the heart of the city
well, that great sprawling complex of palace and harem, but
of the areas that fed nourishment into it through its many
tributaries I was ignorant.

Hunro had taken me into the markets once, but we had
lain on our litters and chattered, and though we had occasionally alighted to finger the wares for sale, I had taken no
note of the streets through which our escort had forced a
way for us. Why should I? For I was the Lady Thu,
pampered and protected, the soft soles of my feet need
never tread the rutted, burning surfaces over which the rest
of the populace surged, and there would always be soldiers
and servants to cross the gulf between me and the dust and
stench of Pi-Ramses.

Always. I came to myself with a grimace. Always was a
long time. The pretty litters were gone, the soldiers and
servants withdrawn, and I was about to cross that gulf
myself on feet so toughened by years of neglect that they no
longer cringed at heat or pain. Pharaoh had decreed that I
should go unshod into my exile and so remain, and that had
been the hardest shame, for the wealth and position of a
lady could be judged on many things, but the condition of
her feet was the final test of breeding and nobility.

I remembered how shocked Disenk had been at the state
of my feet when Hui first placed me in her obsessive care,

how day after day she oiled and abraded them, soaked and perfumed them, until they were as pink and pliant as the rest of me. I was not allowed to touch them to the floor in the morning without linen slippers. I could not go outside without leather sandals. More than the anxious attention she gave to my neglected hair and sun-browned skin, more than the lessons in manners and cosmetics, my feet were the symbols, to Disenk, of my peasant blood, and she was not satisfied until the day when she came to me with a bowl of henna and a brush to paint their soles on the occasion of my first feast with Hui's friends.

On that day I ceased to be a commoner, became worthy, in Disenk's snobbish but beautiful eyes, of the title Ramses later bestowed on me. Looking down on them now as I turned away from the Lake and sought a way that would lead me into the anonymity of the markets, I saw my mother in their splayed, sand-encrusted sturdiness. In one blistered, bleeding month of my exile all Disenk's work had been undone and my Lady Thu, spoiled favourite of the King, vanished once more beneath the flaying of Aswat's arid soil.

I had slowly forced myself to accept the deterioration of my body. It had been the least of my worries, faced as I was with the sudden transition from a life of idleness to one of hard labour in Wepwawet's temple, cleaning the sacred precincts and the priests' cells, preparing their food, washing their robes and running their errands every day and then returning to the tiny hut my father and brother had erected for me where I would tend my pitiful garden and perform my own chores. Yet it had caused me the most grief, not only because I was a vain creature but also because it symbolized all I had gained and then lost. I would grow old and die in Aswat, becoming as withered and sexless as the other women who bloomed early and aged too soon, the juices sucked out of them by the harshness of their lives. No chance to be sustained by the vitality of passion either, for although I was an exile, yet I still belonged to the King and could not, on pain of death, give myself to any other man.

Two things kept me sane. The first, strangely enough, was the hostility of my neighbours. I had brought disgrace upon Aswat and the villagers shunned me. In the begin-ning the adults ostentatiously turned their backs when I went by and the children threw mud or stones and shouted insults, but as time passed I was simply ignored. I had no opportunity to be absorbed back into the social life of the village and so taste again the despair, the feeling of impris-onment, that had tormented me there in my growing years. In spite of my exile I could remain aloof, convince myself more easily that I was not a part of them and the unrelent-ing cycle of their days.

The second was the story of my rise and fall. I began to write it in defence against the longing for my little son that would attack me in the hours of darkness and also to tend the weak but steady flame of hope I would not let die. I did not, could not, believe that I was fated to rot in Aswat forever, no matter how irrational that conviction was, and so night after night I wrote grimly, often through a haze of exhaustion and with swollen, cramped fingers, and hid the sheets of stolen papyrus in a hole in my dirt floor.

That floor hid another secret now, one that would save my son and give me a last chance at freedom if I had expiated my sin in the eyes of the gods and they had relented towards me. Now a hatred for the ruin of my calloused hands, my brittle, unkempt hair, the coarseness of my skin abused by sun and enforced neglect, returned with force. I found myself on the fringes of the crowds that thronged the market stalls. No one glanced at me. With my bare feet and arms, my thick tunic and uncovered head, I was just one more common citizen going about her modest business, and that very anonymity, though promising a margin of safety, filled my mouth with the taste of bitterness.

My first task was to find the Street of Basket Sellers so that I could be at the beer house promptly every third evening as Kamen had suggested. My thoughts, as I hovered beside an awning under which a stallkeeper sat dozing, began to circle him, the beautiful young man who I still could not believe belonged to me, but I thrust them away. The afternoon was advancing. I needed direction, food, a place to hide. Parental joy and pride would have to wait. I felt a sharp tug on my sheath. The stallkeeper had woken up. "If you are not going to buy anything, move on," he grumbled. "Find shade somewhere else. You are blocking my stall."

"Can you tell me how to get to the Street of Basket Sellers?" I asked him, obediently stepping back into the blinding sunlight. He waved behind him vaguely.

"Down there, past Ptah's forecourt," he answered. "It's a long way."

"Then could you spare one of your melons? I am hungry and very thirsty."

"Can you pay?"

"No, but I could mind the stall for you if you wish to refresh yourself with a cup of beer. The day is hot." He looked at me suspiciously and I graced him with the most ingenuous smile I could summon. "I will not steal from you," I assured him. "Besides, how does one steal melons? I have no sack. I do not want to sit by any temple and beg." I held up a finger. "One melon for the time it takes you to drink one cup of beer." He grunted a laugh.

"You have a persuasive tongue," he said. "Very well. But if you steal from me I will set the police onto you." My smile widened. They were after me anyway, but surely they would not be looking for a woman standing behind a stall with a melon held out in each hand to tempt passers-by. I nodded. Tying a linen cloth around his bald head against the sun, he told me what to charge and wandered away, and I took up my post in the shade he had vacated. I longed to take the knife that lay on the table beside the tumbled pile of yellow fruit and split open one of his wares, but I resisted the mouth-watering temptation. Lifting two of them, I began to cry their virtues to the milling crowd, my voice blending with the sing-song shouts of the other vendors, and for a while my troubles withdrew.

By the time the merchant returned, I had sold nine melons, one of them to a soldier who barely glanced at me before using the knife to rend his purchase and walk back into the throng. My new employer slapped down a jug of beer and produced a cup from the folds of his tunic. Rolling a melon towards me and throwing the knife after it, he poured and invited me to drink. "I knew you'd still be here," he said importantly. "I'm a good judge of character. Drink. Eat. What are you doing in Pi-Ramses?" The beer,

cheap and murky, flowed down my throat like a cool blessing and I drained the cup before wiping my mouth with my
hand and slicing into the melon.

I thanked him, and between mouthfuls of the succulent
food I told him some trite story of a provincial family who
could no longer afford to employ me and so I had come
north in search of work. My short tale was interrupted
twice by melon buyers, but the stallkeeper's ears stayed
open to me, and when I had finished both the lie and the
fruit, he clucked sympathetically.

"I knew you'd been in some noble family," he exclaimed.
"You don't talk like a peasant. If you've had no luck, I could
use you on the stall for a day or two. My son usually helps
me but he's away. Free melons and beer. What do you say?"
I hesitated, thinking quickly. On one hand I needed to be
fluid, to be able to come and go, but on the other I had no
idea how long I might be adrift in the city with no resources
other than my wits. Perhaps this man was a gift from my
dear Wepwawet.

"You are kind," I said slowly, "but I would like to wait
until tomorrow to give you an answer. I must find the Street
of Basket Sellers tonight." He was visibly offended.

"Why do you want to go there?" he said. "There are
indeed many basket sellers, but there are beer houses and
brothels too, and at night when the basket sellers go home
the street is choked with young soldiers." He looked me up
and down. "It is no place for a respectable woman." My dear
melon man, I thought with an inward twist of anguish, I
ceased to be a respectable woman the night I decided to
offer Hui my virginity in exchange for a glimpse into my
future. I was thirteen years old. I swallowed the pain away.

"But I met someone who told me that they might have work for me there," I answered, "and though I appreciate your offer, a position in a beer house would mean a place to sleep as well."

"It's your business I suppose," he said less stiffly. "But be careful. Those blue eyes of yours could lead you into trouble. Come back tomorrow if you have no luck." I thanked him again for his generosity and took my leave. I also took his knife, my thoughts returning briefly to Kamen as my fingers curled around its hilt and I thrust it into my belt and pulled a fold of my sheath over it. He had killed to save me, but this time I might have to save myself. The sun was beginning to wester, turning the dust motes hanging in the air to darts of light. Quickly I waved without looking back and lost myself in the press of people.

The Street of Basket Sellers was indeed a long way, and by the time I had found it I was tired and thirsty again. Narrow and winding, the buildings to either side of it crowding together and leaning over its crookedness, it snaked into dimness although the sun still shone red in the square before Ptah's temple. The basket sellers were loading their unsold wares onto donkeys, and the street echoed with the animals' petulant braying and the curses of the men. Groups of soldiers already wove in and out of the turmoil, young men for the most part, loud and eager, seeking the doors through which a gentle, secret lamplight fell.

As I moved slowly along, I heard music begin suddenly, a happy lilting tune that sent the blood quickening through my veins, and a little of my weariness left me. In spite of my situation I was alive, I was free. For the present, no one could order me to go this way or that, no one could command me to scrub a floor or haul water. If I wished to loiter and watch the crowd, I was free to do so, to lean against a warm wall and draw deeply into my lungs the mingled aromas of animal dung and spilled beer, male sweat and the faint sweetness of the rushes used to weave the hundreds of baskets that were piled here every day. Such a choice felt strange and intoxicating to me after so many years when my will was not my own and I savoured it carefully, putting away the thought that, of course, it could not last.

All at once my way was blocked by a soldier who came to a halt squarely in front of me and looked me up and down with a bold stare. Before I could draw back, he was fingering my hair and fumbling with my sheath in an obvious attempt to judge the size and fitness of my body. He gave me an impersonal, swift smile. "Beer and a bowl of soup," he pronounced. "What do you say?" Shame and a hot loathing coursed through me, directed not at him but at myself. For the second time that day my price had been assessed at no more than the value of the barest necessities to sustain life. If I am now worth so little, the words came whispering into my head, why not accept? What can it matter? You need sustenance, and this young man has accurately estimated the cost of the thing you would give in exchange for it. I drew myself up, although I wanted to crawl away and hide.

"No," I replied. "I am not for sale. I am sorry." He shrugged and did not argue, his lust a momentary impulse, not yet fuelled by a few hours of drinking and the jokes of his companions, and stepping around me he sauntered off. My mood of exaltation had gone and I did not linger. One last long red tongue from the setting sun slid towards me as I walked, until it came up against a bend in the street and soon faded. A jostling, whistling pack of soldiers crossed in front of me and disappeared into an open door. I looked up. The scorpion painted on the wall above seemed to want to scuttle down after them. I had found Kamen's beer house.

With some trepidation I slipped inside. It was a small, unpretentious establishment crammed with tables and benches, well lit and seemingly clean. It was still half-empty, but even as I stood on the inner step, more soldiers pushed by me to be greeted with shouts. A few quiet whores sat together in a corner. They noticed me at once and eyed me suspiciously, afraid, I suppose, that I had come to steal business from them, but after a short while they lost interest in me and went back to their appraisal of the room.

I had begun to attract the attention of the soldiers as well. Their eyes flicked over me and away and I scanned them cautiously, looking for a spark of recognition or speculation. It was possible that Kamen had already given a message to his friend to pass to me, but one by one the faces turned away.

I could not stay there. I did not know if any of them belonged to Paiis's guard but surely sooner or later someone would remember my description and rise to ask questions. This street was not a good place for me to be. The smell of soup was wafting into my nostrils from somewhere in the rear of the room and my mouth began to water but I turned and left, walking quickly away from the lamplight and into the lengthening shadows. Tomorrow I could easily steal food, and one night without it would do me no harm. I was thirsty, but the Waters of Avaris lay not far away and I could drink my fill of it if I did not care about the refuse flung into it. Better to take water from one of the temples where the priests kept huge urns filled for the use of pilgrims and worshippers. I found myself back on Ptah's forecourt with a sense of relief.

Spending a moment in prayer to the Creator of the World, I drank deeply of his water and then began to wander the city, moving gradually towards the quays and docks where I intended to shelter for the night. At first I found myself often dodging into the darkness of recessed doorways while some richly hung litter passed by, its escort before and behind to clear a path and protect its rear, a servant calling a warning before it swung into view. Often the curtains would be raised and I would catch a glimpse of thin, gleaming linens bordered in gold or silver, a jewelled and hennaed hand fluttering, the stirring of oiled and coroneted braids. I did not want to take the chance of being recognized, even after seventeen years, by any of my former harem cellmates, though it was unlikely that any of them would know me without long consideration. Sometimes I thought I saw a face I had known, painted and closed, aloof in its beauty and its privilege, but my heart told me that what I perceived was the familiarity of my past, not one small fragment of it. As I grew closer to the docks and warehouses of Pi-Ramses, the torches and processions became less frequent and I walked more freely, but my hand crept to the hilt of the knife I had stolen and remained there, for the streets and alleys were dark and the people I encountered more furtive.

At the water's edge, with the black silhouettes of barges and great rafts before me and the towering and jumbled heights of the warehouses behind, I found a sheltered corner under a pier and there I lay down, pulling my sheath close around me. At the end of the tunnel formed by the churned ground beneath me and the underside of the pier over my head, I could see the peaceful glint of moonlight on the hypnotic rippling of the Lake. My thoughts turned to Aswat, to the moon casting black shadows down the sides of the sand dunes where I shed my clothes and danced each night, danced in defiance of the gods and my fate.

A picture of my brother's face rose before my inner vision. We had always been close. He had taught me to read and write, coming home from his own lessons in the temple to share them with me in the stolen hour of the afternoon sleep. In the first flush of my ascension over Pharaoh, when I had seen Egypt coming to my feet and the future had seemed to glitter with promise, I had begged him to come to Pi-Ramses and be my scribe but he had refused, preferring marriage and work in the temple at Aswat. I had been selfishly hurt, wanting to gather him to myself as I wanted to greedily gather everything my heart and my fingers touched. But his loving detachment had been my balm and my support in the nightmarish weeks after my return in disgrace to the village and he was still my rock.

My last parting from him had been painful. He had agreed at once to lie for me, to put it about that I was lying ill in his house, although we both knew that his punishment would be severe if all did not fall out as I had hoped. Now here I was, lying sore and shivering under a pier with my life once more in ruins, and where was he? Our subterfuge had surely been discovered. Had he been arrested? Or would the mayor of Aswat, according him the affection and respect the whole village felt for him, allow him to walk free until I was either returned to my exile or vindicated before Pharaoh? Pa-ari. I murmured his name as I shifted on the hard ground. He had given me a selfless love I had not deserved and I was still repaying him with trouble.

Of my parents I dared not think. My mother scarcely spoke to me any more, but my father had borne my dishonour with the same inner dignity he had always shown, bringing me such material comforts as he could. Still, there was a wounding awkwardness between us that restricted our speech to everyday things and did not allow us to probe the wounds the years and my wickedness had opened.

The knife had worked its way against my hip and I drew it out and lay with it in my hand. What were the others doing, Kamen and his pretty Takhuru, and Kaha, who had been a welcome substitute for my brother during my months in Hui's house? And Paiis? Hui himself? I needed sleep but my mind raced on, one image replacing another, all of them carrying their burden of anguish. In the end I clutched at the vision of Kamen as it went fleeting by, Kamen before I knew that he was mine, his eyes huge in the dimness as I pressed my manuscript into his unwilling hands, Kamen kneeling on my cot, a dark shape above me as I struggled up from unconsciousness, Kamen's face, pale and contorted as blood spurted from the assassin's neck, the feel of Kamen's hand in mine, Kamen my son, my son, drawn to me against all odds, a sign of the gods' forgiveness. I was calm then. My eyes closed. Drawing my knees to my chest, I slept and did not wake until the clatter of busy feet above and the creak of taut rope disturbed me.

No one paid me the slightest attention as I crawled from my hiding place, tucking the knife out of sight and stretching to ease the stiffness out of my limbs. The early sun felt good on my face, warm and clean, and I let it bathe me for a moment before setting off towards the markets once again. I did not intend to stand behind the melon stall. I would steal what I could from other stallkeepers and then perhaps spend some time in one of the temples. Their forecourts were always crowded with worshippers and gossipers and I could sit at the base of one of the columns and pass the time listening to the talk. If soldiers appeared, I would slip into the inner court where there would be a dusky silence. I hoped that the priests would not turn me out before the hunters had withdrawn. I had not anticipated that boredom would be my enemy along with anxiety, but I could see that it was going to be hard to fill the three days before I must go to the Golden Scorpion. Perhaps I might visit Hui. The thought brought a bubble of laughter to my lips and my pace quickened.

There were many small market squares in the city, and after several wrong turns and an altercation with a man whose patient donkey, loaded with tiers of large clay jugs, was blocking the cramped alley down which I had strayed, I found myself emerging into a sunny space alive with cheerful activity. Tables were being set up, awnings unfolded, children unloading panniers of everything from freshly garnered lettuce whose delicate green leaves still quivered with drops of moisture to crudely painted images of various gods set out to catch the awestruck eye of devotees from the country nomes. Servants were already moving among the half-erected stalls, empty baskets under their arms as they scanned the produce that would end up on the dining tables of their masters, and a small group of men and women had begun to gather in the shade at the far side of the square to await the prospect of employment.

Few glanced at me as I threaded my way through them all. The mouthwatering smell of broiling fish enveloped me as I sauntered past a man bent over the brazier on which it sizzled but I could not snatch hot food. Nor was there any point in running away with one of the ducks piled limply on another stall, for even if I had used the knife to gut one, I could not build a fire on which to cook it. I settled for a handful of dried figs, a loaf of bread and a few discarded leaves of lettuce, for though the owners of the fig and bread stalls had been engaged in their morning gossip and had not noticed my nimble fingers, the man on the lettuce stall stood behind his wares with a stony expression of vigilance on his face and all I could do was gather up the leavings scattered about behind him.

Retreating from there quickly with my meal, I walked a short way until I came to a Hathor shrine. At that hour the goddess's small domain was deserted and I was able to sit on the ground with my back against her niche and eat in peace. By the time I had finished, however, a few women had come to do homage and I was forced to escape from their disapproving looks. My stomach was now pleasantly full, but after my night under the pier I was filthy, my hair full of dust, my feet and legs grey, my sheath stained, so I began to move towards the Waters of Ra on the west side of the city where I hoped to be able to bathe in relative privacy. I knew that military barracks were strung out along part of the Lake of the Residence and the Waters of Avaris on the east side and also beside the Waters of Ra, but to their south were the conclaves of the poor, spilling north from the ruins of the ancient town of Avaris, and there I would be entirely ignored.

I went slowly, my way impeded by the necessity of evading the small patrols of soldiers bent on business that probably had nothing to do with me but who I feared nonetheless, so that I did not come upon the western edge of the city until the sun stood overhead. Here, on the muddy verge of the water, I paused. Far to my right through the few stunted, drooping trees I could see the protecting wall of the military establishment. To my left and behind me was a maze of mud brick shanties set without order in a hot, grass-less waste of noise and confusion. I had strode through it boldly, for the inhabitants were for the most part harmless, unlike the night denizens of the docks. They were peasants who had left their villages for the imagined delights of the city or the poor of the city itself, law-abiding and self-suffi-cient. The patch of packed earth on which I stood was deserted, baking in the sun, but I knew that in the evening the women would bring their laundry here, beating it on the stones just beneath the surface of the water while their naked children shouted and splashed around them.

For the present I was alone. Untying my belt I pulled the sheath over my head with relief. I buried the knife temporarily in the wet sand where the water lapped, and with my sheath in my hand I waded quickly past the rocks, feeling with a gasp of mingled shock and delight the blessed coolness creep up my thighs and over my stomach to caress my breasts. I could not help gulping it down as my head went under.

For a while I simply hung there, letting the water insinuate itself into every crevice of my body, loosening the soil even as it woke and restored me, then I did my best to scrub myself and my sheath. I had no natron, no brush, only my hands. When I had taken my fill of the water, I clambered out, dressed myself in the clinging, sopping linen, and sat in the thin shade of a sickly acacia bush, forcing my fingers through the tangle of my hair. When it lay in a semblance of tidiness below my shoulders, I got up and followed the water in the direction of the barracks. Fed and cleansed, I wanted to sleep.

The rear of the military enclosure was already casting a shadow as the sun slipped from its zenith, and I kept close to the wall, hearing on the other side the occasional neighing of chariot horses, shouted commands, the startling bray of a horn as the army pursued whatever occupations filled its time when the country was at peace. Coming to the vast gates and the paved way leading inside, I crossed it without a tremor and went on. Paiis's soldiers were not quartered here but in the barracks on the other side of the city. If things had not changed, it was Prince Ramses' Division of Horus and the Division of Set performing the manoeuvres drifting to my ears, twenty thousand men to be fed and watered and kept occupied lest their unrest spill over into wanton violence. I wondered how many of them were rotated to the eastern and southern borders and whether the Prince had any more interesting plans for them once his father died.

Fleetingly I thought of Pharaoh and experienced a moment of vertigo. How could it be that I had ever lain beneath him on his fine white sheets in that vast bedchamber, my nostrils full of the scent of incense and perfume and his sweat while about the golden walls, discreetly invisible, his servants waited to answer the snap of his fingers. Ramses! Divine King, with your large kindnesses and your unpredictable callousness, do you ever think of me and regret that I was nothing but a dream?

For some time now I had been aware of another wall that had appeared on my right, higher, smoother than the one on my left, and suddenly I realized that beyond it lay the palace and its gardens, the city within a city that sprawled, forbidden and enclosed, across the whole breadth of Pi-Ramses until it met the Lake of the Residence on the other side. I had come upon its rear, and surely if I tossed a pebble it would rattle down upon the roofs of the concubines' cells. Straining my ears, I listened, with a mixture of revulsion and longing, for those remembered sounds that had sometimes troubled my sleep in my hut at Aswat—the laughter of women, the cries of the royal children playing by the fountains, the music of harp and drums—but it was the hour of the afternoon sleep and the precincts were quiet. I trailed my fingers along the wall as I went, as though their tips could see through the stone when my eyes could not. Did Hatia, mysterious Hatia, still sit motionless just within her door, swathed in black linen, the ever-present jug of wine beside her and her slave behind? Were the two little concubines from Abydos, Nubhirma'at and Nebt-Iunu, still in love with each other and did they still spend the hour of the sleep, this precious hour, satiated in each other's arms? And what of Chief Wife Ast-Amasereth with the voice of mixed gravel and honey and the curiously attractive uneven teeth? Did she still inhabit the spacious apartment above the cells of the lesser women and spend this hour sitting silently in her ornate chair, her full, outrageously hennaed lips slightly parted as she pondered the complex web of spies she had woven about us all?

Then there was Hunro the dancer, lithe, restless Hunro with whom I had shared a cell and a lethal secret. Her seemingly artless friendship had been a sham. Beneath her warmth was a deep disdain for my peasant roots, and when I had failed to murder the King, when I became useless, she had turned from me with relief. At the thought of her my fist clenched and my contact with the wall was broken. It was a place of terror, the harem, as well as unimaginable luxury, and I never wanted to see its lush interior again.

I had come at last to a corner and peered around it cautiously. The wall ran on, shielding the kitchens and palace servants' quarters, but I did not want to follow it for ahead of me, across an expanse of lawn dotted with doum palms, was the familiar bulk of Amun's temple. The air above it was shimmering from the myriad incense stands that poured out their silent prayer to the greatest of all the gods, and the sound of chanting came to me, faint but clear. Gratefully my punished feet sank into the cool grass. At the back of the sanctuary wall I found a secluded corner screened by bushes, and placing the knife against my chest, I curled up and was almost instantly asleep.

I woke with something cold and damp being thrust against my cheek, and even before I had opened my eyes the knife was in my hand and I was struggling to my feet with a thudding heart. The culprit was a sleek brown dog with a long, enquiring nose and a collar studded with turquoise and carnelian around its neck. I could hear an imperious voice calling, and I did not wait to see who might come looking. Pushing the animal away, I sidled around the bushes and then ran, coming with a startling suddenness upon Amun's wide forecourt. It was crowded with evening worshippers, and I realized that I had slept the afternoon away, miraculously undiscovered. I had been very stupid.

For a moment I stood shaking on the edge of the milling people, then pulling myself together, I skirted them and headed once more for the centre of the city. Kamen must send me some encouraging message on the following night, for I was becoming nervous and tired. Fits of despair stalked me and panic itself was not far away. I could not evade Paiis's soldiers or continue to wander aimlessly about forever, and at that realization the idea of retreating to the one place Paiis would not expect to find me returned.

I would wait until dark, and then I would slip into Hui's grounds. Perhaps right into Hui's house. After all, I knew it as well as I knew my miserable little hut at Aswat. Better, in fact, for its tiled floors and painted walls had often been more real to me than the rough box in which I had endured the last seventeen years. Why not? I asked myself as I joined the vociferous throng pushing to acquire the last produce of the day. He has no guards. He is too arrogant for that. The reputation of his wizardry keeps the populace away from his door, but I am not afraid of the power of his gift. I can easily avoid his porter, and then I will be in the safety of his garden, away from crowds and dirt and soldiers.

But such reasons were spurious, I knew, for deep within me was a thirst to see him again, the man who had been my father and mentor, lover and destroyer, and the need was greater than sense. Would I kill him, or bury my face in his beautiful white hair? I did not know.

Once the idea took hold of me, I could not be still. My appetite fled, and so did my desire to hide myself in crowds. Taking the alleys, I worked my way east and slowly, slowly, the light went from dazzling to muted, from pink to pale orange to red, and by the time I reached the long path that ran behind most of the great estates the sun had gone.

I could not scale Hui's wall, and his gardeners assiduously trimmed the trees that might have hung over into the alley. The only way in was under his pylon, and that meant circumventing the Lake guards. As the sky darkened, pale stars became visible one by one, and under their white pricking I retraced the short way I had come along the path and headed for the water. I did not yet attempt the guards. I would stay hidden under the spreading sycamores that shaded passers-by until their watch changed and hope that in their momentary relaxation I could slide beyond them.

With the knife in my lap I waited for a long time. Through the tracery of leaves I could see the two men, one each side of the path, and hear their sporadic conversation. They were bored and tired, ready for a hot meal and their own hearths. The traffic on the water grew as the inhabitants of the Lake embarked in their skiffs and decorated barges for a night of feasting, and for a while the same was true of the path. Torchlit groups sauntered past me like glittering butterflies, speaking of light, thoughtless things, and I envied them their privilege with a bitterness I had conquered during my exile but that came back to me now in all its evil power. I had been richer than they, greater than they, and I gritted my teeth and reminded myself that it was through my own fault that I had lost it all.

Nevertheless, not my fault alone. I watched the night guards approach with a cold anticipation.

The four men drew together and the watch being relieved began to give the report. Quietly I got up, and stepping into the water, not taking my eyes off them, I waded past. I had to go slowly so that my steps made no sounds of washing, and in the space between the trees I crouched so as not to be silhouetted against the sky. But I regained the path further on without incident. They were still talking. Rounding a bend in the path, I drew a sigh of relief and set off for Hui's entrance.

The night was still young and it occurred to me that Hui might be entertaining. So much the better. I could wander about the garden, perhaps sleep a little, and by the time he took to his couch he would be less likely to wake at any small betrayal of my presence. I began to examine the layout of the house in my mind as I walked, wondering where I might best enter, and by the time I had decided on the secluded rear entrance I was standing before his pylon.

Despite the assurance I had given myself earlier that I was not afraid of his Seeing power I paused, for in spite of an almost moonless sky the pylon cast a gloomy and vaguely threatening shadow and the garden beyond was lost in blackness. I looked to where the old porter lurked in his alcove just past one of the stone uprights and saw the faint glow of a fire. If the man was cooking a meal or even just gazing into the embers, his night vision would be temporarily ruined. Stupid Hui, I smiled grimly to myself as I glided under the pylon and immediately sought the grass to either side of the path where my footsteps would be muffled. Stupid, arrogant Hui. Every gate in this district has its guards but yours. What makes you so sure that you are invulnerable?

I was momentarily disoriented as the shrubbery closed around me, but my feet knew where they were, and I had not gone far before the confusion left me. I was behind one of the hedges that lined the path to the house. I could see it all laid out in my mind's eye: the shrine to Thoth, the fish pond among the flower beds to the left, the larger pool where I had swum my lengths every morning under the lash of Nebnefer's critical tongue to the right, across the path and over the other hedge. And at the end a low wall dividing garden from courtyard and house. Keeping to the grass, I padded beside the fish pond, the lily and lotus pads indistinct shapes on the surface of the cloudy water, and pushing through the thick bushes that flourished between the trees along the wall, I looked out on the deserted courtyard and the mass of the house beyond.

Nothing moved. The gravel of the courtyard gave off a faint luminescence, but under the pillars fronting the house all was dark. There would be a servant sitting before the door, of course, to receive guests and summon litters when they wanted to leave. No litters or bored bearers waited in the courtyard. Silence filled all the spaces my eyes tried to pierce, a silence I remembered suddenly as being peculiar to Hui's domain, full of the quality of timelessness. I had to fight against the feeling of womblike security it brought to me. Once this had been my home, a whole world of safe dreams and exhilarating discoveries under the mantle of the Master's protection. Or so I had thought.

I withdrew and lowered myself onto the lawn. It was not possible that he had gone to bed. It was too early. Perhaps

he was working in his office and I could not see the glow of
his lamp from where I was. And then I remembered that he
did employ one guard, a man who stood outside the office
door every night, for inside the office was that other room
where Hui kept his herbs and physics. And his poisons. The
door to that room was secured by the intricate knots he had
taught me, but a determined knife could sever rope and the
guard was an extra insurance against anyone foolish enough
to attempt to break in. The outer office opened directly
onto the passage that ran from the rear of the house
through to the entrance hall and if I tried to enter that way
I would be seen at once. I would either have to go in before
Hui closed the office or wait until the servant at the foot of
the pillars left his post and slip in the front.

At that moment there was a commotion on the path,
torchlight and the murmur of voices, and I crawled to peer
over the wall once more. As I cautiously lifted my head, the
house burst into life. The doors opened, pouring light onto
the gravel. A large shape appeared and stood expectantly as
the gate to my right creaked and four litters swayed across
the courtyard to be set down in front of the pillars. The
curtains were pulled apart and a cold shiver took me, for it
was Paiis emerging with the impudent grace I remembered
so well, and I had no eyes for the other guests also setting
their sandalled feet on the ground and walking towards the
figure waiting to greet them.

He had not changed much. His body was perhaps a little
thicker, and I could not tell whether his mane of black hair
was shot through with any grey, but the face he turned briefly
to the woman behind him was as startlingly handsome as
ever with its alert black eyes, its uncompromisingly straight

nose and the full mouth that always seemed on the verge of a sneer. He was wearing a thigh-length kilt of scarlet linen and his chest was hidden under a mat of gold links. His animal allure no longer fascinated me as it had when I was younger, for I knew it for the shallow thing it was. All the same his blatant, rather tawdry beauty still made a purely physical impact. He put an arm around the bare shoulders of the woman and raised the other in greeting. "Harshira!" he called. "Pour the wine! Are the nut pastries hot? I am in the mood to celebrate tonight. Where is my brother?" The woman reached up and muttered something against his ear that made him laugh, her own hand going to his muscular stomach, and they passed into the hall followed by the other revellers. The doors were closed, but light now diffused through the side windows, and I heard distant music begin.

I gave them time to settle before their low, flower-laden tables, to exchange pleasantries with their host, to down a quantity of the wine I knew was the best to be had in the city. I gave Harshira time to cross and recross the hall, shepherding the servants with their laden trays, and then to take up his station behind the closed doors of the dining room. I gave the litter-bearers time to put their backs to their conveyances and become drowsy. Then I unfolded from the grass, climbed easily over the wall, and walked across the courtyard.

As I had surmised, the man under the pillars had retired. I pushed open the main doors, entered the house, closed the doors behind me, and strolled over the spotlessly gleaming tiled floor with its evenly spaced white columns. Nothing had changed. Hui's elegant furniture, the cedar chairs inlaid with gold and ivory, the little tables topped with blue and green faience, were still scattered artfully about. The walls still smote with their profusion of frozen men and women with cups raised to their mouths and flowers in their hair, inscrutable cats beside them and naked children tumbling at their feet.

The stairs ran away from me into darkness on the far side of the hall, and as I approached them, I could hear the buzz of laughter and conversation interspersed with the trilling of a harp and the clatter of dishes coming from my right. I did not try to eavesdrop. A mood of icy calm was on me, a feeling of almost impudent omnipotence. One of the servants had dropped a sweetmeat from his tray and I picked it up and ate it as I went. I did not even concern myself with the slap slap of my bare feet on the tiles. Moving deliberately, I mounted the stairs. I did not need illumination. Times without number I had gone up and down these steps, not running, for Disenk did not allow me to proceed in anything but a sedate and ladylike manner, and memories rose with me as I gained the upper landing and passed confidently along it.

Coming to the door of my old room, I pushed it open. The window was uncovered, and the dull light of the stars was diffusing through it so that I could see the surface of my table under it where I used to eat with Disenk hovering behind me to make sure that I observed the proper manners. She would sit at it in the red flush of sunset, her head bent over my sheaths, sewing up the seams I had rebelliously torn, for my stride was long and I did not like to take the mincing little steps she required. Eventually Hui had reprimanded me and I had capitulated mutinously to the dictates of gentility.

The couch was still there also but it had been stripped to its bare wooden frame. The mattress, the smooth linen sheets, the deep pillows, had gone. No covering was on the floor, no chests, no evidence of occupation. For a moment I imagined fondly that Hui had ordered the room to remain unused out of sentiment, but then I laughed softly aloud. Thu you are still a conceited idiot, I told myself. There are no tender emotions for you lingering here. Two of your would-be murderers are downstairs, feeding off dainty victuals and congratulating themselves on yet another scheme, and you are here only for revenge. Grow up!

Yet I stood there for a long time in the almost complete darkness, probing the atmosphere for some trace, however faint, of the girl I had been. But no scent of the myrrh with which Disenk had anointed me came to my nostrils, no briefly glimpsed flick of gossamer linen disturbed the shadows, no cry of delight or pain or remorse echoed to my inner ear. The only familiarity lay in the dimensions of a room that had otherwise become dumb and anonymous. It did not even seek to reject me, but presently I sighed and left it, regaining the passage and turning away from the stairs to where another set of steps led down to the bath house. They too were full of a close blackness, but the bath house itself, open along one side to the small courtyard at the rear of the house with its single palm tree lifting stiff branches, was relatively light.

Here I sucked in a long, slow breath, for the damp aromas were a combination of perfumed oils and scented essences holding only sensuous memories. How long had it been since any hands other than my own had touched my body to perform the wholly gratifying rituals of cleansing and massage? Every day I had stood here on the bathing slab while servants had scrubbed me with natron and poured sweet warm water over me, and then with rosy skin and tousled wet hair I had gone out into the courtyard where the young masseur waited. Disenk would carefully pluck out my body hair and the masseur, his hands ruthlessly expert, would stroke and pummel the fragrant oil into every pore. Life had been good then, full of promise for a beautiful and ambitious girl.

I circled the room, the soles of my feet welcoming the wet coolness of the stone floor, and lifted the lids from the many pots and jars on their stone ledges. Shedding my sheath, I dipped a jug into one of the great urns full of water, took a handful of natron, and stepping up onto the slab I abraded and rinsed myself, working the salts into my hair as well. When I had finished, I plunged my head directly into the urn, then reached for the oil. My skin drank it greedily, and so did my hair. I sat on the slab and braided my tresses.

There was a chest just by the foot of the stairs and I opened it and drew out the contents. There were a couple of male tunics and crumpled male kilts but there was also a long, light summer cloak and a narrow sheath, so sheer that only my eyes told me that my fingers caressed it. Harshira thought of every comfort for his master's guests, including the possibility of a bath after a night of strenuous feasting. Tossing my coarse servant's attire into a corner, I drew on the sheath with reverent hands. It slid down my freshly oiled body and settled against my curves as though it had been made for me alone. With its silken texture pressed against me I wished I had a mirror, for I felt for the first time in years the stirring of the Thu I had been. I rummaged again in the chest for sandals but could find none, and then decided it was just as well. Sandals would be too noisy, and besides, my feet had become unaccustomed to wearing them and if I was forced to run they would slow me down.

I was ready. Retrieving the knife from the place where I had laid it, I went back up the stairs, along the passage, and brazenly down into the entrance hall. The outbursts of laughter and talk were louder now, the music more strident. Hui's wine was flowing freely in the veins of his friends. At the foot of the stairs I turned sharply left and joined the passage that ran straight through to the rear gardens. I passed the office door, the smaller door that probably still led into the cell of Hui's body servant, and came to the imposing double doors of Hui's own bedchamber. Without pausing but without haste I pushed them open and went in.

I had been here in his sanctuary only once before on a day I did not wish to remember, but I could not help glancing right first, towards the connecting door that led into the body-servant's room. Kenna had died in there, Kenna the sulky with his venomous tongue, jealous of Hui's attention to me, hating me and protective of the master he adored. I had murdered him in my panic lest he should drive a wedge between Hui and myself and I should be sent away. I had not intended to kill him, only make him very sick, but I had been an amateur in those days and the mandrake had been too strong. I need not have resorted to such a desperate measure after all, for I did not realize that I was far more valuable to Hui than his body servant. Kenna's death sat on my conscience with a weight that my attempted murder of Pharaoh did not. It had been a cruel and senseless act.

The connecting door was shut, but I had no doubt that the current body servant was behind it, waiting for Hui to see his guests off and come to bed. I would have to be very quiet. I looked to the centre of the room. The massive couch still stood on its dais. Its sheet had been turned down. A lamp burned steadily, filling the space around it with an inviting glow. The walls were still alive with the paintings I remembered, lush depictions of the joy of living: vines, flowers, fish, birds, papyrus thickets, all in shimmering colours of scarlet, blue, yellow, white and black. A few gilded chairs sat about, flanked by narrow mosaicked tables set with other lamps, unlit. Someone had tossed a woollen cloak over one of the chairs. Its soft white folds pooled on the ground.

A full goblet had been placed on the table by the couch. I could see its blood-red contents glinting. Gliding across the cool, blue-tiled floor to the dais, I stepped up and thrust my nose close to the liquid. I inhaled carefully but could detect no hint of a soporific mixed with the wine so I picked it up and drank. The taste was pure Hui, dry, expensive, utterly slaking, and before I realized it I had drained the cup. Shrugging, I set it down then looked about for a suitable hiding place. There was none. A few ebony chests lined the walls, but though they were large, I did not think I could fit into any of them.

The cloak caught my eye. Voluminous and thick, it gave me an idea, and I went and stared at it thoughtfully then grabbed it up and carried it to the chest farthest away from the lamplight. I draped it this way and that over the edge until I was satisfied that I could crouch in the angle between it and the side of the chest. Then I crawled beneath it. On hands and knees, my face pressed to the tiny slit I had left in order to see into the room, I felt it resting gently on my shoulder, and all at once my nostrils were invaded by the delicate scent of jasmine, Hui's perfume. I closed my eyes as a wave of longing for him swept over me, and taking the soft fabric between my fingers I drew it to my lips.

It was no good. Only the first thirteen years of my life had been spent without the knowledge of him, and the time before that was nothing more than an ephemeral mirage to me, without clear form or substance. He was the grounding, sometimes conscious, sometimes unwitting, of everything I had been and was now and would be until I died, no matter how hard I tried to exorcise him from my ka. I put my back against the wall, drew up my knees, and set the knife beside me. Then I waited.

II

I CROUCHED there for a long time, sometimes sitting, sometimes kneeling, gritting my teeth against the cramps that soon began to shoot through my protesting limbs but afraid to leave my hiding place and stretch them for fear I would be discovered. Once the doors opened without warning and my heart leapt into my mouth, but it was only a servant come to trim and replenish the lamp and he left again without so much as a glance into the rest of the room. I tried to doze, but my position and my state of mind made any relaxation impossible, so I continued to huddle with the knife cradled between thighs and stomach, wondering in the end what madness had impelled me here.

But he came at last, stripping the wilted kilt from his waist and tossing it onto a chair as he approached the couch. Sighing, he passed both palms over his face then pulled the white ribbon from his braid and shook his hair loose. He called sharply and the other door opened to admit the body servant. Silently the man reached up and unfastened the moonstone pectoral from his master's neck and slid the silver bracelets from the outstretched arms. Hui stepped out of his sandals. "I'm tired," he said. "Leave all this until the morning."

"Do you require poppy, Master?" Hui shook his head.

"No. And I don't want any more wine either. Take the cup away. Drink it yourself, if you like." The man went to the table and lifted the vessel, then paused. From my narrow vantage point I could see his face quite clearly. He was about to speak but then thought better of it, for it was obviously his responsibility to see that the goblet was left full. He looked puzzled, held it high against his chest, turned, and bowed.

"Thank you, Master. If there is nothing more, I shall go." Hui gestured, and a moment later he was alone.

He moved out of my sight, but from the sounds he made I presumed that he had gone to the window. In the span of quiet I hardly dared to breathe. Presently I heard him sigh again and murmur something. The rattle of his fingernails against the frame was distinctly recognizable, and immediately afterwards he was back in the line of my vision, standing by the couch. He was still startlingly, exotically beautiful with the unrelieved whiteness of his skin, the ashen ivory of the hair that rippled down his spine and tendrilled against his collar bone.

He bent to blow out the lamp, curving his long fingers around it, and his features were fully illuminated in that instant. The lines to either side of the soft, sharply delineated mouth I had dreamed of kissing and that had only twice been laid against mine were perhaps deeper. That was all. Time had been kind to him, the man who was himself the Master of the future, and I was so suddenly and painfully flooded with the helpless, remembered desire for him that I must have made some sound, however small, for in the act of extinguishing the lamp he stopped, still bent, and stared straight ahead. For one delirious moment his hooded eyes seemed to gaze directly into mine, glittering red and suddenly alert, but then he exhaled and the flame died. In the blinding darkness I heard him get onto the couch. I closed my eyes so that they might adjust more quickly, and when I opened them again I could make out the square of lighter greyness on the floor from the uncovered window and a portion of the dais.

Hui's breathing slowed and became regular, but the conviction that he was not sinking into sleep, that he was lying there with his eyes open, waiting for me, gradually took hold. With a sickening wash of terror I remembered the first time I had confronted him. He had come to Aswat to consult with the priests of Wepwawet on behalf of Pharaoh. The village had been in a frenzy of speculation about the famous and mysterious Seer whom few had seen, how he always went about swathed in linen from head to toe like a freshly wound corpse in order to conceal some dreadful deformity. I had already decided to seek him out and ask him to see into my future, for my desperate fear of remaining in Aswat for the rest of my life, birthing babies like my mother and growing coarse and old before my time, was greater than my dread of the monster the women's whispers had magnified. I had left my parent's house at Aswat in the middle of the night and swum to his barge, clambering onto its deck and creeping into the dark, stifling confines of the cabin. But then I had stood staring at the vague mound under the sheet, paralyzed with the same terror sweeping over me now, for he had known, even in his sleep, that someone was there.

Swallowing, I fought the panic. Be sensible, I told myself. How can he possibly know that you are here? The man who trimmed the lamp did not know. Neither did the body servant, and nothing has changed since he left the room. All the same, the certainty that he was aware of me grew until I felt myself shrinking against the wall, urgent for invisibility. The knife grew slippery in my grasp. I wanted to cry.

Then, just when I knew I must fling the cloak aside and scream and scream, he spoke. "Someone is there," he said, his voice perfectly calm. "Who is it?" In the pause that followed I bit my lip and squeezed my eyes shut in a paroxysm of dismay. All at once he began to laugh. "I rather think that it is Thu," he went on conversationally. "You had better show yourself so that you may deliver whatever acrimonious speech you have prepared and I can get some sleep. "

Pushing the cloak aside I crawled forward resignedly, biting back a groan at the ache in my legs as I willed them to move. Coming shakily to my feet, I stood trembling, such a tumult of emotions churning in me—love, rage, fear and the unwelcome familiarity of a child's hesitation—that I could hardly think. "I was right," his voice continued out of the gloom. "It is my little Thu, come home to roost like some bedraggled desert bird. Not so little now, of course, are you?"

"You betrayed me." I wanted the words to be strong and forceful, but I heard myself croak them instead. "Damn you, Hui, you used me and betrayed me and left me in the harem to face humiliation and trial and a sentence of death. You raised me, you were everything to me, and you abandoned me to save your own skin. I hate you. I hate you. I have spent the last seventeen years thinking about killing you and now I am here to do it." The knife was no longer clumsy in my grip. Tightening my hold on it, I stepped towards the dais, but as I did so I was half-blinded by the dazzle of light that flared suddenly. Hui was sitting up with tinder in his hand, and the flame in the lamp once again steadied to a yellow glow.

For what seemed like an eternity we stared at one another. His expression was one of mild amusement, yet behind it I could sense wariness and perhaps, yes perhaps, a little sadness? I felt my fingers grow numb around the hilt of the knife. As before, so very long ago, I was frozen in place, unable to move.

I remembered him standing naked in the river under the moonlight, all glistening silver as he raised his arms to his totem, the moon. I remembered him sitting behind his desk in the office, framed in the greenery outside the window, his face stern as he reprimanded me. I remembered the way his hair fell over his cheek as he bent above his pestle, all his concentration fixed on the herbs he was grinding, while around us spun the sweet and acrid aromas of that inner sanctuary where he was most himself. I swallowed. "Well?" he prompted, his eyebrows rising. "Is your knife not sufficiently sharp? Shall I call for a whetstone? Or is your will not sufficiently hardened? Are you remembering the good things instead of those times that must surely sear your honest peasant soul? Memory is an implacable weapon, my Thu. Are you going to stab me or not? You have had plenty of practice in murder you know. This should be easy." As always, he had shown an uncanny ability to read my thoughts. My shoulders slumped.

"Oh Hui," I whispered. "Oh, Hui. You have not changed. You are still arrogant and cruel and insanely self-confident.

Did you not wonder, even once, how my life was unfolding in Aswat? Do you feel no remorse for what you did to me?"

"Of course I wondered," he answered crisply, sliding from the couch and reaching leisurely for the kilt he had discarded earlier. "But I know you very well. You survive, my Thu. You are the tough little desert flower that can suck life from the most meagre surroundings. No, I did not worry about you. As for remorse, you failed your task in the harem and I did what I had to do. That was all."

"Make up your mind," I said drily. "A moment ago I was a bedraggled desert bird." He looked me up and down with a cool, deliberate assessment, and in spite of my half-humorous retort I had to inwardly steel myself for the mocking comment I knew would come.

"How old are you now?" he demanded. He had finished fastening the kilt about his waist and had flung himself into a chair and crossed his legs. His calves were still taut, the white feet high-arched and long. I did not dare do more than notice them out of the corner of my eye, for I did not want my weakness to show.

"I am in my thirty-third year," I said. "But you did not need to ask. I was thirteen when you picked me up out of the Aswat mud and seventeen when you flung me back into it."

"Your temper has not improved," he commented.

"Evidently not," I snapped, "for if it had I would not be standing here without paint or jewellery or a pair of sandals on my feet. Why don't you say it, Hui? You cannot wait to tell me how much of a wreck I have become." To my credit, the tremor I felt did not reach my voice. He began to smile, but his eyes remained unreadable.

"So the temple drudge is still vain," he drawled. "Your skin is as rough as a crocodile's. Your feet have spread. They are no longer delicate and the bones can no longer be easily seen. Your hair is only fit for bees to hive in. You are a rather disgusting shade of cinnamon and no noblewoman would dream of employing you in any other capacity than that of kitchen assistant. But, my Thu, the ghost of the woman who fired Pharaoh's lust can still be seen and with care she could be resurrected. Her blue, blue eyes could still trouble a man's dreams." I searched his face, not knowing whether he was sincere or indulging in the viciousness peculiar to him. Did my eyes trouble his dreams? For though his smile was gentle, I could not tell if it was also patronizing. "Do not fret," he went on smoothly. "You look no worse than when you first came to my house. A few months with someone as skilled as Disenk and you would hardly recognize yourself."

"Do you think I care for nothing more than the ruin of my youth?" I said. "Aswat has burned away such frivolous concerns." I must have spoken with too much bitterness, for his smile widened.

"Now you are being pompous, and untruthful too," he said. "No woman born has been free of the vice of vanity." He leaned forward. "But of course you have more pressing concerns, do you not?" He spoke solemnly, but his red eyes suddenly lit with sarcasm. "You have found your son. Or rather, he found you. He came to consult me. Did you know? How did you manage to produce such an upright, sober young man?"

I stilled the retort that rose to my lips. I could have pointed out that Kamen was a credit both to Men's upbringing and to Egypt, that Hui and Paiis were trying to destroy something strong and good, that if they succeeded Egypt would be finished as an example of true Ma'at in the world. But I was no match for Hui in the art of verbal sparring. "Please do not taunt me, Hui," I said quietly.

He stared at me for a long time, the gleeful light in his eyes fading to a brooding opacity. Beside me the lamp crackled. Outside the window a breeze came up, making the leaves of the shrouded trees rustle for a moment before becoming still once more. I was tired and drained, wishing I had resisted the urge to come here, for he was more powerful than I and always had been.

Then he stirred, uncrossed his legs, and rose. "Are you hungry?" he queried, and without waiting for an answer he strode to his body-servant's door and rapped on it loudly. After a while the man appeared, sleepy and swollen-faced. "Bring whatever is decently left from the feast, and a jug of wine," he ordered. He turned back to me. "I did not want to command the assassination attempt on you and your son," he said quietly. "I had little choice when Kamen returned alive to Paiis and Paiis warned me of the new danger lurking on our complacent horizon. If you had remained mutely in Aswat, if by some quirk of fate Kamen had not stopped there while fulfilling his duties, none of this distasteful mess would have come about. But the gods have placed in your hands the tools of revenge and you have picked them up. However, dear sister, you cannot use them."

He had come so close that his breath fell warm on my face and the odour of his jasmine-drenched skin filled my nostrils. He had addressed me in the most loving and familiar terms. Never before had he used the word "sister," reserved for an adored wife or mistress, and if it had fallen from any other lips but his, I would have been disarmed. As it was, I became alert at once in spite of the almost overwhelming desire to close my eyes and lift my mouth for a kiss, and I slid the knife deliberately between us.

"Save it for your brother's witless whores, Hui," I said loudly, pressing the fist that held the hilt against his naked breastbone. "Doubtless they can be easily manipulated, but if you want to throw me off my guard you will have to make a greater effort than this. I know perfectly well that you do not want my body. Besides, I still belong to the King, or had you forgotten? And it is to the King that Kamen and Men, yes and Kaha too, are going, with the copy of my manuscript Paiis did not know existed and a tale of attempted murder pharonic justice will not be able to ignore. Step back or I will run you through." He did as he was told, but not before his red eyes had flared with what I knew to be a momentary lust coupled with admiration. I smiled. "Danger has always aroused you, hasn't it, Hui?" I said, and realized for the first time as I spoke the words that they had sliced through to the mystery of his core. "Danger, plots, all of it, an escape from the burden of the gift the gods bestowed. Then you should be on fire, for you are in greater peril now than ever before. Paiis cannot silence all of us."

He retreated to the chair and sat with his customary unhurried grace, then propped his elbow on the armrest and put his chin in his palm. He regarded me speculatively.

"Kaha too?" he murmured. "That hurts me. A scribe's loyalty should be above question."

"His loyalty is above question," I retorted, wanting savagely to shake him out of his self-control. "It rests with Ma'at and justice."

"It rests between his legs when he looks at you," he flashed back. "If I wanted to, I could have you pinned to the floor in a moment." I took the knife's hilt in both hands and pointed it at him.

"Try it, Hui," I taunted him. "I have less to lose than you."

We were saved from further outbursts by a discreet knock on the door. The servant entered bearing a tray which he set on the table beside the couch at Hui's curt order, then he retired to his room without so much as a glance at me. "Help yourself," Hui said.

I went to the table. The wine jar was still sealed. Turning to the chest where I had hidden, I wrestled the lid open and fingered the contents until I found a linen bag with a drawstring. Going back to the table, I filled it with the wine, the loaf of bread, a handful of figs and some goat cheese. Hui watched me in silence. When I had finished, I faced him. "Do not say it," I warned him. "I am wearing your sheath and taking your food, but you owe me a great deal more than these things. You owe me seventeen years of hard work and despair, and when you are arrested I will be at your trial to collect the rest of the debt. I hate you, and my fervent prayer is that you are handed the same sentence I endured because of you, that you are shut up in an empty room until you die of thirst and starvation. I shall sit outside the door and listen to your pleas for mercy, and this time there will be no merciful Pharaoh to restore you to life."

He did not stir. A slow, lazy smile spread over his pale face and one white eyebrow twitched upward. "Darling Thu," he said. "You do not hate me. In fact you love me with a passion and constancy that enrages you, and that is why you came here tonight. Why else would you warn me of my imminent arrest? Presuming, of course, that Paiis is unable to wipe you all out, a task he will probably accomplish in spite of your bluster to the contrary. And in the unlikely event that I am tried for treason and commanded to end my own life, what would be left to you apart from a sweet but rather unsatisfying relationship with your son? For you are me, Thu. I made you, and without me you would be an empty husk. The seed of life would be gone."

I did not look at him again. Clutching the bag in one hand and the knife in the other, I went to the door. "May Sebek crunch your bones," I whispered, "and then may the eternal darkness of the Underworld close over your head." Fumbling, I gained the dark passage beyond. The guard had taken up his station outside the office but I brushed past him, hardly aware of his presence. The entrance hall with its tall pillars was deserted and I hurried across it, but it could have been peopled with a thousand merrymakers and I would not have noticed.

For Hui was right. I loved him, and hated myself for loving him as a prisoner will both loathe and worship his torturer. No edict of Pharaoh, no decree of the gods, could make him love me back, but I would go on aching helplessly for him until I drew my last breath. I wanted to gouge out his hypnotic red eyes. I wanted to push my knife deep into his vitals and watch his blood run hot over my hands. I wanted to put my arms around him and feel his body relax into acquiescence against mine. Blinded by the tears of fury and loss pouring down my cheeks, I stumbled out onto the courtyard, found the small gate, and pushed through it into the rustling haven of the garden. By the time I came to myself, I had waded past the sleepy guards on the Lake path and was approaching the centre of the city.

Half-dazed I stood flattened against the rough wall of an alley while a succession of laden carts rattled past. My feet and legs were caked with river mud and the delicate sheath I had stolen from Hui's bath house was drying grey and stiff against my thighs. It was time to approach the Golden Scorpion again, to seek a message from Kamen, to make plans, but for a long time after the carts with their shriek-ing donkeys had creaked away I could not move. My thoughts were scattered and my courage gone. Not until I found myself wishing fervently and pathetically that I was lying on my cot in the miserable little hut I had called home in Aswat did I come to my senses and force myself into the stream of humanity parading by.

He had not said that he did not love me, in fact he had not expressed any emotion at all. He guarded his ka more closely than the King on a royal progress, but in times past I had seen that guard weaken when he looked at me, and as I wended my way through the torchlit turbulence of the city streets, I deliberately recalled them to soothe the aching wound his words had left. In lifting me from my village as formless clay and moulding me into the shape he wanted, in fashioning my thoughts and directing my desires, he had become enmeshed in his own creation. If he was in my mind and heart, the architect and originator of everything I became, then I too was in his blood, a disease he had inflicted inadvertently upon himself.

We had made love once, in his garden, on the night my anguish and despair had come to a climax and I had decided to kill the king. The recklessness of that decision had fuelled our sudden lust, it was true, but Hui was not a man to allow himself to be carried away by the urgency of the moment alone. Under our mutual excitement and guilt there had flowed an undercurrent of genuine feeling. But he had denied it, was still denying it, for the sake of his survival, and the yearning in my own heart had been overwhelmed by the drive for revenge.

And revenge there would be, I told myself as my hurt receded and I approached the open door of the Golden Scorpion. No memory would be as sweet as the taste of Hui's downfall on my hungry tongue. Pausing to brush as much soil from my legs and sheath as I could, I slipped the knife inside the linen bag and stepped down into the friendly yellow lamplight.

The room was comfortably full. As before, a few heads turned, and I stood for a long moment to allow my presence to become obvious to anyone waiting for me, then I threaded my way to the far corner and slid along one of the benches. The proprietor came at once, but I told him I was waiting for someone. He hesitated, obviously puzzled by the contrast between the quality of the linen I wore and my dishevelled appearance, but having satisfied himself that I was not trying to sell my body in his establishment, he went away.

I watched the customers come and go, a steady, happy stream of young officers and city commoners with their women. Sometimes one would glance about the increasingly stuffy premises and I would tense and lean into the light, but I was not approached. I began to be anxious. Kamen had definitely said that he would send word to me on every third night, but the hours were wearing away, the proprietor was making it clear that he would rather have a drinker in my seat, and I was too conspicuously alone among soldiers who, though not on duty, had surely been given my description.

I began to strain to hear the conversations around me, expecting my name to issue from one of the many mouths. In the eyes that flicked over me I thought I read vague suspicion, a doubtful weighing of recognition, and in the end I could bear it no longer. Rising abruptly, I made my escape, emerging into the shadowed alley with a gasp of relief. Something had happened to Kamen. I was sure of it. I knew by now that he was a man of his word and besides, his attitude to me had been touchingly protective. He would be aware of my anxiety, and there must be a very good reason for his silence.

No, not a good reason, I thought as I blended with the dimness and began to walk towards the end of the Street of Basket Sellers. A bad reason. Something sinister. Paiis has found him. Paiis has killed him. A surge of panic made my heart jump. No. Do not think of that. Think only of his arrest. Presume that he is in hiding and cannot show himself. He cannot die, or the burden of guilt will kill me too. Surely the gods would not be so cruel as to allow me to find him only to have him snatched away from me. Oh Wepwawet, Opener of the Ways, help me now! What shall I do?

A hand fell on my shoulder and for one idiotic moment I thought that the god himself had come up behind me in answer to my prayer. My breath hitched. The pressure of the hand increased and I was forced to halt, turning away from the glaring torchlight of the larger street and back into the dimness.

A young man stood before me, his grip changing to my upper arm as I faced him. I recognized him immediately as one of the roisterers in the beer house. Kamen's messenger, I thought with relief. He did not want us to be seen together and he has waited until I left. Yet I had no intention of giving myself away prematurely, for I did not like the way he kept a firm hold on my flesh. "What colour are your eyes?" he asked abruptly.

"You have mistaken me for a whore," I answered calmly. "I am not for sale." He leaned forward and peered at me intently, then he pulled me, politely but determinedly, towards a door through which a little light was spilling. Angrily I tried to shake free, but he simply held me more tightly, scanning me with care.

"Is your name Thu of Aswat?" he demanded. A wave of terror broke inside me.

"No, it is not," I said, "and if you do not let me go, I will begin to scream. There are laws against accosting women in public places." He did not seem in the least perturbed and his clutch did not loosen.

"I think it is," he replied. "You fit the description my captain was given. Tall, blue-eyed, a peasant who walks with the grace of a noblewoman and speaks an educated tongue. I followed you from the Golden Scorpion because I was not sure I recognized you, but now I have no doubt. You are under arrest." Quickly I glanced about, but as luck would have it the street was temporarily empty of even the most persistent whore.

"And you are drunk," I said loudly, insultingly. "If you let me go at once, I will not report your behaviour to the city police. Otherwise you will wake tomorrow with more than a sore head full of regrets."

"I am not drunk," he insisted. "I am sorry, but you must accompany me to the authorities." I knew then that I had no hope of talking him into a doubt he obviously did not have, but out of my desperation I tried once more.

"What authorities?" I spat. "You are no soldier. Where is the evidence of your rank?"

"My authority comes from the order passed to my captain by His Highness the Prince Ramses. I am not on duty tonight."

"Then you cannot take me anywhere. Do you think I am stupid?" He did not even smile.

"Far from it," he acknowledged. "The Prince's Division and the city police would not have been mobilized to search all over Pi-Ramses tonight for a stupid peasant woman. I must confess I am curious to know what heinous crime you have committed, although it is none of my business. You might as well submit yourself to whatever fate awaits you, Thu of Aswat, for having found you, it is my duty to pass you to my superior. I may not be in rank this night, but he is."

The terror had turned to a cold sweat that flooded my spine and sprang out over my scalp. I forced my body to relax, my shoulders to slump. "Very well," I said tiredly. "Lead on." I would have groped for the knife but it was still

n Hui's linen bag together with the food and my other arm
was imprisoned. However, the young man's grip lessened at
my words and he took a step forward. At once I turned my
head and sunk my teeth into his forearm. He yelped, and as
he pulled his arm away I pushed him hard in the chest and
ran towards the brightness of the larger thoroughfare.
People were there. I could lose myself in the crowd. I could
hide.

But I had reckoned without the damnably fashionable
sheath I had stolen from Hui's bath house. Tight from hip
to ankle it acted like a hobble and before I knew it I had
stumbled and was on my knees in the dirt. Frantically I tore
at the one seam running up the side of the garment but the
thread resisted my feverish nails while the soldier, already
recovered, began to shout for assistance and a group of his
friends burst from the doorway of the Golden Scorpion.
Stumbling to my feet I hitched the thin linen around my
thighs and fell towards freedom but it was too late. Rough
hands grabbed at my hair, hauling me back, and an arm
went around my throat. "Consider yourself a prisoner of the
Horus Throne," the young man panted.

They tied my hands and marched me through the city.
Although some of them were indeed drunk, and laughed
and joked at their good fortune in apprehending such a
dangerous criminal, the one who had followed and
arrested me was not and he made sure that I was closely
hemmed in by the others. One went ahead to warn the
citizens to clear a path and I walked through lakes and
eddies of inquisitive faces, some pitying, some hostile, all
staring at the dishevelled woman whose fate, thank all the
gods, was not theirs.

I did not look at them. I looked beyond them to where dark doorways invited, or dim alleys wound into invisibility, but no opportunity for flight presented itself and finally, exhausted and resigned, I was ushered into a small mud brick building and deposited before a desk from behind which a uniformed man was rising. My captors vanished after untying my hands and relinquishing my bag.

After a brief pause, during which the man's gaze never left my face, he nodded, came around the desk, and placed a stool behind me. I sank onto it gratefully and waited while he opened my bag, examined the contents, and drew out the knife and the unopened wine jar. "Good Wine of the Western River, year sixteen," he said. "It is yours?"

"Yes."

"May I open it? Will you share it with me?" I shrugged.

"Why not?"

"Thank you." He pried off the wax seal imprinted with the source and year of the wine, reached to a shelf behind him, and set two cups on the table. While he poured, I summoned up enough energy to study the insignia on his leather helmet and bracelet. He belonged to the Division of Horus, the Prince's personal Command. And had the young soldier not said that the warrant for my arrest came from the authority of the Prince? In my fear I had passed over the words, but now I remembered them.

"You are not under General Paiis," I blurted. He glanced up in surprise, then handed me a cup.

"No, of course not," he replied. "What made you think that you were arrested on the General's orders? It is Prince Ramses who signed the warrant. Drink. You look completely spent."

"Did the Prince order my arrest on the advice of the General?" He blinked at me quizzically.

"I have no idea. All I know is that some hours ago the city police and all men from the Prince's Division who were on duty or watch were commanded to begin a search for you. You are badly wanted. For good or ill?" I managed a smile and raised the cup to my mouth. The wine smelt of Hui, and slid down my parched throat like one of his elixirs.

"I do not know," I said honestly, replacing the cup on the desk. I was beginning to feel better. If the Prince wanted me found, it surely meant that Paiis had failed to keep his filthy murder plot to himself. Or at least he had been compelled to come up with some pretext for my arrest that would limit his power to get at me and Kamen. And where was my son? Had he reached the ear of the palace after all? I was suddenly hungry. The captain saw me eyeing the bag and pushed it towards me.

"Eat then," he said. He regained his seat. I poured more wine for myself and fell upon the bread, figs and cheese.

"You may keep the rest of the wine for yourself," I told him. "Now where am I to spend the night? And have you any word of my son?" He frowned.

"Your son? No. I did not know that you had a son. I know nothing about you, Thu. As for where you are to spend the night, my orders are that when found you are to be conveyed at once to the royal harem."

The cloud of my euphoria condensed into a heavy weight of undigested food and hurriedly drunk wine and a surge of nausea made me swallow convulsively. Feeling suddenly faint, I groped for the edge of the desk. "No," I whispered. "No! I cannot go back there, not now, not after so many years. The harem is a prison, I will not be able to escape it a second time, there is death in that place, oh please put me anywhere but there!" My voice had risen. My fingers curled around the wood. This has nothing to do with Paiis, I thought to myself frantically. This is the Prince's doing. He will take a vicious delight in seeing me trapped there once more, and this time there will be no one to protect me. I will disappear into that huge herd of perfumed cows. I wanted to run from the room but my limbs were trembling so hard that I could barely lift my head. The captain leaned over and pried my hands loose, holding them warmly.

"I do not know what peculiar tale you could tell me if you wished," he said deliberately, as though he was speaking to a frightened child, and indeed at that moment I was a child, undone by the prospect of a fate far worse than the death I had imagined at Paiis's hands. "What I do know is that the Prince is a fitting and merciful Heir, worthy to ascend the Horus Throne when his father goes to the gods. He is neither petty nor spiteful. Nor are his punishments greater than the crimes he judges. You are understandably distraught after being paraded through the city. Calm yourself."

I am distraught because my punishment will come from a Prince whose advances I once repelled and who was instrumental in having me condemned to death, I thought wildly. In the harem I will never have a chance to even speak to him. He will drop me into that ocean of anonymous women and I shall be lost, forgotten for ever, and he will ponder the ironies of fate and smile to himself.

But under the captain's touch my sanity gradually returned and I was able to sit straight. "You are right," I said shakily. "Forgive me. I am very tired." For answer he rose, and going to the door, rapped out a sharp summons.

"You can ride to the harem in a litter, I think," he said. "Here is your escort. It is time to go."

I had to use the desk to pull myself to my feet and I stood there weakly, loath to leave the bare room that had in so short a time become a haven of safety. Beyond the door a torch flared into life and I saw the litter resting on the ground, its plain, heavy wool curtain raised, its interior like a dark mouth without teeth, open to devour me. So my life has come full circle, I thought dismally. But I go to the harem as a prisoner this time, in an unadorned public conveyance, and I must bid farewell to a soldier not a Seer. Such are the jokes of the gods. The captain was waiting by the door, his arm extended. I took a moment to straighten, to breathe deeply, to lift my chin. Then I walked past him, clasping his hand as I did so. "Thank you for your kindness," I said.

"May the gods go with you, Thu," he replied, and the door closed behind him. I do not want the gods to go with me, I thought mutinously as I climbed into the litter and twitched the curtain down. There is no justice in the heavens. Let them spy out some other victim on whom to practise their idle malice, and leave me alone.

The litter was lifted and began to move. I peered out, hoping that at least the guard might be thin and I might tumble out and escape, but a soldier walked to either side, sword drawn, and I heard one ahead crying a path and the crunch of sandalled feet behind. There would be no unpremeditated halts on this journey.

There were no cushions in the litter, only a hard straw pallet on which to recline. I curled up and squeezed my eyes shut, pushing away the threatening phantoms of the future that tried to take command of my mind. I am alive, I told myself firmly. I have survived much. I can survive this too. The scorn of the women who remember me as Pharaoh's would-be killer will be no different than the hatred of Aswat's upright villagers. Remember Kamen, Thu. Remember your son. You gave birth to a Prince, and nothing that might happen to you can alter that glorious fact. So I fought to gain some confidence while my heart beat a tattoo of fear and my brave thoughts shredded like wind-blown tatters even as I unfurled them.

I must have dozed in spite of my feverish imaginings, for I came to myself with a jolt as the litter was set down. The curtain was lifted and a face peered in at me, limned in torch-light. "Get out," the soldier barked, and I scrambled onto the ground. Another soldier appeared, words were exchanged, and my bearers and escort went away. I looked about me.

I was standing on the vast stone concourse before the main entrance to the palace. The watersteps and the canal were behind me. To right and left, large trees raised their shrouded branches over lawns that ran away under them into darkness, but the pillars of the entrance were fixed with many torches that cast a garish light over the richly apparelled litters sitting on the paving like beached skiffs. Their bearers waited patiently for their masters to return from whatever royal feast or ministerial conference was taking place within. I could hear the gentle suck of the water where the orange glare rippled beside tethered craft and the subdued voices of the sailors attending them.

Nothing had changed. I could have been standing here eighteen years ago, resplendent in yellow linen and gold, my hair netted in silver thread, my hennaed palm uplifted imperiously to summon my litter while behind me Disenk hovered, my embroidered cloak over one arm and a box of cosmetics tucked under the other to touch up the kohl around my eyes or the blue shadow on my lids should I be indelicate enough to sweat during the evening. A longing that was like the most refined homesickness went through me in the moment before the soldier took my wrist, and I fancied that my other self, that ghostly vision of youth and power and beauty, turned and smiled at me with a scornful superiority. I allowed the soldier to lead me away.

I knew where we would go. A broad stone path led towards those rearing, lighted pillars under which a crowd of royal soldiers and servants were clustered, but before it reached them, it divided. The right-hand fork went to the gate that gave onto the palace gardens and the columns of the banqueting hall and further still, to Pharaoh's office.

My captor took me along the left-hand way. The path cut through more verdant lawns, and I caught a glimpse of the pool where Hunro and I had swum every morning after I had gone through the series of exercises Nebnefer had taught me and Hunro had danced beside me. Hot and dishevelled, laughing and invigorated, we would race each other out the harem gate, across the grass, and plunge head-long into that clean, cool water. At that same gate the soldier let go my wrist, knocked twice, and left me, but before I could collect my wits and dismiss the insidious visions with all their unwanted resurrections, before I could dash for the trees, the gate opened and I was drawn inside.

The man even now closing the gate behind me was dressed in the ankle-length, flowing sheath of a Steward.

Beside him a boy stood eyeing me with frank curiosity, holding a torch, and the light glittered on the Steward's golden armbands as he faced me and beckoned. He did not introduce himself. And why should he? I asked myself as I trudged after him and his slave. I am less than no one, a peasant to be delivered to the kitchens or the laundry and given a kilt and a sleeping pallet before being consigned to oblivion.

I could see little as we went, but I knew what we were passing. On the left would be more trees, grass studded with bushes, a lily- and lotus-dotted pool, and then at right angles to the narrow path my feet were already recognizing, a mud brick wall with an outside staircase leading to the roof of the queens' quarters. Two high walls began, hemming me in, and I felt the first intimations of suffocation in my chest, for the wall on the left ran a very long way until it ended beyond the whole length of the harem buildings and the one on the right hid the palace itself. Struggling for air, knowing it was memories clutching at my lungs and nothing else, I paced steadily after the bobbing torch.

The harem had been constructed in four enormous squares with narrow alleys running between each one. Each square had an open courtyard in the centre with lawn and a fountain, and around the courtyard were the two tiers of cells for the women. At the far end was the block reserved for the royal children. We had already passed the first block, a heavily guarded and quiet enclave for the queens. The second and third were full of concubines. The Steward paused at the entrance to the second and swept through. I hesitated, not knowing whether to follow him or not, for surely he had been ordered to deliver me straight to the servants' cells beyond the Royal Nurseries. But looking back, he saw me halt and waved me forward with a jerk of his thumb.

I had lived here, in this block. I had shared a cell with Hunro. I did not need the torch to show me where the fountain stood or where the grass gave way to the path that ran past each small doorway. I looked up. The same stars stood above the black edge of the roofs. The same wind stirred the grass under my feet and filled my nostrils with the same faint odours of perfume and spices. If I had come there in daylight, I might have been able to hold onto reality. But slipping through the warm darkness, my mind receiving the vague shapes of my surroundings and accepting them as immediately and unremarkably familiar, my nostrils, the soles of my bare feet, the rest of my skin, feeding my senses with impressions that obliterated time in an instant, I became for one horrifying moment insane. The Steward stopped in a pool of yellow light pouring from the open door of one of the cells. "The Keeper of the Door awaits you," he said, and turned on his heel. I stepped into the lamp's glow.

He had hardly changed at all. I had always thought him ageless, for he carried himself with an easy grace and authority, and only the deeper grooves around his alert black eyes and sober mouth told me that seventeen years had passed. He rose from his seat as I went dazedly towards him, the blue kilt I remembered so well falling softly about his ankles, the black wig with its many rigid waves cascading over his shoulders. Thick gold armbands went from his elbows to his wrists and rings winked on his long fingers as he slid from the chair. He smiled. "Greetings, Thu," he said.

"Greetings, Amunnakht," I whispered, and bowed to him, according him the profound respect I had always felt for his intelligence and wisdom. The most powerful man in the harem, he was responsible for the peace and good ordering of the hundreds of women in his charge and he was answerable to Pharaoh alone. If he wished, he could foster a concubine to the height of royal favour or condemn her to remain forever obscure. He had liked me, and out of love for his royal Master had promoted my cause with the King, believing that I would do him good. But I had done him harm. I had betrayed Amunnakht's trust also, yet it had been he who, on Pharaoh's command, brought the life-giving water to me as I lay dying in prison, and had held my head and soothed and comforted me. I had not deserved such forgiveness. "I did not thank you for your unmerited kindness to me when last we met," I said to him haltingly, "nor for taking upon yourself the task of making sure my totem Wepwawet went with my son to his new home. Because of you I have found him. I disappointed you deeply and I am sorry. It has been on my mind all these years that I did not thank you."

"Come forward, Thu," he invited. "Sit. I have requested a simple meal for you. It is very late, but you may want to eat before you sleep. I had not much warning that you were found." I did as I was told, still in the grip of that lingering dislocation, so that his words and my own seemed to come from other mouths, in another time. "Whether you disappointed me or not is unimportant," he went on, regaining his own seat and crossing his legs. "I regarded you as my greatest failure and I sorrowed over both your fate and my lack of judgement at the time. I do my duty to my Lord and see to his needs to the best of my ability, and it was his disappointment that caused me the most grief." He arranged the filmy blue folds of his kilt across his knees. "He commanded your death and I assisted in the distribution of your belongings. Then he commanded that you should live and I was pleased to enter your cell and minister to you."

"You could have sent a Steward."

"I said I was pleased to enter your cell," he pointed out. "In spite of your great crime and your flagrant ingratitude to the One, I still had much affection for you. Why I do not know."

"Because I was not like the others," I responded. "Because I refused to behave like one of His Majesty's female sheep. Because I would not be cast aside for the mistake of bearing him a child."

"I see that you have not changed much," he said. "You are still arrogant and sharp-tongued."

"Not so, Amunnakht," I disagreed softly. "I have learned patience and many other bitter lessons during my exile. I have learned to love revenge."

There was a silence during which he studied me without agitation, his body quietly relaxed, his whole attitude one of unselfconscious confidence, and I stared back at him while gradually that hideous sense of displacement began to fade. The years between my sixteen-year-old self and the present re-formed in their proper order, and I was able to put the lamplit cell, the scent of the unseen lawn outside, the constant susurration of the fountain water, the man who sat thoughtfully opposite me, into the perspective of a returning lucidity. Somewhere in this vast complex of buildings Hunro slept, but not the Hunro I had known. In the queens' apartments Ast lay. Was she still elegantly beautiful? And Ast-Amasereth, that cunning and mysterious foreigner who shared the secrets of the state with Pharaoh, her husband, was she still alive? Time had not stood still here as it had not spared me during those endless years in Aswat. I had not been trapped in a loop of hours and the past was gone for ever.

I leaned forward at last, a question on my lips, but the doorway was shadowed by a servant who entered, bowed to the Keeper, and set a laden tray on the table beside me. Steam rose from the onion soup, the hot brown bread dripping with butter, the two pieces of broiled goose from which a tantalizing aroma of garlic wafted, and beads of moisture trembled on the leaves of young lettuce, sliced radishes and mint. The woman unfolded a napkin, and with a murmured and formal request for permission, spread it across my filthy lap. She held out a finger bowl in which a single pink blossom floated. When I had rinsed my fingers she poured a brown liquid into a clay cup, set it by my hand, and retired behind my chair, ready to serve me. But Amunnakht signalled her and she bowed again and left us as noiselessly as she had come. I picked up the cup and felt my throat grow tight with unshed tears. "It is beer," I said huskily. "You did not forget my liking for the drink of my upbringing."

"I am an excellent Keeper," he said imperturbably. "I forget nothing that might bring happiness to Pharaoh's concubines. Eat and drink now. The food has been tasted." At the stark reminder of the dangers lurking in this place where every luxury was taken for granted and yet the screen of ease and indulgence hid the darkest passions, my mood changed. I sat with the cup cradled in both hands and looked across at Amunnakht.

"Why am I here in this cell and not lying on some miserable pallet under a kitchen bench?" I asked. "Did the Prince command you to receive me like this only to make my ultimate destination more bitter?" He hardly stirred. One carefully manicured fingernail was drawn along his eyebrow.

"I saw the list of names you gave the King at the time of your previous arrest," he said. "His Majesty enquired of me whether I had any deeper knowledge of them than he, or whether I had heard whispers of a seditious nature about them. He was distressed. He had condemned you to death but doubt fluttered in his august mind. I was forced to tell him that I knew nothing untoward about those listed, but I did not believe that you had dictated their names maliciously, without foundation for your accusation. In his mercy the One stayed your execution so that he could investigate your claims of a treasonous conspiracy. He said that once dead and yet proved right you could not be resurrected to this life and he would have committed a grave sin against Ma'at."

"He said that?"

"He did. So you went into exile. You should have been whipped first for attempting to murder the Good God, but he would not have it. His rage against you and his hurt were great, but I think he also felt guilt because he had loved you more than any other and had cast you away. He appointed the Prince to investigate the Seer and the others, but no evidence of their culpability came to light."

"Of course not!" I retorted hotly. "They lied, their servants lied, everyone lied but me!"

"Such self-righteousness from a regicide!" he commented wryly. "The matter was closed, but Pharaoh was not fully convinced that it should have been. As a precaution he demoted the Butler Paibekamun to the rank of Steward in the palace and made him taster to Great Royal Wife Ast." I laughed aloud at that delicious irony. Paibekamun had disliked me from the first, thinking me common and ignorant, and I was glad to hear that his arrogance had suffered such a blow.

"Am I here because I violated the terms of my exile, Amunnakht?" I asked. "Am I to serve in the harem instead of in Wepwawet's temple for the rest of my life?" His features slowly broke into a wide, unaffected grin and for a fleeting moment I saw a Keeper I did not know existed, a man of humour and delight.

"No, you evil woman," he chuckled. "For tonight a most extraordinary thing happened. Three men begged an audience of the Prince as he was preparing to preside in the banqueting hall. Luckily for you, he granted it. Then he heard such a tale of attempted assassinations and ancient plots as has never before been told in this place of many secret crimes and violent acts." I slammed the cup back on the table so hard that the beer slopped over my hands.

"Kamen! Kamen pleaded our case to the Prince! Where is he now, Amunnakht?" The Keeper sobered.

"No, Thu, it was not your son who held the ear of the Heir captive. It was his adoptive father, Men, his betrothed's father, Nesiamun, and the Scribe Kaha." I clenched my teeth in a sudden paroxysm of misgiving.

"Why was he not there? Something terrible has

happened to him, I knew it! Paiis ..." Amunnakht held up an admonitory hand.

"Paiis is confined to his estate. Kamen was found chained in his house. He has suffered no harm, but I do not think he would have been allowed to live through this night if the Prince had not moved swiftly to contain the General."

"I don't understand."

"All those named on your list so long ago are under house arrest, Thu, pending the report that will be brought back from Aswat concerning a body buried under the floor of your hut. If it is there, you will be vindicated. You are to be allowed the freedom of the harem and your hurts will be attended. The Prince will see you as soon as his men return from Aswat."

"I want to see my son!"

"Kamen has been delivered to Men's house. The Prince does not wish you to leave the harem at present."

"But Hunro is here, Amunnakht. If she knows I am also here she will try to do me harm."

"You have not listened," he reproved me. "Hunro was on your list. She may not leave her cell and a harem guard is at her door continually." A bewildering gladness spread in me. I wanted to close the space between us and throw my arms around the Keeper, but of course I did no such thing.

"So I was not arrested for punishment, I was captured for my safety!" I cried out. "And they will find the body because Kamen and I put it there ourselves! I am hungry now, Amunnakht!"

"Good." He rose in one fluid motion. "Eat then, and sleep. Tomorrow when you wake you will find a body servant outside your door, waiting for your orders, and if you lack anything, send me a message." I laughed at him for sheer joy.

"It will not be Disenk, will it?"

"No," he responded gravely. "Your previous servant is now in the employ of the Lady Kawit, the Seer's sister. And concerning the Seer, there is one thing …" A hand squeezed my heart, very gently.

"Yes?"

"The Prince's soldiers went to Hui's estate but he was not there. The house and grounds were searched but he has gone. His Steward does not know where." So Hui not only heeded my warning, I thought bitterly, but acted on it as soon as I left him. I was a fool to go there. I should have remembered how wily, how clever he is. Am I to be cheated of the one portion of my revenge that would taste the sweetest? Where has he gone?

"He has holdings in other parts of the Delta," I said slowly, "and he is well known in all the temples of Egypt."

"Every hiding place is being explored," Amunnakht assured me. "The harem is well guarded, Thu. He cannot possibly reach you here." No, but I want to reach him, my thoughts ran on. I want the royal hands to go around his white throat at last, at last, I want to see his damnable self-assurance crumble. I want to see him suffer.

"How is the King?" I asked diffidently. "Will I be allowed to see him?" Amunnakht shot me a shrewd glance.

"He is very ill," he said. "He does not often leave his couch. I fear he is dying. But the Prince went to him this evening and told him all that had passed."

"He knows I am here then. He may send for me!"

"He may, but I do not think so, Thu. After all, you did try to kill him once."

"He was happy with me," I said softly. "In spite of all the pain we caused each other, he may remember that at the last."

"Perhaps. Dream well, concubine."

He was gone in a swirl of blue linen and I was alone. Drawing a deep, satisfying breath I turned to the table and raised the beer to my lips. Kamen was safe. I was safe. And the King would remember his little scorpion. The gods had been kind after all. They would allow me to kneel before their kinsman and beg forgiveness for the harm I had done him. Drinking quickly, I reached for the soup.

12

BEFORE CRAWLING between the pristine smoothness of the sheets on the small but luxurious couch, I pulled Hui's grubby sheath over my head and tossed it out the door. Then blowing out the lamp, I lay down. The familiar silence of a harem night enveloped me, its quality of smug insularity heightened by the reassuring murmur of the fountain, and I sank under its spell with a sigh of sheer abandon. Briefly I thought of the docks where I had slept previously, of my anxious wait in the beer house, of the unexpected kindness of the captain, of Amunnakht and his words, but most of all it was the King's face that hovered before my inner vision and his voice that lulled me. He lay a mere stone's throw beyond the wall of my compound. Was he awake and thinking of me? Or had I been in the end so inconsequential to him that he could barely remember my name?

And what of Hui? Where could he have gone? Perhaps he had left Egypt altogether, but somehow I did not think so. He would not betray his guilt so blatantly. He would hide and wait to see what happened, and if my affairs went badly he would return with some innocuous story of where he had been. At the moment I did not care. My couch was soft, my belly full of the best food I had eaten in seventeen years, and my son within the guarded walls of his father's house. I slid contentedly into unconsciousness.

The sounds of female voices passing my door woke me, and for a while I was not sure where I was. I heard a child scream with momentary rage followed by the scolding voice of an adult. My room was still dark, but when I swung my feet to the floor and moved drowsily to the door, tugging it open, a blast of dazzling sunshine half-blinded me. The morning was far advanced. Before me the wide lawns were dotted with groups of women who sat knee to knee, talking, or sprawled under white canopies that flapped lazily in the refreshing breeze. Servants flitted between them. Brown children splashed in the fountain or chased the dogs that barked frenetically. As though renewing an ancient habit, my eyes were drawn to one particular spot on the far side of the huge square but it was empty.

Something stirred by my feet and a young woman uncurled, smiled at me, and bowed. "Greetings, Thu," she said. "I am Isis, your servant. You slept well?" I licked my lips and suppressed a yawn.

"Thank you, Isis," I replied. "I have not enjoyed such a good sleep in years. Now, as you can see, I am naked and sadly in need of a bath. Have you the authority to bring me anything I want?" Her eyebrows rose.

"But of course," she said. "Anything at all. You are the Prince's honoured guest." I forbore to mention that if indeed I was a guest of royalty I would not have been sequestered in the harem, but I did not want to spoil this child's sense of her own importance.

"Good!" I exclaimed. "Then go and fetch me a robe, and tell the bath-house attendants to prepare hot water. Find a masseur and a cosmetician. Bring food to me after I have bathed. Are there clothes for me?" She blinked.

"I will have a variety of sheaths, sandals and ornaments laid out on the couch for your selection," she said, and bowing she prepared to leave.

"One more thing," I added. "I see that the concubine Hatia is not in her accustomed place. Where is she?" The girl frowned.

"Hatia?" Then her brow cleared. "Oh, Hatia! She died five years ago. I was not employed here then, but it is said that from the time she entered these precincts to the time she was found stiff on her couch she remained silent. None of the women heard her speak one word."

Neither did I, I thought sadly. Her servant, a man equally mute, came to me once to ask me if I would attend her in my capacity as a physician, but Hatia turned her face to the wall when I entered her cell and I was left with an overwhelming impression of great misery and quiet suffering. Hatia the drunkard. I had suspected her of spying on me for the Great Queen Ast-Amasereth in exchange for unlimited amounts of vintage wine. I had even wondered if it had been Hatia who had placed the poisoned fig on my dish when but for Disenk's vigilance I would have eaten it and died. But in all probability the glazed malevolence of her scrutiny encompassed all of us, the healthy, beautiful women who came and went before her. I should have tried harder to treat her, to draw her out, but I had been too selfish and utterly involved with my own affairs.

At my dismissal the girl strode away and I retreated to my couch. I could not help Hatia now, could not undo the many thoughtless acts I had committed during my stay among these privileged and yet restricted women, and even now, when a few short steps would take me to the cell I had shared with Hunro, I gave thanks that I was not really one of them. I had not changed much. I simply knew myself a little better than I had all those years ago.

But a chilling thought struck me. Was I in fact not one of them? I still belonged to the King. I was still a royal concubine. I had lain with no man since my forbidden coupling with Hui, that insane hour in his garden. Ramses had the right to order me returned to the harem for as long as he lived, and his son could then retire me if he wished to that dreadful place in the Fayum where the old and used-up concubines lived out their final days. A sense of desperation brought me to my feet and exploded the bubble of self-satisfaction in which I had been congratulating myself. The King must send for me, and when I had apologized for what I had tried to do to him, when I had wept and knelt by his couch, I must ask to be released from his service. The strange twists of fate that had made up my life must not dribble away into the stultifying boredom and despair of an unwanted slave!

My gloomy thoughts were interrupted by Isis's return. Over her arm she had a filmy cloak of semi-transparent linen which she shook out and draped around my shoulders. "You are expected in the bath house," she said, and I forced away the fear, determined to revel in this chance to regain something of the youth I had lost.

They bathed me in scented water and combed lotus oil through my neglected tresses. They plucked the coarse hair from my body and massaged more oil into my parched skin. They abraded and dressed my poor abused feet, coaxed honey and castor oil into my hands and face, scraped and washed and oiled me again. I submitted with the deepest joy. These were the delights whose memory had nourished my days of drudgery in Wepwawet's temple and my nights of near-hopelessness when I fought to believe that exile in Aswat was not the end. They signalled my rebirth into a life that was more than work and the sleep of exhaustion, and no matter what, I did not believe that Aswat would ever be a part of my destiny again.

I returned to my cell on bandaged and sandalled feet, my body tingling, my hair gleaming, to find the cosmetician waiting for me, her chest open, her brushes and vials laid out. She waited politely while I sat at the table and broke my fast. Isis served me with the easy competence of experience, and as before, the manners Disenk had drummed into me during my first months in Hui's house came back to me. Every morsel was a blessing, every drop of milk a promise.

When I had finished, Isis removed the tray and the cosmetician put a finger under my chin, lifting my face to her assessing glance. "Do not flatter me," I told her shortly. "Do not tell me what arresting blue eyes I have or how well-formed my mouth. I do not know if the ravages of sun and time can be erased but please try." One corner of her own mouth lifted in a wry half-smile. She was an older woman, already greying, and I was not surprised when she said, "I remember you, Thu, though of course you do not remember me. When you were in residence here I was attached to the Lady Werel. You were fortunate to have the services of Disenk for your painting. She is an artist." She is also a snobbish little rat who left me to drown like the rest of them, I thought. "Your complexion is distressingly brown," the woman went on, "and I do not know what can be done to restore a bloom to your face. Perhaps much, with time. Are you taking up residence here again?" I sighed.

"Please all the gods I hope not," I answered her honestly. "Nor do I know how much time there will be for your work to take effect. But do your best." She nodded and turned to her potions, and I sat back, closing my eyes.

She worked quietly and methodically and when she had finished she handed me a copper mirror. I did not want to look at myself. For years I had avoided my reflection in the Nile, in the irrigation canals bordering Aswat's fields; I had even refused to glimpse myself in the water of my one drinking cup. The villagers had turned their faces from me and I had done as they did. It was not only vanity. It was an unwillingness to see my besmirched soul condemning me from behind my own eyes.

Yet now I took the elegant instrument and with trembling fingers lifted it. She had painted my lids silver above the sweeping black lines of the kohl, and dusted my cheeks with gold. My lips glistened with red henna. Framing the whole I saw the dark, shining lines of my hair, subdued and luxuriant. I caught my breath and the Thu I used to be, the young and vibrant Thu, began to laugh softly somewhere deep inside me. "I will return each day for as long as you wish," the woman said, beginning to pack her belongings. "Make sure they continue with the honey and castor oil, Isis, and they can add a little myrrh to hasten the fading of the dark colour. Rub oil into her hands and feet every night and do not let her use them much." She bowed to me gravely and was gone.

She had forgotten her mirror. I still clutched it close to my face. What would Pharaoh see? I wondered. A battered thirty-four-year-old peasant or a lovely girl grown to a glorious maturity? Oh gods. I thrust the mirror at Isis and reached for my first cup of wine. "The man is here with your sheaths," she said. "Do you wish to dress now? He has also brought a sunshade the Keeper himself sent for you, with a message that you must not venture out without its protection." So Amunnakht also believed, though he had denied it, that Ramses would eventually send for me. I nodded.

"Let him come in."

The linens the man poured upon the couch were like rivulets of iridescent water. The ornaments—necklets, bracelets, rings, anklets, thin, delicate coronets—glinted and flashed in the shaft of sunlight pouring through the open doorway. Gold, silver, turquoise, jasper, carnelian, moonstones, even the leather sandals he was placing in careful pairs on the floor were encrusted with gems. I approached this sumptuousness with reverence, fingering linens of the twelfth grade, so fine that my still-rough fingers could scarcely confirm their texture. Isis and the man waited while I picked up and put down one precious thing after another, trying, in a mood of astonished humility, to choose just one sheath, one pair of sandals, from this profusion of riches. Finally I decided upon a yellow sheath bordered in silver thread and sandals with tiny clustered balls of silver set between each toe. Gold bracelets mounted with turquoise scarabs went around my forearms and I set a pectoral of linked golden scarabs around my neck. Lastly I lifted a thin fillet of gold and settled it on my forehead. Its circle was engraved with ankhs to symbolize to myself my entry into a new life. "What of the rings?" Isis asked, but I shook my head, spreading out my hands in front of her.

"These are not yet fit for adornment," I said. "They are thick and swollen. Perhaps tomorrow." The man began to gather up the articles.

"The yellow was a good choice, Lady," he told me. "It suits you." I thanked him and he hefted the treasures and went out. I turned to Isis, feeling rather lost.

"What shall I do now?" I asked, more to myself than her. "I want to see my son but I cannot. I would be content, but for that. How long will it take for the Prince's soldiers to return from Aswat I wonder?"

"I can erect a canopy for you on the grass or under a tree," Isis suggested. "We can play board games. I do not think it would be good for your feet to walk around the precincts though. Not until they are a little softer. I will take these papyrus sandals back to the bath house." I knew then what I really wanted to do.

"Yes," I said. "Set up a canopy just outside this door, not too close to the other women, and then send a scribe to me. I will dictate letters." She hurried to do as I had requested, eager to please me, the Prince's guest, and soon I was sitting amid a pile of bright cushions in the shade of the wide white linen roof, the cell behind me and the vivid, sun-dappled lawn before. Was it my imagination, or were some of the women pointing my way and whispering? It would be too much to hope that those who knew me in disgrace would all be dead or banished to the Fayum or moved to other quarters. But none of them approached me, and before long a scribe came up to me and bowed, his palette tucked under his arm, and for a while I forgot their curious stares.

I dictated a letter to Men, thanking him for the stand he had taken on my and Kamen's behalf. He had done so out of his trust in Kamen's word no matter how ridiculous the story had sounded, and I admired such loyalty. I also spoke through the scribe to Nesiamun and his daughter, thanking them for their kindnesses. After draining the beer Isis had left by my elbow, for so much talking after so long had dried my throat, I dictated a short letter to Kamen himself, telling him that I was well, eager to see him, and anxiously awaiting news of our fate. I was careful for the sake of the woman who had raised him not to express my newly found love for him too strongly, for I did not want to pierce a heart that was surely already aching with loss. I knew exactly how she must feel. I had believed him lost for nearly seventeen long years, not knowing whether he was alive or dead, healthy and adored or unhappy and rejected. And while I suffered, she had watched him grow, cuddled and nourished him, delighted in every small change that signalled his slow progress towards the intelligent, kind young man I had discovered. Now she, in her turn, must let him go, for could I not claim him now as my own? Was it not my turn to relish his existence? I did not want to hurt Shesira, but Kamen was mine. When all this was over, he and I would leave Pi-Ramses together. Exactly where we would go I was not sure, but having found him I had no intention of ever saying goodbye to him again. He could marry Takhuru, if he liked. She was beautiful and of noble birth and I approved of her spirited disposition, so like my own. But she would have to live with us.

Lastly I dictated a long missive to my dear brother, telling him of all that had happened since I had begged him to lie for me and assuring him that at last his care for me over the years of my exile would bear fruit. The scribe wrote steadily and of course without comment, pausing only at the end to ask me whether I wished to sign the sheets of papyrus myself. I did so. Then he stoppered his ink, put away his brushes, and rose. "The letters within Pi-Ramses will be delivered today," he said, "but the one to Aswat will not go out until a Herald is sent south on imperial business. Probably tomorrow."

"But that is wonderfully prompt!" I laughed. "I had forgotten how efficient the harem staff can be. Thank you." He shot me an inscrutable glance and left.

For a while I sat lazily watching the ebb and flow of the bright women patchworking the grass. I was conscious of the flutter of the gossamer yellow linen against my calves, the gentle weight of the golden circlet pressing into my forehead, the dull gleam of the scarabs forever crawling towards my wrists. All was complete. Nothing more was required of me at present. No temple chore to be done, no garden to be weeded, no Herald to be approached with beating heart and hidden shame. No more panic, no more hiding, no more need to quell those gusts of near despair that had been the companions of so many nights. Everything in me was beginning to unwind, loosen, grow fluid with life again. Settling back, I gazed up into the ethereal ceiling of the canopy while my eyes grew heavy and then closed. I slept, and did not hear Isis kneel beside me with a tray laden with the delicacies of the noon meal. She was still there when I woke an hour later, protecting the food that had been officially tasted in the kitchens and must remain inviolate.

For three weeks I lived a lazy, pampered life, rising whenever I woke, spending long hours in the bath house and under the hands of the masseur and the cosmetician, adorning myself each day in whatever rich attire I chose. My skin began to gleam again, my hands and feet to soften, my hair to lose its brittle, unkempt wiriness. The copper mirror held before my face increasingly showed me the returning bloom of health and I no longer shrank from my reflection.

The month of Khoiak slid into Tybi. The first day of Tybi signalled the commemoration of the coronation of Horus and also that of our ailing Pharaoh. The harem emptied as the women, dressed in all their finery, got onto their litters and were carried from one celebration to another in the city, but no invitation came to me and I was glad. It was said that the King had rallied for his coronation remembrance and was presiding over the homage of his ministers and the congratulatory gift-giving of the foreign delegations. I could imagine him seated on the Horus Throne, the Double Crown on his head and the crook, flail and scimitar grasped in his large fists. The pharonic beard would be strapped to his uncompromisingly square chin. Cloth of gold would hide his wide girth. But his hennaed eyes would be puffy with fever and tiredness no matter how skilled his cosmetician and I did not think that Queen Ast, surely seated beside him like a stiff and dainty doll, would spare him a great deal of sympathy. Her own kohled eyes would be on her son the Prince, virile and handsome, exuding a vitality that the guests would not be able to help comparing with his father's increasing decrepitude.

Perhaps I was doing the Queen an injustice but I did not think so. I remembered her as coolly self-contained and full of the arrogance of her pristine blood. Poor Ramses, I thought as I wandered to the quiet bath house through the deserted courtyard. I loved you once, an emotion basely mingled with pity, some awe and much greedy irritation, but I do not think that you have ever been loved whole-heartedly by any save perhaps Amunnakht. It is a lonely thing to be a God.

Once during those three weeks I sent to the Keeper for any news of Hui, for one night I dreamed that he was drowned and I was standing on the bank of the Nile looking down on his peaceful dead features as the water rippled over them. But Amunnakht replied through one of his Stewards that though the search for the Seer was being conducted with exemplary thoroughness, he had not been found.

Yet the dream continued to haunt me for some time. I knew that if it had been myself I had seen floating dead in the Nile's slow washing, the omen would have been a good one, it would have meant a long life for me. Or if I had seen Hui plunging into the river, it would have signified the absolution of all his ills. But to have watched him thus in my sleep, already dead and unmoving, for that there was no easy interpretation. Did it symbolize my eventual triumph over him or was it trying to tell me something darker, something more terrible and literal? The possibility that he had killed himself occurred to me, causing me a few moments of extreme agitation, but I quickly calmed myself. Hui was incapable of suicide. He would retreat or feint, manouevre or compromise, he would always want to know what came next, right up until the instant when for him there would be nothing more. In the end the details of the dream faded and I ceased to fret over it, attributing it quite rightly to the rapid change in my circumstances and the fact that Hui's shadow was always lurking behind my thoughts.

I received letters from Kamen and from my brother, Pa-ari, who must have sat down as soon as he read my words to him and composed a reply. He told me that he had been able to keep my absence a secret for almost two weeks but then a priest from the temple had insisted on seeing me, and my mother had pushed her way into his house, demanding to diagnose and treat my illness. This surprised me, as my mother had been vociferous in her condemnation of me, and though she had not forbidden me to enter her house, she had made it plain that she did not wish to see me. Pa-ari wrote that he had done his best to keep both of them away but without success. He had been brought before the mayor of Aswat and charged with complicity in my escape. He had been held briefly in Aswat's one tiny prison while the mayor had sent for advice to the governor of the nome but had been released soon afterwards. The village was buzzing with speculation about me. He was overjoyed and relieved to know that I was well and that I had been reunited with my son. He expected word on his punishment at any time. I let his scroll roll up with a small rustle. By now the Prince's men would have found the body and be on their way back north. Pa-ari would be safe to return to his pretty wife and his three children and the work of scribe he loved. That was one debt no longer dragging on my conscience.

When two weeks had gone by, I went to see Hunro. My motives were wholly selfish and unworthy of me but I could not help myself. She had pretended to befriend me. The memory of her secret superiority, her calculated lies, still burned me with humiliation and I wanted, not to gloat perhaps, but to confront her with the reality of my triumph. Of course she would not need reminding of her situation. It may have been that I needed reminding of mine.

Accordingly I requested permission to do so from Amunnakht. He sent a servant to tell me that my petition had been passed to the Prince. I waited. A reply came with surprising speed. His Highness had granted a meeting between Hunro and myself, providing both guards on Hunro's door were present. I had expected Ramses to allow this. I had known him quite well and it seemed that he had not changed much. It would give him a secret pleasure to think of a confrontation between accused and accuser and perhaps, just perhaps, he believed I had a right to look into the eyes of the woman who had despised me and then abandoned me without regret. He had dictated his permission so that there would be no misunderstanding at Hunro's door. I had no doubt that every word passing between us would be reported to him, but I did not care. He was welcome to any entertainment he might derive from them.

I chose a morning when I had slept well. I selected a pale azure sheath whose elegant folds accentuated the deeper blue of my eyes, and all the jewellery I put on was silver. I wore my hair loose but covered in a net of silver thread into which small turquoise flowers had been sewn. It lay shining and thick just below shoulders that had by now been buffed to the sheen and colour of fine gold. I would have commanded that my palms and the soles of my feet be hennaed but my title had been taken away from me long ago and with it the right to display the badge of nobility. I knew that I no longer resembled the peasant who had walked up the ramp and onto Kamen's craft, but was my metamorphosis complete enough to cause Hunro distress? I hoped so. Isis anointed me with lotus perfume. I had sent her to find out in which precinct my old enemy was being held, and I was not surprised to hear that she had been placed in the children's quarters. I too had been relegated there after I had forfeited Pharaoh's interest by inadvertently becoming a mother.

I set off for the short walk with Isis beside me, holding the sunshade over my head. Word of my position in the harem had by now become the subject of common discussion, although how such news spread had always been a mystery to me, and the women who had stared at me with a caution almost amounting to hostility now greeted me affably. I called back to them as I crossed the lawn. Gaining the far side, I stepped into the brief gloom of the short passage that led to the narrow way between the four harem buildings and the palace itself and turned left. The children's quarters were at the end farthest away from the main entrance, and soon Isis and I were plunging into a maelstrom of noise and activity.

I could see the guards at the far side of the open square standing on either side of a closed cell door. I approached them and halted. Both of them bore the insignia of the Prince's Division of Horus, not that of the regular harem guards, and one of them wore a captain's armbands. I addressed him. "I am Thu, guest of His Highness in this place," I said formally. "I wish to speak with the prisoner." He looked at me thoughtfully.

"Do you have evidence of the Keeper's permission or that of His Highness?" he enquired. For answer Isis passed me the Prince's scroll and I handed it to him. He read it carefully then made as if to tuck it into his belt but I forestalled him.

"I would like to keep it," I said firmly. "In the event of any trouble resulting from my visit it is the proof that the Prince allows me to be here." I was no stranger to the perfidy of royalty and had no intention of trusting solely in Ramses' goodwill. The captain raised his eyebrows but after a slight hesitation handed the scroll to Isis.

"My trust in you is greater than yours in our Prince," he commented acidly. "Your servant must remain outside. You already know that my soldier and I must accompany you." I nodded. He turned to the door, untied the rope holding it closed, and pushed it open. My heart had begun to race but I willed it to slow. Straightening my shoulders, I walked inside, the men with me, and the captain closed the door behind us.

One narrow shaft of white daylight arrowed down from a slit window cut high in the far wall, just below the ceiling. It diffused softly through the room where its immediate ray did not touch, but my first impression was one of dimness after the brilliance of the morning outside. A woman was sitting cross-legged on the floor directly beneath the spear of sunshine, her head bent over something she was sewing. I thought at first that it was Hunro herself, but as she scrambled to her feet, linen in hand, and bowed, I saw that she was a servant. My glance barely grazed her, scanning the indistinct recesses beyond. Then someone stirred and I half-turned as Hunro took form out of the greyness and stepped before me.

She had changed. In the brief moment while we regarded each other I noted, with a mixture of satisfaction and dismay, how the long lines of her dancer's body had lost their definition and become perilously curved. Her mouth, once generous with laughter and full of opinion, was now grooved with a mild peevishness and the skin that had once reflected flawlessly her exuberant restlessness had an unhealthy, sallow tinge. She was still beautiful but her beauty had become a thing without edge, without that sharp, bright sparkle I had envied so much. "The years have not been kind to either of us, Hunro," I blurted. Her eyes narrowed and she smiled slowly, coldly.

"Well, well," she said. "It is Thu, the woman who has achieved the impossible and returned from the dead. If I had known I was to be so honoured, I would have had myself kohled and hennaed. Your sojourn in the grave has obviously improved neither your appearance nor your disposition, for in spite of the coddling you have received from whatever cosmetician assigned to you, you still resemble a desiccated corpse under your paint." One corner of her mouth rose in a sneer. "As for your disposition, you still have the manners of a peasant. No noblewoman would demean herself by entering my cell merely to gloat over my fate. I presume that is why you have invited yourself here."

"You are right," I said steadily. "But I am not here only to gloat, for no final verdict on your fate or mine has yet been pronounced, Hunro. I wanted to stand before the woman who lied to me, who betrayed the trust and friendship I thought was offered to me, and who showed her contempt for me in the end by turning her back. I do not think that those are the qualities of a true noblewoman." Her eyes darkened and her tongue appeared, running slowly along her upper lip.

"I will not stoop to excuses," she said. "Nor will you trick me into discussions or recriminations concerning the past, not with these men present to record every word I say. You have stood before me. Now go."

I hesitated, wishing now that I had not come, feeling ashamed of my base greed for such a petty little revenge. The light, perfidious phantom that had flitted mockingly through my dreams no longer existed. In its place I found a bitter, defeated woman under whose defiance lurked a cloud of fear. Where was the carefree dancer? "What happened to you, Hunro?" I asked her. "Why did you stop dancing?" She glanced down at her body with an involuntary expression of distaste which she immediately controlled.

"Because I realized suddenly that I could not dance my way out of the harem," she answered dully. "Ramses refused to let me go, and then there was nothing more." She looked up into my face. "When I was young, it seemed so much more wonderful to be the concubine of Pharaoh than the wife of a mere nobleman. I did not see into my future. I did not know."

"Neither did I," I whispered, and as I spoke, it came to me that my life, no matter how hard, had been more fortunate than hers. I had sinned and yet been given my freedom, but Hunro would not escape the consequences of her guilt so easily. "Forgive me for coming here, Hunro," I said forthrightly. "Even though I know you planned to kill me and probably still would if given the chance, it was a cruel thing for me to do." She took a step towards me, fists clenched.

"Oh how magnanimous you are," she said in a low voice that nevertheless trembled with scorn. "How gracious. How kind. The victorious Thu condescends to her fallen enemy. Save your pity. You are right. Ramses should have let you die. I disliked you from the moment you darkened the door of my cell all those years ago and I think no better of you now. Leave me alone!" She flung away from me in a clumsy parody of her former grace, walking through the brief illumination of the column of white light before disappearing into the shadowed corner, and I turned obediently to the door. One of the soldiers pulled it open for me and I went past him.

On the threshold I paused, taking deep breaths of the pure, hot air and letting the sun beat on my upturned face. Isis came hurrying with the sunshade raised and I felt the captain's hand on my elbow, impelling me gently away from the cell's entrance. Nodding my thanks, I set off across the grass of the courtyard, all at once aware of my parched throat and an ache of tension between my shoulder blades. There was a glory in my flexing knees, a consciousness of solemn privilege in the movement. I did not dare to look back.

I spent the remaining week before news came from the Prince in an indolent haze punctuated by bouts of shame regarding Hunro that alternated with a sense of the implacability of Ma'at. Justice would be served on her, on all of them, in spite of their efforts to pervert Ma'at's course to their own ends. The great cosmic balance in which truth, judgement and the bond between celestial and earthly government were held would be reasserted in Egypt. My sentence was over. Ma'at had ground me down and spat me out, chastened but free. Now it was rolling over the conspirators, and my shallow pity for Hunro did not extend to the others. I hoped that the weight of Ma'at would crush them entirely. Except, perhaps, Hui. Always my thoughts returned to him, and when they did I wrenched my mind back to whatever was solidly before me—food or wine or the feel of hands massaging my feet. All was in the hands of the agents of Ma'at, our Pharaoh and his son, and the matter would be adjudicated, stored in temple archives, and ultimately forgotten.

On the eighth day following my visit to Hunro, as I was sitting unclad and damp on my couch after my bath and waiting for Isis to bring my meal, the bright morning light was cut off by a tall figure who entered and bowed. Amunnakht was smiling. With an exclamation I grabbed up a discarded cloak and came to my feet, fumbling to wrap it around me in my excitement. "The news is good, isn't it Amunnakht?" I said breathlessly. "It is good?" He inclined his head and went on smiling in his usual urbane way.

"It is good," he agreed smoothly. "The Prince has asked me to tell you that a body was recovered from under the floor of your hut in Aswat. It had dried somewhat. It was brought to Pi-Ramses buried in sand so that it would not deteriorate further. It was examined by the palace physician to determine whether or not the wounds inflicted on it were as you and Kamen described and by three generals and several officers from various divisions." He paused, for effect I was sure, and I could see that the mighty Keeper of the Door was as ecstatic beneath his calm exterior as I was.

"Well?" I prompted him, my bare toes curling in anticipation. "Do not tease me, Amunnakht!"

"Several of the officers recognized the man as a Libu mercenary. Some years ago he was attached to the Division of Amun. When his time of indenture was over, he did not renew it. His general believes that he then went west, back to his Libu tribe, after letting it be known that he was available for hire as an assassin. Paiis obviously took note of his offer for any future use." He bowed again. "It seems that you will be pardoned for leaving your exile, Thu, and Paiis and the others will be put on trial for conspiracy to commit treason against a god."

"Then I may leave the harem? I may see my son?" He shook his head.

"No. You will be required to give evidence before the judges and so will Kamen. The Prince has decreed that you and he are not to confer with each other over this case. Besides, whether you like it or not you are still a royal concubine and as such you belong here until Pharaoh dies and his Heir revises the harem lists. You might like to know that the accused have all been brought within the palace compound and have been incarcerated in the barracks cells." He paused. "General Paiis is occupying the same room that held you seventeen years ago." I squeezed my eyes shut.

"Oh thank you Wepwawet, greatest of greatest," I murmured in a wave of powerful relief that rendered me temporarily weak. Then Amunnakht's words pierced my euphoria and I opened my eyes. "All the accused?" I demanded. "All of them?"

"No." Amunnakht had sobered. "The Seer cannot be found. Only the gods know where he is." I stared at him, perplexed yet somehow not surprised at his words, and spread my hands.

"What happens now, Amunnakht?"

"Now we wait. All the servants of the accused are being questioned. When the Prince is ready he will summon the judges, the accused and the accusers."

"But I thought that according to law the accused may not be present at a trial!" Amunnakht's blue-draped shoulders lifted in a shrug.

"His Majesty wishes an exception to be made. These are important people, Thu, and the charge is grave."

"I was not important enough to be present at my condemning," I remarked bitterly, and Amunnakht folded his arms and looked at me with disapproval.

"Nevertheless the rendering was just and your punishment deserved," he said sternly. "Self-pity does not suit you, Thu, not now. Will you stay a child forever? The King wishes to see you." I blinked.

"He does? Oh, Keeper, I have hoped … prayed … How is he? Is he well enough to receive me? What shall I wear?"

"You will decide on something appropriate," Amunnakht said. "I must be about my duties. Enjoy your triumph, Thu. The King's health is precarious. One day he rallies and the next he takes to his bed. You will not be given much warning of when you are to be summoned. I see that Isis is here with your food. Be well." He was gone. Light burst about my feet only to be cut off again as my servant entered with a tray. Seeing my face, she stood still.

"You have had a satisfactory visit from the Keeper?" she enquired. Pulling the cloak about me calmly, I backed to the edge of the couch and sat. All at once the full import of Amunnakht's message fell upon me. I felt it swirling dizzily about my head, brushing my heart so that it began to race, fingering my limbs so that they trembled. "Yes, Isis, most satisfactory," I managed through chattering teeth. "But I am suddenly cold. I will eat outside in the sunshine." At once she was concerned.

"Are you ill, Thu?" she wanted to know. "Shall I send for a physician?" My teeth were still chittering against each other and I explored, bemused, the violence of my reaction. Seventeen years of tension and anguish were being spewed forth and the process was beyond my control.

"No. It will pass," I gasped. "Take out the cushions and the canopy, Isis. Everything is all right."

But Hui, I thought. Hui. Wherever you are, in whatever anonymous place you have found refuge, you are the missing link in the chain of events that are surely leading to my vindication. If you cannot be found, then I cannot be completely healed from the wounds you inflicted on the child that I was. Unless you stand before me in the flesh and ask for my forgiveness for using and deceiving me, as I shall plead with the King for his pardon, I shall never be free of the gnawing worm of revenge. And that, above all else, is what I truly desire. I am tired of the anger and bitterness that are eating my heart away.

13

THE SUMMONS CAME three days later. I had spent the time as quietly as possible once the peculiar fit that had seized me was over, but I did not sleep well. In spite of my efforts to calm my thoughts they revolved anxiously around my audience with Ramses. How should I behave? What should I say? What would he say? I was as insecure at the prospect of this long-desired opportunity as I had been the first time Hui had taken me into the royal presence. My agitation became so great that I sent to one of the harem physicians for an infusion of poppy. The drug dulled my apprehension, but it still throbbed numbly under the somnolence induced by the draught.

But the moment the blue and white liveried Royal Under Steward appeared at my door, bowed, and delivered the command to stand before the Lord of All Life the same evening, all my doubts fled. Calmly I thanked the man, and when he had gone I sent for Isis. We discussed my apparel, perfume, jewellery, and when those things were decided upon I sent for a priest. Behind the closed door of my cell he lit incense, and while I prostrated myself before the small statue of Wepwawet I had managed to acquire from the harem storehouses, he intoned prayers of praise and supplication to my totem. I had an overwhelming sense of the god's affectionate concern. Yes, I thought with my nose against the floor matting and my eyes tightly closed, I have always relied on you, Opener of the Ways, to get me out of every foolish predicament I put myself in and you come to my aid because from the time of my youth I have never failed to honour and sacrifice to you. You have allowed me to be disciplined but not destroyed, and for that I owe you everything. Be with me now as I make yet another atonement. And may Ramses pardon and release me, I added, but briefly, secretly. I apologized to the priest for having nothing of my own to give him, either for his services or for Wepwawet himself, but I promised to offer what I could whenever I was able to lay claim to more than my own body. He merely smiled accommodatingly and left. The priests of Wepwawet, I reflected as I stood at my door amid clouds of fragrant grey smoke wisping out into the court-yard, are not greedy. Unlike the mighty servants of Amun.

Just before sunset I ate a light meal, and then Isis dressed me. After much deliberation I had chosen to wear a simple white sheath which fell from a wide silver collar, crossed over my breasts, and was gathered to my waist by a silver belt before folding about my ankles. I was not attempting a seduction. Those days were long gone. There would be no games. I would approach Ramses as myself, as honestly and sincerely as possible. The cosmetician brushed blue shadow on my eyelids, painted black kohl around my eyes, and reddened my mouth with a little henna. Isis gathered my hair behind my head and braided it, winding a silver ribbon through the now gleaming tresses, and fastened one silver and blue enamelled lotus over my ear. Large silver ankhs hung from my lobes and I slipped onto my wrist one band of silver onto which a gold ankh had been soldered. I had rejected the heavy sensuality of myrrh in favour of lotus perfume, and I sat still while Isis pressed the oil to my neck and dabbed it on my braid. Then I carried a chair to my doorway, and seating myself and folding my hands in my lap, I waited while Ra slowly descended into the mouth of Nut and shadows began to seep across the grass before me.

When I saw the Under Steward approaching, I rose and went to meet him, following him through the courtyard and along the short, roofless passage to the narrow path that divided harem from palace. Quickly he crossed it, spoke to the guard on the small but very high gate set in the almost unbroken wall that formed one side of the path, and I found myself, for the first time in seventeen years, placing my feet on the avenue that led to the royal bedchamber. At its end were massive double doors of cedar chased in gold. Steadily, with only the merest flutter of my heart, I walked towards them, fiercely denying the flood of memories pouring into my mind and threatening to unhinge me. The Under Steward knocked. One of the doors swung open. The man bowed, gestured that I could proceed, and went back the way we had come. I was on my own. Taking a deep breath, I stepped inside.

Nothing had changed. Great wooden lamp stands still marched across the lapis-inlaid expanse of the floor, the yellow flames glinting where their flickering light found the flecks of pyrite in the dusky blue of the tiles. Chairs of silver and electrum still sat haphazardly between low ebony tables whose surfaces gleamed with gold. The far walls of the huge room were lost in dimness but as always the shapes of stolidly waiting servants could be seen, ranged against them. The royal couch still rested on its stepped dais, the small table beside it a jumble of medicinal pots and jars.

I heard the door thud shut behind me. At once I went to the floor, kneeling and then bending over so that my forehead met the coldly beautiful lapis, and as I did so my nostrils filled with an odour I recognized only too well from my days as a physician. Foul and yet thickly sweet, it sent a tremor of shock through me. There is death in this room, I thought. He is dying. Ramses is really going to die. Until that moment the reality of his final illness had not been brought home to me, but now, as a voice somewhere above me called out, "The concubine Thu," and the echoes went rolling away to be lost in the gloom, my nerve almost failed me. He cannot die, I protested silently. He is Egypt, he is a god, he has been Ma'at for more years than I can count, his presence has brooded over everything from the smallest seed in my father's fields to the flowing of the Nile into the Great Green. His shadow fell across every day of my exile. Ramses! Then my good sense reasserted itself.

"Is it her?" His voice, weak but oh so familiar, broke on my ears like a blow. "She may rise and approach." I came to my feet, and slipping out of my sandals I paced to the dais, mounted it, and intended to kneel once more beside the couch. But as I looked down on it, I found myself paralyzed by a rush of such powerful emotion that I could not move.

He was lying propped up on many pillows, his shaved scalp covered, as was proper, by a linen cap. His barrel chest rose and fell, rose and fell under the welter of disordered sheets. One naked arm lay across the vast mound of his hidden belly. The other rested flaccidly against his thigh. In the glow of the one small lamp on the table beside him I saw that his face was puffy and sheened in sweat. His eyes, those brown eyes I remembered so well, always alive with a shrewd humour or cold with the sharp acuity of supreme authority, were now dully filmed with fever and exhaustion and I had the immediate and profound impression that here was a man not so much dying as used up. Nevertheless he was staring at me with full recognition and after a moment he lifted one hand. "The years of your exile have not taught you better manners, Thu," he wheezed. "You always were a law unto yourself." His words released me and I knelt, taking his cold fingers and pressing my lips to them.

"I am sorry, Your Majesty," I said. "Forgive me. You are right. I was distressed to see you like this. Something overcame me, shock or sadness or memories, and I forgot to reverence you. May I?" I rose, and sitting on the edge of the couch, reached over and laid my palm against his forehead. His skin fed an immediate high heat into my hand. "Do you have competent physicians, Majesty?" I wanted to know. He smiled faintly as I withdrew.

"Competent or not, they are unable to cure what ails me," he said. "They fuss and prattle, but they are all afraid to tell me the truth. That I am old and dying. I had always thought that you were a courageous girl who would rather brave my displeasure than lie to me, but I was wrong, wasn't I?" He moved pettishly.

"Not altogether, Majesty," I responded. "I did not lie to you when I spoke of Egypt's plight under the rapaciousness of the Houses of Amun, but my motive for doing so was evil. I did not lie to you when I confessed my love for you, but it was not as strong as I pretended. I did not lie when

I intended you to die." Those swollen, rheumy eyes wandered over my face.

"It was all so long ago, my Thu," he said. "Long ago and now so unimportant. I did not die. I believed I did not love you after you bore my son, but I was wrong. I sent you away and gave the boy to Men, but you troubled my dreams and it was I who felt the guilt, not you."

"Not so," I said swiftly, sudden tears pricking behind my own eyes. "For guilt became my bedfellow, Ramses, and I have waited for seventeen years to beg you for your forgiveness. Will you forgive me for what I did to you, the Holy One? I deserved the death you decreed for me."

There was a silence, and then he began to cough. Groping for my hand, he held me tightly, struggling for air. There was a stirring behind me as servants came forward out of the shadows, but with his other hand he waved them back. "It will be better tomorrow," he gasped finally. "This is not a prelude to death, not yet. I have some time left." Mastering himself, he let go my hand to push himself higher on the pillows but when he had done so he took my hand again. "I note that you ask for forgiveness not pardon," he whispered. "You have changed. My little scorpion would have wheedled a pardon out of me, but this woman, still lovely enough to stir me if I were able to be stirred, asks for nothing more than a word. Perhaps your exile taught you much after all, for I see no guile on your face, Thu." His fingers clenched around mine. "I forgive you. I understand. I did not forget the names you gave to my son and lo, the wheel turns, Ma'at lifts her head, and the names become traitors even now awaiting my august judgement." A sly little smile flitted across his ruined features. "You lusted after my son, didn't you, Thu? You thought to hide it from me but I knew."

"Yes, Lord."

"Did you sleep with him?"

"No, Lord. Neither he nor I was so perfidious."

"Good. Would you like me to command him to sign a marriage contract with you?"

I glanced at him sharply, all at once alert. Ill as he was, he was surely not above putting me to some kind of test. Or was it that with the door to the Judgement Hall slowly creaking open and the wind from the next world already soft on his cheek, he wished to bestow some last favour on me? Or had he discovered by some mysterious means that once I had forced the Prince to sign a document that would have made me one of his queens after his father's death? The Prince had asked me to use my influence with Pharaoh to have him designated the royal Heir, for my star had been high and bright at the time and Pharaoh was refusing me nothing. After my arrest the document had disappeared, reclaimed and doubtless burned by the Prince who did not want to be associated, even by inference, with a murderess. Ramses was watching me, a gleam in his eye that reminded me forcefully and bleakly of the tremendous zest for life that used to fuel his every action. I shook my head.

"No thank you, Ramses," I said. "I no longer desire your son. Nor do I wish to be a queen in Egypt."

"You lie when you say you do not wish to be a queen," he croaked, "but I congratulate you. That is the second time you have refused to take my bait. Oh, Thu, I did not realize until now how deep the wound of your sting had penetrated me. I not only forgive you, I pardon you also.

And I will have Amunnakht draw up a declaration of manumission so that you may leave the harem a free woman. Is there any man you do desire?" The tone of his voice was heavy with sadness. It touched an answering grief in me and I felt the tears begin to slide soundlessly down my face. I was still young. I would live and be fulfilled if the gods willed it so, but he was dying, relinquishing his hold on all he had come to love. The curious, twisted cord that had bound us together would soon be broken, and he would exist only as a fading ghost in my memories that would grow dimmer as I myself moved towards my end.

"I thought it would be different," I said huskily. "I dreamed for years of coming into this room and falling down before you and begging your forgiveness, and you would be the Ramses I remembered, and I would still be that impetuous, brazen child. Or better still, that one day you would come to Aswat and lift me out of the dirt and restore me to your bed and give me back my title and my pretty things. But it is not like that at all." I found myself beginning to sob, great spasms that hurt my throat. "The past is really dead, isn't it, Pharaoh? For you are ill beyond healing, and I am lost even in the midst of my vindication, and everything has changed."

"Come here," he rasped, and I crawled up onto the couch and laid my head against his shoulder. "I am not a fool, Thu," he said. "Take your freedom. Take whatever pretty things you want from the harem when you go. Take back your title. I will make it so. For am I not a god, and do the gods not shower us with blessings whether we deserve them or not? I loved you, but not enough. And you loved me, but not enough. We cannot alter what has been. In a few days the trial you have waited for will begin. Sit with your son, hold up your head, speak out at last against those who used you so remorselessly. And when it is over, go where you will and put it all behind you. Ask Men to allow you to stay for a while on his estate in the Fayum, so that you may rest and recover. Go with the goodwill of this old god." His voice trailed away and he sighed. With my ear against his chest I could hear the crepitation in his lungs as he breathed, yet under the rank odour of his sickness his skin gave off the faint aroma I remembered so well. Laughter and sex, fear and exultation, worship and betrayal, it all came back to me in waves and I cried until I was spent. Then raising myself, I looked down on him. His eyes were closed and I thought he was asleep. Bending, I kissed his half-open mouth.

"You are a good man, Ramses," I whispered. "A good man and a great god. Thank you. Think of me when you take your place in the Heavenly Barque." He opened one eye.

"What else will there be to do?" he murmured drowsily. "Go now, my Lady Thu. May the soles of your feet be firm." Slipping off the couch, I touched his shoulder and turned. The distance to the door seemed to grow as I walked over the dark tiles but at last I reached my sandals. Putting them on, I turned again and knelt, prostrating myself. The lamps twinkled like tiny stars lost in that hushed vastness. No sound from the watchful servants disturbed its peace. I closed the door quietly behind me.

Once Isis had undressed and washed me, I lay on my couch thinking that I would be unable to sleep but I did, falling suddenly into a sodden unconsciousness from which

I woke late with the aftermath of my tears still marking my face. It is a sign of aging, I said to myself as I held the copper mirror and critically inspected myself. When you are young you can laugh, cry for hours, drink yourself into a stupor, and still rise the next morning looking as fresh and unlined as you did the day before. Or the week before. Or even the year before. I sighed, considering that truth, and found in my mind no twinge of anxiety. Only yesterday I would have been thrown into a panic by the sight of my puffy eyes and irritated skin but now it did not matter at all, it was a trivial vanity beside the dreadful reality of the King's slow dissolution.

I had loved two men and lusted after a third. One had denied the depth of his feeling for me so that he could use me. One had loved me for my virgin beauty and then tossed me away. And the Prince? Last night I had ended any possibility of being possessed by that tall, muscular body and I did not care. It was true. I did not care. My words to Ramses had been sincere. Today I was as old as he, as spent as he. I no longer wanted power, over men or the kingdom. I simply wanted to see justice done and then retire to some quiet backwater, far from both Pi-Ramses and Aswat, and live in seclusion with Kamen and Takhuru. Last night Ramses and I had healed the wounds long open in both of us and I felt, right to the heart of my ka, the change in me. It was as though I had been flooded with colour when grey was all I had known.

I went to the bath house for cleansing and massage, but afterwards I did not bother to send for the cosmetician. I ate and then wandered about the courtyard talking to the other women. Rumours of the arrests were circulating, causing ripples of excitement and speculation, but I did not speak of my part in the affair. I had no desire to satisfy the curiosity in the eyes that both welcomed and followed me.

Late in the afternoon a Royal Herald bowed before me and held out a thin scroll. Thinking it was a message from Kamen I broke the seal without examining the wax and discovered a few lines of hieratic script written, astoundingly, in the King's own hand. "Dear sister," I read. "I have instructed Amunnakht to deliver to you whatever pretty things you wish to own and I have commanded the Keeper of the Royal Archives to find and destroy the document rescinding your title. When you choose to leave the harem, my Treasurer will give you five deben of silver so that you may buy land or whatever else you choose. Perhaps a small estate in the Fayum will be available. Be happy." It was signed simply "Ramses."

I nodded my thanks to the Herald and entered my cell, a lump in my throat. So I was the Lady Thu again. I could henna the palms of my hands and the soles of my feet. I could hunt ducks in the marshes with the throwing stick if I liked. Five deben of silver would feed me for the rest of my life or ... I tried to swallow away the lump that had become as big as a egg and threatened to force more tears. Or it would purchase a house and land, a place where I could grow vegetables and keep a cow and have a steward and labourers of my own.

Twice Ramses had mentioned the Fayum. So he remembered the estate he had deeded to me, teasing me and calling me his little peasant. We had visited it together. The land had been neglected, the house dilapidated, but he had allowed me to sleep within its empty womb for one night and when we returned to the palace I had set about hiring men to transform it. How I had loved it! The fields would nurture me, I had believed. We would own each other and it would reward my care with luxuriant crops and the safety and security of something that would not rust or fade or be lost.

But it had been taken away from me after my disgrace. Everything I had thought was mine had been snatched away and given to others. Who owned it now? I did not know. But Pharaoh had remembered how much his gift had meant to me, how although I had worn fine linen of the twelfth grade and gone about hung with gold, my heart was the heart of a peasant to whom land was a living thing, and he had moved now, quickly, before he was unable to make any more decrees, before … I sat for a long time, the papyrus cradled in my lap, and stared unseeingly at the far wall of my cell.

Another week went by before the trial began, and in that time Amunnakht took me into the huge, heavily guarded harem storehouses, opened an empty chest, and told me to fill it with whatever linens and jewellery I liked. I took not only sheaths, rings, necklets, anklets, earrings and arm and headbands but precious oils and fresh natron too. I found a cosmetic table with a hinged lid and stacked it with pots of kohl and henna. In a small room devoted entirely to medicines I took a box and put in it a mortar and pestle before selecting such an array of herbs and salves as I had not seen since I worked for Hui. "Am I being greedy?" I asked a patient Amunnakht, my eyes on the crowded shelves, one of the royal physicians standing by anxiously. I did not feel greedy. I felt quite calm and detached. I was collecting a future, and Ramses would know this.

"No, my Lady," the Keeper replied, "but even if you were, it would not matter. The King wishes it." He had addressed me by my title. Its restoration must be common knowledge then. Lifting down a small sack, I opened the drawstring and found myself looking at layers of dried kat leaves. I laid them on top of my other acquisitions.

But the discovery that gave me real pleasure was a scribe's palette complete with several unworn brushes of various thicknesses, a stack of papyrus, a sturdy scraper to smooth the sheets and pots of ink. Clutching these things to my now rather dusty breast, I smiled at Amunnakht. "Tie up the chest and seal it and store it for me," I requested. "I will have to send for it when Kamen and I are settled somewhere. But I will take the scribe's tools back to my cell with me. I want to write to the King." He bowed without speaking and I left him then, stepping out into the heat of the day and walking quickly towards my courtyard. I had written nothing in my own hand since I had finished the story of my life in far away Aswat and I longed to feel the familiar shape of a brush in my hand and the palette across my knees. I would honour these things by pouring out my gratitude to the King.

I was warned the day before the trial began, and so I was ready when the two soldiers came in the early morning to escort me into the palace. Now, arrayed in blue linen and gold, my hands and feet were proudly hennaed and I wore rings at last, for my fingers had grown thin and soft again with Isis's daily care.

We left the harem by the main gate and began to pace along the paved way that joined the wider avenue running to the imposing pillars that marked the public entrance to the palace, and all at once I realized that the lawns between the watersteps and the towering outer wall of the royal precincts were crowded with people. A murmur went up when I appeared, and the front line surged forward. Immediately more soldiers came running to surround me, roughly pushing through the press. I went on steadily, head high, while ripples of excitement shook the throng. I heard my name several times. "Captain, how do they know?" I asked the man at my elbow. He shrugged.

"The General Paiis is popular in the city and his arrest could not be hidden. The rest is rumour and speculation. They have come because they smell blood. They are not sure whose." At that moment a voice called, "Mother!" and I had time for a brief glimpse of Kamen's strained face before I was enveloped in his embrace. I held him tightly while his escort and mine struggled against the swell of bodies around us. He set me away smiling, but I thought he looked unwell. His eyes were bloodshot and darkly circled in spite of the kohl enhancing them. "The last time I saw you, you were barefoot and dressed in nothing but a coarse kilt," he said. "I hardly recognize you now. You are truly beautiful."

"Thank you, Kamen," I said. "But you do not seem well."

"No," he responded shortly. "The waiting has been hard."

"We must move, my Lady," the Captain cut in urgently. "I do not wish to order violence to be done to these people." Kamen raised his eyebrows at me.

"My Lady?" he queried. I nodded.

"I have made my peace with your father," I said, "and he has given me back my title." Behind him stood his adoptive father and Nesiamun and I greeted them briefly as together Kamen and I turned towards the pillars.

"Takhuru has offered prayers for our vindication every day since you and I parted," Kamen told me. "She sends her blessings today." For some reason this news annoyed me.

"That was kind of her," I said more sharply than I had intended, and he put an arm about my shoulders and laughed.

"I am flattered by your jealousy," he chuckled.

There were more soldiers fronting the pillars, swords drawn and spears extended. As we drew near them and they parted cautiously to let us through, I said, "Kamen, would you like to know the name that was chosen for you by the palace astrologers when you were born?" He glanced down at me, startled.

"Gods!" he breathed. "That is something I have never considered, but of course I was named before I was taken from you. Why now, Mother?" We had passed the protecting guard and entered the cool shadows of the pillars. At once the turbulent noise behind us fell to a muted mutter.

"Because when the Overseer of Protocol calls the names and titles of both the accused and us, the accusers, he will use both your original name and the one you bear now. I did not want you to hear it first from him." In the pause that followed I could feel him tensing, preparing himself for what I would say.

"Tell me," he said. I kept my eyes on the broad shoulders of the soldier in front.

"You were named Pentauru." The tension went out of him and he grunted.

"Excellent scribe," he said. "It is a peculiar choice for the son of Pharaoh, and not at all suitable for the soldier that I am. I do not like it. I will remain Kamen."

We had come to a halt before the doors to the Throne Room. Usually they were kept open to accommodate the constant flow of ministers, petitioners and delegations, but today the Captain strode up and banged on them with one gloved fist. Evidently the trial was to be held here. They were pulled open, and with our escort now ranged behind us, we passed through. I do not like it either, I thought as the slap of our sandals echoed in the sudden vastness. I never liked it. Kamen is right to want to keep a name that honours the man who raised him and loves him, but I wish that Ramses had asked to see him, even though he is merely one royal bastard among dozens. How will this court treat him? With the deference that should be accorded to a half-brother of the Heir? An Under Steward was leading us to seats placed along the right-hand wall and Kamen removed his arm from me. We sat in a row, Kamen, Men, Nesiamun and I. Footstools were produced. The soldiers took up their stations behind us.

I watched Kamen's eyes explore the sheer magnificence of this hall. The cavernous expanse of its floor and the walls as well were tiled in lapis so that one felt that one was deep under dark blue water shot through with golden sparks from the flecks of pyrite caught in the holy stone that only the gods were allowed to wear on their person. Golden bases as tall as I held large alabaster lamps and censers swung from gold chains, filling the air with fragrant bluish smoke. Servants arrayed like gods themselves, their blue-and-white tunics bordered in gold and their sandals jewelled, stood their watches at intervals around the walls, waiting to be summoned.

At the far end of the room, facing the entrance, a dais ran from wall to wall. It held two thrones of gold standing upon lions' feet, their backs sheets of beaten gold depicting the Aten, its life-giving rays spreading out to embrace the divine spines that would rest against them. One, of course, was the Horus Throne, sacred to Pharaoh. The other was for the Great Royal Wife and Queen, Ast. I noticed that a third chair sat beside them. Here was the heart of Egypt's power. Here the Holy One came to be worshipped and feted, to receive foreign dignitaries and send forth his decrees, and the soaring dimensions of the place were heavy with an atmosphere of awesome authority. Behind the thrones, to the left, was a small door leading, as I knew, to a modest robing room. I had been that way with Hui on my first visit to the palace when he had brought me into Ramses' presence. I supposed that I should have to speak of that. I was here, after all, to accuse the Seer. But I did not want to think about it then.

The small door opened and there was a stir as about ten men filed through, crossed the dais, and took their places on chairs on the floor fronting it. I did not recognize any of them. "The judges," Nesiamun whispered in response to a word from Kamen. "All formidable men but not all impartial I believe. Three of them are of foreign blood. We shall see." I stared at them openly as they settled themselves, folding their ankle-length kilts about their calves and talking to each other in low voices. Their whispers ran around the hall in sibilant echoes. Most of them looked to be middle-aged or older apart from one, a rather good-looking young man with a keen eye and ready smile.

Their conversation died away. I could see them casting contemplative glances at me. Of course they knew who I was, having already read and heard all the evidence collected, but I could deduce nothing from their cool expressions. I felt a pang of anxiety. Perhaps they had considered the evidence inconclusive. Perhaps they had decided that it was impossible for such mighty and influential men as Paiis and Hui to be guilty of treason and I was lying and must now, after seventeen years, see my sentence fully carried out at last. But Ramses had pardoned me. The Prince had thought the evidence against those men strong enough to convene a trial. I was being foolish, allowing my surroundings and a few solemn-faced men to shake my security.

The rear door opened again and this time all the company rose and bowed, arms outstretched, for a Herald had emerged and was calling, "The Horus-in-the-Nest, Commander of the Infantry, Commander in Chief of the Division of Horus, The Prince Ramses, Beloved of Amun," and behind him the Prince came, resplendent in ceremonial military attire. Flanked by his aides, he strode to the third chair on the dais and seated himself, crossing his legs and gazing down the hall. "Rise and sit," the Herald concluded, taking his own place on the edge of the dais at Ramses' feet, and I regained my chair and studied the man for whom my body had burned.

He had been somewhere in his early twenties when I first saw him in his father's bedchamber and had mistaken him for Pharaoh himself. With his perfect soldier's body, the grace of his movement, his wonderfully even features dominated by a pair of piercing brown eyes, he had fulfilled my girlish fantasy of everything I believed I would see when I came face to face with Egypt's god. But he had been merely a prince then, not even the oldest royal son by birth, and in competition for his father's favour with two of his brothers, also named Ramses. The man Hui had brought me to see, the god in whom the real power resided, had been a bitter disappointment. Rotund, lascivious and seemingly genial, it had been a long time before I saw past Pharaoh's indifferent body and dismayingly ordinary personality to the dignity and clear-sighted intelligence of a god beneath. Prince Ramses had liked to spend much time alone in the desert, hunting or communing with the Red Land. He had cultivated an image of kindness and impartiality, but I had discovered that this mask hid an ambition as great as my own had been. He was as ready to use me to gain the approval of his father as Hui was to gain Pharaoh's death, and I had taken the disillusionment very hard.

Studying him now, I could see the first mild encroachments of middle age. Though he obviously still took his exercise regularly and his body had remained taut, he had thickened about the waist and his face had lost something of the clean lines that had drawn the eye so irresistibly. Flesh puckered slightly over the golden commander's armbands gripping his upper arms, and as he bent to address a brief word to the Herald, the suspicion of a fold appeared under his chin. Yet he was still an almost perfect example of masculine pride and beauty. I could appreciate the sight of him, although he no longer shortened my breath. He must have felt my long regard, for he turned his head in my direction and our eyes met. Raising one dark, feathered eyebrow he smiled, the salute of one survivor to another, and I smiled back. It was going to be all right.

The Herald had risen, and at his signal the main doors were pulled open. Soldiers paced briskly through and behind them came the prisoners, flanked and herded by more soldiers. I had thought they might be chained, but they were walking freely, a concession, I supposed, to their exalted rank. The doors closed behind them with an ominous, echoing thud. They were ushered to the stools ranged along the wall opposite to us, and at a word from the Herald they sat.

There they were, my old friends, my old enemies, clad not in the sweat-stained, dusty plain kilts I had expected but their own sumptuous garments. All of them were painted and bejewelled. Paiis had on his General's insignia. I was momentarily indignant, for when I had been arrested and placed in the cell from which Paiis had just come, I had been deprived of everything. The judges had come to me and I had been forced to face them unwashed and barely clad. But you were only a concubine, I reminded myself. And besides, these men, and Hunro too, have not yet been condemned. I looked them over unabashedly.

Paiis had not changed much. He still exuded an air of rather grubby salaciousness. He was over-painted, his mouth too orange, his eyes too thickly encircled with kohl. As soon as he sat down, his gaze became fixed on me with a mixture of threat and challenge intended to cow me but it left me unmoved. I had once thought him a romantic figure. How innocent I had been!

My glance slid to Paibekamun. His face was pale. He was staring straight ahead, his hands folded in his lap. You I hate, I thought fiercely. You I will be glad to see go down, you arrogant, disdainful man. You took every opportunity to silently remind me of my peasant roots, even when in your capacity of Royal Butler you had to admit me to Pharaoh's bedchamber, and in spite of your desire to see Ramses dead you took an evil pleasure in my downfall. I hope they flay the skin from your body before they execute you.

When I looked at Hunro, the rage within me became tempered with a little of the pity and shame I had felt when I had confronted her in her cell. She was rigid but composed, her back straight, her tiny feet together in their delicate sandals. Her hand rested in the hand of the man sitting next to her and I realized after a moment of puzzlement that it was her brother Banemus, the General who had spent most of his life commanding Egypt's southern garrisons and holdings in Nubia. Burly and weatherbeaten, yet I remembered his open, frank face and how I had warmed to him on the one occasion he had been in Hui's house. I do not want to see him die, I thought. Surely he cannot share the full load of guilt with Hui and Paiis. He has been away from the centre of their machinations for too long. As for the others, Mersura, Panauk, Pentu, I hardly noticed them. They meant nothing to me and I did not spare them one thought.

A waiting silence filled the hall. Someone cleared his throat. Someone else's bracelets clinked loudly. Then the little door slid open for the last time that morning and an official came swiftly out, bowed low to the Prince, and stepping off the dais, went to stand in the centre of the floor. He wore a long blue and white kilt and a wide white sash across one shoulder. His shaved skull was bare. Behind him a scribe carried a thick stack of papyrus and a servant a collapsible table which he set up before the official. The pile of paper was placed on it. The scribe sank cross-legged beside it and the servant glided away.

The official turned to the dais and bowed again. The Prince raised one beringed finger. My heartbeat quickened. "In the name of Amun Greatest of Greatest, King of all gods, and by the divine authority of Ramses User-Ma'at-Ra, Meri-Amun, Heq-On, Lord of Tanis, Mighty Bull, Beloved of Ma'at, Stabilizer of the Lands, Lord of the Shrines of Nekhbet and Uatchet, Mighty One of Festivals like Ta-Tenen, the Horus of Gold, Mighty One of Years, Protector of Egypt, Vanquisher of Foreign Lands, Victor over the Sati, Subduer of the Libu and Enlarger of Egypt, I declare this Court of Examination in session," the official half-chanted. "I am the Overseer of Protocol. This trial will be presided over by His Highness the Prince Ramses, the Horus-in-the-Nest, by the command of Pharaoh, who has dictated the following statement."

The scribe at his feet had laid his palette ready across his knees, opened his ink, and selected a brush. He waited. The Overseer of Protocol selected a papyrus sheet and read from it in the same sonorous voice. "I, Ramses User-Ma'at-Ra, Beloved of Ma'at and upholder of the feather of justice, charge the judges in this case to behave with impartiality to all stations of men brought into the Court of Examination. Be assured of the guilt of the accused before condemning them. But remember that as for all that they have done, their deeds are upon their own heads whereas I am privileged and immune unto eternity since I am among the righteous kings who are in the presence of Amun-Ra, King of the Gods, and in the presence of Osiris, Ruler of Eternity."

What a curious statement, I thought. What is Ramses trying to justify himself for? Displaying faulty judgement for elevating these men to positions of power in the first place? Doing little more than casting a desultory eye over their movements in the years since my list was placed in his hands when a more vigorous investigation might have freed me from exile sooner? They were words of excuse no god would use and they unsettled me. The Overseer was continuing. "Nevertheless, if they are found to be guilty of the crime of which they are accused, it is my desire that they should not be executed but die by their own hands."

I knew that such a sentence was customary for those of noble rank, but I could not help wondering whether in commanding them to kill themselves Ramses was indulging in a moment of wholly ungodlike vengeful spite. Although he had been a great warrior in his early days, defeating the host of tribes who had attempted to invade Egypt, he had been unable to wholly wrest the power that should have been his within Egypt itself from the greedy hands of the Amun priests. Thus in his impotence he had occupied the throne uneasily, being forced to defer often to the richer and more influential High Priest of Amun, and the strain of such unremitting diplomacy had taken its toll. He trusted few men, and it occurred to me that in turning so deliberately to bite the royal hand which had fed them unstintingly, Paiis and the others had sunk their teeth into the one existing wound guaranteed to cause the King the most pain. Ingratitude. I glanced at Paiis. He was twisting his foot to and fro and watching the light glint on the jewels of his sandal.

The Overseer of Protocol had handed the King's charge down to his scribe. At his signal the judges rose to be named. In a loud voice the Overseer identified them one by one, and as he did so, each regained his seat. "Baal-mahar, Royal Butler," he called. One of the foreigners Nesiamun mentioned, I thought. Syrian perhaps. "Yenini, Royal Butler." Another foreigner, this one a Libu. "Peloka, Royal Councillor." This time I had to guess the man's roots. Lycian, I surmised. "Pabesat, Royal Councillor. May, Royal Scribe of the Chancery. Hora, Royal Standard Bearer." This one was the younger man with the brisk manner and lively eyes. "Mentu-em-taui, Royal Treasurer. Karo, Royal Fanbearer. Kedenden, Royal Councillor. Pen-rennu, Royal Interpreter." They were all seated again, ten judges in all. There was a pause while the Overseer bowed to the Prince. Ramses nodded his acceptance of the men on the chairs ranged below him and the Overseer turned back into the room.

The Herald stood. "The accused will kneel," he intoned. "His Royal Highness will state the charges." The prisoners did as they were told, Paiis with nonchalance, Hunro clumsily and clearly distressed. When they had touched their foreheads to the floor and were once more upright, Ramses continued. He remained seated, his brown legs crossed, his arms lying loosely along the arms of his throne.

"The Overseer has the formal charges," he said, "and we all know what they are. I do not need to accuse you indi-

idually. You are all indicted for the same offences. The first
is one of conspiracy to commit treason by the murder of the
King, using an ignorant and misguided girl as your instrument. The second is yet another conspiracy, this time to
destroy the evidence, both human and recorded, that
threatened to bring you to justice. You are in Egypt, all of
you, not in some barbaric backwater, and in Egypt even
Pharaoh is not above the law of Ma'at. It saddens me to see
such noble blood brought low."

But he does not look sad, I thought. Only relieved. He
must make a public example of Paiis and the rest and do it
so finally that in years to come, when he is the one sitting
on the Horus Throne, men will remember the price of
treason.

"Depositions have been taken from your servants, your
families and your friends," the Prince was concluding. "The
judges have read them all, but the Overseer will recount
them aloud so that the accusers may note any discrepancies
in their contents. You may take your seats." He nodded
once, brusquely. The Overseer selected a sheet of papyrus
and took a deep breath.

"The statement of one Disenk," he said, "cosmetician, of
the house of the Lady Kawit in Pi-Ramses, once cosmetician in the house of Hui the Seer." It was the first time
Hui's name had been mentioned and besides, this was the
dainty, snobbish little Disenk's account of the days when
she had taught me how to behave like a noblewoman and
had slept outside my door to keep me from straying, but my
attention became fixed on Paiis. He was leaning back with
his arms folded and he was smiling. That man knows something that we do not, I thought suddenly, and a shiver went

through me. He believes that he will be exonerated. Why? Does he know where Hui is? Have they plotted some surprise for us together? Or has he somehow managed to shift all the blame onto Hui's shoulders, for it seems that Hui is safely out of the reach of this court's decisions and cannot be questioned? I began to feel a frightened anger. If Paiis was set free, what would happen to Kamen and me? Would Paiis hunt and kill us out of sheer vindictiveness? I believed so. I tried to wrench my mind back to Disenk's statement and failed.

The reading of the depositions took a long time, and the hall had become close and hot by the time the Overseer, his voice now ragged, placed his hand on the tall pile and said, "These are the words recorded. Does anyone wish to refute them?" There was a heavy, almost drowsy silence. I had not been giving them the attention I should. My thoughts were still revolving around the General. He seemed to sense my discomfiture. When I glanced covertly at him, I found that he was looking at me with an open, impudent stare.

The Overseer repeated his question. No one answered. The Herald came to his feet. "The court will resume in two hours," he called. "Make your obeisances." The Prince had also risen and was striding to the rear door accompanied by his entourage. We all bowed. The judges stretched and began chattering to each other. The Herald appeared at my elbow. "Food has been prepared for you in the gardens," he said quietly. "You may all follow me."

"I would rather sleep than eat," Nesiamun remarked as we left the hall by the main entrance. He fell to talking with Men. I slipped my hand through Kamen's arm. Before coming to the palace's public doors, we turned left and soon found ourselves pacing across the banqueting hall, forested with pillars and sunk in an echoing gloom at that time of the day. A faint odour of stale incense filled my nostrils, and then we were passing between the row of columns that served for a wall and out into blinding sunshine.

Ahead of us, beyond the paved path that ran on, I knew, past Pharaoh's private office to the offices of his ministers, was an expanse of lawn in the centre of which a large fountain spurted water into its stone basin. Beside it an awning had been erected, shading a table laden with dishes. Servants stood waiting to attend us. Kamen pressed my hand and then shook himself free to inspect the fare. I lowered myself onto the cushions scattered about and immediately a servant appeared, bending to pour me wine. Another laid a square of linen across my lap and set a tray of food beside me.

I looked about. Our guards had followed us and had formed a loose circle about the lawn, not, I knew at once, to keep the curious away but to make sure that we had no commerce with anyone else. The accused perhaps? It was more likely that we were not going to be given a chance to bribe or subvert the judges.

Kamen sank onto the grass beside me. "The depositions were interesting," he said after taking a sip of his wine. "How did the interrogators persuade the servants to tell the truth? It all tallies with your manuscript, Mother, but they lied after you were arrested."

"Their masters were in positions of strength then," I answered, fondly watching his strong fingers rifle through the appetizing dishes on the tray. "There was no evidence to endanger them. Today it is different. Kamen, have you noticed the General?" He shot me a speculative glance.

"Yes," he said shortly. "Paiis has some sort of information of which we are ignorant. I do not like it. And where is the Seer?" My appetite had left me. Draining my cup, I held it up to be refilled.

"Not only is he absent but the Prince made no reference to him at all when he spoke the charges," I replied. "Surely even if the authorities cannot find him, he should still have been included. Disenk's and Kaha's depositions dealt with him of course, but, Kamen, where are Harshira's words?"

"He has disappeared as well," Kamen said. "Didn't you know? I think he and Hui are somewhere safe together."

"Does Paiis know where they are?" He shrugged.

"Perhaps. But I have the strangest feeling that the Prince knows." I stared at him in horror and grabbed his arm.

"Gods, Kamen! Has Hui made a secret pact with the Double Crown? Sacrificed Paiis and Paibekamun and Hunro to save himself? Or even ..." My fingers tightened around his warm flesh. "Even persuaded the Prince to condemn me also?"

"Now you are being foolish," he chided me. "Pharaoh has pardoned you. You have served your sentence for your part in the conspiracy. Nothing can harm you now." I released him and stared out from under the awning at the brilliant early afternoon. I think you are wrong, I said to myself. Hui can, if he chooses. I know this. Paiis is a crude blunderer compared to Hui's slow, subtle thoughts. Hui has done something. But what?

At Kamen's urging I choked down a few morsels of the delectable food the palace kitchens had produced for us and then lay back on the cushions, watching the linen roof of the canopy billow in the fitful breeze. Men and Nesiamun were engaged in some discussion involving the export of faience. Their voices and the mundane nature of their conversation were lulling, but I was tense with fear, caught in a formal and ponderous proceeding that must grind to its end and from which I could not escape.

"The Lady Hunro is not as beautiful as you described her in your account of your early days," Kamen said. He was lying beside me, propped on one elbow, his head resting on his palm. His dark eyes smiled into mine. "I had expected to see a woman slim and willowy as a marsh reed, but there is already an air of old age about her. Has she been ill?"

"Only with disillusionment and regret," I told him. "The years cannot be kind to a woman whose heart has shrivelled for want of loving." He looked at me shrewdly.

"Then what strange love has kept you young, O my mother?" he murmured. I had no reply and was saved from having to think of one by the peremptory summons of the Herald. We filed after him back into the Throne Room.

The accused were already in their places. I did not know whether they had been fed or not. The judges were coming in and behind them six servants carrying fans. Taking up their stations, they began to move the air around us, the quivering white ostrich plumes noiseless as they lifted and fell. The Overseer and his scribe paced to the table, the scribe going to the floor and preparing his palette. The soldiers closed the doors and went to stand about the walls. From the back of the dais the Prince came forward, slid into his chair, and acknowledged our reverence absently. His glance went at once to Paiis. His smile held something smug, unpleasant. "Proceed," he said to the Overseer. The man turned to me.

"Lady Thu," he said. "Will you now rise and accuse the prisoners on the matter of the first charge."

I had longed for this moment, longed for it, dreamed of it down all the hard years of my exile. In Wepwawet's temple, cloth in my hand and painful grit under my bare knees, I had imagined how it would be while I scrubbed at the stone flags. Sometimes in the tiny garden I had managed to scrape out behind my hut, I would pause from my weeding and sit back on my haunches while vivid pictures rolled through my mind: myself creeping into Hui's bedchamber, knife raised; myself seducing Paiis and then slitting his throat while he slept, satiated beside me; myself with a handful of Hunro's hair, forcing her to the ground while she screamed and clawed at me.

But after these disturbing scenes, in which, I knew, lay the seeds of madness and a true despair, would come the saner but no less improbable vision of myself standing before Pharaoh and a room full of shadowy people, telling the story of my own seduction and the cold, deliberate plot that had lain behind it. The reality was smaller somehow, less dramatic, but my moment had come. Vindication was at hand. Rising, I bowed to the Prince, lowered my head to the Overseer, and turning towards the judges, I began, "My father was a mercenary ..."

I spoke while the afternoon wore away, stopping occasionally to drink the water placed in my hand, pausing when emotion thickened my throat and threatened to undo me. I ceased to see the line of attentive men, the Prince slumped behind them with his eyes fixed on my face, the vague shape of the Overseer to my left. I forgot Kamen, breathing gently beside me. Gradually my words took life,

perhaps my life was lived again through my words, and
with them came the images, sharp and clear, infused with
fear or joy, uncertainty or surprise, panic or pride. Once
more I sat in the desert with Pa-ari and cried out to the gods
in my frustration. Once more I stood in the dimness of
Hui's cabin, Nile water dripping from my limbs, my nerve
almost failing me. I remembered my first glimpse of
Harshira, standing on Hui's watersteps to bring order out of
the chaos of disembarkation after the long voyage from
Aswat to Pi-Ramses.

And I told of the darker things, my education at the
hands of Kaha and then Hui, all calculated to prepare me
for my entrance into the harem, changing my girlish ignorance into a violent prejudice against the King and a disillusionment with government in Egypt that would lead to
my attempt on Ramses' life. I did not spare myself, but
neither did I cloak the purposes of the accused who had
trained me like a hunting dog to one purpose and who had
had no more regard for me than handlers with a valuable
living tool.

Only once did I cry. When I described how I obtained
the arsenic from Hui, mixed it in the massage oil, and
presented it to Hentmira, the girl who had replaced me in
Pharaoh's affections, I could not prevent tears of remorse
from spilling over. I did not try to wipe them away. This too
was a part of my punishment, this public atoning, the final
act to bring healing and wholeness to me. I had known that
Hentmira would probably die. I had told myself that her
fate was in her own hands, whether she chose to use the oil
on Pharaoh or not, an evil argument that now filled me
with self-loathing. At the time my hatred and panic had

engulfed all else, but over the years of my exile I had come to deeply regret the callousness that had deprived a young woman of any chance to see her own hopes and dreams fulfilled.

I did not tell of my arrest or sentencing. Those things had little to do with the crime. The court knew how everyone from Hui down to his lowest kitchen slave had lied and left me to die alone. Nor did I speak of the Prince's bargain with me where I should gain a queen's crown if I kept the Prince's virtues before his father. That was a private matter. The Prince might even have forgotten all about it. By the time I sat down, trembling and exhausted, I had laid bare the full dimensions of the plot against the throne. My part was over.

Another break was ordered, and as before, we were escorted out into the garden. I was shocked to see that the sun had almost set and the water in the fountain was splashing red. The evening air was cool and sweet with the aroma of unseen flowers. Suddenly I was ravenously hungry, and ate and drank immoderately. It was almost over, all of it. Tomorrow I could begin my life anew.

When we re-entered the throne room, the huge lamps about the walls had been lit and the fanbearers did not return. The judges took their seats looking listless and tired. The accused, too, seemed weary. The day had begun early for everyone. Only the Prince and the Overseer appeared fresh. They conferred briefly before the Overseer strode to his table. He motioned to Kamen. "King's Son Pentauru, otherwise known as Officer Kamen, will you now rise and accuse the prisoners on the matter of the second charge."

So Kamen in his turn bowed to the Prince and the Overseer and began his share of our story, his voice ringing

out strong and clear. I listened attentively as he spoke of
our first meeting when he and his Herald put in at Aswat
and he undertook the responsibility of my manuscript not
knowing that I was his mother. He did not falter when he
described how he had taken it to General Paiis, his superior,
and how shortly thereafter he had been commissioned to
return to Aswat with orders to arrest me but his suspicions
regarding the man accompanying him had grown as he
proceeded further south. His words regarding the attempt
on our lives and how he had killed the assassin and we had
buried him under the floor of my hut were steady.

This is my son, I thought with a rush of wonder and
pride. This intelligent, able, upright young man is flesh of
my flesh. Who would have thought that the gods would
grant me such a gift? I felt gratitude towards Men, sitting on
Kamen's other side with his arms folded and his head down
as he also absorbed Kamen's tale. He had been a good father
to my son, and Shesira a worthy mother, raising him with
a greater discretion than he would have received if he
and I had remained in the harem. Kamen had learned self-
reliance, modesty, an interior discipline that even now I
myself could not lay claim to, and I knew that if I had been
responsible for his rearing, young and selfish as I was, I
could not have inculcated those things in him.

If I closed my eyes, I could hear faint echoes of his royal
father's tones as his recitation of the facts drew to a close,
and I had already noted, as surely all in the room had noted,
the striking physical similarity between the Prince listening
on the dais and his earnestly gesticulating half-brother. The
blood of a god coursed through Kamen's veins. If the King
had signed a marriage contract with me as I had begged him

to do in a frenzy of desperation, the prospect of incarceration in the harem for the rest of my life driving me to the inevitable humiliation I had suffered in the presence of many of his watching ministers, then my son would have been fully royal and entitled to all the riches and deference the Prince enjoyed. He might even have been named the Horus-in-the-Nest, the Heir. Firmly I quashed the thought that had begun to curl inside me like thin smoke. You really are an ungrateful and greedy woman, Thu, I chided myself. Will you ever stop wanting everything?

14

AFTER KAMEN HAD SAT DOWN, with a smile for me and a low word to his adoptive father, Men himself and Nesiamun rose in their turn and spoke briefly of their involvement. It had been slight and they soon fell silent. When they had finished, there was a general loosening throughout the room. Men yawned and stretched surreptitiously and the judges fell to whispering among themselves. But the moment did not last long. The Overseer called for order. "The evidence has been heard," he said. "The time for condemnation is at hand. His Highness will speak." Ramses stirred. He leaned forward, his face blank.

"Stand up, Paiis," he said. Paiis's head swivelled in his direction. An expression of puzzlement flitted across his face, a mere twinge of surprise, before he obeyed. The protocol of a court proceeding required that after the evidence was presented the judges, who had been acquainted with it before the case was heard, would rise one by one and immediately give their verdict. It would be left to whatever dignitary was presiding to decide on and pronounce the sentence. Ramses flicked a hand over the line of men beneath him. "Look at them, General," he commanded. "What do you see?" Paiis cleared his throat. He had taken up a soldier's stance, legs apart and hands behind his back, but now his fingers were creeping towards his jewel-studded belt.

"I see my judges, Highness," he replied, his voice husky from disuse. Ramses smiled grimly.

"Do you indeed?" he snapped. "Then how fortunate you are, General. Unhappily I must tell you that your eyes are deceiving you. Shall I clarify your vision? It will give me great pleasure to do so. Or perhaps you would like to assert that I am the one under the influence of a mirage while your sight remains clear. Well?" The room was no longer full of drowsiness. The silence was breathless with anticipation. I looked in complete confusion from the Prince to the judges and then at Paiis. What was happening? Paiis's fingers were now twined tightly around his belt. He had gone very pale. One blue-painted eyelid twitched briefly.

Suddenly the Prince came to his feet. "Speak, you cur!" he shouted. "Whine and cringe while you explain how you can see ten judges while I can only discern four! Shall I name the phantoms of my mirage or shall you?" Paiis licked his lips. The henna had worn off them as the day had progressed. Now they were a sickly white. The judges were sitting like ten wooden dolls, staring at him stiffly.

"I do not understand, Highness," Paiis managed. The Prince gave an exclamation of disgust.

"Egypt has poured her blessings into your hands," he said, "and in return for her trust you have done your best to pervert her heart and render her impotent. Ma'at cannot survive in a country bereft of justice, and justice cannot survive in a country where judges can be corrupted. Or Generals. Do you agree?"

Judges corrupted. "... not all impartial I believe ..." Nesiamun had said. My perplexity began to resolve itself. No wonder Paiis had looked so smugly confident. A decision of six against four would have meant that he could leave the court a free man. But how had Prince Ramses known? Paiis was saying nothing. "I wish to add another charge to the two already levied," Ramses went on. "That during the time of your house arrest you secretly invited to your estate two of the men you knew to have been appointed to judge you. You offered them food and drink. You offered them gold if they would find you innocent following these proceedings. They agreed. You used another judge, one chosen from among the ranks of the army, to extend your invitation. Stand up, Hora." The young Standard Bearer got to his feet, his expression solemn. Turning, he prostrated himself before Ramses. "You have incurred the extreme displeasure of the God by not reporting the General's intention before the judges entered his house," Ramses said harshly. "For that, you are relieved of your position as Standard Bearer and your military commission is revoked. However, you were honourable enough to report the General's contemptible ploy to the Overseer of Protocol, therefore you will suffer no physical punishment. Leave this room." Hora came to his feet.

"I did wrong, Highness," he said in a low voice. "I am sorry. I thank you for a clemency I do not deserve." He backed down the hall and as he passed me I thought, Yes, you are being spared because you are like me. You betrayed the betrayers. The doors swung open and closed again behind him.

I looked at Paiis. He had regained his former stance. His chin was up and he was gazing fixedly at a point on the wall above my head. He must have known that his attempt to subvert the court was in itself a grave crime and its discovery, added to the already existing charges, would confirm his guilt and make his sentence inevitable. But his self-control had faltered only momentarily and he had recovered it in a way I could not help admiring. Ramses spoke again.

"Pabesat, judge and Royal Councillor, May, judge and Royal Scribe of the Chancery, on your feet," he said. "Do you have anything to say to this court?" The two men struggled up, and turning to the dais, fell on their knees. As one of them, it was May I think, bent over to place his forehead on the floor, he broke out in a gush of nervous sweat that drenched his long kilt and dripped audibly on the tiles. The shape of his buttocks could be discerned through the now sopping linen clinging to them. Both men were breathing loudly.

"Have mercy on us, Lord!" one of them burst out. "We were weak. The General is a powerful man against whom no accusation of wrongdoing has ever been made. He persuaded us that the case had been brought by a jealous and vengeful woman who wished to destroy him."

"But you read the evidence," Ramses objected coldly. "You heard the words of the officials who examined the body of the assassin this same General hired. Your love of gold was greater than your love of the truth. You are little better than the man who deluded you. Because you abandoned the instructions given to you, I command that you should be taken at once to a place of seclusion and there your noses and ears are to be struck from your bodies. Captain!" A soldier detached himself from the shadows, and signalling to others, came forward.

May began to flail about on the floor, sobbing, "No! No! It was not our fault! Mercy, Prince!" but Pabesat rose and stood shaking, his hands clenching the folds of his garment. The soldiers took hold of them impassively. They were forced to lift May from the ground and carry him out of the hall. His wails echoed briefly against the roof, and then he and the sounds of his terror were gone.

Ramses slid back onto his chair and crossed his legs. I reached for Kamen's hand, feeling sick. Three judges had been dismissed, but what of the other three? The Prince lifted a cup that sat by his foot and drank slowly, reflectively. He set it down. Was he marshalling his thoughts or deliberately drawing out the moment? I could not tell. When he spoke, it was quietly, calmly. "Baal-mahar, Yenini, Peloka," he said. "Leave the seats you are not worthy to fill, and join the scum in whose filth you have wallowed. Do not argue or protest. You saw the birth of the plot against the God, many years ago. You discussed it with the other accused. You suggested ways in which it could be carried out. The fact that you took no active part in its slow unfolding does not excuse you. Paibekamun and Pentu the scribe came and went from the General's house and the Seer's house to the palace, sharing such information as you all needed. I shudder to think that all of you had access to my father, and if it had not been for the protection of the other gods, who love him as one of their own, you might have succeeded in warping the course of Egypt's history and bringing Ma'at into disgrace. Fortunately your servants have proved to be more loyal than you. When questioned and assured that this time there was evidence to support the claim of the Lady Thu, they capitulated."

I had been in a state of shock until the mention of my name brought me to myself. For all these years I had imagined that I knew all the conspirators, but it seemed that the web Hui and Paiis had spun and cast abroad had drawn in others, even a Royal Councillor. The Prince is a cunning man, I thought with a chill. This trial is very advantageous for him. He is sweeping out the house that will soon be his, and in the process he both lets all Egypt know that treason will bring the inevitable consequence, and assures himself that when he ascends the Horus Throne he is surrounded by loyal ministers.

While these words had been passing through my mind, the men had risen and crossed the floor to stand beside Paiis. They looked dazed, even uncomprehending, and for a moment I pitied them. They had lived in a comfortable safety, doubtless knowing nothing of the new danger confronting them when Kamen returned with me from Aswat. After all, if the Prince was correct, they had not been in the forefront of the plot and Paiis would not have bothered to keep them informed. The order commanding them to serve as judges at this trial must have seemed not only a fine joke to them but also an opportunity to free their compatriot and proceed with their lives. Ramses' investigation had been too thorough for them, a far more rigorous exercise than one his father would have conducted.

Ramses nodded at the Overseer of Protocol. There were to be no more surprises. Straightening his shoulders, his hands flat on the pile of papyrus on his table, the man repeated the words he had intoned earlier. "The evidence has been heard," he called. "The time for condemnation is at hand." He faced the four remaining judges.

"Mentu-em-taui, judge and Treasurer, what is your decision?" Mentu-em-taui stood.

"All are guilty," he said flatly and sat down again.

"Karo, judge and Fanbearer," the Overseer said. "What is your decision?" Karo rose.

"All are guilty," he agreed, and resumed his seat. The final two judgements were the same. The scribe on the floor beside the Overseer scratched industriously.

Following this there was a heavy silence. Ramses sat with his chin resting in his palm, staring broodingly at the accused. They stared back at him as if hypnotized, reminding me forcefully of hares trapped in the predatory glare of a cobra. At last he stirred and sighed. "I do not like to do this," he said. "No, not at all. You are Egypt's bane, all of you, when once you were Egypt's young glory. But I must root you out like the poisonous plants you are. May the Feather of Ma'at judge you less harshly." A tiny sound escaped from Hunro, both gasp and cry. She was holding her brother's arm with both hands, her eyes riveted on the Prince.

"I want to speak, Highness," she choked, her voice thin and tinged with panic. "Please, may I speak?"

"It is against court protocol for the accused to have anything to say," Ramses replied flatly. Hunro came to her feet, arms out and palms uplifted in the ancient gesture of supplication.

"I beg you, Horus-in-the-Nest," she said brokenly. "A few words. Before death silences me forever." Ramses thought and then fanned his fingers.

"Be brief." Hunro gulped.

"I plead for my brother Banemus," she began, and beside her the man looked up sharply. "It is true that in the beginning, many years ago, he heard the treasonous words fall from the mouth of Paiis, and out of his own frustration he acceded to them. He agreed to foment rebellion against your father's administration among the troops stationed in Nubia once the God was dead, for he believed, as we all did, that Ma'at was wounded under your father's hand. But he returned to his duties in the south and did nothing further. He would not attend …"

"No, Hunro!" Banemus broke in angrily. He had come to his feet. "I will not let you do this! I have been judged as guilty as you! I will not accept mercy at your hands!"

"If mercy is granted, it will be at my hands, Banemus," the Prince interjected. "Sit down. Go on, Hunro." It was impossible to tell from his expression whether or not her plea was moving him.

"He would not attend the meetings we held to air our grievances and further our plans on the few occasions when he came home to Pi-Ramses." She swallowed, swaying, and I was afraid that she was about to faint. But she rallied, stood straight, and looked defiantly at Ramses. "He is guilty of nothing more than an hour of temporary madness, soon over. He did not want to hear how we crept slowly towards our goal."

"How is it, then, that his regret at being even temporarily involved did not translate into the loyalty to his King that should have compelled him to report the matter to the Vizier?" Ramses queried drily. "And it is not true that he refused to attend all feasts. The Lady Thu has written and testified that she met him at the house of the Seer."

"But the plot was not mentioned that night," Hunro said eagerly. "Thu knew nothing of it then. The men had gathered to assess Thu's suitability to … to impress your father. Banemus did not know. I swear he did not."

"Peace, Hunro," Banemus said, grasping her arm. "Of course I knew. I thought the whole thing foolish, doomed to fizzle out and die like a poorly made fire, but I knew. Do not demean yourself by lying any more." He pulled her down. She burst into tears and sobbed, laying her head in the hollow of his shoulder. His arm went around her.

Ramses stood. One hand went to the ceremonial dagger at his belt. The other rested on his hip. "Baal-mahar rise," the Overseer called. The man obeyed.

"Baal-mahar, guilty in this matter, you are to be taken to a place of execution where your head will be severed from your body," the Prince said, and immediately the Overseer shouted, "Baal-mahar, you have been awarded your punishment." The Prince turned to Yenini who had already come clumsily to his feet.

"Yenini, guilty in this matter, you are to be taken to a place of execution where your head will be severed from your body." At once the Overseer called, "Yenini, you have been awarded your punishment." The same terrible words rang out to Peloka, smiting my ears and beating on my heart.

I have done this. The words formed in my head with dreadful clarity. I have brought death to all these people. It no longer matters whether or not they are guilty. Their plans came to nothing in the end. The King lives. I live. How ironic! But their blood will spurt from their necks and splash the executioner's legs and puddle the earth outside the row of cells I remember so well, all because I met Kamen one evening in Wepwawet's temple at Aswat. I shuddered. All these lives. It is just, but will their blood pour onto the scales of the Judgement Hall when my own heart is weighed, and force the balance against me?

I was very tired. The great lamps, tended by soft-footed servants who glided unobtrusively from one to the other, burned steadily in the centre of the wide pools of yellow light they cast. In the darkly gleaming floor, the golden specks of pyrite alternately took fire and dulled as the flames wavered. The ceiling of the vast room was shrouded, and a lake of dimness separated me from the condemned before the opposite wall, as though the sentences of death had already been carried out and I was peering at pale ghosts across the chasm that divided the dead from the living.

Mersura, Panauk, Pentu and Paibekamun were also to die by beheading. They received the judgement listlessly. I could see that the reality of the Prince's words had not penetrated their own weariness. They craved rest, food. Perhaps their backs were aching and their ankles swelling from a day of enforced idleness. Their bodies knew nothing of the moments that could no longer be squandered on appetite or sensation, and their minds were still closed to the horror of the annihilation looming.

The Prince also seemed exhausted. The hollows beneath his kohled eyes had deepened and the lids had swollen slightly. It was as though a smothering blanket had descended on the whole company. Only the Overseer showed no sign of flagging. Patiently he waited for the last pronouncements. "General Paiis, rise," Ramses said. Paiis came to his feet in one graceful movement. His one loss of dignity was behind him and he stood to attention now, a senior officer facing his ultimate superior, handsome and still proud. "General Paiis, guilty in this matter, you are to be taken to a place of incarceration and there you are to take your own life in any manner you choose, within a period of seven days from now, according to the law governing the disciplining of those of noble blood. Your arouras and estates are as of this hour khato, and your crops, cattle and other riches also revert to the Double Crown. Remove the armbands of his command."

"General Paiis, you have been awarded your punishment," the Overseer said, addressing him by his title for the last time as an officer strode to Paiis. But Paiis stripped the golden symbols of his military position from his arms himself and handed them to the man. As he did so, his face flushed crimson and then the colour receded as rapidly as it had come, leaving him white as salt. He remained on his feet.

"Lady Hunro, rise." The Prince's voice was husky, but I did not think its tone had changed from emotion, merely from tiredness. Hunro rose but one hand pressed against Banemus's shoulder for support. Her legs were trembling. "Lady Hunro, guilty in this matter, you are to be taken to a place of incarceration and there you are to take your own life in any manner you choose, within a period of seven days from now, according to the law governing the disciplining of those of noble blood. Your arouras and estates are as of this hour khato, and your crops, cattle and other riches also revert to the Double Crown. Your title is void."

"Where is Hui?" Hunro burst out hysterically over the drone of the Overseer's voice, telling her that she had been awarded her punishment. "What about him? Why is he not condemned also? It is not fair!" Ramses ignored her.

"General Banemus, rise," he ordered. Banemus got up and lowered Hunro onto her chair before turning to face the Prince. But Ramses did not speak the expected sentence. He blew out his lips and regarded his fighting man resignedly. "You are a problem, General," he said. "By the right of Ma'at I should condemn you to death along with the others, but you are the ablest general Egypt has, and oddly enough, the most honest. You spoke out many times to my father against the foolishness of putting Egypt's best soldiers where they could do the least good. You have served in Nubia with intelligence and foresight. There is no evidence that you carried out your thoughtless threat to rouse Egyptian soldiers to revolt against their betters, a threat, I believe, made impulsively as a result of your extreme frustration. You heard of the plot and said nothing, a damning blow against you. But the same can be said for the servants of these other accused and I pardoned them for their misguided loyalty and their common blood. Therefore I will command thus. Your General's armbands will be taken from you, and you will be demoted to the lowest rank of the infantry. Your secular title is also revoked. You will labour under the most junior officer in the division to which I shall assign you. Your holdings will be placed under the jurisdiction of the Double Crown until such time as you have worked your way back up to the privileged position you have heretofore enjoyed. I have spoken." Banemus stared at him.

"Highness, I do not deserve such generosity," he protested. "Yet if in your omnipotent mercy you deign to let me live, then in that same mercy consider my sister. She …" He got no further.

"I have spoken!" Ramses shouted, coming to the edge of the dais. "Hunro dies! I am the Hawk-in-the-Nest, the Heir of my father the God! My voice is the voice of Ma'at! Remove his armbands! And take the condemned away. I am sick of the sight of them." He strode back to his chair and flung himself into it.

Banemus surrendered his armbands, and then Hunro hurled herself at him, screaming unintelligibly. He staggered, holding and trying to soothe her, but she was past all reason. A captain barked an order and two soldiers tore her away from him. She was struggling maniacally as she was dragged down the hall.

"I have not lived! I have not lived!" she was shrieking. "Banemus, save me!" He stood looking after her, arms hanging at his sides, then at a touch from Paiis who was passing with his own escort he turned and walked unsteadily away. The Herald faced us as the doors closed and the suffocating atmosphere in the room seemed to lighten.

"This Court of Examination is now completed," he called. "Do reverence to your Prince." Those of us who were left straggled to our feet and made our obeisances. The rear door was opened for Ramses to pass through, but on its threshold he paused and turned.

"Men, I wish to see you at once in my apartments," he said. "And Lady Thu, you may not accompany your son tonight. You are to go back to your cell in the harem and wait for my summons in the morning."

What now? I thought resignedly. I had hoped to slip away with Kamen, ask Men for a room in his house until my future became clear to me. I wanted to have done with this place. Hunro's frenzy had clawed at my heart, reminding me vividly of the day the judges had come to my cell to tell me that I was to die of starvation and thirst. I too had momentarily lost control. I had shrieked and cried while servants stripped my cell of everything. They had even torn the sheath from my body. I had descended into the pit Hunro saw yawning before her, but just as the hand of death closed about me I had been resurrected. There would be no such miracle for her. My hatred seemed a hot and ignoble thing to harbour in the face of such suffering, and exploring myself I found that it had vanished.

We straggled out of the Throne Room into a peaceful, star-strewn night. Pausing before the pillars of the palace's public entrance, I sucked in deep breaths of the sweet, cool air. I am alive, I thought deliriously. My flesh is warm. My skin feels the brush of this breeze, the touch of my son's kilt as it stirs against my thigh. I see the shadows of the trees lying still on the damp grass and the faint pattern of starlight on the surface of the canal. And seven days from now these things will still delight me. Thank you, Wepwawet.

Men bade us a subdued good night and disappeared back in the direction of the Prince's private quarters. Nesiamun took my hand, smiling into my eyes. "Congratulations, Lady Thu," he said kindly. "Your triumph will become an example of the impartiality and sure implacability of Egyptian justice for our children long after you and I are in our tombs. Come to my house when the Prince releases you and we will celebrate together, all of us." I thanked him and watched him stride away.

"Everyone seems to forget that I too am a criminal, having committed blasphemy by trying to murder a god," I murmured, Hunro's distorted face before me.

"No," Kamen said. "You have already paid for that blasphemy with seventeen years of exile. But you are an enigma, Thu, a criminal blessed by the gods. No one knows quite what to make of you." He kissed me on the cheek. "I will wait for my father and go home with him. Send to me as soon as the Prince gives you leave. Go and sleep now." I had presumed that he would come to my cell and talk to me for a while. I wanted to speak of Paiis and Hunro, of the Prince and of the past, but most of all I wanted to hear Hui's name passing between Kamen's mouth and mine. Instead I nodded, returned his kiss, and joined the Herald waiting to walk with me back into my courtyard.

Isis was waiting to wash off my paint and see me to my couch. I submitted to her attention absently, and when she had dowsed the lamp and gone away, I lay on my back and stared up at the ceiling. The night was so still that the monotonous sound of the fountain came to me clearly, and occasionally a brief puff of air from the open door brushed over my face, but that was all. My body was weary but my mind was fully alert, racing over the events of the day and slowing only to contemplate the present.

The sentence on Paibekamun and the other palace dignitaries would have been carried out by now and the dusty expanse of the parade ground outside the detention cells would be dark with their freshly spilled blood. Had they been executed before Paiis and Hunro had been returned to their cells, so that Hunro's tiny feet were compelled to step around the carnage? Or did they kneel on the hard ground under the flare of torches while Hunro's horrified face was pressed to the bars of her door? Poor woman. Better not to think of that, or of the grim fact that criminals were not embalmed. Their bodies were buried anonymously in the desert without even a stone inscribed with their names so that the gods could not find them.

My mind and my body turned from such a ghastly fate and I closed my eyes to reflect on safer things. Why had the Prince summoned Men to his apartments? What did he wish to say to me tomorrow? What were the prisoners doing at this hour, alone in their cells? Was Paiis dictating a last letter to his sister Kawit, and perhaps a missive to Hui also, to be delivered by her secretly? And Hunro. I hoped that Banemus was with her, giving her comfort, trying to infuse her with courage. I did not think that the terror of dying had precipitated her painful outburst, but the insupportable awareness that her life was over before it had really begun. "I have not lived!" she had screamed, and I shuddered at the torment in those words.

I slept at last, deeply and dreamlessly, and woke to full sunlight and a sense of joyous well-being. The courtyard was full of happy noise. Children released from their quarters ran about beside their gossiping mothers or plunged in and out of the fountain's basin with shrieks of delight. Servants moved to and fro across the grass carrying cushions and sweetmeats or adjusting the canopies that fluttered like captured birds of every hue over the heads of the women clustered beneath them. Here and there a lone woman sat beside her scribe and her steward, dictating letters or conducting business.

The bath house too was echoing with feminine activity, cool and dark and redolent with the moist fragrances of scented water and precious oils. Several of the women engaged me in conversation. Word of the trial and its outcome had spread rapidly and mysteriously during the night, as all such news does, and they were curious and eager for any details I might choose to supply. I talked to them freely while I was scrubbed, massaged and oiled. One even asked me if I would return to my practice of physician to the women now that I was back among them. I told her frankly that although Pharaoh had given me my freedom and I had been allowed to select medicinal herbs for my personal use, he had not lifted that particular ban, and in any case, I planned to settle somewhere quiet with my son.

Back in my cell I ate with full appetite, reflecting that when I had first taken up residence in the harem, I had kept myself aloof from the other inhabitants. I had treated their various small complaints, but I had regarded them as enemies, competitors for Pharaoh's attention, potential challengers in the pitiless combat between jealous and ambitious concubines. Such tensions had been absent from the Children's Quarters when I had given birth to Kamen and been banished permanently to that section of the harem, but I had been so angry and despairing that even there I had kept the others at arm's length, regarding them as has-beens, docile and accepting as sheep. Fear, arrogance and the insecurity of a peasant in the company of her betters had been the source of my disdain. I supposed that I was still arrogant and always would be. Vanity and pride had dogged me since my childhood. But I no longer feared what life or my fellows could do to me, and as for insecurity, their titles and bloodlines had not saved Paiis and the rest of the condemned from disaster.

I was not summoned until the evening. In the meantime I had dictated another letter to my brother, and asking for one of the land surveyors attached to the palace, I had questioned him closely about available farms and estates throughout Egypt. There were several in the vicinity of Thebes to the south, but I did not want to live in close proximity to Amun and his powerful priests. Middle Egypt also offered a few estates with large houses and prosperous fields, but again, I did not want to feel Aswat close by.

There was some khato-land and, of course, all Paiis's vast arouras had already reverted to the Double Crown, but I would crouch in another hovel before I would ever approach Pharaoh in order to benefit from the General's downfall. Let other vultures pick the meat from his bones. I thought with longing of my pleasant little estate in the Fayum. Someone else owned it now. Its fertile soil nurtured strangers, and its house, the house I had planned to restore with such love and care, now sheltered other dreams than mine. I requested a list of all properties from the surveyor, together with their costs, and sent him away. I felt discouraged. Perhaps I would show Kamen the list and ask him where he would like to live.

I retired for the afternoon sleep, ate again, and had Isis bring me the cosmetician and the dresser with his array of sheaths and sandals. It was while I was holding out my arms so that Isis could tie the golden plaited belt around the blue sheath I had chosen that the Prince's Herald darkened my door and bowed. I was ready, my hair wound with golden streamers, my eyes blue-shadowed and black-kohled, my mouth and palms and the soles of my feet hennaed.

I followed the Herald along the path beside the lawns, out of the courtyard, and across the paving that ran all the way from the main harem gate to the servants' quarters in the rear. The guard on the gate leading into the palace let us through and we angled right, away from the double doors of Pharaoh's bedroom to the stairs that hugged the outside wall of the Throne Room and led up to where the Prince lived. We mounted, turned in at the first door, crossed the narrow passage that used to lead left to Ramses' brother's rooms, and the Herald knocked on the inner door. I wondered briefly whether the far apartments were still occupied. A servant opened for us. The Herald went in and I heard him calling my title and name. He beckoned and I entered.

The Prince glanced up as I halted just inside the door and made my reverence. He had been conversing with two men beside a table littered with scrolls and now he motioned them away. They bowed to me as they passed, murmuring greetings before slipping out the door with the Herald and closing it behind them. Ramses and I were alone.

I looked around apprehensively. The room had not changed. It was still sparsely furnished although the furnishings themselves were of the highest quality, and it still held a peculiar atmosphere of impermanence, as though it was merely the setting for some obscure play while the Prince's real life was lived elsewhere. I supposed that now it was, for Pharaoh could no longer attend to matters of government and Ramses as his Heir was shouldering much of the responsibility weighing down the Double Crown.

He gestured me forward, looking me up and down with a thoroughly masculine appraisal. He himself seemed rested, his eyes clear. Coming around the table he leaned against its edge, then folded his braceleted arms across his broad chest. "Well, my Lady Thu?" he said peremptorily. "Are you satisfied at last?"

"A strange question, Highness," I replied. "Perhaps. Although the consequences of my persistence to have the truth revealed are more horrifying than the imagination could ever make them." His black eyebrows rose.

"The accused were sacrilegious, treasonous god-killers," he said flatly. "So were you, but theirs is the more heinous sin. I am amazed that you can pity them. They used you with a coldness and deliberation I find utterly abhorrent."

"You tried to use me too," I pointed out impulsively, my damnable tendency to blurt out the first thing that comes into my mind betraying me yet again. "You promised me a queen's crown if I would keep the scent of your virtues under your father's nose."

"Ah yes." He came back at me so swiftly that I knew he had been expecting this accusation. "But I was honest regarding a need that had only Egypt's welfare as its end. You were deceived as well as used for an evil purpose." I wanted to tell him that his self-righteousness was as delusory as mine had been but this time I bit my tongue. After all, he would soon be a god.

"I daresay you are right, Highness," I sighed, "and anyway, it is all behind us now. May I ask you a question?" He nodded once. "Why was Hui not indicted with the rest? He was not mentioned in the charges at all and yet he and his brother were equally guilty. Even though he has managed to evade capture he should have been awarded his sentence. It seems ..." I hesitated, wanting to tell him that I was still a little afraid, that Hui was entirely capable of effecting some strange punishment on me if he was still at large, that I was both relieved and incensed that he had in some mysterious way slipped through the net, but all I could do was finish lamely, "It seems unfair."

Ramses stared at me for a moment before turning behind him to the table where two goblets and a jug of wine sat. Carefully he raised the jug and poured, then held out a cup to me, his rings clinking against its golden curve. "So your vengeance is not complete," he said. "Not even the blood that was spilled last night, that will be spilled sooner or later by the end of the next six days, can fully slake your thirst. Your wounded rage has not been directed at Paiis, who tried to have you murdered together with your son. No. It has always been the Seer, hasn't it, Thu? The man who took away your innocence and filled all your world with himself while playing you for a fool. Do not forget that I have read your account of those years. I know to what extent your heart was engaged by him as well as that thing in you that can hate so efficiently." His words were sympathetic, yet his eyes had narrowed and held no warmth and his wide mouth curved upward shrewdly. "What an irony, that only he has evaded the judgement. Of such is the incomprehensible humour of the gods. All the same, let us drink to vengeance, yours and the Horus Throne's. May it one day be fully accomplished."

The wine was dry and heady, sliding easily down my throat. "It was not so simple, Highness," I said. "He did not regard me altogether as a fool and I neither love nor hate him as much as you suppose. He no longer fills my world. He occupies a corner where the wall is unfinished and the door unhung. My youthful self also inhabits that space, and it was of my youthful self, the wrong done to her and the wrong she did, that I wrote."

"And yet the loves and hates of youth burn with such ferocity that we can still be singed with their fire in our later years," he pointed out carefully. "We are seldom strong enough to exorcise them ourselves. Others must do it for us. You are not being wholly honest, Thu."

"Neither are you, Highness," I retorted, acutely uncomfortable at his perception. "You have still managed to give me no reason for the omission of Hui's name in the proceedings. You cannot believe he carries no guilt!"

Ramses took another judicious sip of his wine, watching me carefully over the rim of his cup. He licked his lips with deliberation, frowning as though the gesture required conscious attention. Several times it appeared that he would speak, but he checked the urge. Then he seemed to shake himself. His gaze went to the crimson liquid in his cup and he began to swirl it around and around.

"My father thought that it would be better for you to learn of this later," he said quietly, "but I cannot see what difference it will make whether you hear it now or not." His scrutiny suddenly left the cup and became fixed intently on me. "The charges against the Seer were indeed read, Thu, and a condemnatory judgement was pronounced. It was done in private, before my father himself."

With a kind of numb fascination I saw his mouth form the words and it was a few moments before they made sense to me. When they did, I went cold with shock.

"Charges? What charges?" I tried to demand, but my voice came out a thin croak. "For Set's sake, Ramses, what judgement? And why in private?"

"Because my father wanted Hui set apart for reasons of his own," Ramses said. "The charges were the same as those for the others. I am not permitted to tell you the judgement imposed but if you knew it, you would approve I think."

"Then what was it?" My head came up, and as it did so I saw something in his face, something almost furtive, that made me say the words that had burst into my mind without any warning. "Hui was present at this secret proceeding, wasn't he!" The Prince's gaze met mine calmly.

"Yes," he said brusquely.

"Was he condemned to death, then?" I asked sarcastically. "Was he flogged first? Did the executioner take his head before the public hearing began? Or did Pharaoh thank him very much for being such a fine physician, such a mighty Seer, and let him walk out of the palace a free man? I want to know! I have a right to know!" Ramses held up a reproving finger.

"Be careful," he cautioned. "You are close to committing blasphemy. What makes you think you have a right to know anything more than that you are pardoned for your own heinous crime? Pharaoh in his wisdom has found the perfect sentence for Hui. You will know it in due time. Be patient."

"I want to see the King," I pressed, distraught. "I want him to tell me these things himself!" The Prince shook his head.

"He will not see you again," he said. "He is very low and he knows that such a meeting would only bring him anguish. He has done everything for you that was in his power, forgiving you so that his heart may receive a favourable weighing and also because with the sentiment of old age he remembers how he loved you. Have faith in his prudence. He is a good man."

"I know." I breathed deeply in a whirl of confusion and distress. "I am sorry, Highness. This wound goes very deep."

"It will heal eventually," Ramses said wryly. "Now, no more questions. Here. Finish your wine."

When I obediently lifted the cup that had been forgotten in my grasp, he took my other hand and gently placed it also around the curve of the goblet, guiding the rim to my mouth. As I surrendered to his ministration a tranquillity seemed to spread through me from the warmth of his palms. When I drew away, he let me go, taking the cup and setting it on the table with a decisive click. Then he turned back to me. "There is something else," he said, and a faint smile lit his features. "My father regrets that he did not accede to your plea for a marriage contract between the two of you all those years ago. He feels that if he had done so he might have spared you from attempting to commit murder, and your son would have received the upbringing and deference due to a legitimized prince. You should know, Thu, that I disagreed with an old man's misplaced guilt. He no longer sees the past as it was, all the ruthlessness and desperation with which those days were imbued. You would not have made a trustworthy queen. I am telling you this for the sake of our old bargain, so that you will no longer think of me as entirely devoid of sympathy."

I heard him out with a growing sense of futility and sadness. Once I would have traded my ka for that honour. I had begged Pharaoh to marry me and legitimize our son but he had refused. I had forced a similar arrangement from the Prince and that too had come to nothing, along with my feverish and lustful desire to possess his body. Perhaps if the King had married me, I would have abandoned Hui and his schemes, but eventually there would have been greater heights to scale, more power to be scrambled for on my own behalf, with Egypt becoming nothing but my playground. I did not deserve to be a queen; indeed, in those days it would have been impossible for me to understand the responsibility that accompanied the title. Now I did not want either a crown or the Prince's embrace.

"I think you will make a wonderful Mighty Bull," I said quietly. "Thank you for telling me this. You are right, of course. I have never been worthy of a title, let alone the position of queen. Do not let Pharaoh fret over one of the wisest decisions he ever made." He came to me, and raising my chin he kissed me gently.

"Thus do the gods see their mysterious desires fulfilled," he commented. "I wish you well, Thu. Your past sins will be buried with the man around whom they gathered."

"Not so," I objected bleakly. "For they gathered around Hui, and where is he? Have I your permission to leave the harem now, Highness?"

"I want you to stay for another six days," he said. "Then you will be free to go wherever you wish." He held up a hand as I began to protest. I did not want to be sitting in my cell on the day when the last prisoner took his life. I wanted to be far from Pi-Ramses, on the river perhaps and sailing to a destination full of promise, with a wind stirring my hair and sunlight glancing off the water. "This is not a request," he warned me. "It is a command. There is a final arrangement to be made before you go. Be patient and all will be made clear to you in due time. And when it is, I beg you to remember the mercy and forgiveness of the god whose days in Egypt are almost done. Go back to your cell now. I dismiss you." At once I bowed and backed to the door. "I doubt that I will see you again before you leave the city," he added. "But if there is ever anything the Lord of All Life may do for you in the future, you have only to send a message. There was a time when you stirred my blood also, Thu, as I know I heated yours. But our destinies were not meant to move along the same path, only to brush each other as they have done. May the soles of your feet be firm." A lump had formed in my throat.

"Long life, health and prosperity to you, Horus," I said. I glanced at him one last time. He had lowered himself into a chair and was sitting back with his legs crossed and his hands folded on his knee. In the encroaching dimness of sunset I could not make out his expression. I opened the door and left him.

15

I DID NOT SLEEP that night. I ate a late, quiet meal, and by the time I had finished and Isis had tidied my cell, the courtyard had emptied. I had no desire to go to my couch. In spite of the wine I had drunk with the Prince and the shocks, both pleasant and wounding, I had suffered, my body was not tired. I felt empty and peaceful, drained of all feeling. Isis loosed and combed my hair, washed the paint from my face and the henna from my palms and feet, and helped me into a shift. She extinguished my lamp, and bidding me a good night, she went away. I waited until the sound of her footsteps had faded before leaving my room and walking out onto the cool grass.

It was soft and yielding to my now tender soles, and as always, I relished the sensation. The air, too, was silky with a caress the day could not bestow and I moved through it gratefully, aware of the press of the shift against my body, the slight flutter as the linen billowed behind me. Approaching the fountain, I settled beside it, my back against the basin. At once I felt the vibration of the pounding water thrumming soothingly through my spine. Now and then a thin spray misted me. I was aware of it beading in my hair and netting in the fine down of my arms but it did not trouble me.

The courtyard lay in a dreaming darkness, the moon above half-full, the stars around it faint but strengthening further away from its pale light. Most of the cell doors were closed. One or two still stood ajar, the lamps within giving off sullen orange glows that did no more than waver on the stone path before being dissipated in the lush blackness of the lawn.

I drew up my knees and gave myself fully to the strange mood possessing me. I was alert, responsive to every hint of breeze that grazed my skin, every private rustle in the grass, as though with the emptying of my emotions had come a heightening of the senses. My mind shared this peculiar, almost delirious state. No wisps of unfinished thoughts, no vague, drifting chaos of images filled it with noise. Scoured and clear, it was a vessel waiting to be sanely filled.

Hui engaged it first, and beneath the anger and shock that had exploded from me at the Prince's revelation regarding the private hearing he had been accorded, I was now able to acknowledge the lack of surprise that had underpinned my reaction. There was a familiarity about the news, as if my ka had expected nothing less from a man who had always been mysterious and unpredictable.

Somehow Hui had managed to have himself admitted to Pharaoh. Not only that, but he had convinced the King to allow him a secret pleading. No judges, just the God Himself to hear and pronounce sentence. How had he done it? Had he seen his danger in the visionary oil and slipped into the palace before the warrant for his house arrest was issued, gambling everything on the belief that he would be able to negate the evidence and influence Pharaoh? After all, he had been the King's personal physician for many years. Such a relationship fosters trust in the one and authority in the other. And yet the Prince had assured me that if I knew what sentence had been imposed I would approve.

No, not if. When. What did that mean? For I knew deep in my belly that Hui was alive somewhere. And why was I being kept here until the time allotted for the other sentences had run out? What possible arrangement was there to make that might have a bearing on my future? The King himself had made it secure with his generosity. And what had the Prince wanted with Men? Was it a matter regarding Kamen? The only answers to these questions were speculative, and in the end I laid them aside. All I knew was that Hui was alive. Was I glad or sorry? Both and neither. Where Hui was concerned I could have no single well-defined emotion. I ceased to ponder all these things and gave myself up to the beauty of the night. I was still sitting hunched by the fountain when the first greyness of dawn began to deaden the stars.

The following three days were uneventful and I spent them thinking of Pharaoh, for whispers regarding his failing condition were rife among the other women and the mood in the harem was a melancholy one. I wanted to do him honour, this man who had bound my life to his for so short a time and yet whose shadow had fallen across every moment of the last seventeen years, but he did not wish to see me again. My only homage could be a silent one, a reverence of the mind. Accordingly I kept a vision of him before me, his voice, his laugh, the feel of his hands on my body, the stony coldness of his rare angers, and each night I lit incense before my totem and prayed to the other gods to ease his passing and welcome him joyfully into the Heavenly Barque.

But many of the inmates spoke less of their dying master than of their fate, for the new King would take an inventory of the Women's House and those concubines he did not wish to keep would be moved from the precincts. Some would be given their freedom. The younger ones would probably be required to stay. But the older women, the aging, the infirm, would find themselves conveyed to the Fayum. I had once visited the harem there with the King and seen a fate that one day might have been mine. It was a quiet place but its peace was the emptiness of impending death, its cells harbouring the dried-up husks of what once had been the flower of Egyptian womanhood, and I had been so horrified that later I had been unable to make the proper sacrifices to Sebek, who had a temple in the oasis. That terrible destiny would not now be mine and I pitied those around me for whom such banishment, no matter how benign, was certain.

On the fourth day a Herald came with a scroll, and standing in the centre of the courtyard he proclaimed that the criminals Mersura, Panauk and Pentu had carried out the sentence imposed on them. There was no mention of Paiis or Hunro. I felt nothing as the sonorous words rolled from cell to cell, only a slight lifting of a weight I had not known was there, and after the man had gone to call the news in the next courtyard, I went to the pool just outside the harem precinct, stripped, and lowering myself into it, I swam up and down until my limbs shook from the effort.

Afterwards I lay in the grass to let the sun dry my body, feeling the heat burn through the droplets of water and into my flesh, the light almost insupportable even through my closed eyelids. The air was fiery in my lungs. Alive, I breathed. Alive, alive. What bliss to be alive! When I could bear it no more, I rolled into the shade of the nearest tree and sprawled naked and uncaring in a kind of ecstasy.

On the fifth day another Herald entered the courtyard, but this time his message was for me. I was sitting just outside my door enjoying a pot of beer, having been freshly painted and dressed, when he halted and bowed, glancing about to make sure that no one was within hearing. "Lady Thu," he said in a low voice. "The Prince has received a plea from the prisoner Hunro. She has asked to see you. As you know, nobles condemned to take their own lives are allowed to request whatever is reasonable be it fine wine or delicacies or final visits from their loved ones. The Prince does not command you to fulfil Hunro's desire. He merely acquaints you with it and gives you his full permission to do what you will. You may refuse if you wish."

"But what can she possibly want of me?" I asked, puzzled and uneasy. "There has been no love lost between us. I cannot comfort her. Is her brother not with her?"

"He attends her every evening and stays until dawn. Hunro is unable to sleep. She is unable to do … anything."

"Oh no," I murmured, the breeze that had been pleasant a moment ago now making me shiver. "No. That I cannot do. Will not do! How dare she presume! Does she still think that I am no better than the murderer they made of me? Does she still regard me with so much disdain?" The hurt was immediate and I wanted to cry. I would never be free of the taint of guilt, never. I might enjoy forgetfulness for a while, perhaps even a semblance of wholeness, but the stigma would always be there like an invisible brand. Murderess.

The Herald waited without comment as I buried my face in my hands, struggling to regain control of myself. When I did, I spoke without looking at him. "Tell His Highness that I will wait on Hunro," I said unsteadily. "Tell him to send me an escort this afternoon." After all, I thought bitterly as I watched him walk away, that is what murderers do. They murder. Hunro is lucky to have such an accomplished murderer on hand. I rubbed at the tiny bumps on my cold arms. Oh gods, I prayed, help me not to beat at Hunro with vicious words when her distress must already be past all describing.

An hour after noon a soldier came, and together we walked through the palace gardens and out behind the servants' quarters to the huge, dusty expanse of the army's training grounds. Isis held the sunshade over my head, its shadow a thin pool around my feet in the full glare of midday. On the far side, shimmering in the haze, the barracks lay in neat rows with the stables adjoining them. I could discern a few soldiers lounging in the shade of the buildings but there was no other activity. It was the time of the afternoon sleep and the churned earth between us lay hot and empty.

The prison cells backed onto the rear wall of the servants' domain. I remembered them well. In spite of myself, my eyes were drawn to the one I had occupied, the one that now held Paiis. Two guards flanked its door but I could see no movement behind the grill. My escort led me to the adjoining room, and at his nod, one of the soldiers on duty began to untie the thick knot that kept its door closed. I waited, suddenly overcome with the fear that Paiis might choose this moment to fall on his sword or cut his own throat, that I should hear the scuffles and cries of his last agony, but the knot was unravelled and the door pulled open without incident. I turned to Isis. "Wait for me over there, in the shade of that tree," I said. "Do not stand out here in the sun." Then I followed my escort inside.

The smell hit me at once, a foetid combination of urine, sweat and terror so powerful that for one desperate moment my guard was my jailor and I was a young concubine again, about to be condemned to death. The door rasped shut behind us. I did not need to examine my surroundings. There was nothing much to see. A dressed couch with an open tiring box full of sheaths at its foot, a table containing a lamp and several rather pretty cosmetic pots and jars, a rush carpet covering the dirt floor and edged by several sets of sandals. Hunro's possessions seemed garish and frivolous in this stinking, hopeless ante-room to eternity. Gathering my scattered wits, I looked about for her.

She was crouched in the corner, behind the table, and when she saw me she gave a cry and flung herself at me, clutching both my hands and babbling incoherently. She was barefooted and clad only in a filthy, streaked sheath that once had been white. Her hair, unwashed and uncombed, straggled down her back in dishevelled tails. Her fingernails were black with accumulated grime. Whatever vow of dignity she had made to herself when this heavy door had closed behind her had disappeared when her nerve broke, for it was obvious that the collection of face paints, oils and henna had not been used.

"Hunro, where is your servant?" I asked sharply. She stood away a little, trembling, but she did not let go of my fingers.

"I couldn't bear to have her around," she half-whispered. "Always asking me, Hunro, will you wear this, Hunro, will you wear that, Hunro, what colour of paint would you like on your eyes, as if I was going to a feast at the palace instead of ... of ... And insulting me, not using my title. Banemus made me wash and dress. It was stupid. Why should I wash and dress just to die? I sent him away too." She was speaking increasingly calmly but I could see that the lull was precarious. Madness haunted those wild eyes fixed on my face.

"You sent for me," I reminded her, careful to keep my voice as steady as possible. "What do you want?" She cast a wary glance at the soldier behind me, and sidled close.

"I can't do it, Thu," she muttered. "I can't. In the night I get so scared and I cry. In the morning I think I can and it will be all right. After all, my ka will go on into the paradise of Osiris and sit under the sacred sycamore tree, won't it? But then I ask myself, what if there's no paradise, no tree, no Osiris waiting? What if there's only oblivion? And the moment when I might be brave passes and I tell myself I will try again the next day. But I only have two days left!" She had begun to wail, letting go my hands to pull at her already tangled hair. "If I don't do it, they will come in here with swords and hack off my head!"

"Listen to me, Hunro," I said firmly, though my spirit was quaking at this awful falling-apart. "You have been sentenced to take your life. You must face the fact that you are going to die. You can do it with courage and composure or you can let them dispatch you like a dog, but it will be better if you have yourself cleaned and arrayed like the noblewoman you are and light incense to your totem for he journey you must make. There is no use waiting for a miracle. Rescue will not come. It is life itself fighting in you, a powerful, mindless thing."

"But rescue came to you!" she shouted. "A miracle happened for you, and you are a murderer, you killed Hentmira and almost finished Pharaoh! I never even touched him! Why do I have to die? It should have been you!"

I could have tried to reason with her, but any word I might have spoken would have only heightened her hysteria, and besides, I had no desire to justify myself before this despairing woman. It would have been cruel and selfish. "Yes, it should have been," I agreed. "But it wasn't. I am so sorry, Hunro. Let me order your servant back to tend you, and send for your brother."

"It sickens me to see you aping your betters," she sneered. "Order my servant. Send for my brother. Fine words and an educated tongue will never disguise your thick peasant blood!" I turned without another word and walked to the door. My escort reached to open it, but at that she began to scream, "Don't leave me, Thu! Please! Please! Help me!"

I did not want to help her. I wanted to leave her to her cowardice and dirt and regrets. But I knew that if I stepped through the door, I would not be able to put any of this behind me. Striding back to her, I slapped her sharply on one cheek and then the other, then I put my arms around her as she slumped against me, sobbing. Lowering her onto the couch, I cradled her for a long time until the frenzied note went out of her cries, then I stroked her hair. At last she sat up and looked at me with streaming eyes that no longer flared with unreason. "It is so hard," she whispered and I nodded.

"I know. But there are the palace physicians, Hunro, and Banemus too. Why have you not asked for help from them?"

"Because I don't trust them," she choked. "I have been convicted of treason and blasphemy in plotting to murder Pharaoh. They would take their revenge by giving me a poison that would kill me slowly and painfully."

"That is nonsense! And Banemus would not do such a thing!"

"But Banemus would not know what to ask for." Her hands were lying in her lap, twining about each other. "I know it is a great deal to ask of you," she said haltingly. "I do not deserve your kindness. But you are a physician, Thu, and well acquainted with potions. Will you prepare one for me? Something that will put me to sleep without pain so I can just … just drift into death?"

Did she understand the enormity of what she was asking? The dreadful irony of her request? It was almost too much to bear. I really am less to you than the dust beneath your feet, I thought sadly. Nothing more than a tool, an instrument to be used and used again for the same sordid purpose. "I will do this if you will recall your servant and Banemus and a priest, and ready yourself honourably," I said quietly. "You come of an ancient and noble lineage. Do not betray your ancestors by grovelling before your fate." I got up and she rose with me, her eyes now feverishly eager, and tried to touch me again but I evaded her.

"I will!" she promised. "Thank you, Thu."

"Do not thank me," I replied without looking at her. "To bring death is not a matter for gratitude, you fool. I will send a draught tomorrow evening." I did not know whether she had heard me or not. I came up to my escort. "Let me out of here," I whispered. But Hunro must have caught my last words to her, for she called after me, "You will bring it yourself, won't you, Thu?"

"No," I managed to reply as the blessed sunlight flooded over me. "That is something I cannot do. Farewell, Hunro."

The door thudded shut behind me. Across the training ground I saw Isis scramble to her feet, the sunshade in her hand, and start towards me and I had to force myself to stand and wait for her. I wanted to flee, run frantically from Hunro's pathetic need and my own disease, shut myself in my own safe little room and get drunk on Pharaoh's good wine.

But as I was poised tensely for flight, there was a stirring in the next cell and a familiar voice said, "I heard Hunro screaming and I thought I recognized your tones, my Lady Thu. How kind of you to visit the condemned." I closed my eyes. Not now, I thought desperately. Please, not now! Isis had almost reached me and I turned to her swiftly.

"You are a wonderful sight," Paiis went on softly. "Beautiful and vibrant and quivering with indignation. Do not be cold towards me, Thu. It took you a long time, but you have won. You have defeated me. Can we not share a few last friendly words?" Isis was there. I felt the shadow of the sunshade fall over me and glanced towards Paiis. He was watching me through the bars of his door, the rings on his fingers glittering in the strong light. As I caught his eye, he gave me a smile of singular sweetness.

"It was not a contest," I said to him tersely. "Not a game. My life was at stake. So was Kamen's, a young man who guarded your house for you honestly and dutifully. You are a ruthless man. Why should I share words of friendship with you? Where were you when I was left in that cell to die?"

"I was at home getting drunk and regretting the fact that I had never bedded you," he said promptly. "That is the truth. You are right. I am a worthless piece of refuse best thrown away. I doubt if even the gods will want me, but until they are forced to decide, I eat and drink and summon my musician to play my favourite songs. Will you join me in a cup of wine? A good vintage I assure you, from the vineyards that used to be mine." To my own astonishment I found myself drifting towards him. Impatiently he gestured to one of his guards and the man began to untie the door.

"You are not obliged to accept, Lady Thu," my escort reminded me quietly and Paiis cut in, "Oh yes, you are. Only a hard heart would refuse the last request of a dying man."

"Stay with me," I said to my soldier, and Paiis stood aside and bowed as I entered, after seventeen years, the cell where I should have died.

He had brought luxurious things in with him. Two cedar chairs inlaid with gold and ivory stood beside each other and in front of them was a low table, also of cedar, topped in grey and white veined marble. A small gold shrine sat on it, the doors open to reveal a delicate statue of Khonsu, chief god of war. A silver-handled censer lay beside the shrine, and the inescapable stench of previous prisoners was overlaid with the scent of myrrh. A tall stand topped with an alabaster lamp fashioned like an open lotus bloom rested in one corner. His couch could hardly be seen for the profusion of thin white linen sheets and cushions on it. A large carpet was underfoot. What little space was left was taken up by several bowls and dishes on which were piled various pastries, sweetmeats, dried fruits glistening with honey, a selection of cold cooked meat, coils of butter and slabs of bread. I picked my way through this profusion to the chair Paiis indicated, and he slid onto its companion, bending to lift a chased silver jug.

"I will not fall on my sword until the last moment of the last hour before the eighth day," he said as he poured wine into two wide-mouthed silver goblets, "and until then I intend to indulge myself. To your remarkable good health, my Lady. May you enjoy it in safety." He drank, his kohled eyes fixed on me over the rim of the cup, but I did not raise my wine. Was his gaiety a kind of derangement or a genuine acceptance of his end? I decided that it was the latter. His will had temporarily wavered in the Throne Room when his attempt to subvert the judges had failed and been unmasked, but he had recovered his self-control and would not weaken again. Lusty and cynical, crafty and intelligent, he was nevertheless a disciplined soldier and an aristocratic Egyptian. When the time came, he would run the weapon through his belly with dispassion.

Putting down his cup, he sat back and crossed his legs, his expression sobering. "She cries and sobs all night," he said. "I hear her through the wall. I would comfort her if I could but I am not allowed to leave my cell. She was a thing of loveliness once, with her restless dancer's body and her independence. Who knows what she might have become if our scheme to unseat the King had succeeded?"

"You are completely unrepentant," I remarked, and he smiled at me, his handsome face lightening.

"Completely," he replied promptly. "If Ramses had died of the arsenic you gave Hentmira to so innocently slather over him, and Banemus had done what he was supposed to do and ready the army in the south to march in revolt, we would have been in control of Egypt. Able to put the priests in their place, re-establish true pharonic authority under someone of our own choosing, begin to recover something of the empire our forebears ruled." He sighed. "It was a glorious dream, but like most dreams it did not have enough substance to coalesce into reality. A pity. Why should I repent, dear Thu? I am an Egyptian patriot."

"Did it never occur to you that if Ma'at was indeed corrupt and needed healing you would have succeeded? That it has a way of using us to further its righteous ends, and if such a thing is not necessary and we try to compel it to change, it simply abandons us to the consequences of our vanity?"

"Thu the philosopher," he mocked me gently. "Thu, defender of the right. Such words ring slightly hollow in the mouth of an ambitious and unscrupulous woman like you. Oh, do not mistake me." He held up a hand as I was about to make a quick rejoinder. "I do not mean to insult you. When you were young, your ambition was a capricious force, dangerous and unpredictable and entirely selfish. How else were we able to use you? But now it is channelled, purified, directed towards the righting of a wrong and the furthering of good order, in your life as well as the life of Egypt. So was mine. This is wholesome ambition, Thu. But it is still ambition. How then are we different? Here we sit, two people whom the gods have fashioned to be alike. Even our motives have been similar. Why, then, are our fates so different?" I could not answer him. To cover my disquiet I leaned forward, picked up my wine, and sipped it slowly. I had an ominous feeling that he was right. "I do not know," he went on. "Perhaps it is simply because the gods have decided to favour a courage in you that I do not have." I met his eye, wanting to express the sudden burst of sympathy I felt for him, but all I could say was, "Such humility does not suit you, Paiis. I think I prefer you arrogant and full of self-confidence." He laughed and the moment of closeness was gone.

"I tried very hard to have you silenced," he said. "I am glad now that killing you proved impossible. You have been often in my thoughts since I first saw you at that feast Hui gave to enable the rest of us to judge your potential as a royal concubine."

"I saw you long before that evening," I said sadly. "I had not been long in Hui's house. I used to sit on the floor of my room and gaze out of the window after Disenk had extinguished my lamp and gone to her mat outside my door. One night, very late, after one of Hui's feasts, I watched his guests leave. You came out of the house and stood in the courtyard. A drunken princess was trying to persuade you to take her home with you but you refused. You kissed her. You were wearing red. I did not know who you were, but you were so handsome, Paiis, so godlike, laughing in the glare of the torches! And I was so young, so full of naïve, girlish fantasies. I will never forget it."

I had not intended to tell him that. The memory, so clear and unsullied by events still in the future that should have muddied and besmirched it but did not, was somehow precious to me and I dreaded a trite, lascivious response that might destroy its purity. But he went very still. I kept my gaze on the table before me as the silence grew between us. After a long time he stirred.

"Damn you," he said huskily. "Why must you remind me that I too was once young, a boy full of that same fresh simplicity that can take such a sordid little incident and transform it through sheer ignorance and innocence into the stuff of a romantic dream. That child had gone, buried under the gradual accumulation of need, necessity, the distasteful decisions and experiences of soldiering, the insidious lure of self-indulgence. I did not want to see him resurrected now. Not now! It is too late!" I remained still, and after a struggle I sensed rather than saw, he mastered himself and turned again to me. "I am so sorry, Thu," he said. "Sorry that I did not measure up to the image you created for me, sorry for having had a hand in your corruption. I think that is my only regret. Come. Finish the wine and we will part."

Shaken, I lifted the goblet to my lips. Paiis did the same, and all at once we were enveloped in an atmosphere of solemn ritual. It was as though his confession had altered the very air of that squalid room, giving it a majestic peace. A serenity descended on me so that I forgot the repugnant task I had shouldered for Hunro, forgot that I had wanted to drink myself into a stupor. We drained the wine and rose with one accord in a strange and fleeting companionship. Paiis put a hand against my neck, and bending he kissed me firmly, the gesture warm and oddly familiar. "If you ever find Hui, greet him for me," he said as he released me, and I realized that my mouth had recognized his because of his brother's. "Oh yes," he went on. "I know that he is alive, but not where he is. His threat to the stability of Egypt is not as great as mine, you see. I have a feeling that you and he are not done with each other yet."

We had moved to the door. I turned to my escort, and in that moment Paiis put both palms and his forehead against the sturdy wood. "Ah freedom," he murmured, his voice catching, and I saw his fingers curl inward with the intensity of his emotion. "Pray for me, Thu, at the Beautiful Feast of the Valley. Shout my name. Then perhaps the gods will find me." There was nothing left to say. I touched his shoulder, still round and firm and hot with life, and he retreated. The door swung open. This time Isis was there and I walked away at once. I did not look back.

I drank deeply when I had regained the sweet security of my cell, but it was water, not wine that I poured down my throat. Then I lay on my couch and wept, quietly and without any storm of sentiment. I did not cry for Hunro or Paiis or even for myself. The tears came because life was the way it was, dull and hard for some, full of promise and ease for others, a journey fraught with unfulfilled dreams and broken hopes for many. When I was spent, I slept without agitation and woke simply and naturally to a westering sun and the aroma of the hot broth and fresh bread Isis had brought.

While I ate, I thought about what poison to give Hunro. I did so with as much calmness and deliberation as I could, forcing a separation between the tumult of hurt and anger that threatened to revive and the purely reasonable processes of my mind. At the time of my own arrest the box containing the medicines Hui had given me, together with the scrolls listing various ailments and their prescriptions, had been taken away, and during my exile I had been forbidden to practice the craft I had been so expertly and disastrously taught. Lately, in the storehouses of the harem, I had filled a chest with physics but I had taken nothing that might prove harmful. Now, as I placed the food slowly into my mouth and concentrated on chewing it carefully, I allowed myself to try to remember those things I had shied away from for so long.

It was not easy, for I had to recall the circumstances under which I had learned them, and that in itself brought forth exquisite pain. Hui's large office and the tiny herb room adjoining it, its shelves crowded with row upon row of clay pots and jars, stone phials, flaxen bags stiff with dried leaves and roots. Myself beside him, pen poised over papyrus as he wielded his mortar and pestle, his deep, quiet voice explaining what he was doing and why. The aroma of the ingredients themselves, some powerful enough to make my head ache, some no more than a delicate whiff of severed petals that mingled pleasantly with Hui's own perfume, jasmine.

Jasmine. I pushed my empty dish away and laid my arms upon the table, staring at the way the golden lamplight caught in the fine hairs on my skin. Yellow jasmine would kill. Every part of it, flowers, leaves, roots, stem, was deadly. A high dose worked quickly but it brought on unpleasant symptoms including anxiety and convulsions. The mandrake, too, would be efficient, but amounts large enough to end Hunro's life would also bring acute distress. I knew this from experience. With a jolt to my heart that could have ended my contemplative state I remembered Kenna, Hui's body servant, whom I had murdered with an infusion of beer and mandrake out of nothing more than a jealous panic. He had died amid the horrifying stench of his own vomit and the sick effusion of his bowels.

Then what of the passion flower? I exhaled and the flame in the lamp quivered, making my hunched shadow gyrate briefly against the wall. It was used in bait to destroy hyenas, and something in me woke and assented to the irony its use would mean before sinking once more beneath the rigid steadiness of my will. No matter that its symptoms were kind, leading from drowsiness to paralysis to death. That stab of glee must be denied for the sake of any peace I might be able to achieve afterwards.

My thoughts moved on. The dog button was very effective. It could be swallowed, inhaled as powder, or rubbed on the skin. But like so many other toxic substances it caused spasms and then convulsions so extreme that the victim ended his life as stiffly arched as a bow.

I laid my cheek against my outstretched arm and gazed into the gently lighted room, considering and then rejecting one possibility after another, and with the increasing anxiety came a gradual lessening of my control. Whispers and echoes seeped through the cracks, coiling up from the darkness where my soul was howling in self-loathing and despair at its daunting changelessness. When I knew that the sound of its keening was about to reach my mouth, I got up, pulled on my sandals, and flinging a cloak around my shoulders, I went out.

I was praying that the Keeper of the Door was still in his office as I strode quickly past the adjoining courtyard and the Children's Quarters and pushed through the small gate at the end of the path leading to the servants' crowded cells. The night was still young and the area before their rooms was noisy with activity and full of the smells of cooking from the nearby kitchens. Those who noticed me bowed uncertainly, doubtless wondering what I was doing in their domain, but I ignored them.

A turn to the right and a few steps brought me to another gate, this one guarded, for it led into the palace grounds themselves. Asking one of the soldiers to go and see if the Keeper was in his office and would grant me an audience, I waited, my back to the happy tumult behind me. Presently the man returned and waved me through. I was in luck. The Keeper was indeed still working.

The offices of Pharaoh's ministers backed at right angles onto the two walls dividing the palace from servants and official guests, and it was a short walk from them to the King's own office and the Banqueting Hall. Leaving the gate, I went forward, swung left, and paced steadily until I came to the open door which sheltered the man whose hand lay over every aspect of harem life. I could see him within, piling scrolls into a chest, and as I paused in the doorway, he looked up and saw me. He bowed, closed the lid of the chest, and spoke to his scribe. "These can go to the records room now," he said. And to me, "Come in, Lady Thu. How can I help you?" The scribe hefted the chest and edged past me, sketching a reverence as he did so. I watched him walk away for a moment, the gathering darkness soon engulfing him, then turned and entered the office.

Amunnakht stood smiling expectantly, one hand resting on his desk, and all at once I did not know what to say. Seeing my hesitation he gestured to a chair and then to the wine jug beside him but I shook my head. Swallowing, I found my voice. "Amunnakht," I said, the words thin and high in my own ears, "Hunro has asked me to help her end her life." His smile vanished and he looked at me solemnly.

"That was cruel of her," he commented. "Cruel and unnecessary. I am so sorry, Thu. Such a request must be causing you great distress. If I had known of her cowardice, I could have provided her with one of the palace physicians."

"She is insane with grief and terror," I went on, impelled for some reason to defend Hunro. "She will not call a palace servant for fear that out of spite he will cause her to die in agony. She is not able to imagine any emotions but her own any more."

"She never could." Amunnakht came to me, and taking my arm he drew me to the chair. "Do not pity her Thu. And for your own sake you must not comply with her ridiculous request." I lowered myself into the chair and glanced up at him.

"I have already agreed to help her," I said. "What else could I do? Prince Ramses left the decision up to me, and when I saw her dishevelled and wild and crying I knew that I could not be reasonable. Her nerve has gone. Tomorrow is the sixth day. If I do nothing, she will die in blood and disgrace." He looked down on me thoughtfully and then he sighed.

"Some might say that you are both reaping the harvest you sowed in the past," he commented. "Hunro will die at the hands of the woman she used to murder another and you will have your revenge on her entirely legitimately. Thus the circle of your fates is closed at last. Hunro has learned the law of consequence too late, and you, dear Thu, no longer harbour the heart of a killer. I know this. The King knows it. Only you are still in doubt. What do you want me to do in this matter?"

I listened less to his words than the tone of his voice, soothing and reassuring. It was the instrument he used to calm hysterical concubines, reprimand fractious ones, or proclaim pharonic decrees, yet I did not believe that his intent was to manipulate me. We knew each other too well. He spoke with sincerity and concern, and thus I was comforted. "I want you to witness that the plea came from Hunro herself," I told him heavily. "The soldier who accompanied me into her cell will bear me out. I want you to prepare a document setting out her words and the Prince's knowledge and my agreement. Then I want you to come with me into the storehouses with one of the palace physicians and observe while I do the work, noting the ingredients I use." I clenched my fists and met his eye. "No one must say that I acted without permission, hers or the Prince's, or that out of revenge I gave her a vicious poison that caused her to die painfully. It is bad enough that all will know, and remember my past, and say it is as they expected!" He nodded.

"I understand." Suddenly and startlingly he squatted, and taking my face between his palms he brushed my lips softly with his thumbs. "In two days the Prince will release you," he said quietly. "It will all be over. All of it, Thu. Then it will be your task to live again, to find friends to coax you into laughter and good black soil to nurture you and perhaps a man who will pour over you the healing oils of love so that you may look into your mirror once again and see a woman cherished and revived. But you must want these things. You must vow to make the past thin and shred and blow away like an outworn sheath. Will you do this?" I pressed my own hands against his, overcome by the surrender of his customary detachment.

"Oh Amunnakht!" I choked. "In spite of everything you have supported me." He smiled with amusement and rose, his face falling into its usual lines of polite objectivity.

"I have been Pharaoh's faithful servant," he said, "and you have proved impossible to ignore." Going to the doorway he shouted a sharp word into the darkness and presently a servant appeared. "Fetch my scribe," Amunnakht ordered, and coming back into the room he retired behind the desk. "Now," he breathed. "You will dictate a scroll in whatever words you wish and I will sign it and send it to the Prince with a request that he sign it also. Then we will go to the storehouses."

When the scribe appeared, I did as the Keeper had suggested, and when I had finished he put his name and titles beneath my words. "Take it to Prince Ramses at once," he told the man, "and when he has set his seal on it, place it in the archives together with the other correspondence relating to the royal concubine the Lady Thu. As you go, find Royal Physician Pra-emheb and ask him to meet me at the harem storehouses." Filling a cup with wine, he held it out to me. "Come," he invited mildly. "We have a little time to wait. Let us drink to the future, and give thanks for the bounty of the gods. I have a plate of pastries here somewhere, probably stale but tasty enough. Would you like one?"

We toasted and drank and nibbled on sweetmeats, so that by the time Amunnakht set his empty cup on the desk with a click and bowed me to the door, I had regained my equilibrium.

We walked to the storehouses through a peaceful night and found both the scribe and the physician waiting for us outside the cavernous entrance. A servant with a lamp stood by. "It has been done as you commanded, Keeper," the scribe said in answer to Amunnakht's query. "I found His Highness in the gardens with his wife. The scroll has been sealed and now reposes in the archives." I sighed inwardly with relief, wondering what Ramses had thought of my desire to have my part in Hunro's suicide officially recorded. Doubtless he remembered another scroll, the one promising me a queen's crown before it so opportunely vanished.

"Did the Prince comment on my words?" I could not help asking the scribe.

"No, Lady," he replied. "His Highness merely remarked upon reading it that all was as it should be." An ambiguous and wholly typical response, I thought wryly, turning to the physician as Amunnakht introduced us. Pra-emheb inclined his head to me, his eyes alive with curiosity.

"Do you minister to the King directly?" I wanted to know as we all moved inside the building. "How is His Majesty's health?" Pra-emheb pursed his lips.

"I am in attendance on him during the day," he replied. "There is nothing to be done but to ease his decline. I do not think he will live much longer. He eats only a little fruit and that with difficulty and will only drink milk."

"Does he still rise? Sit beside his couch? Is he in pain?" And does he crave Hui's expert touch? I wanted to add. Is he wandering in the past when my body was warm beside his and the fires of lust ran through his veins instead of the frigid and mysterious fluid of death? The physician shrugged.

"He likes to be propped up on his couch from time to time, but such efforts exhaust him," he said. "I do not think he feels much pain. We drug his milk with poppy. The members of his family are with him but the priests give him more comfort now." Poor Ramses, I thought sadly, and fell silent, following the pool of lamplight falling from the hand of the servant and Amunnakht's regal, blue-clad spine.

When we reached the room where I had so recently chosen medicines to take away with me, we came to a halt. The scribe settled his palette on a bench and laid out a fresh piece of papyrus. "I want you to make a draught," I told Pra-emheb. "I will tell you what to do. It is so that I may not be accused of deception, of secretly substituting one ingredient for another. I will ask you also to witness the account the scribe will write, together with the Keeper. Do you agree?" He frowned.

"I have no idea why I am here," he protested. "What draught? You could have requested a physic from me without all this fuss, Amunnakht."

"The Lady Thu is an accomplished physician," the Keeper explained imperturbably. "She has been retained by the Prince at the urging of one of the condemned to prepare the poison that will allow the condemned to take her own life. Understandably she wants the distasteful task fully and properly recorded."

"Oh." Pra-emheb stared at me blankly. "Then you have my sympathy, Lady Thu. What do you require?" The scribe was ready, his pen poised above the papyrus. I strove to keep my voice and expression firmly neutral.

"Nothing very complicated," I replied. "I have decided to use the bulb of the dove's dung, ground and mixed with a good quantity of poppy. What do you think?" I could see the alternatives being assessed behind his eyes as he nodded slowly.

"It is a good choice for a painless death," he said. "No convulsions, no vomiting or diarrhea, simply a rapid stopping of the breath. The bulb is of course the most lethal part of the plant, and ground up it will probably provide one ro of powder. How much does the condemned weigh?"

"Not much," I said swiftly. "She has become ... emaciated since her incarceration. But I will use two bulbs to make sure. I do not want her to suffer." I was hating this cold, impersonal conversation, this objective discussion that could have been about the best treatment for worms in the bowels but instead concerned a prescription for annihilation. I would have preferred the decision to have been an interior one, a quick and shameful conclusion in the secrecy of my mind and then the barest of instructions spoken hurriedly. But Pra-emheb seemed to relish the airing of his knowledge, or perhaps the spurious importance it brought.

"Two bulbs will do," he said. "And then it will not matter whether they are fresh or dried. Of course if fresh, the method of preparation will have to be ..." I cut him off sharply.

"I know how to prepare every poison and physic available in Egypt and many outside it," I snapped. "I do not need a lesson. You are not here to teach me but to follow my instructions." He took a step away from me and looked to Amunnakht, offence in every line of him, but the Keeper, after giving me a dark glance, smiled placatingly.

"It is a distressing matter," he purred. "We are all upset. Forgive her, Pra-emheb, and let us conclude the business as soon as we may." I bit back the retort curdling on my tongue.

"Hunro is not business," I whispered but the physician had already turned to the shelves and was murmuring, "Dove's dung, dove's dung." All at once his hand froze in the air. "I know who you are!" he said loudly. "I remember the scandal. I was a young apprentice in the palace at the time, treating the servants, but the story spread everywhere. You ..." Again I forestalled him.

"Do not say it, Pra-emheb," I half-begged, half-threatened. "I do not care to hear it any more. I was awarded my punishment and now it is over. Over!" Suddenly I felt a wave of sick dizziness, and turning I sank onto one of the chests cluttering the floor. "Please, just do this thing and go away." Amunnakht's hand descended on my shoulder, warm and steadying. Pra-emheb's hand began to move.

I watched as, stony-faced, he lifted down a box, extracted two bulbs of the plant, and opening the small sack hanging from his belt, took out a knife. Expertly he stripped the withered, crackling remains of the stem and cut off the dried roots. He took mortar and pestle, and slicing the bulbs, he dropped them into the pestle and began to grind them. They released a bitter, earthy odour and I knew that no matter what they were diluted with they would taste the way they smelled, harsh and dangerous. Sweat began to bead on his forehead, for the work, as I well remembered, was arduous. Amunnakht spoke to the servant. "Set down the lamp and fetch natron and a bowl of hot water," he ordered. The man went away, his footsteps echoing in that dim, vaulted place, and I got up and began to scan the shelves, seeking a pot in which to pour the finished liquid. I found a stone jar with a wide mouth just as the sound of Pra-emheb's grinding ceased.

"What now?" he said, setting the pestle aside and wiping his face on his kilt. I handed him the jar.

"Find poppy," I told him. "Fill this half-full with the powder. Add the dove's dung and then I will top it up with milk."

"Half-full of poppy?" he exclaimed. "But that in itself will be enough to make her heartbeat falter!"

"Exactly," I said wearily. "I want her to succumb to the soporific effects of the poppy and drift to sleep before the dove's dung acts." I could not blame him for what seemed like stupidity. His reaction had been a physician's shock, unthinking and immediate. I wished that mine could be the same. "Have you recorded all this?" I asked the scribe. He nodded and went on writing.

Pra-emheb found the poppy and tapped the white powder into the jar. The ground-up bulbs followed. As he passed it back to me, the servant reappeared bearing a steaming bowl and a dish of natron, and the physician plunged his hands into it and began to wash himself vigorously. He was trying to cleanse more than his flesh, I knew. I wanted to do the same. "Thank you, Pra-emheb," I said to his bent back. He did not reply. Holding the jar, I walked out of the storehouse.

I did not realize that Amunnakht was behind me until he spoke. "Do not think badly of him, Thu," he said. "It is a hard thing for a physician to do."

"You do not need to tell me that!" I shouted, rounding on him. "Am I not a physician also? Or have you forgotten?

Do you imagine that this causes me no more pain than a thorn prick to the finger? Must I pay for the evils of my youth forever?" He did not answer. Instead he leaned forward and took the jar from my fingers.

"How much milk must be added?" he asked. At first I did not hear him for the rage making my pulse race, but then I understood and the hurt went out of me.

"You do not need to do this, Keeper," I said huskily. "I made the promise, not you."

"You have done enough," he replied. "I am the Keeper of the Door. All women within the palace precincts are my responsibility. I will fulfil this duty on your behalf. How much?" The night was fine, dark and sweet with the scent of wet grass, with showers of stars, with gentle eddies of air that fluttered my sheath and lifted my hair. I inhaled deeply.

"Half a cup," I said. "Then shake it well and add more milk, leaving room only for the stopper. You will take it to her, Amunnakht?"

"Yes. And I will stay with her while she drinks it."

"It must be shaken again just before it is poured out, and she must drink it all at once or its bitterness will prevent her from draining the rest," I told him. "But after you have added the first half-cup, let it stand overnight so that every grain may be softened. Do not let it out of your sight, Amunnakht. If a servant mistook it for milk, I would never forgive myself."

"Nor I," he smiled. "I will send you word when it is done. Good night Thu." He did not wait for more. He walked away, enveloped in the invisible cloak of confidence and dignity that was so uniquely his, and I made my way back to my cell with a lighter heart.

Once there I stripped off my sheath and sent Isis for wine, and while she was gone I went to the deserted bath house and scrubbed myself feverishly, grinding the rough crystals of natron into my skin and then upending jug after jug of pure water over my head. Returning to my room, tingling and yet shivering, I crawled onto my couch. The wine was there on the table, a cup already filled for me, and Isis was hovering. Thanking her, I told her I would not need her until the morning. She bowed and left, and before her heel had vanished around the door jamb I had emptied the cup and was pouring myself another.

I lay drinking, half-propped up on my cushions, allowing the wine to heat my stomach and loosen my mind from the grip of the all-too vivid images afflicting me. It was a harmless indulgence, a minor and temporary refusal to face the stresses of the moment, and I let the spell of the alcohol take me where it would.

It did not carry me into the past where loss and despair might have claimed me. It floated me into the future, Kamen and Takhuru and I on a quiet estate where the gardens were lush and shady and the flowers splashed colour beside the paved paths and pink and white lotuses heaved gently with the ripples on the fish pond. There would be a white craft tethered to our modest watersteps, with a bright yellow sail tied to the mast. Sometimes we would board it and be rowed to Aswat to visit Pa-ari and Kamen's grandparents, but more often we would simply drift on it in the scarlet sunsets, watching the white cranes spread their wide wings and the crested ibises stand contentedly among the tall reeds bordering the riverbank.

There would be neighbours, pleasant people with whom we might feast occasionally, inviting them into our small but beautiful reception room where we would all sit on cushions before our little blossom-strewn tables and sip wine and eat the delicious food our cook would prepare and gossip happily of local people and affairs. Perhaps Prince Ramses, no longer Heir but Mighty Bull, would honour us with a visit, causing a stir of excitement and envy among those neighbours. Men and Shesira would come, and Kamen's stepmother and I would share anecdotes about the son we shared, while Kamen himself traded light-hearted jokes with his stepsisters.

I would practise medicine again but not every day, for there would be my overseer of cattle and crops to consult with and accounts of yields and profits to be kept. Besides, there might be grandchildren, babies with Takhuru's delicate patrician features and Kamen's intelligent gaze, who would grip my hands in their chubby brown fingers and totter about the lawns after butterflies and blown leaves.

Yet under this pleasant, wine-induced daydream into which I plunged with the relief of a hounded rabbit chased by a pack of dogs was the disquieting throb of a present reality.

Hui was out there somewhere.

And tomorrow was the seventh day.

16

IN SPITE OF THE WINE I had drunk, I did not sleep well and woke with a jolt of anxiety to the cacophony of the dawn chorus and the first cool rays of sun on the glittering grass beyond my door. I had tossed and sweated in the night. My sheets were plastered to my body and I had a raging thirst. Leaning over to the bedside table, I picked up the jug of water that was always kept full and emptied it down my throat, then I lay back and watched the quality of light change on my ceiling.

How many thousands of times has Ra lifted himself from the womb of Nut since Egypt rose from the primordial darkness? I mused. How many people down through the ages have lain on their couches or pallets, as I am doing, and heard the birds greet the day, and felt the air heat around them, and thought—today I will labour, I will eat and drink, I will swim in the Nile, I will make love to my wife, I will return to my couch when Ra is again swallowed? Surely they should be saying—today I breathe, I hear, I see, I am alive, and tomorrow if the gods wish it to be so I will again open my eyes to life.

And how few have known the hour of their death? Have opened their eyes, still half-drowned in dreams, and gazed drowsily into the swiftly growing dawn with the thought—I will do this today, I will do that—until the fragile moment of half-consciousness receded before the onslaught of terror. I am to die today. I must count the number of breaths I have left, for they are fleeting. Tomorrow will not exist for me. I will not wake to another sunrise.

The courtyard was stirring now. Servants pattered along the path bearing the first meal of the day to their sleepy mistresses and the aroma of fresh bread wafted with them. Their voices were cheerful as they called to one another. Would Hunro eat this morning? I wondered. Had the horror of her waking faded and been replaced by the hope that even now a reprieve might come? And what of Paiis? He had told me that he would wait until the last possible moment before ending his life. How would he spend his final day? In eating, drinking and whoring? Probably.

Isis darkened the doorway, greeting me brightly and setting my food across my knees. While I picked at it, she busied herself in tidying the room, chattering all the while. When I could bear the flurry of activity no longer, I sent her to prepare my bath, and pushing away the remains of the meal, I left the couch and went to stand by the open door.

The sun was already bright and warm. A few of the women were wandering on the grass in their sleeping shifts, yawning and blinking up at the deep azure sky. The clatter of dishes came from many of the cells, together with an occasional sharp word of reproof or a burst of laughter, and I sucked it all up like a famished beggar. I would not relinquish one moment of this until the last drop of water had run through the clock, I said to myself passionately. Neither will Hunro, even though she sits in prison. If Amunnakht is wise, he will not approach her until after night has fallen, for as long as the sun shines today she will refuse to drink.

When Isis returned, I went with her to the crowded bath house, but after I had been washed and massaged, I refused paint and jewellery. I was not sure why. Certainly such a gesture did nothing for either Paiis or Hunro but it seemed impertinent, even insulting to the dark solemnity of death to indulge in such frippery. I could feel its approach in an unrest that took hold of me as the morning progressed, invading me and seeming to spill over into the courtyard until a brooding apprehension gradually hushed the women's conversations and made the children quarrelsome.

In the middle of an afternoon imbued with a peculiar quality of timelessness a servant delivered to me the list of properties available for sale that I had requested from the surveyor. I received the scroll with surprise, having forgotten all about him, and quickly skimmed the contents. But the words and numbers passing under my eyes seemed to have nothing to do with me. They belonged to a different world, where one hour followed another and led into a future as foreign to me as the barbaric lands beyond the western desert, and I let the papyrus roll up and put it away. My world contained only Paiis, Hunro and myself, all of us consumed in the fire of waiting.

I could not sleep away the noon heat. The courtyard emptied as the women sought their couches, but the weight of unease followed them and I heard them mutter and toss as I too lay wide awake under a thickening miasma of foreboding. One by one they emerged again to sit under their canopies and I rose with them, setting a cushion at the foot of the outside wall of my cell and lowering myself onto it. A kind of reverential stillness fell on us until the thought of any movement became impious. The peace it brought was not tranquil. It was the immobility of creatures threatened by a sensed but nebulous danger and in the end I closed my eyes and surrendered to it.

At sunset the atmosphere lightened a little with the arrival of the evening meal. Isis set the tray beside me but I could not eat. My heart, my mind, everything in me was concentrated on the moments slipping by for Hunro and Paiis. It no longer mattered that they were criminals. Nor was I regretting that they must die.

My ka was remembering the agony of my own dying, the anger, the confident belief that a mistake had been made and I would be rescued, then the panic turning into a sullen acceptance punctuated by bouts of hysterical denial when I would fling myself against the door of my cell and scream to be released.

Later, when I was too weak to rise, I begged for water, for light to drive away the nightmare-infested darkness, for the touch of a human hand to ease the awful loneliness of death. That touch had come at the eleventh hour, and Amunnakht had pulled me back from the brink of eternity. But the eleventh hour would be the last for Paiis, and the Keeper would hold out to Hunro not the water he had held out to me but a cup of oblivion.

Dusk crept into the courtyard, and before Isis removed the stale food on my tray she lit my lamp. Other lights were springing up, twinkling fitfully through the soft darkness, but as I leaned against my doorpost and watched them blur through the translucent curtain of the fountain, I became aware that the usual evening bustle was absent. If there was to be feasting in the palace, the women did not know it. I could see their shapes moving quietly beyond the open doors, but their servants sat or squatted idly outside.

How many hours before Ra passes the halfway point between the jaws of Nut and the moment when her body expels him as the dawn, I wondered, listening to the unaccustomed stillness. The moment when tomorrow begins. Five? Six? What shall I do? I am too distressed to read or even to pray. This is not revenge. The satisfaction of which I dreamed, the fantasies on which I fed, are ashes in my mouth, and if it were possible I would rush to the prison and let the doomed go free. But that is simply another fantasy. Freeing them would not change their natures. And why not? a voice whispered inside me. It changed yours, for are you not speaking of mercy where once there was only greed and fear?

Leaving my doorway, I began to pace, arms folded tight against my chest and my eyes on my feet. I did not want to attract the attention of the other women by passing their cells and risking conversation, so I left the courtyard and turned onto the deserted path that ran between the walls of the palace and the harem. High above, in the narrow strip where the sky opened out, the stars blazed white, but the blackness where I walked was so complete that I could hardly see my bare feet moving on the cool paving. I met no one coming from the other courtyards or entering them. Even the Children's Quarters were quiet.

I do not know how long I glided up and down that long passage, a sense of unreality growing in me, until drugged by the measured regularity of my movement, I felt as light and insubstantial as a phantom. But I was not soothed by the counting of my steps, the tiny ache that began in my ankles, the darkness surrounding me. The very formality of motion served to accentuate the relentless elapsing of time so that each step I took became a moment gone for Paiis and Hunro, minutes decaying with their life.

But at last, having come yet again to the gate leading into the servants' courtyard and turning, I saw a shadow glimmer at the far end of the path and stood still. He came on steadily, an indistinct blur of fluttering linen, a faint whisper of sandals, the dim plains and hollows of his face gaining definition as he approached, and I put a hand gone suddenly numb against the wall next to me.

He halted and bowed. His expression was grave, strained, and when I lifted my eyes to his, I found that my throat had gone dry and I could not speak. "It is done," he said. "All day she waited for a reprieve. I went to her two hours ago but she would not drink until the time had run out and there was no more hope. By then she was so exhausted that she did not protest. You chose the ingredients of the potion well, Thu. There was no struggle." I tried to swallow.

"And Paiis?" I whispered. Amunnakht smiled grimly.

"He was drunk all day yesterday and slept for most of this morning. But then he had himself bathed and painted and his priest summoned. In the last hour he cut his wrists and bled to death before his shrine to Khonsu. It was a fitting ending."

A fitting ending. All at once my mouth filled with bile, and turning to the rough stone of the wall I laid my forehead against it and let the tears come. For a while I cried soundlessly, but then I felt Amunnakht's arm go around my shoulders and he drew me to him. He said nothing. He did not murmur calming words or stroke my hair. He simply held me until the pity and the grief and the strange pain of loss had all spilled over and trickled down my cheeks and been lost in the weave of his garment, then he set me away. "You will be able to sleep now," he said. "And tomorrow your son is coming to remove you from my care. The Prince has released you. I will miss you, Thu."

"And I you, Amunnakht," I replied shakily. "It has been as though the last seventeen years did not exist. I would like to see Pharaoh once more before I leave. Can you arrange it?" He shook his head.

"Ramses has only a few days of life left," he said. "Already the palace is preparing to mourn him and the sem-priests are readying their instruments of embalming. Let him depart in peace. It is a time of endings." That word again. I wiped my burning face on the sleeve of my shift, and as I did so a wave of healthy tiredness swept over me. I took a deep, ragged breath.

"Thank you for your care of me, Keeper," I said huskily. "I wish you much life and continued prosperity." Swiftly I leaned forward and kissed him on the cheek, then walking quickly over the long stretch of pavement sunk in gloom, I left him. I felt his eyes on me as I went, and as I turned into the entrance of my courtyard I glanced back, but he was gone.

I fell onto my couch and into a dreamless sleep almost simultaneously, awaking sprawled in the same position I had taken when my head found the pillow. Yawning and then stretching until my limbs cracked, I swung my legs onto the floor. "Isis?" I called, and before I had shrugged off my crumpled shift, she was beside me, a question in her eyes, her brow furrowed.

"Is it well, Lady Thu?" she asked hesitantly. I nodded.

"It is very well," I answered. "Today you will be assigned another mistress. I am leaving the harem forever. I will go to the bath house by myself while you find me food, for I am lamentably hungry, but hurry." She did not follow my order, however. Picking up my sleeping robe she stood there bunching it absently and biting her lip. "Is there something else?" I urged impatiently.

"I had not thought that you would be going so soon," she blurted. "Forgive my impertinence, Lady Thu, but I have enjoyed serving you and with your permission I would like to go on doing so. If you have no body servant awaiting your pleasure, then please take me with you." I stared at her, taken aback.

"But, Isis, I have no home yet. I do not know where I am going. You might find yourself isolated on some arid farm in the wastes of Nubia. Here in the harem you reside at the centre of power. Your duties are few and gentle. You come and go about the city. You would be bored and unhappy with me." She shook her head violently and gripped the linen even tighter.

"I know all about you," she said. "I have heard the gossip. Some of the women fear you. Some envy you your closeness with the Prince. Their lives are ..." She paused, searching for words. "... are very small, Lady Thu, and their servants become small also. I have not been here long and I do not want to spend the rest of my life moving from one unsatisfied concubine to another."

"Then what do you want?" I asked curiously. "Do you not fear me also, Isis? Or do you see me as an adventurer who will take you into turbulent waters? For I assure you that I myself want nothing more, now, than to sit in my own garden, drink my own wine, and punt on the Nile in my own skiff every evening while the sun goes down."

"I will erect the canopy in your garden," she said eagerly. "I will pour your wine and arrange the cushions on the deck of your skiff. I will massage you and paint you. I will be efficient and unobtrusive. I do not fear you, Lady Thu. I am afraid to die never having known what it is to be alive."

Like a pinprick to the heart I heard Hunro's voice, silenced now forever, and looking into the young and pleading face of this girl made me feel suddenly old.

"Very well," I sighed. "But do not come wailing to me in the future when you discover that I have no intention of moving in the circles of the wealthy and you have become bored. Talk to the Keeper and get his permission in writing. Now fetch me food!" Smiling happily she bowed and rushed out, and I made my way to the bath house through the sparkling morning.

Scrubbed and oiled I returned to my cell and ate with relish, savouring every mouthful Isis set before me. I was dipping my fingers in the bowl of warm water she held out to me when one of the stewards presented himself and there was a commotion outside. He handed me a scroll.

"It is a list of all the effects you requested from the store-houses," he said in answer to my query. "The boxes are here. The Keeper begs you to be ready to depart at sunset. He also reminds you that the King's gift of five deben of silver is in a separate casket within one of the chests, together with two scrolls dictated by the One Himself. You are not to unroll them until you arrive at your destination."

"But I have no destination!" I shouted after him, to no avail. He and the servants had gone. I turned to Isis. "Open the chests," I said. "You will find sheaths and sandals and paint. Select what you will and come and dress me. I will go through these gates clad in my own belongings. Then you can hunt for the Keeper and persuade him to give you to me."

Retiring to my chair, I listened to her delighted exclamations as she rummaged about. I have no destination, I thought on a tide of elation. I am free. Tonight I will see the lights of the harem and the palace recede behind me for the last time. Where will I go? It does not matter, for I do not care.

I was ready to leave long before the appointed time, sitting outside my door on one of the huge chests while behind me Isis, ever conscientious, cleared the cell of my occupancy. I could have remained in it until the last moment but from the time Isis closed the lid on the pretty cosmetic box I had chosen in the storehouse and placed it in the larger chest its atmosphere had changed, become alien to me. I was no longer the woman who had taken up residence within it such a short time ago, and it had mutely begun to shut me out. For my part, its dimensions, its furnishings, even its odour, became all at once foreign to me and I shed it like a cocoon, stepping out onto the path that would take me not only out of the women's quarters but also into a new life.

I was wearing clothes and jewellery I had not put on before: a diaphanous sheath of a peculiar dark crimson colour shot through with gold thread, a belt of linked golden lotuses, bracelets of golden leaves whose veins were thin tracings of carnelian, and a band that rested on my forehead and showered my loose hair and my neck with droplets of hung gold. A single large scarab carved in bone and encased in chased gold graced one finger, and gold dust glittered on my eyelids.

So I waited, arrayed as though I had been bidden to a great feast in the banqueting hall instead of an unknown future, my feet together, my hennaed palms on my knees, the aroma of the expensive perfumed oil Isis had rubbed between my breasts enfolding me in its musky cloud. There was no one to whom I wished to say farewell. I had taken my leave of Amunnakht, and Pharaoh was not strong enough any more to face another encounter. Neither was I. If the Prince had wished to see me again, he would have sent for me. I should have summoned a scribe and dictated a letter to my brother and family in Aswat, but I did not want to disturb the mood of solemn, joyful anticipation I felt.

I sat motionless in the gently blowing airs of the court-yard while Isis completed her scouring and came out to join me. I told her to get her belongings from her own quarters and say whatever goodbyes were needed and she soon returned, afraid, I think, that I might go without her, a large leather sack over her shoulder and the precious scroll ending her employment in the harem in her hand. Carefully she set her bag beside a chest and sank to the grass across from me but she did not let go of the roll of papyrus. I did not speak to her and she did not look at me. Each of us was engrossed in our own thoughts as the after-noon wore away.

At last, when the sky above the courtyard had faded from deep blue to the delicate pink that preceded the scarlet of sunset and the shadow of the fountain pulsed long across the grass, I heard the footsteps for which I had been yearning and I turned my head and watched him come. Smiling, he held out his arms and with an answering cry I rose and went gladly into his embrace. "How lightly you are travelling, Mother!" he said with mock sarcasm as he gestured to the men with him to pick up my chests. "Is the bag to go as well?"

"It belongs to Isis," I explained, tucking my hand beneath his elbow. "She has been released from the harem to serve me. Oh, Kamen, it is so good to see you, to hear your voice! How has it been with you? Is Takhuru well? Are you taking me to Men's house?" We began to walk towards the entrance, Isis behind.

"I am very well," he replied. "The Prince has granted me a commission in his own Division, and he has placed Banemus directly under my authority. It was a wise decision although uncomfortable for both of us. Banemus is, was, a great general and I hope to learn much from him. He will redeem himself quickly I think. Takhuru ..." I pulled him to a halt.

"I had planned that we should live together, you and I and Takhuru!" I protested, anxious and disappointed. "That hope has sustained me through all the horror, Kamen, but if you have taken oath under the Prince you must remain in Pi-Ramses! I need you! I have a list of estates I want you to look at. Without you, what shall I do?"

"I am not going to disappear from your life again," he said, taking my hand from the crook of his arm and kissing it softly. "But I must carve out a career for myself, marry Takhuru, raise a family. I cannot live with you, my mother.

It would be wrong for you as well as for me. I understand a little of what you have suffered and you must trust me when I tell you that I will not allow you to suffer any more. A home has already been prepared for you. I think you will like it. If not, I will help you find another."

"A home? But where? I wanted to do the choosing with you, Kamen. Please!" For answer he indicated the chests.

"You have the two scrolls Pharaoh gave you?"

"Yes. But what…?"

"Enough. Your craft awaits you at the palace watersteps and soon the light will be gone. We must make haste."

He vanished along the entrance passage, and I paused before following him and looked back. The fountain was still cascading into its wide basin. Its glittering red water was catching the last of the sun and the constancy of its sound, a music that had quietly accompanied the passionate and despairing days of my first confinement in this place and was still weaving its melody as I left it for the second time, was like the voice of eternity itself, obscure and enigmatic.

Around it the women sat or lay talking while their servants folded up the canopies that were no longer needed. Somewhere someone was plucking lazily at a lute, its plangent notes drifting in the warm air. More servants went to and fro bearing laden trays whose tantalizing odours spoke of an evening of good food and red wine, of sharing the small details of the day, of lamps lit and couches rumpled and then the silent hours before another dawn when it would all begin again.

But without me. Thank all the gods. Without me. Some other concubine would peer into my cell with trepidation and desire while her servant opened her boxes and began to unpack all her pretty things. Would she sometimes lie on the couch in the darkness and wonder whose body had weighted the mattress before her? Would she dream of love and a queen's crown? The ghost of Hunro called to me. I have never lived, it whispered. Never lived. With a final ache of pity for her, for myself, for them all, I turned and walked away.

Kamen was already speaking to the guards on the main gate, and by the time I came up to him, it was open and Isis and I were waved through. On my right the pool where Hunro and I had swum together lay black and motionless, already absorbing the colour of night, and the trees that shaded it during the day loomed over it now with sinister enquiry. After one swift glance at it I hurried to catch up with Kamen. He was striding along the path that ran between lawns to join the wider avenue that many times had taken me through the imposing public entrance of the palace. Imperial servants were already fixing torches to the mighty pillars, and courtiers were beginning to drift under their glare.

Soon I found myself crossing the vast plaza that ended with the watersteps. Here I had to weave between groups of cheerful nobles on their way to the night's revelry in the palace and I thought of Pharaoh alone in his cavernous bedchamber but for the physicians and the pervading stench of his dying, itself an ominous unseen presence, while in this complex and opulent building the pulse of Egypt went on beating.

Kamen led us beside the steps and along the side of the canal where craft of every size and ornamentation were tethered until he slowed at the foot of a ramp leading up onto the deck of a small but graceful vessel. Its planking was of cedar. Its prow and stern were unadorned but its cabin was hung with golden damask and the sail tied against its slender mast appeared to be gold cloth also. A flag flapped limply high above but I could not discern its colours. A helmsman sat with his bare legs hanging one each side of the tiller, watching the activity around him with interest, and several sailors were leaning on the rail.

At the sight of Kamen they sprang to life, pattering down the ramp to help the servants with the chests and bow us aboard. At Kamen's signal the ramp was run in, the rope holding us stationary untied, and the helmsman and the crew began to ease us from our berth.

"Whose boat is this?" I asked Kamen as behind me Isis disappeared into the cabin with an armful of cushions and one of the sailors bent with a pole to push us away from the bank.

"It is yours," he replied. "A gift from the Prince. He did not know what colours you would wish on your flag so he allowed me to choose for you." A wry smile lit his eyes. "I said that seeing I am of royal blood and you have spent the greater part of your life as a possession of the King, the imperial blue and white might be appropriate. He laughed but consented."

"A gift?" I said wonderingly. "How generous of him! I am speechless."

"Generous perhaps," he agreed. "But I think that our future Pharaoh derives much secret amusement from your situation. He awaits a report from me on your reaction to a further gift he and his father have arranged together. No."

He held up a hand as I began to speak. "You may not ask. The two scrolls will make everything plain."

"Then I am not to see your adoptive father or Takhuru or Nesiamun? I have much to thank them for, Kamen."

"We are not going far," he told me. "Men understands what I am doing. Will you rest in the cabin now, or shall I order a stool for you here?"

I asked for a stool, and when Isis had brought it, I sat clasping my knees and looking back while the craft broke free of the other vessels choking the canal and turned her prow towards the river. Slowly the row of tall pillars with their flaring torches illuminating the glittering crowds passing beneath them grew smaller. My vision filled with the dark trunks and tangled branches of the trees lining the canal. The sun had gone, and the lamp hanging in the stern cast shafts of orange light that broke across the oily water and were dissipated in the gathering gloom of the banks. The oars rose and fell cautiously, trailing grey foam.

Soon we turned out of the canal into the Lake of the Residence and the estates of the nobles began to slip by, their watersteps lamplit, their rafts and skiffs also hung with lights. The festive night of the city that was the centre of the world had begun, but I was no longer a part of it. Nor did I want to be. My fleeting melancholy came from nostalgia, a brief and poignant desire to turn back time, and nothing more. I did not think. The motion of the boat soothed me. The deepening darkness enclosed me. I did not realize that Kamen had come to sit on the deck beside me until he spoke.

"We are coming up to the Waters of Avaris," he said. "Wine and cold food have been prepared for you. A salad, some bread and goat cheese, figs and slices of goose. Will you eat while you watch the city go by or come into the cabin?" I put my hand on his head, feeling how thick and strong his black hair was, how warm his scalp.

"I care nothing for the city any more," I said. "What life I had here I left in the palace, and in unmarked graves somewhere in the desert beyond the Delta. Let us go into the cabin."

One lamp bracketed on the wall glowed on the cushions scattered over the floor, the low table laden with dishes, the narrow camp cot already dressed with my linen. Isis was kneeling by the table and waiting to serve us, blushing as Kamen greeted her kindly. Outside I heard the challenge from the guards and our captain's answer and knew that the Lake of the Residence was behind us.

Taking a cup from Isis in which the dark wine trembled, I raised it. "To my totem, Wepwawet, to the Great God Ramses, to his son the Hawk-in-the-Nest," I said. "Life, Health and Prosperity to us all." We drank together and then set upon the food, and I realized suddenly as I watched Kamen's graceful fingers shredding a crisp piece of lettuce that I was happy, really happy, for the first time in many years.

For several hours we lounged on the cushions and talked without tension, Kamen of his youth, his military training, his growing love for Takhuru, his ambitions for the future, and myself of my days with the King. I did not wish to speak again of my own youth in Hui's house or of the months of my exile in Aswat and Kamen, sensing my reluctance, did not press me. There were many jokes told and much laughter before he kissed my cheek and sought his blanket under the awning that had been rigged against the cabin wall outside and I settled down on the camp cot with Isis curled up on the cushions by the door.

When I woke, the Delta was behind us and we had just passed the pyramids that littered the high plateau on the west bank. The morning was cool and bright with promise. Standing blinking in the cabin's doorway, I stared for a while at the dazzling blue sky against which the beige hills stood out as sharply as though their outlines had been traced with a knife. Closer in, a line of palm trees marked the river road. The Nile glinted, reflecting the hue of the sky, and at its edge where the reeds clustered, birds whistled and piped to the new day.

Isis knelt on the deck, an array of bowls and jars around her, setting out food. Across from me the oarsmen's bent backs glistened with sweat as they pulled against the current, for we were going south and the river, although no longer swollen and rushing with the flood, was nevertheless full and flowing. Above me the yellow sail billowed in the prevailing wind out of the north, and the imperial colours of the flag ripped out at the top of the mast.

Kamen was leaning with his forearms on the rail. He was barefooted, clad only in a short white kilt, his hair blowing about his neck. He must have sensed my scrutiny for he turned and, seeing me, came striding across the deck. "You slept well," he observed. "With only one night on the river you look better. Some of the strain has gone out of your face. Come and eat under the awning. The fare is much the same as before and I am sorry for that, but we are not travelling far and this evening you may taste hot victuals." I followed him around the cabin to where the awning cast a wide shade, and settling myself on the cushions under it, I tried to reason where we might be going. Isis came, bowing and setting out the dishes, and I had an idea.

"Isis, try and find the scroll I received from the land surveyor," I told her. "Bring it to me. I will guess our destination," I went on, turning to Kamen. "Everything for sale is on that list. If we are not going far, I should be able to tell you where my new home is to be. But Kamen, estates this close to the Delta are prized and very expensive. Most of them are hereditary anyway. To whom do I owe my silver? And I am angry that I have not been allowed to make this choice myself." I picked up the beer Isis had poured for me, took a long drink, and bit into a piece of cheese.

"I have told you," he answered with indulgent deliberation. "You must trust me. If you are not delighted with what has been done for you I will take you back to Men's house and we can pore over this list of yours."

"Well at least we do not appear to be going as far as Aswat," I muttered. "This vessel is not fitted for such a long haul."

I took the scroll Isis extended and unrolled it. The surveyor had grouped the properties according to the districts in which they lay. I ignored everything south of the Fayum. We had already sailed beyond several places listed, and in the Fayum itself, nothing was available. I was not surprised. The oasis was lush and beautiful, rich in orchards and vineyards, its soil black and fertile. Royalty owned much of it and the rest was tended by the stewards of the nobility.

"It must be somewhere between the entrance to the Fayum and where we are now," I remarked, handing the scroll to Kamen. "Only two estates qualify, and one does not run down to the river. Therefore it must be the other." Kamen took the papyrus but let it roll up without looking at it and handed it back. He squinted at me, grinning.

"You are an intelligent woman," he taunted me. "If you can tell me where we are going, I will personally dig in your garden for a full year."

"Then you must be very confident that I will not arrive at the truth," I said, and laughed, but I was genuinely mystified and occupied my mind with trying to solve the puzzle for the rest of the day.

We docked briefly in the evening, putting in at a narrow, sandy bay so that the sailors could rest. They built a fire on the bank and swam and later sat in the glow of the embers, drinking beer and talking together. Kamen joined them.

I sat on the deck in the peaceful twilight, cradling my wine and listening to my son's intermittent, lusty laughter, feeling a harmony grow between my body and my heart that had never been present before. I seemed to be at one not only with myself but with my surroundings, blending thought and emotion into the scent of the cedar planks beneath me, the soft lapping sounds of the river against the shoal and the rustle of shy creatures in the underbrush, the white stars above, irregularly blotted out by the stiff black fronds of the palms. I had become accustomed to the constant background noises of life in the harem. Even at night, when the women and their children and their servants fell silent, the city would make itself known as a distant rumble.

But I had been bred to the land. It was in my very bones and tonight its call came flooding over me, whispering and cajoling. In my youth I had been desperate to escape the life of hard labour and inevitable ignorance that prematurely aged the other young girls in Aswat. I had succeeded, but I had not exorcised the spell of the soil itself. I no longer wanted to. I had become a noble, the Lady Thu, well educated and rich, but like so many other minor nobles living on their country estates far from Pi-Ramses I was also a provincial with one hennaed foot in the muddy earth of the Inundation. I was at peace. I would accept whatever house and land my son had purchased on my behalf and retire into a blessed anonymity.

Just before I retired for the remainder of the night, Kamen came back on board and I saw the ramp being drawn up behind him. "We will go on," he said. "I want you to sleep, Mother, and in the morning you must stay in the cabin until I come for you. Isis can see to your needs. Put on your most sumptuous clothing and the best jewels you have. Make sure she paints you meticulously. You are beautiful, but I want you to look irresistible."

"I am not going to meet a lover, Kamen," I said crossly. "And you should not be giving me orders like a bullying husband. Will a few arouras of land care how I am arrayed?" Something in his manner had made me suddenly uneasy.

"You must make a good impression on your new Steward," he insisted. "He is a very able man but temperamental. You must gain his admiration at once or you will be forced to terminate his employment."

"In my time I have dazzled a king and bested the most beautiful concubines in the harem!" I said hotly. "And now I am reduced to strutting before a mere Steward? I do not think so, Captain!"

"Please, Mother," he begged softly. I did not reply. I rolled my eyes, shrugged, and went into the cabin, twitching the curtains closed behind me.

For a while I lay listening to the low voices of the sailors as they manoeuvred us out into the river once more. I felt the craft falter and quiver in the moment when the current tried to drag it northward but the dipped oars strove to pull towards the south, then it slid forward. Isis, dozing on the cushions, sighed and shifted her position. My eyes closed. I had intended to stay awake, to try and sense where we were going in the speed and direction of the vessel, but its movement and the rhythmic sound of the oars rising and falling lulled me and I slept after all.

I knew before I even opened my eyes the following morning that we had berthed somewhere. The boat rocked gently. No one was calling a beat for the oarsmen. Pearly light was seeping through the tasselled curtains of the cabin. It was very early. The din of the dawn chorus was still filling the air; therefore, I concluded, we must be close to many trees. A fragrance came to me, very faint but unmistakeable, the scent of orchard blossoms and the delicate tang of vine leaves. We have returned to the Delta, I thought in shock. Oh surely not! It cannot be!

I left the cot and stood, intending to tear open the curtains and look out no matter what Kamen wanted me to do, but at that moment Isis entered bearing a bowl of hot water. Before I could catch a glimpse of what lay beyond, she pulled the drapery closed again, smiled a greeting, and came to remove my sleeping shift. "Where are we, Isis?" I demanded. Her hands did not falter as they drew the garment over my head.

"I am sorry, Lady Thu, but I am not permitted to tell you," she said calmly. "Your son told me that he would have me whipped if I did."

"Such impertinence!" I snapped. "You are my servant not his. This had better be the last time you disobey me." She was trickling the water over me and reaching for the natron.

"Yes, Lady," she said humbly. "I am sorry. What sheath shall I fetch today?"

I submitted to her hands more willingly than I would have admitted. I was less annoyed than curious, and after my body and my hair were washed and I had been plucked and oiled and scraped, I did not attempt to see out when she left me to bring my clothes. Let Kamen have his fun. I would pretend surprise and delight no matter what sight met my eyes when he came for me.

Isis seemed to be overcome by the solemnity of the occasion. Her touch was reverential as she draped me in the white and silver sheath, heavy with tiny golden ankhs, and hung the filigreed silver pectoral around my neck. I wanted her to braid my hair, but she ignored my request, combing it loose and setting on my brow a wide silver coronet surmounted with an ankh from whose arms hung tiny feathers of Ma'at. She had kohled my eyes and hennaed my mouth, touched me with myrrh, and was slipping jewelled sandals on my feet when Kamen pushed through the curtain and surveyed her handiwork. All that was left were the gold rings to slide onto my fingers when the henna had dried on my palms. "Very good, Isis," Kamen said after eyeing me critically. "Now, Mother, command her to go and bring the two scrolls Pharaoh dictated for you." Isis glanced at me and I nodded. When she had gone, I rose.

"My son," I said quietly. "I love you, but I have played your puppet long enough. I want the truth." He inclined his head, and coming up to me, he took my face between his hands. His eyes were warm.

"Oh, my mother," he murmured. "Do you know how proud I am to be your son? Or how happy this moment makes me? I have marvelled often at the strange workings of fate, but never with more astonishment than here in this cabin where you shine like the goddess Hathor herself." He dropped his arms as Isis came back, and at a second nod from me, she gave Kamen the scrolls. Breaking the seals on them both, he read them quickly. "This one," he said, passing it to me. "But come outside before you look at it." He held the curtain open. With a deep breath I brushed by him.

The bright waters of the lake of the Fayum opened out before my eyes, spreading away to be lost in the distance where the encircling hills met the sky. Pleasure craft already skimmed its surface, white sails shaking in the morning breeze, white foam breaking in their wake. Its verge was dotted with watersteps, gleaming bone-white in the sparkling sunlight, the paths leading to them from the low houses lost in a riot of luxuriant vegetation. Blossoms blown from the thick orchards floated across my vision. Palm groves swayed. "But, Kamen," I stammered. "There are no estates for sale in the Fayum."

"No," he said quietly, taking my fingers in his own. "Turn around, Mother. Look behind you." Dread took me then, an awful, powerful surge of fear and foreknowledge and disbelief so that even as I was turning I knew what I would see and my heart began to pound and my breath stopped in my throat.

It lay as I remembered it, the pretty watersteps against which we were tethered, the paved way through arching trees, the high shrubs to either side protecting it from the fields themselves and the two temples that flanked them. I could see the clustering pomegranates and sycamores that sheltered the house itself, so thick that the strip of desert beyond was invisible. I knew where the date grove lay, and the orchard and the vineyard. I knew that the lines of tall palm trees marked the irrigation canals that had brought life to my fields.

My fields. My ten arouras, deeded to me so long ago. Many times I had wondered painfully whose feet were treading the path, whose voice called to the Overseer over the burgeoning crops, whose hands cupped the clusters of grapes at harvest time. I pulled my fingers from Kamen's grasp, and stumbling across the deck, I clung to the rail. "I do not understand," I whispered. "Help me, Kamen." He came up beside me and put an arm around my shoulders.

"When I was given to Men as a baby, Pharaoh deeded ten arouras of khato land in the Fayum to him in exchange for his promise of secrecy," he said. "The house was in disrepair but the previous owner had had the fields cleared and had planted a barley crop, chick peas, some garlic. It was a good estate. Father had the house restored and the outdoor shrine and other outbuildings repaired. It became our second home. Every Akhet we came here to swim and fish. I always loved it, from the first time I set foot on these watersteps. I grew up here. I did not know, none of us knew, that it had once belonged to a famous concubine who had fallen from favour and into obscurity." He put a finger under my chin and lifted my face. "Do not cry, Mother. You will ruin your paint and Isis will have to start all over again."

"Go on," I managed.

"After the trial the Prince summoned Men. Pharaoh wished this estate to revert to you. He offered Men an alternative, something on the Nile at the mouth of the Fayum. To his credit, Men agreed. We have moved out, Thu. The house has been furnished from the palace storehouses on Pharaoh's command. I think he loved you very much." Kamen waved. "It is yours. The original deed is in your hand."

Through a blur of tears I unrolled the scroll. Sure enough, it was the same document the King had presented to me with such delight all those years ago. "Oh Ramses," I choked, and could say no more. There it lay before me, peaceful and stately and vibrantly green. Mine. Mine forever this time. And he had done this knowing that he would not live to see my gratitude. I did not deserve such overwhelming and unselfish affection.

Kamen gestured and I sank onto the stool a sailor had brought. Isis thrust wine into my hand and steadied it while I drank. I was recovering. "As soon as possible I will travel back to Pi-Ramses and offer Men my heartfelt thanks," I said shakily to Kamen. "I do not know what to say. I will dictate a letter to Pharaoh and hope it reaches him before …"

"I think it is already too late," Kamen said. "But he would not want you to fret about it, Mother. It gave him pleasure to put a peasant back on her land, or so he said to the Prince. Besides, there is this." He held up the other scroll. "When you are ready, you are to take it and go into the house. You are not to open it until you are told."

"Told by whom? The Steward? There are servants within, Kamen?"

"Yes. If you do not like them you have Pharaoh's permission to rid yourself of them." I came slowly to my feet and regarded him thoughtfully.

"There is a trick here, isn't there?" I said. "Will I lose the estate if I do not accept the staff? Is the Prince toying with me?"

"No!" I saw a flash of pity in his eyes. "The deed is in your hand. No one can take it away from you. Pharaoh is a very wise man, Mother, wise and compassionate. You are feeling better? Good. Go now. I will remain here on board until you send me word that all is well." He handed me the second scroll. There was a message in his expression. Worry? Expectation? I could not decipher it. Wordlessly I walked to the ramp, took the sailor's steadying hand, and set my feet upon my own piece of Egypt.

I had not gone far along the shady path when the house came into view, set in its shelter of tall trees, its pretty white-painted façade gleaming in the morning light. The last time I had seen it, approached it, its mud bricks had been crumbling and the stone beneath me had been cracked and heaved. Men had restored it all with a sensitivity I found remarkable in a wayfaring man, but then, I reflected, I did not know Kamen's adoptive father well at all.

My thoughts had begun to race, and I slowed them with an effort, conscious that they were trying to scatter under the weight of tension growing in me. The house loomed nearer. The dappled light through which I moved gave place briefly to full sunshine as I passed the fish pond. Its surface, once scummed, was now clear and dotted with lotus and lily pads. To the left of the path, opposite the pool, the outdoor shrine cast a shadow over the grass. Its tiny doors stood open and the shrine itself was empty, waiting for me to install my dear Wepwawet.

Now the entrance to the house was directly before me, two white pillars between whose sturdy girth there was only dimness. No door guard rose to greet me. The silence was palpable. I hesitated, overcome suddenly by a wave of foreboding. Something was not right.

I peered into that cool opening, trying to interpret the instinct that told me to turn and run, back to the boat, back to Kamen's protecting arms, back to safety. Sweat broke out along my spine, dampening the scrolls I was clutching. You are being ridiculous, Thu, I told myself. You know what is within. The reception room, wide and pleasant, with doorways in its far wall that will lead you to a bedchamber, guest quarters, Steward's office, a passage to the rear garden where you will find the bath house and the kitchen and the servants' quarters ...

Servants.

The Steward.

Taking a deep breath, I gathered my courage, mur-mured a quick prayer to Wepwawet, and strode across the threshold.

In the moment that it took my eyes to adjust to the gloom I became aware of two things. First, the scent of jasmine, very faint but unmistakeable, insinuated itself into my nostrils and froze the blood in my veins. Second, I was not alone. There was a shape even now rising from the shadows.

Tall.

Grey-skinned.

Grey-skinned …

It came forward, halted, and one stray beam of light from the clerestory window struck its head in a halo of purest white. My heart stopped, and in that moment of shock and panic I fought to breathe.

He stood there staring at me with his red, kohl-rimmed eyes. He was naked from the waist up, his moon-kissed hair falling over one pale shoulder in a thick braid, the folds of a thin kilt brushing his ankles. A silver snake bracelet clung to his upper arm.

I rammed one fist against my ribs and with a jolt my heart began to race again.

"No," I said. "No."

Then my mind fled. I threw myself forward and beat at him clumsily, showering his face, his chest, his stomach with blows, raking him with my rings, reaching to tear out his hair. He fielded me silently, trying to grab hold of my wrists, grunting when I found a target, but at last he succeeded. Panting and sobbing, I found myself imprisoned against him, my arms locked behind me.

"This is my house!" I shouted. "Get out of my house!" I felt his grip relax and flung myself away from him. He spread his hands and raised his white shoulders. Blood from a cut I had made below his ear was trickling down his neck.

"I cannot," he said apologetically. "I am afraid that the orders of Pharaoh and the Prince must supersede yours. You may read the scroll now."

"Do not speak!" I croaked at him. I was trembling with shock and buffetted by a torrent of emotions: fury, fear of what he might do, relief that he was alive, anguish that he had somehow survived, and a gush of sweetness at the sound of his familiar voice. With clumsy, hot hands I tore open the scroll.

The words leaped out at me with horrifying clarity. "My dearest Thu," I read. "Having been privately tried and found guilty of treason and extreme blasphemy, the Seer and Noble Hui has been condemned to take his own life. However, with a regard for the years in which he served as my personal physician and Egypt's greatest visionary, and also, my lovely concubine, with the thought that you should be given a man worthy of your talents and your passions, I have decided to spare his life only if you will deign to have him as your debentured servant for as long as you wish. If you choose to send him away, he must award himself the punishment I have decreed. Be happy." It was signed by Ramses himself and sealed with the royal imprint.

For a long time I gazed down at the papyrus, then I tossed it savagely away and lowered myself into the nearest chair. "This is madness," I said tonelessly. "You are an evil man, Hui. How did you do it?" He came and squatted beside me, bringing with him a cloud of his perfume, jasmine. I closed my eyes.

"You must believe me when I tell you that I made no attempt to bring about this most quixotic judgement," he said urgently. "On the night when you hid in my room and taunted me, warned me, I realized that we, Paiis and Hunro and the rest, we could not avert the hand of justice this time. I went at once to the palace and confessed everything. I expected Ramses to place me in a cell at once, which he did. I also expected to be hauled before a public tribunal with my brother and Hunro, but it did not happen."

"It should have!" I cried out. "I was there, Hui! I waited in the harem until your brother and Hunro died! I know what they suffered. You were just as guilty as they. By what right do you still live? If you had any honour you would have killed yourself regardless of Pharaoh's machinations!"

"Ah yes," he said softly. "Honour. But we know that I have little of that dubious virtue, don't we, Thu? What is honour compared to the vital satisfactions of life? You of all people are aware that the sheer joy of living outweighs every other consideration. After all, you were deprived of everything but the elementary tools of survival for seventeen years."

"You made sure of that," I whispered. "Go on."

"I was brought to Pharaoh and the Prince shortly before the trial was due to begin. Ramses told me that he desired—that was the word he used. Desired. He desired to spare my life for your sake. He said he knew that although he had possessed your body, I was the one who held your heart in thrall and he did not want you to spend the rest of your life mourning me. Perhaps he knew your heart better than you knew it yourself."

Abruptly I pushed myself out of the chair and began to pace. "You arrogant men," I said bitterly. "Complacent, prideful, superior. You threw yourself on the King's mercy, didn't you? You offered all the evidence he could wish for in exchange for your life. And he was reluctant to see you destroyed. After all, you tended him in the most intimate ways as his physician. He liked and trusted you above his sense of justice. But he had to do something. He could not free you and execute the others. So he thrust the decision on me. The coward! I hate you both, and you most of all! Ramses is dying, without my help this time, and you can die too. I don't want you here. Get out. Go and fulfil the terms of that stupid, wicked bargain!" I gestured at the scroll lying in a corner.

He had risen to his feet and was standing with his hands behind his back, watching me soberly. "It was not like that, Thu, I swear. You do Ramses an injustice. If your decision has been made already, I will honour it, but hear what I have to say before you condemn me. Will you let me speak?" I nodded grimly.

"Say what you like," I retorted. "But I am no longer the innocent girl who hung on your every word, Hui. Remember that."

"I remember much," he said softly. "I remember the first time I saw you, stark naked and dripping wet in the cabin of my boat, your eyes huge with fear and determination. I remember the night you kissed me and I ached to respond, to take you in my arms and let my schemes wither. I remember the smell of you when you leaned close in my herb room, your whole attention fixed on the lesson I was trying to teach you.

"But most of all I remember the darkness in my garden when you came to me distraught and we planned Pharaoh's murder, and we made love, not with tenderness as we should have but in greedy exaltation at what we were going to do." He paused, and for the first time since I had known him I saw him falter, at a loss for words, awkward and unsure. Was it an act? I could not tell. "You have changed, Thu, but so have I," he went on carefully. "My little plans came to nothing years ago, vanishing under the weight of time. Egypt survives, as I should have known she would. Ramses survives to die a natural death and his son will make a capable Pharaoh. Nothing is left to me but the bitter realization that I threw away the one thing that might have made me happy.

"I taught you to live only through me. I invaded and captured your mind and your heart, deliberately and callously, but I did not know that in the process you had also captured me. When you were banished to Aswat, I believed that you would also be banished from my thoughts, that the whole miserable affair was over and the memories of you would fade." He smiled ruefully, and this time I thought I saw genuine pain behind his eyes. "For seventeen years I waited for that to happen, strove to make it happen. And when Paiis came to me with your manuscript in his hands, I saw a final chance to obliterate the past. We planned your deaths, yours and Kamen's. Paiis pressed for such a solution because his security was threatened, but I saw it also as a way to exorcise a tormenting ghost. I continued to delude myself until I saw you on the night you confronted me in my bed chamber, the night I ran to the palace in the hope that Ramses would order me slaughtered on the spot. I knew then that I would never be free of you, that I was ensnared forever in the net of my own making. I did not want to live any more. And if you turn me away now, I shall die with an eagerness I would not have thought possible. I love you."

"You are still trying to save your life," I said drily. "It is too late to talk of love, Hui. You have always worshipped self-preservation."

"I still do," he replied straightforwardly. "But I no longer want it at any cost. We are two of a kind, Thu. We always were. I am not asking you for equality. According to the terms of Pharaoh's edict I am to be your servant, quite literally. You may do with me what you like."

Oh gods, I thought despairingly as we faced each other in the increasing heat of that charming little room. What should I do?

Well, what do you want to do?, a voice within mocked me. Do you want to exact your full revenge and call Kamen to arrest him so that he must endure what you have seen with Paiis? Hunro? Do you want him grovelling before you, ready to fulfil your every whim, afraid to disobey you in case you send him away to die? Or do you want to love him freely and joyously, the way it should have been from the beginning, before your greed and his cold ambition got in the way?

But is it possible to lay aside the past with all its lies and pain, its dead dreams and thwarted hopes? my thoughts ran on. Are protestations of love enough to silence the whispers of faithlessness and mistrust that sounded through all the days of my exile and filled the darkness of my tiny hut night after night? How can I still the cruel memories, so many more than happy ones, that even now crowd my mind and chill my heart? It would be like trying to regain my virginity. Is it too much to expect that he is speaking the truth at last? Can we learn to trust each other against all odds?

He was looking at me patiently, calmly, a sliver of moonlight in the middle of the morning, an exotic and still mysterious creation of the gods, a complex and beautiful man, and my love for him was a wound I could not cure. Ramses had been right. Right and astute. Out of his goodness he had given me the one gift beyond anything in his treasury. Walking to the scroll, I picked it up and tore it in two.

"You are free to go, Hui," I said matter-of-factly. "You can leave Egypt if you want. I refuse to accept any of the terms of this so-called bargain. I will not alert the authorities. I will do nothing at all. I do not desire your death or your servitude." I pointed at the door. "Freedom, Seer."

He did not move. He did not so much as glance in the direction of my finger. "Freedom to do what?" he said huskily. "Return to my house in Pi-Ramses where my brother's voice still echoes and the oil waits to show me dead visions and useless fantasies? Where my garden is filled with the scent of the lost years, yours as well as mine? I do not want that kind of freedom. Death would be preferable. I can hide from myself no longer, Thu. I need you. My heart, my soul is incomplete without you. You must believe me. You say you desire neither my death nor my servitude. But if you force me to walk out the door, you condemn me to both, for no one can live who only serves the time that has gone."

Looking into those fiery red eyes, it came to me that it did not matter what I believed. He might be lying, or the truth might be beating at last beneath the agitated rise and fall of his naked white chest. All I knew was that I had no choice. Life without him would be nothing more than a pointless round of little responsibilities, little pleasures, devoid of the rich depths of either passion or pain, and I would glide through the shallows of a meaningless existence until my end. The thought was insupportable. "Then summon Harshira," I said. "I presume that he is here also. Tell him to bring refreshments, and we will discuss what we are to do. But before that, there is a question you must put to me. Something I have longed to hear, Hui. Words that must come from your mouth if the past with all its dark power is to be rendered impotent and we are to begin again." His brows drew together and his eyes narrowed. He did not blink. Outwardly calm, I waited while everything in me was tight with the tension of knowing that my whole life, my whole future, now depended on what he would say.

Then the ghost of a smile flitted across his face. "Dear Thu," he murmured. "Can you forgive me for the grievous wrongs I have inflicted on you? For using you and deserting you? For plotting to destroy you and taking away your youth? Are you able to forgive me? Will you try?"

For a long time neither of us stirred. We stood staring at each other while the day grew drowsy with heat and the birds fell silent in the garden beyond.

THE END